Courttia Newland is the author of the critically acclaimed novels *The Scholar* and *Snakeskin*. He has contributed to the anthologies *Disco 2000*, *New Writers 8* and *AfroBeat*, and is editor of an anthology of new black writing in Britain, *IC3*. He lives in west London. You can visit his website at: www.myvillage.co.uk/urbanfactor

'Fairly crackles with depictions of teenage temptations . . . after the white-wash better known as *Notting Hill*, the antidote couldn't be better timed'
i-D Magazine

'Pulls no punches in its description of estate life as a mixture of community and ghetto . . . his strength lies in the depiction of violence and menace'
Independent

'It is the ambition and scale of Newland's book that really impresses. Every one of the stories has some kind of engrossing and subtle moral point to make; almost all the characters are alive with tenderness and hope . . . an impressive achievement'
Guardian

'Newland writes with a compelling lightness, utterly lacking in hyperbole or machismo . . . it is quite easy to imagine Newland becoming one of this country's most important social commentators in years to come'
Glasgow Herald

'Newland has a sharp curiosity that gives him both a maturity beyond his years and an energy that reinforces his youth'
Independent on Sunday

'Britain's brightest black writer'
Evening Standard

'Plenty of local dialect, bags of intrigue and characters you've sat next to on the bus. Moreish'
19

'As a literary culture, we are chronically short of this sort of fiction. Voices like Newland's provide a vital counterpoint to the likes of Bridget Jones'
Financial Times

'"Young, gifted and black!" If the phrase hadn't already been kicking around for a few decades it would have been invented for Courttia Newland . . . Newland has held up a mirror to a part of our society that many people, especi   otherwise not know about – or wo
Touch

Also by Courttia Newland

The Scholar
Snakeskin

This book is dedicated to the memory and family of Stephen Lawrence

Contents

Elisha (I)

Straining with the heavy cardboard box, Elisha dolly-stepped sideways centimetre by centimetre; when her head touched the doorframe, she sucked in her non-existent stomach and eased through the door into her new room. Her face was a deep red, and her arms were aching, even though she'd only carried the box from the lift on the landing. This was the last of their things, she was glad to say; her muscles felt limp and tired, as she'd been lifting and carrying since eight that morning and it was nearly lunchtime now.

Once past the frame, Elisha walked carefully towards the centre of the room, easing her load down slowly and placing it amongst its fellow boxes with a grunt. Pulling her fingers from underneath, she got to her feet and flexed her right arm, tenderly feeling at the bicep with a miniature smile. A set of pink women's dumbbells was one of the few items from the old flat she still possessed, and although she'd bought them for twenty pounds almost six months ago, she'd only been using them half-heartedly since. Today was the second or third time (she couldn't remember which) that she'd lifted the weights. Her smile grew wider; so much for keeping fit.

Well, I can make a fresh start here, she thought to herself, unable to deny the wriggle of pride that shot through her, despite her initial reaction to the room. *I'll do press-ups, and sit-ups and maybe even aerobics at that fitness centre I saw down the road . . .*

There was a crash and a tinkle of glass next door, and Elisha heard her older sister cursing in her own unique and highly descriptive manner. She went to the bedroom door and poked her head out to see what was up.

'What happened?'

Her sister Tawanda, a tall slender girl with smooth light-brown skin, was squatting over a small Sainsbury's box that had fallen on its side, spilling its contents across the bare wooden floor. A lamp glazed with a light blue marble effect was obvious amongst the mess – it was broken in two, and little shards from the glass shade lay around it in a rough circle, like debris from a miniature bomb blast. Tawanda was pushing thin strands of hair from her eyes while picking up the larger pieces and holding them against each other to see if they matched, presumably so she could glue them together. Elisha crouched beside her, still waiting for an answer to her question. Tawanda shot her a disgusted glance.

'I stood on one ah your friggin' tapes,' she snapped angrily.

Elisha instantly frowned. '*My* tape? Nah, sorry luv, my tapes are in my box, don' even try it.'

'Den what's that please?'

Tawanda pointed at the wooden floorboards by the front door. A TDK D90 lay there like a crushed beetle, its transparent casing cracked through the middle. Elisha walked over and studied the tape. A low groan came from the depths of her being as she read the label.

'Shit Tawanda!'

'See!'

'Why'nt yuh look where you was goin'! Dat's my new R 'n' B tape man, Sheri gimme it as a leavin' present. I ain' even listened to it yet!'

'So what!' Tawanda looked livid, though this was a common expression for her. 'Your stoopid tape made me break Mum's favourite lamp. Dat means the money's comin' outta your pocket man, 'cos it ain' comin' outta mine.'

'So you feel,' Elisha replied tartly. She picked up her precious tape delicately, as though it were an injured child. 'You shoulda bin lookin' where you was goin' wid yuh big foot dem.' Kissing her teeth loudly she went back towards her box-filled room. 'I'll never get another one ah dese widout payin' for it Tawanda! I hope you're satisfied!'

'You're so fuckin' selfish . . .' Tawanda started, but she stopped abruptly when she heard footsteps on the landing.

Elisha stood firm by her door, knowing that is she disappeared now, her mum would only have to come looking for her, and then she'd probably be twice as angry. Veronica, a doll-pretty fair-skinned woman, stepped through the threshold, her vision obscured by the large box she was carrying; she was closely followed by Linton, her long-time boyfriend. She put the box down, looked at her broken lamp and her silent daughters, then frowned and sighed all at once. Linton put his load down behind her and peered over her shoulder.

'OK. What happened to my lamp?'

'Elisha an' her stoopid self wen' an' dropped a tape on the floor an'—'

'Don' watch her man, Tawanda tripped over her own big feet Mum, how can you trip on a tape? She jus' don' wanna take the blame for her own clumsiness—'

'All right, all right, all right!' Veronica shook her head with fatigue, clearly not able for the added stress of arguments on her moving day. 'Forget it – something was bound to get broken today, it's jus' one of those things. Let's all forget it, all right?'

'Fine by me,' Elisha agreed. Tawanda snorted, but didn't bother making a reply.

'Can I get inside, Ronnie, please?' Linton's deep voice asked from behind their mother. Veronica laughed and giggled in the girlish way both daughters had confessed they hated, then moved slightly to allow her boyfriend to come in.

Mind you, Elisha thought, *I'd be gigglin' if I was dealin' wid summick like him.* Blatant.

Linton was yet another bone of contention between the sisters, who loved one another dearly, but couldn't see eye to eye eighty per cent of the time, and fought like cat and dog the other twenty. Elisha thought he was a dream – tall, broad like a rugby player, with hazel eyes and rugged good looks. Tawanda thought he was a vain, self-opinionated, arrogant, lazy prick. And that was the edited version.

Her mother (in Elisha's view) obviously loved him, and even Tawanda reluctantly agreed Linton was here to stay . . . though she put her sister's defence to the man down to plain and simple puppy love. Elisha thought that at the age of eighteen she was far too old for such things. Tawanda, at twenty-one, claimed that eighteen was the most vulnerable of ages – the age at which you were on the edge of adulthood; the age at which you felt you knew more than you actually did.

'So's dat everyting?' Linton asked their mother, in his strong Trini accent.

Ronnie nodded. 'That's the lot!' she trilled, before looking towards her younger child, her face filled with excitement. 'So how'd you like your new room 'Lisha?' she wondered happily, wrapping an arm around Linton's considerable waist. As usual, Tawanda cut in before Elisha could reply.

'I suppose she likes it jus' as much as she says she did two weeks ago, when we all came roun' wid the guy from the council, Mum,' she sneered loudly in her smarter-than-thou voice.

Linton winced as if he'd only just realised what he'd let himself in for, moving in with a young woman with a lethal weapon for a tongue. He managed to control his own, and merely eyed her with disdain. Although he'd been seeing Veronica for a while, Linton had only decided to move in with them following the fire that had swept through their old home with the speed of a gale-force wind. The girls agreed their mum must've begged him quite a bit, as Tawanda had made her feelings towards him very plain a long time ago.

Ronnie's lips curled in a strained smile, determined to continue playing happy families. Elisha glared at her sister, then grinned a sickly sweet smile at her mother. 'Yes Mum, I'm very happy with my room. It's got a wicked view,' she told her.

'Oh yeah, wonderful! I love the sight of mud!' her sister said sarcastically, as she picked broken pieces of lamp from the floor. 'Where can I put these den? We ain' even sorted out our bin yet!'

Elisha cut her eye in her sister's direction and went back to her room before she said something she'd regret.

She walked over to her bed and sat on the bare mattress, feeling the hard springs on her arse, and looking around herself dispiritedly. Although her sister could be a bitch at times, Elisha knew she'd been right about the room. It was large, but the size only accentuated the darkness. It was painted, but the paint was orange, and peeling everywhere she looked. There was a built-in cupboard, but one of the doors had fallen off, and the drawers were crooked, as if they were broken too.

At least you got your own room now, she told herself. *Dis's a damn sight better than sharin' wid Tawanda in dat hostel. Ain' it?*

Not daring to answer that, she got up and went over to the window, looking over her new estate – her new manor. Greenside seemed no different from Winton, the Fulham estate she'd lived on previously. The view made her sigh discontentedly – she'd lied about her pleasure at looking from her bedroom window. The local council was building another set of blocks behind her own, expanding the estate in the run-up to the Millennium. Huge piles of bricks, cement mixers, and yellow industrial vehicles were dotted over the bare earth. The view from the windows in the kitchen and living rooms was marginally better; from there you could see the old estate, though Elisha knew that view wasn't too great either.

Mum's happy though, I mustn't stop her from being happy . . .

As though she'd been mentally summoned, Ronnie entered her daughter's room, treading carefully, as though stepping through a minefield. When she reached her daughter's side, she looked out of the window too, then kissed Elisha's cheek, squeezing her shoulder, her expression saying she knew the effort her daughter was making not to speak her mind. Elisha rested her head on her mother's shoulder tiredly.

'Mum. I . . .'

'Ssssh . . .' her mother whispered. 'I know. Don't worry. Things'll change and we won't be here long.'

They stood at the window in silence, looking over the emptiness. Ronnie let go of Elisha's shoulder.

'All right 'Lisha, back to work girl. Can you go shops for me?'

'OK, sure.'

Ronnie dug in her jeans pocket, her face screwed up as she grunted and pushed. All at once, Elisha felt as though a thick curtain had been lifted; she noticed how tight the jeans were, and how much weight her mother was putting on. *She's getting older*, she realised with a shock. The picture of her mother she'd carried in her head since she was a kid was gone; now Elisha saw the tiny little crow's feet, the early signs of middle-age spread, and the thin, almost unnoticeable strands of grey hair.

'Take this an' get me . . . some washing powder, toilet roll and some Super Glue for the lamp. Will a tenner be enough?'

'More than enough,' Elisha replied. 'You cookin' later?'

Veronica gave her a strange look. 'Are you mad? I'm too tired to cook girl – ain' there a chippie aroun' here or sumthin'?'

'Dat's what I'm sayin' innit? I seen a West Indian takeaway by dat little row ah shops. I can get us sumthin' from out dere.'

Her mother smiled, then dug in her pockets some more, until she retrieved another ten-pound note. 'Good idea! OK, jus' get four dinners an' four drinks, you know what everyone likes. There should be enough money. Don' bother ask Tawanda what she wants – you'll be here all night, an' I wanna fix my lamp as soon as possible. You sure you'll be OK out there on your own?'

'Yes Mum,' Elisha drawled, heading out of the room. 'Soon come.'

'You be careful,' her mother warned, pointing a finger her way.

'Yes Mum . . .'

Elisha pushed her way out of her new block's electric doors, held one open for an elderly black lady, then walked the straight road towards the cluster of shops she'd seen earlier. Zipping up her puffer jacket, she shot quick glances left and right, checking out her surroundings while attempting to look as much like a local girl as possible. Rows of four-storey blocks stretched out in front of her, and she shivered, though she didn't know why.

Her best friend Sheri, who'd lived two floors below her in the old estate, had seemed to know every spooky story Greenside had to offer. When she and the rest of the girls heard that that was where Elisha and her family were being moved to, they began to reel them off, one after another, with no thought for their friend's feelings. They spoke of murders, drug deals, prostitution, and at first Elisha had been deeply affected. She'd laughed along with their stories, smoking her cigarettes nonchalantly, then as soon as she was alone fear began to take over, seeping into her bones and fuelling her paranoia.

When she'd come here with her mother to see the flat two weeks ago, Elisha instantly felt better. The streets were relatively quiet, the screaming hordes of kids looked no different to the ones who played on the streets of Winton, and there was a vibe in the air, transmitted like a radio wave, that let her know she'd fit in here and be made welcome. The estate wasn't perfect, and it wouldn't have suited everyone, but Elisha felt she'd be all right. That was when she'd told her mother it was cool with her if she accepted the council's offer.

She passed the last block on her side of the road, then looked up, squinting at the nameplate high up on the brick wall. Belsize House. As she crossed the road, she peered to her left and saw a group of boys loafing, their hands in their pockets, cracking jokes, smoking and sipping from bottles of Dragon Stout.

Oh God, Elisha thought as they spotted her. Elisha was tall, with a marzipan complexion and a curvy figure that only the baggiest of clothing could hide. Her features made her pretty in a youthful way, though she often complained about her nose, which she thought was too small for her face. Her skin was clear, and she had the kind of smile that would unconsciously make people want to smile back. It was almost impossible for her to avoid the attention of the opposite sex. She walked a little faster. The youths began to call.

'What'm baybi! Baybi!'

'Hello! Hello!'

'Ay – ay, don't go on like dat! Yuh lookin' nice y'nuh star! Me only waan chat t'yuh, wha' gwaan?'

Ignoring their cries, Elisha walked on until she could hear them no more. She was sure they were nice enough when you got to know them, but as she was a newcomer their hormones would be screaming at them to 'try a ting'. Elisha was kind of between boyfriends at the moment, but nevertheless she was one of those girls who didn't respond to catcalls. Putting the youths to the back of her mind, she eased her pace as she caught sight of the shops.

The West Indian takeaway was called Smallie's. It had gleaming white surfaces and pictures of Barbados on the walls, as well as autographed photos of Omar, Lennox Lewis and Ian Wright. A few people were waiting for their food by counters set on the right- and left-hand sides of the wall, and Elisha joined the queue, looking at the menu to make sure the shop had everyone's favourite dish, before glancing at the other customers.

A brown-skinned woman sat on one of the stools by the right-hand counter, humming softly to the beautiful child on her lap. Two white men in suits stood beside the woman, arms crossed, holding clipboards bearing the letters 'BBC'. On the left, two bandanna'd boys talked in low tones, while keeping a close eye on their mountain bikes, which leaned against a wall outside. Beside them were three black girls dressed in jeans, jumpers and the shiny black raincoats that were currently so fashionable. Elisha had had a jacket like that – before the fire.

She flicked her eyes over the girls quickly, not wanting them to think she was screwing them, then turned her attention back to the menu. A large dusky black woman, strands of curly perm peeking out beneath her hairnet, stepped out from the kitchen area.

'Two rice an' peas wid chicken curry!'

The suited men smiled gratefully, the walked up to the counter and handed over a pink raffle ticket, before leaving with their containers of food. The large black woman waved goodbye, and dealt with the next customer in line.

''Ello, what would yuh like?'

'Can I 'ave the rice, peas an' curry goat dinner, please.'

Two minutes later Elisha stepped up to the counter.

'Good afternoon, what would yuh like, me dear?'

'Uhh . . . Can I 'ave two rice, peas an' curry chicken dinners, one rice, peas an' steak, an' one rice an' curry goat—'

'No steak – steak done.'

'Oh, OK. Can yuh make dat steak order a curry goat, please?' Elisha paused as the woman wrote this down. 'An' can I also have three Guinness punches, a pineapple punch, an' four bakes.'

'Four dumplin' . . .' the woman was saying. She went to the till and added it all up.

'Dat will be . . . sixteen pounds exac'ly.'

'Cheers,' Elisha muttered, as she handed over the money. A man from the kitchen brought two small packages to the counter.

'Two chicken rotis!'

The woman and child picked up their food and left. The large black woman gave Elisha her change and her raffle ticket, then told her the food would be two minutes. She went over to the left-hand counter to wait, feeling faint hunger bite at her belly. One of the three black girls finished her conversation, then looked over.

'Hi,' she smiled prettily. She was tall and skinny, with Elisha's fair complexion and finger waves in her hair.

'Hi,' Elisha grinned in eagerness.

'You moved in Bartholomew ain' yuh?' one of the other girls asked. She was short and dark, with an earnest face and stunning long eyelashes. Her hair was pulled back in a long jet-black ponytail. The last girl was dark too, with gold hoop earrings and thin blond plaits. Elisha nodded.

'Yeah man – how'd you know?'

The girl smiled. 'I saw you an' yuh mum goin' in dere wid a whole 'eap ah boxes not long ago.'

'Oh – you should've said 'ello.'

'I would've, but you guys looked so busy . . .'

The other girls laughed at that, but the laughter felt warm to Elisha, with no trace of bitchiness. She joined in, even though the friendly Greensider wasn't laughing with her friends.

'I din't wanna disturb yuh,' she continued. 'What floor you on den?'

'Ninth.'

The girl nodded. 'I'm on the twelfth! My name's Valerie by the way.'

Elisha shook hands and introduced herself. The tall girl gave her name as Lilliane, and the blonde as Leonora.

'D'you all live in Bartholomew?' Elisha wanted to know.

'Uh-uh. We live in Woodcrof',' Leonora said, pointing at Lilliane and herself. 'My mum don't like tower blocks.'

'Innit,' Elisha agreed. 'My las' drum was in a tower block an' the lifts were never workin'.'

'Why'd you move here den?' Valerie asked, blinking slowly. She had very clear and round brown eyes.

Elisha shrugged a little pitifully. Why indeed?

'Our flat burned down. No one knows what happened, but it destroyed almost all our possessions. The council moved us.'

The three girls covered their mouths dramatically.

'Oh, I'm sorry,' Valerie breathed. 'Nobody was hurt was they?'

'Nah, nah. I was at my ex's, my mum was out wid her man, an' my sister was ravin', so nobody was physically hurt. My mum's a bit upset about it all though. My gran's dead – she died a long time ago I mean, an' a lot ah the stuff she give my mum wen' in the fire. Mum's copin' though, dat's the main ting.'

'What about yuh garms?' Leonora looked pained, as if the question had taken some effort.

'Gone innit? All ah dem. The council gave us some money though, an' the flat was insured, so we should get somethin' back, but—'

'—It's not the same.' Lillian finished sympathetically. 'I dunno how you managed. I couldn't live knowin' all my bes' clothes were gone forever. Min' you, you don't look too bad . . .'

'Thanks,' Elisha said gratefully. She'd worried about her appearance ever since the fire. 'I lef' a few ah my things at my ex's house. I tell you what though – I had a cris' pair ah Versace jeans dat got bun up. I'm screwin' about dat, believe.'

The girls gave a sympathetic moan. The man from the kitchen came back. 'Three chicken dinners!'

'Dat's ours,' Valerie smiled. 'Hol' on, we'll be back in a sec'.'

The girls went to the counter, laughed and joked with the woman at the till, then came back while Elisha watched them, feeling happy.

'We might as well wait for your food an' walk back wid you,' Valerie proposed.

'Seein' as we're virtually neighbours now.'

'OK,' Elisha smiled. She'd made her first new friends.

After purchasing the other items her mother wanted, Elisha and the three girls walked back to Bartholomew, chatting in a relaxed and easy way.

'So what's it like here?'

'It's OK,' Lenora allowed carefully.

'It's *borin*'!' Valerie cried loudly. 'Nuthin' happens. Even the youth club's closed down 'cos they reckon it's full ah asbestos. If dat goes, there'll be nuthin' left for us yout's.'

'Mek dem close it, I don't care,' Lilliane sneered. 'I wouldn't go dere if yuh paid me luv.'

'I bet Lacey an' Trisha care,' Leonora told her thoughtfully. 'Don't forget, they'd both be out of a job.'

The girls made sympathetic noises but no one had a reply to that.

'We didn't even have a youth club in Winton,' Elisha sighed mournfully.

Leonora looked up at her. 'What, you used to live on Winton estate in Fulham?'

'Uh huh.'

'D'you know a girl called Bianca Davis? She lives in Cossham House.'

'Nah . . .' Elisha looked vague.

'What about Sasha? Sasha Miller, lives in Linden?'

She brightened. 'Yeah, I know Sasha, her mum's name's Beverly innit? We went secondary.'

'Sasha's my cousin,' Leonora said proudly. 'Beverly's my mum's second cousin or summick like dat. I never understan' all dat shit anyway.'

'Sasha' safe man,' Elisha told the girl. 'She keeps herself to herself an' she's quiet, but she's one ah dem people everybody gets on wid.'

Leonora smiled as they passed Belsize, where Elisha had seen the group of boys hanging about. Another quick look told her what she'd expected – they were still there. The boys saw them crossing the road, and began calling Lilliane. She blushed, smiled, then sauntered over. Leonora followed. Valerie and Elisha hung back. Lilliane and Leonora began to talk to the boys, breaking into loud laughter every now and then. Elisha watched them awkwardly, while Valerie stood in silence by her side.

'Don't yuh know dem?' Elisha gestured in the direction of the boys.

'Yeah, but I didn't wanna leave yuh here on your own,' Valerie replied. After a moment, she looked into her new-found friend's eyes and decided to tell her a kind of truth. 'Anyway, I don't get on wid one ah the guys over dere – his name's Raymond. I used go out wid him, but he's a e-dyat man, smokes too much bone.'

'Which one's dat?' Elisha muttered, peering over.

'The one in the blue cap and brown leather.'

'Mmmm . . .' He didn't look too bad to Elisha.

Another boy came out of the dark staircase in the centre of Belsize, looking harassed and slightly annoyed. He was quite short, his golden-brown skin contrasting deeply with the dark black of his eyebrows and beard. He walked over to the group, and after what looked like some manly gossip, he started talking to the girls, who were now posturing and skinning teeth shamelessly. Elisha, who'd been watching the boy closely, saw him look their way, then point over and tug Lilliane's sleeve. She shifted a little and looked away.

'Who's he?' she asked Valerie.

Valerie squinted, then kissed her teeth. 'You don' wanna know.'

'Yeah I do!'

Valerie sighed. 'I tell you what – wait till Ray's not around an' I'll gladly introduce you. His name's Orin. He's OK I suppose, jus' loves playin' badbwoy, dat's all.'

'He's cris',' Elisha said plainly. Valerie gave her a sympathetic ↻ce as Lilliane and Leonora wandered back.

'Lyun lot was askin' about you Elisha,' Lilliane told her. 'They wanned to know how come you two never come over.'

Everyone looked at Valerie.

'Ray an' Johnny said hi . . .' Leonora started tentatively.

Before she could finish, Valerie turned and walked off towards Bartholomew without saying a word. Leonora and Lilliane frowned at each other, then, pulling at Elisha's sleeve, they ran to catch her up.

The Yout' Man and the Ki

His pager started beeping the second the front door closed behind him. He groaned, cursed and pulled it from his waist, convinced he knew who it was. The message was short and curt: ORIN I NEED TO SPEAK TO YOU URGENTLY LOVE SISSY. Sighing, he clipped the pager back on to his jeans and fished for his keys.

The house was echoing with Usher's 'My Way' when he walked down the passage, which only served to rile him more. He blasted into the living room, where Sissy and Carolyn were sitting goggle-eyed, watching *The Box*; they looked at his angry face, then at each other, before starting to laugh in high-pitched, crazy-sounding giggles. He rolled his eyes and waited for them to finish.

Gemma, alias Sissy, was Orin's fourteen-year-old sister, but no one had called her Gemma since she was two. Orin had given her the nickname Sissy as an infant, using the word as a much-preferred shortcut to saying 'my sister'. The nickname suited Sissy so well that her Christian name was discarded like a soiled nappy. Only her father still called her Gemma, when he was really vex.

Orin narrowed his eyes and gave the girls a measured stare, reducing their laughter to quiet giggles. His sister was smart, beautiful and witty; she was also loud and foul-mouthed, a fact of life he couldn't stand. Carolyn was her closest friend, and of the same mould, except that she had a strange maturity about her; she was like a forty-year-old trapped in a teenager's body. Orin didn't approve of her friendship with his sister, but as nothing untoward had happened yet, he'd decided to let it be.

'I think he's vex y'nuh,' Carolyn muttered in a hushed semi-laugh. Sissy cut her eyes at the wall.

'Cha man, wassup wid you now Orry? I only wanned you to do me a favour.'

He sighed again and came further into the living room. 'Wha' d'you want? I gotta go sign on!'

Sissy got up and crossed the room towards him, holding five one-pound coins in her palm. 'Can you get me a Pink Protection relaxer kit from the Indian guy in the market—'

'Pink Protection relaxer kit?' Orin spluttered disbelievingly. Behind his sister Carolyn began to laugh once more. 'You paged me sayin' "urgent" for dat?'

Sissy put her hand on her hip and pouted. 'Ah, wha' you goin' on stoopid for man, you couldn't have taken more than two steps out the door. C'mon, it ain' gonna hurt you.'

Knowing she was right on all counts, he took the coins with a grunt and pocketed them with no more argument. Sissy smiled and danced a couple of steps to the beat of the TV.

'Thank you, thank you,' she sang brightly. 'An' make sure yuh get regular an' not super, OK?'

'OK,' he mumbled. 'Wha's all dis for anyway?'

'I'm gettin' my hair done innit?' she replied glibly.

Orin gave her a push. 'I know *dat*, but how come you ain' goin' dat place in Grove?'

Sissy shrugged. 'Shannon's doin' it,' she replied, pushing him back, but not quite as hard. He let it slide because she was the bearer of good tidings for once.

Shannon, a door-to-door hairstylist from Denver House (the estate's second tower block), was a goddess – a black queen who was a little too old for a prince like him, but there was no harm in looking was there? Orin planned to be around later to bus' some small talk and check her out.

'Oh, OK,' he said in the most nonchalant tone he could manage. 'I gotta run, I'm late as it is.' He nodded at Carolyn and made for the door. Sissy followed, calling, 'Remember regular, not super!'

'Yeah, yeah,' he growled, stepping into the sunshine again and slamming the door behind him. Although it was bright, it was very cold. He fumbled in his pockets for a cigarette and found a chip. When he'd lit it and taken a few puffs, he started out on his fortnightly journey to the Job Centre.

He stepped past the brick enclosure for a large metal dustbin that stood at the bottom of the Belsize landing chute, and immediately saw his block's regular loafers cooling in their usual spot – Johnny Winsome, Ray Miles, Ryan Wilson and Alex Carter (who'd just been released from Feltham for the third time, after a three-month stay). And from the neighbouring blocks, Benji, Robby, Mak and Little Stacey. They began hailing him on sight. As he got closer, Orin noticed the two girls in amongst all the males. Lilliane and Leonora. Not bad looking, but dumb as fuck.

Definitely not in Shannon's league, he thought with a smile.

'Yeah yeah,' Alex drawled as he caught sight of him. Orin touched fists with the youths.

'Whassup?'

'Chillin',' Alex replied easily, 'Yuh hear 'bout Jason Taylor? He got knock out las' night yuh know.'

'Yeah?' Orin shook his head as the youth offered him the Dragon bottle. 'Nah man, too early. So who knock 'im out?'

'Lawrence innit. Dem man lash a 'lex togevva an' Jason was supposed to take it to Lionel's an' split the wong wid Larry. 'Stead ah doin' dat, my man tell him he got robbed by some cat, den kep' the suttin' an' sol' it to the Ol' Man y'get me? Lawrence mussa fin' out star – when I see 'im las' night he was coarsin' Jason up.'

The Old Man was an aged fence who lived in Belsize House,

and a vibrant, respected figure on the estate. Although he maintained an honesty that was surprising in his line of work, wily youths like Jason Taylor couldn't quite manage the same – which often resulted in violent clashes between former friends.

'Man's gettin' too bright these days,' Orin commented disgustedly. 'It's like yuh can't trus' man in the manor no more.' The others grunted agreement. 'How much did Jay get for the Rolex anyhow?'

Alex hawked and spat a thick wad of phlegm before replying. The girls groaned in disgust; he smiled thinly. 'I think the Ol' Man gi' 'im four hundred.'

Orin laughed and shook his head.

'Dem lot're fools anyway,' Ryan broke in savagely. 'Bere back-stabbin's bin goin' on between dem fuh ages. I wouldn't do fuck all wid none ah dem man star. None ah dem.'

'Can't you speak den Orin?' Leonora sneered over their conversation, worming her way back into everyone's attention. The surrounding boys said nothing, letting them get on with it.

'Yeah yeah, wha' you sayin'?' Orin smiled, moving a little closer. Looking over her shoulder he spotted Valerie and Elisha standing across the road, talking amongst themselves. At the sight of the new girl, his eyes widened considerably. 'Hey – who's dat wid Val?'

Everyone barring the girls looked over.

'Oh! Dat's Elisha,' Lilliane gossiped eagerly. 'She moved in Bart dis mornin'. She seems OK.'

'She look *good*,' Ryan emphasised, his lips moving as though they had a life of their own. Leonora rolled her eyes.

'So how come they're standin' over there?' Orin asked.

Leonora wrinkled her nose. 'I dunno, I never asked her.'

Now every head was twisted that way. Valerie and Elisha fidgeted unconsciously, very aware of the attention they were getting. Orin was watching Elisha openly, wanting her to see him. Elisha looked over occasionally, but generally put on an air of disinterest. He didn't mind . . . as long as it didn't last.

'She got a man?' he probed Leonora further.

'She don't *know*,' Lilliane sighed. 'Why we gonna ask the girl suttin' like dat?'

'So you can show man like *us* the ku, y'get me?' Johnny cried, cracking up and touching fists with the others. The girls gave each boy a hard look, then kissed their teeth and moved away, clearly annoyed by all the macho business.

'See you lot later man . . .'

'Bye . . .' Leonora waved.

'Yeah, piss off yuh bitches,' fifteen-year-old Little Stacey muttered. He was rewarded with a loud roar of laughter, and grinned widely until he caught sight of Orin's face. When his smile had vanished, the older youth turned and watched the girls walk towards Bartholomew until he could see them no more.

'Dat new girl's the lick,' he breathed, in sincere admiration.

'Tell me nuh,' Ryan agreed, also looking their way. Stacey nudged his best friend Benji's side and pointed at the boys. They both grinned.

Orin arrived at the Job Centre half an hour late, but it was no big thing; the advisers weren't usually bothered, so he wasn't about to start worrying. The Centre was an open-plan, plush office area. The cards advertising jobs were on metal stands by the main front doors, while at the other end were five desks – three on the left-hand side of the room, two at the far end facing the front doors. Suited men and women of various colours and creds sat behind them, looking uneasy at the prospect of facing another day of the unemployed. Musak floated from unseen speakers; it was meant to be soothing, but always ended up pissing Orin off.

A long snaking queue almost reached the reception desk, and Orin joined it with a sinking feeling, preparing to wait. He'd been signing on since he left school three years ago. Although he hated the routine, there was no way he was going to go for the kind of job they advertised on the employment cards. He didn't think he was being snobbish or anything, he just believed he could do a lot better than *Trainee Chef*, or *Painter and Decorator*, or *Assistant Dental Technician*. Those jobs were fine if that's what you wanted to do – if that's what you enjoyed. But Orin neither wanted nor enjoyed any of the jobs on display. He'd decided to continue doing a little hustling and selling a bit of greenery until he found something better.

After a long wait, he made it to one of the desks at the far end. He sat down and smiled at the black woman before him.

'Y'all right?'

'Hiya!' she beamed back. 'Now don't tell me, I remember, I remember . . .'

'I'll gi' yuh a clue if yuh want,' he said helpfully.

She shook her head and closed her eyes. 'Nah man, hol' on, I got it, I got it . . . McKnight, yeah?'

His eyebrows lifted in surprise. 'Hey! I din't think you'd remember!'

'I never forget a face, or a name,' she replied, giving him a sassy wink before walking over to the rows of cardboard boxes bearing the signing-on slips and flicking through *Mc*. Orin watched her firm behind with dull interest, wondering if she was flirting with him. She was a bit old, but he'd give her the wuk same way – it'd just have to be an undercover wuk, that was all.

'Here we are . . . McKnight,' she said, pushing the slip in front of him. He grabbed for the pen on a shoelace, trying to banish his thoughts.

'Have you done any work in the las' two weeks?' she asked in a bored monotone. He thought about it as he signed, then stopped dead.

'As it goes I did. My uncle got me to do some buildin' site work, it paid really good as well. Does dat affec' my dole or—'

'Don't sign dat den!' the woman screeched, before looking down at his slip. 'Oh. You've signed it. *Shit*. I gotta get you a whole new form, I'll jus' be a sec' . . .'

She got up from her seat, then froze when she noticed he was laughing. A sarcastic smile appeared on her lips, and she sat down again.

'Ha, ha, ha.'

'I tell yuh the same ting every week innit.'

'Well, your circumstances might've changed.'

She was talking like a typical social security worker now. Orin didn't really check for that.

'Dere yuh go,' he said, passing her the form. He sniffed once, then again. 'I like dat scent man.' He sniffed some more, mainly for effect, but stopped when he felt the tingles of a sneeze. 'Whassat, Poison? Chanel?' The woman beamed.

'You're jokin' ain' you? This's Boots' own darlin' – a Christmas present from my mother. Hardly in the number five league.'

'Yeah?' Orin managed to appear shocked, as though he hadn't smelt the same scent coming from his sister's room many times in the past. Not that Sissy would ever admit it. 'You must have naturally sweet-smellin' skin or suttin'. I never smelt a high-street perfume like dat before!'

'Thank you,' she said, clearly pleased, forgetting her former irritation.

He got up to leave while he was ahead, feeling good, the way he always did when he left this place.

'See yuh in two weeks!' he called over his shoulder.

'I hope so,' she murmured, just loud enough for him to catch it.

Orin smiled confidently and headed for the door. When he got there, a black youth was just coming inside. It took a moment before he recognised him as Nathan Walters, a Greensider who had attended his secondary school. They smiled at each other in greeting and touched fists.

'Yes man, yuh cool?' asked Nathan, a small bullet-headed youth with a cheeky face and an amiable nature. Orin shrugged.

'Yeah man, jus' makin' my mark y'get me?'

'Yuh know dem ones.' Nathan grinned in understanding.

'Suh wha' yuh bin up to?' Orin enquired, moving back from the doorway. The youth rubbed his nose and followed.

'Ah, the usual yuh know, survivin' innit? I was doin' a little paintin' an' decoratin' a few weeks back, but since dat all finished I'm back signin' on again. Pisses me off man, I hate dealin' wid all these sour-faced people every two weeks.'

'Some ah dem are all right,' Orin admitted, looking back towards the counters. His client adviser was busy with someone else.

Nathan sighed. 'Yeah I suppose so . . . But I ain' gonna be on dis signin' on shit much longer. Between me an' you, I'm thinkin' about settin' up a little pirate station.'

Nathan was looking at Orin hesitantly, as if he wasn't sure he was doing the right thing in telling him. Orin held his serious gaze, though the conversation was already losing him. Pirate radio stations were great to listen to, but Orin was only interested in the idea of instant money – long-term plans simply held no appeal.

'Yeah man dat soun's like a ruff idea. What, you gonna do it aroun' Greenside?'

'Course man. It all depends on whether mans pitch in an' help me out, but I'd love to get suttin' together soon . . .'

Orin nodded automatically, though by now he was only half listening. Nathan read his expression correctly, and decided to break out of the subject before he bored his audience any more. He lifted his fist again.

'Ay Orin, I better hol' my place in the queue before I affa wait the whole afternoon.' He touched his friend, then moved back towards the counters.

'All right man safe. Dere's veg about if yuh on it?'

'Yeah? I might check yuh later still . . .'

'Bell me,' Orin stressed, before making another stab at leaving. As he went he took a last glance towards the counter, just to see if his adviser was watching him. She was. When she saw him turn her way, she raised a hand to her lips and blew him a quick kiss, making him grin and respond with a tiny wave of his hand.

Wah, he thought to himself, *big tings* . . .

He strolled out of the Job Centre like a Lord.

Orin stopped off at a shop for a pack of king-size blues and a copy of *The Voice*, then visited the local bakery for an apple Danish and jam doughnut. With these items in hand, he made his way to the park in the centre of Greenside for his usual spliff, cake and read.

This outing had become routine – he loved relaxing in the outdoors, watching the other Greensiders go by and reading about his people. He also loved the way his weed sold a lot faster while he was out there. The quicker he sold, the quicker he could go back and see Lionel, his supplier, for more of the good stuff. When he thought about it, the park wasn't just routine – it was a necessity.

Once inside, he found his usual spot, checked for dog shit, then took off his jacket and lay down on it. The park was fairly empty. The only figures Orin could see were the workmen bustling around the dilapidated youth club opposite. He wrapped his zook carefully, then lit it and opened out the paper. Soon he was engrossed, though he looked up every now and then, just to make sure no police were clocking him.

Twenty minutes later he was turning the sports pages when he saw two white men enter the park. They strolled around the pathway, not talking to each other but looking tense. Orin watched them come his way suspiciously; there was no way they were from the manor, and he was pretty sure they were CIDs. The two men passed, casting a disinterested glance his way, but dismissing his presence immediately. When they were far enough away from him, he relit the remainder of his spliff and continued to watch.

They seemed very agitated. The shorter and younger looking of the two started waving his arms about and pointing at the park gates. The older man did less talking, but every time he opened his mouth he'd shake the Tesco's carrier bag he was holding. When they reached the wooden benches that stood in front of a row of bushes beside the youth club, they sat down.

Orin watched them some more, but as they continued to do nothing but talk, he rapidly lost interest. He turned back to the paper. When he finished reading, he ate his cakes. He checked his pager. Nothing.

Orin was getting ready to leave the park when he realised the white men were making their way back towards the gates. He decided to wait until they'd left, as he was still a little suspicious; this park was notorious for dealing and he didn't fancy reminding them of his presence.

Just as they reached the tall gates, a panda car slowly rolled past, then came to a halt. Orin stiffened. Two policemen got out and walked over to the two men. They talked. The policemen split the men up and began talking into their radios. The younger one started shouting.

That was when Orin realised the Tesco's bag was gone. He watched the policemen search the men, but after a little while it was clear there was nothing to be found. Orin saw the men hurl insults at the policemen, then walk slowly down the road, looking back every now and then. The Met men got back inside the car, watching them with hard eyes. After five minutes they started the panda up and drove off in the direction the men had taken.

Orin frowned deeply, trying to make sense of the scene he'd just witnessed. Where had the bag gone? Why had the police stopped the men?

He got to his feet and, warily watching the men in overalls working on the youth club, Orin made his way towards the benches. His nerves jangled, as if some sixth sense was telling him to go the opposite way – but he just couldn't do it. He had to know what was in the bag.

Looking around again, he reached the bench and bent over, peeking underneath it. Apart from empty Rizla packets and cigarette butts there was nothing to see. He stood up and felt the blood rush to his head, making his world go dark. He closed his eyes. When his head felt better, he opened them – then he saw the bushes.

As soon as he got close enough, he noticed the blue, white and red and could read the letters 'TES'. Still checking his surroundings with quick, furtive glances, he reached for it, lifting it from the withered roses and rhododendrons. The weight of the bag surprised him. When it was completely free of the bushes, he opened it quickly and peered inside.

He gasped.

Orin slammed into his house, breathing hard and standing with his back against the door, thinking about what he'd found. The bag was zipped inside his jacket, snuggled comfortably by his stomach. He closed his eyes and inhaled slowly, drawing air into his chest until it hurt. His mind was alive with thoughts and ideas, racing around crazily, careening inside his head – *Did anybody see me? There was all those workmen there but they couldn't have seen anything I was quick I know I was quick. But what about the Rads dem? They was long gone they left the scene long before but what about all dem man outside . . .*

He tried looking out of the frosted window in the front door, but there was only a haze of colours and blurred movement. His friends had been very curious when he walked past them at a near run only seconds before. They'd called him over, wondering what the rush was, but he shook his head and said he'd be back out in a bit. Orin had felt the weight of their eyes on him as he'd unlocked his door, and with his back to the road his renegade mind had been certain the police were appearing by the vanload behind him, fully aware of what he held inside his jacket. When he was sure there was no one outside his front door, he walked into the sitting room. His sister and her friend were still there, but now there was a teenage boy with them, lounging on the sofa, his arm around Carolyn and his feet on the coffee table. His feet were the first thing Orin noticed. The youth rapidly removed them.

'Yes,' Orin said harshly, nodding everyone's way. He didn't wait for a reply and made his way towards his bedroom, while looking back over his shoulder at the scattered videos and tapes. 'You better clean all dat shit before Dad comes back Sissy!'

'Yeah I'm gonna do it later, don't fret yuhself!'

Orin paused by the door. 'When you lot go back anyway?'

'Tomorrow,' they groaned in unison. Carolyn's boyfriend, a tall youth called Clive, kissed his teeth and waved a lazy arm.

'Cha man, I don' see the point in all dis anyway. Wha's the use ah strikin' for one day? The government ain' respondin' to dat! They wanna strike for all . . . a week, or even a mont' at leas'! Den they'd see their money goin' up, believe dat! An' we'd get back jus' in time for the Christmas holiday!'

The girls cackled. Orin shook his head. 'I thought school days were supposed to be the bes' days ah yuh life,' he noted dryly.

'Not my fuckin' life,' Clive moaned. 'I can't wait to get outta dat shithole man, an' I know dem teachers can't wait either, y'get me? The sooner I get leave, the better it'll be for everyone star.'

'Yeah, well you go piss-poor Avery innit,' Sissy replied disdainfully. 'Anyone'd feel like dat goin' dere!'

'So what, Greenside ain' much better than Avery y'nuh,' the youth spat back. 'Anyway, I don't gi' a damn, school's school wherever you go, y'get me. I'm gonna juggle till I leave, so I don't business mate, I'll jus' ride dem mont's till den.'

Clive studied the older boy with a smile in his eyes. 'What Orin – wanna buy a lickle draw?'

Orin smiled, knowing he should feel annoyed, but not caring. 'Nah man, I'm safe. But don't be sellin' no green to anyone else in dis house y'nuh – especially my sister.'

He cut his eye at Sissy as he said this. She stuck out her tongue in reply but remained silent.

'Y'ear me?' Orin warned.

'Yeah man, yuh safe. I never juggle in yuh drum anyway.'

Orin smiled again, recognising the lie but not bothering to chase it up. 'All right den. I'll catch you lot up yeah?'

He walked into his room and closed the door firmly, before locking it and pulling his curtains shut. He took the bag out of his jacket and reached inside. When his hand came out he was holding a dark brown cling-wrapped rectangle which looked like an over-grown brick. He lifted it to his nose and inhaled deeply.

It was exactly what he'd hoped it would be.

He laid the block on the bed, then sat next to it, looking at it closely. Hashish. Cannabis. Ash. Rocky. Pox. Call it what you like, he'd found it, and he was already making plans as to how this little package could make him a small fortune.

The top of the block was almost black in colour, and was smooth and unmarked when compared to the sides. These bore deep ridges, no doubt from the knife that had cut this piece, and were more chocolate brown than black. The aroma was strong. Orin knew without a shadow of a doubt that there had to be just under, or just over a ki, sitting right there on his bed. He couldn't help smiling; there was no doubt about it, he was rich. Selling a kilo of ash on his estate would be as easy as selling binoculars outside a nudist colony.

Unlocking his door and ignoring the wild laughter from the sitting room, he went into his dad's bedroom and picked up the phone, pushing buttons rapidly. His voice was full of urgency when he eventually spoke.

'Yeah Cherina it's Orin. Y'all right? Yeah man, if you could.'

He waited a few moments.

'Yeah Malcolm, wha' you sayin' blood? Yuh still got dem diggys? What, c'n I borrow dem? Now now. Yeah man, I need you to bring dem over quicktime. Aah, don't go on like dat, it's important . . . I can't chat now, jus' come nuh! It's serious, believe me it's serious. All right. Lickle.'

Orin went back to his bedroom and sat on the bed in a daze. He'd sold ounces and halves for ages, and had even played the middle man on a few bar sales in the past, but he'd never had this much ash in his personal possession in his entire life. Between him and his friend Malcolm, Orin was sure they could get rid of the lot and make one hundred per cent profit. His thoughts of the two white men were brief and dismissive.

He switched on the radio and built a spliff from the weed he already had, smoking it from his bedroom window while he waited for his friend. Nearly half an hour later there was a light knock on his door.

'Yeah yeah!' he called over his shoulder.

Malcolm came in. The youths had been friends since for ever – Malcolm was the most trustworthy man Orin knew. He lived in Denver House. He was thin and gangly, dressed in Calvin Klein jeans and a Dolce & Gabbana hooded top. His face was usually expressionless and calm; nothing seemed to surprise Malcolm. Orin was interested to see what his reaction to the kilo would be.

'Yes blood.' They touched fists.

'Nice one,' Orin passed the spliff over. 'D'you bring the diggys?'

'Yeh man.'

Malcolm took a puff and looked towards the bed. His eyes widened. He coughed twice, blew out the smoke as quickly as he could, then moved closer to the bed before sitting down carefully.

'*Fuckin' 'ell*,' he breathed slowly. Orin smiled. There was silence while Malcolm surveyed the block, then smelt it. He looked up at his friend, clearly puzzled.

'Where the fuck d'you get the money fuh dis from?'

The care-free smile wouldn't leave Orin's face. 'I didn't,' he replied happily. 'I found it.'

'Don't lie!'

Success. Malcolm's face was covered in shock.

'Nah man, I ain' lyin'! I was in the park an' I seen these bait white brers walkin' wid a Tesco's bag. When they left they didn't have the bag no more. Two twos, nex' ting I know the Rads are on their case innit! When they left, I wen' over to where they'd bin cotchin' an' foun' the bag! Dat's what was inside!'

His friend was shaking his head, seemingly unaware of the movement. 'Oi bredrin, yuh know dere mus' be at leas' a ki dere star!'

'Yeh man, I know.'

'Who you tol'?'

'No one. You, dat's it. I'll need yuh help to get rid of it man. I reckon sooner or later dem white brers'll come lookin' fuh their tings, so the quicker we do dat the better. Anyting we make, we split fifty-fifty innit?'

'Damn!' Malcolm exclaimed, a huge grin spreading across his features. 'You musta bin skinnin' teet' when you opened dat bag mate!'

'Nah man, I weren't skinnin' no teet', I was narrow. Dem man coulda bin CIDs! It coulda bin a set up or anyting, y'get me. I jus' had to take the chance.'

'Blatant. So what, yuh wanna weigh dis suttin' up den?'

'Yeh man.'

Orin watched as Malcolm retrieved the black digital scales from his pocket and put them on the floor, talking as he worked.

'I reckon Maverick'll take dis off our hands star, no worries,' he said confidently.

'What, today?'

'Boy . . . maybe, maybe not. Depends on his financial situation at the moment. Lionel might be up for it if Mav ain't; my man's always got money fuh dem tings.'

'Yeah man. We could even approach Kenny an' dem man if tings get really tight.'

Malcolm replied with a shrug of his shoulders. 'If you want, but I feel say dem man are on a shit lick right about now.'

'Fuh real.'

When they'd weighed the block, Orin went into the kitchen and returned with a roll of cling-film. Once they'd wrapped it up again, Orin built another zook. Malcolm took his Ericsson out and got dialling

'Yeah . . . Lionel it's Mal, Malcolm Walters. Give us a ring on 0956 227453, I got some business for yuh. Later.'

He turned to Orin.

'Voicemail. I'll try Maverick innit.' Malcolm dialled again and waited. 'It's ringin',' he informed Orin, before turning back to the phone. 'Yeah . . . Mav, it's Malcolm blood . . . Whassup? You in the manor? What, yuh girl's drum? Yeah? C'n me an' Orin come an' see yuh? We got summick yuh might be interested in. Yeh man . . . All right . . . All right, we're comin'.'

Malcolm pressed 'End' and smiled widely. 'Yeah man, he said come an' check 'im now now. I think he's up for it.'

'Come we go den,' Orin urged, putting the block in the bottom of his cupboard, then locking the door. He watched Malcolm as he put away the digital scales and phone, then they left the flat, heading for Rockwood House, just across the road from Belsize.

The youths were still outside the block when Orin and Malcolm emerged from the house. They called out again, but neither boy was in the mood for small talk.

'Yaow, wha' you lot lookin' so serious about star?' Ryan yelled. There was a row of at least four Dragon Stout bottles on the wall behind him, and his eyes were red and glazed.

Malcolm turned his way. 'Serious business blood, serious business!' he yelled back.

'Yuh not kiddin',' Orin said soberly, clutching his sides and shivering. 'Fuck, it's cuttin' out 'ere!'

'Never you min' it'll soon warm up,' Malcolm replied cheerfully.

Orin nodded and walked a little faster.

Rockwood House wasn't Maverick's home block. He lived in Devonshire, also on the eastern end of the estate. He was one of the most prolific young dealers in the area and crack was his main mover, though he didn't mind selling ash or weed. At twenty-one he was just two years older than Malcolm and Orin, but financially there was a world of difference between them.

Beth, Maverick's long-time girlfriend, was the owner of the two-bedroom third-floor flat, which she shared with her five-year-old son, Neil. Beth had lived in Greenside all her life. Her first home had been with her parents in Mackenzie House, until she gave birth to her Neil when she was twenty. Maverick wasn't the child's father, but he seemed content in the relationship. He didn't live in the flat but could be found there on a regular basis.

Orin and Malcolm breezed into the sitting room behind Beth, a chubby black girl with thick extensions.

'How's tricks?' Malcolm asked her amiably.

'Not bad, not bad,' she drawled. 'I'm jus' gettin' back into college again man, it's my secon' year an' there's so much work! Sometimes I regret the day I ever enrolled in dat damn place!'

'Yuh studyin' law innit?'

'Yeah man,' she sighed, flopping down on the leather sofa and flicking channels with the TV remote.

'Good,' Orin told her. 'The sooner you pass all dem exams the sooner you can represent me in court if I need yuh!'

Beth laughed and tutted at the same time, though Orin knew she was just playing. He'd already received probation, a fine and a warning that the next step was jail, the last time he'd appeared in court – almost one month ago. He'd been charged with attempted robbery and conspiracy to rob after he and Ray Miles got caught rolling tourists and prostitutes in Paddington.

His father hadn't been able to afford the bail at first, so after a quick stint in the magistrates' court he'd been remanded in custody for two weeks until the cash was raised. As he was nineteen, he'd spent those days in Wano, and although he wouldn't want to repeat the experience, Orin thought it had done him some good.

Beth pointed at a door to the left of the room. 'Mav's in the kitchen. Go straight through, you lot know the way.'

'Thanks Beth,' Orin said cheerfully. 'Where's Neil?'

'Oh, he's at his granny's gettin' spoilt rotten, lucky sod!'

They eased through the kitchen door to find Maverick weighing and cutting a block of ash about the quarter of the size of the one they possessed. The youths looked at each other, both groaning inwardly. Maverick gestured with his knife as they came further inside.

'Close the door.'

Malcolm complied.

'Wha' you man sayin'?'

'Safe star,' Orin assured him.

'I'm good,' Malcolm joined in. 'So Mav, yuh gyal ah study hard bredrin!'

'Yeh man, an' I'ma make sure I encourage her to pass star.

Dat way I can think about settin' up a little business, and know my legal fees are covered, y'get me.'

'Yeah yeah. So what business yuh wanna set up den?' Malcolm asked, looking genuinely interested. Maverick smiled and talked while he was cutting.

'My own pizza shop man, sellin' West Indian pizzas!'

Looking at the ash with deep concentration, Maverick didn't see the wide smirks Orin and Malcolm shot each other.

'I thought about it when I was readin' *The Voice* one day; a restaurant in Brixton had a pizza called "The Yardie", wid yam an' green banana an' all dem tings. So I thought – why not go a little further. Why not 'ave a whole range ah West Indian pizzas?' He stopped and looked towards the ceiling as if searching for inspiration. '"The Jerk Chicken", tender pieces of chicken covered in a creamy jerk sauce, topped with mushrooms, jalapeño peppers, and pepperoni . . .'

Orin felt sick.

'"The Ackee an' Saltfish". Well, dat one speaks for itself, apart from the fac' you could have it wid or widout hot pepper sauce . . . An' how 'bout dis one – "The Curry Goat"?'

Maverick didn't wait for an answer, and was so caught up in his little dream he didn't see Malcolm and Orin in silent hysterics.

'Y'get me though blood, dere's a worl' ah possibilities, blatant! Beth even thought up one call "The Rice an' Peas", but we couldn't figure out how the peas would stay on the dough widout cheese . . .'

Maverick paused in the middle of his live advert and finally looked at the youths, who were gasping for breath and shaking with the force of their mirth. He stared at them angrily for a moment, then turned back to his ash.

'Ah, fuck you lot man, you don' know nuttin'. Fuckin' baits,' he grumbled, while Malcolm and Orin killed themselves laughing.

Malcolm held up a shaky hand. 'No, no wait, I got one, I got one!' he grinned. 'How 'bout dis Mav – "The Heavin' Stomach"!'

At that, the young dealer gave in. He laughed along with

them, then used the knife to point at a small bag of weed sitting on the kitchen counter next to the cutting board.

'You're a joker man. Wanna buil' it?' he asked amiably.

'Go t'rough Mal,' Orin told his friend between chuckles.

Malcolm found some Rizla and got busy.

Maverick suddenly turned serious. 'So wha' you man 'ave f' me den?' he drawled, looking at the two of them curiously.

Malcolm gestured at Orin. 'I'll let my man show you the ku, y'get me . . .'

Orin cleared his throat and laid it all out for Maverick, beginning to end. At first, the dealer looked a bit dubious, especially when Orin told him about finding the bag. But as soon as he heard the block had been checked and weighed, and Malcolm joined in, verifying what Orin had found, Maverick seemed to think about it, then began to smile.

'Yeah man. Yuh know what mate, dat sounds proper sensible. Yestiday I got a ki off dat brer Cassius, yuh know, the Ol' Man's son? When I get the ting back to my drum an' look – bere Henna star! I was brewin'. When I phoned him he was in Birmingham, but he said he'll gimme my money back sed way, so dat's safe. He'll be comin' back down tommora, so as soon as I get the wong I'll take dat ki off yuh, blatant.'

'Tommora?' Orin didn't look too happy.

'Yeah man, all my wong's tied up in dat Henna; I can't do nothin'.'

'Is dat the Henna dere?' Malcolm asked, nodding his head at the block on the cutting board.

'Nah man,' Maverick replied. 'Dat's some pox I had lef' over from my las' lot – dat's gonna be draws only, so I need a ki, soon as. Look, I guarantee I'll take it off yuh hands. I jus' ain' got all the cash for it now. I couldn't do it before tomorra.'

'Boy . . . we need the wong quicktime man,' Orin stressed. 'Dem white brers'll be lookin' their tings, an' the sooner I get it out my dad's drum, the safer I'll feel.'

'You dunno who sol' dem bluefoots dat pox do yuh Mav?' Malcolm quizzed.

'Nah mate,' the dealer replied. 'It blatantly wasn't me, or I'd buy it back off yuh right dis second – at the right price. How much d'want anyway?'

'Gimme thirteen fifty – jus' fuh keepin' yuh mout' shut,' Orin said levelly.

Maverick nodded.

'So what, yuh gonna save it f'me den?' he asked the youths, looking from face to face anxiously.

That was when Orin realised they'd hooked the dealer. He hadn't believed it would be that straightforward, despite his outward confidence.

'Yeh man, providin' you definitely wannit,' he assured his friend.

'Done!' Maverick said boldly. The three youths touched fists while Malcolm lit the weed.

They stayed in Beth's flat for another hour and a half, before heading for the streets of Greenside charged up to the eyeballs. Orin told Malcolm he wanted to see if Lionel was in, just in case Maverick let them down. Malcolm saw the wisdom in this and they took a left out of Rockwood, walking the long straight road that eventually ran past Denver and out of the estate.

'Wha' d'you reckon of Maverick's pizza idea den?' Malcolm asked Orin seriously.

'Nigga's crazy.'

'Yuh reckon?'

'Yeh man. Dem pizzas soun' disgustin'! I wouldn't fuckin' well eat 'em anyway!'

Malcolm shrugged a little, looking embarrassed. 'Well boy, I thought they was *funny* an' dat, but I didn't think they was disgustin'! The more I think about it, the more I reckon I'd eat 'em!'

'Yeah, well you're sick too,' Orin replied candidly, screwing up his face. 'Maverick's a good businessman an' dat; he *knows* how to juggle, an' he's blatantly a smart brer. But I think he's gone too far. He could think up suttin' better than West Indian pizzas. Dat shit soun's proper corny mate.'

'Dat's the trouble wid us man,' Malcolm started snidely. 'We don't support each other's ideas . . .'

He looked up at Orin, who wasn't paying attention. Instead, his friend was looking straight ahead, his eyes fixed and unblinking.

'Whassup wid yuh now?' Mal sneered in a frustrated tone.

'It's dem,' Orin whispered, trying to talk without moving his lips.

Malcolm studied him closely to make sure he wasn't joking. He didn't seem to be. He turned from his friend and looked in the same direction.

A black Granada was easing up the road towards them at a snail's pace – too slow to simply be passing through. Orin looked at the passengers and saw there were at least four white men, all of them scanning the streets with the utmost concentration. The two in the front were the ones he'd seen in the park that afternoon. Malcolm's voice broke into his thoughts.

'Yuh sure dat's dem?' he said sternly.

'Yep. Positive.' Orin's face had adopted Malcolm's expressionless gaze. Mal kissed his teeth and spat on the floor.

'I ain' runnin', I don't care – not in my own fuckin' manor. I'm stanin' right here.'

'Don't be a fool man. Yuh tooled up?'

'No.'

'So wha' yuh talkin' stoopidness . . .'

Just as the words left Orin's mouth the driver, the older of the two men, looked up and saw them. He shouted something at the others then floored the accelerator.

Orin ran. He bombed it along the pavement adjacent to Goldsmith, the block next door to Rockwood, then darted around a corner, where a large group of kids were enjoying their day off thanks to the National Union of Teachers. They stared as he almost hurtled into them. Although he recognised some faces, he didn't know any names. Orin straightened up and looked around, wondering if Mal knew any of the kids. Then he realised that Malcolm hadn't run with him.

True to his word, Malcolm had stayed right were he was. The Granada roared up parallel to him and the men jumped out. Two large guys who'd been sitting in the back of the car ran off in the direction Orin had taken. The young guy, who looked only a few years older than Malcolm, was in his face in seconds. Mal pushed him away, but he wouldn't leave him alone.

'What, what?' Mal yelled, deciding to feign ignorance. 'Wha' yuh pushin' yuhself up in my boat for?'

'Leave 'im Al!'

Malcolm looked up in surprise and saw the second man casually moving closer. His face was craggy, and thin blond hair hung from his square-shaped head in hay-coloured strands. His nose was badly misshapen, as if it had been broken more than once, and his eyes were sunken and blue, like dead men's eyes or the unseeing orbs of a shop mannequin. He addressed Malcolm dangerously.

'Lissen you, we wan' our hash,' he growled, in a voice that chilled the youth, despite his bravado. 'We wannit dis minute. No excuses, no *lies* . . .' He raised his eyebrows at the word. 'Jus' our fackin' hash. Now where is it?'

'I dunno wha' you're on about mate, seriously.'

The old guy cursed and eyeballed him some more. The two burly men who'd run after Orin came back empty-handed. One of them was a bald black guy. Malcolm tried to give him a dirty look, but the man didn't even glance his way.

'Gone mate,' he panted harshly. 'We wen' roun' the back lookin' for 'im but dere's jus' a coupla little kids playin'. Dis estate's like a fackin' maze. Cunt could be anywhere by now.'

The older man looked around for a little bit, not saying anything. Al glared at the youth in front of him, obviously wanting a row. Mal rubbed his chin, getting a little vex.

'So what, can I go now?'

The old guy gave him a hard look, then turned to his mates. 'Put 'im in the car. Quickly.'

Before Mal knew it, the burly men rushed him and forced him towards the Granada. He fought them all the way, but they had his arms and legs and he just wasn't strong enough to fight against them. Yelling and roaring, Malcolm was edged closer and closer to the car. Some pedestrians were standing and watching, but no one said a word – the youth assumed that they thought the four guys had to be CIDs.

The first stone whistled past the car as he was yelling, so Mal didn't pay it much attention. The second hit the bonnet just as Al was trying to push Mal's head down to squeeze him inside.

The next minute, stones, pebbles and rocks were raining down on them, like some freak weather system. A huge corner-piece of scaffolding hit the windscreen, shattering it into star-shaped cracks. Mal saw and heard a headlight tinkle into nothing over the sound of the men's curses and painful shouts. Soon enough they had to let him go to cover their own heads, and they darted for the comparative safety of their vehicle like frightened rabbits into burrows.

Watching the falling objects carefully, Malcolm made a head-long run for Goldsmith, pumping his legs and arms as hard as he could. Behind him, he heard the Granada reversing down the road at high speed. He bounded to the top floor of the four-storey block to see Orin in the midst of a group of eight children, all watching the Granada and cheering loudly. Doors opened all over the landing, adult faces appearing and shouting at the kids until they quietened. Mal apologised for the noise, then laughed with joy and approached the youths.

'Buy y nuh, respec' for dat my yout's,' he cackled, touching every available little fist, including the girls. Orin glared at him, but couldn't help smiling through it.

'So what, I don' get no thanks? After all it was my original idea spee!'

'Respec' blood!' Mal said gratefully, offering his fist to his friend.

'We better get out of here blood, before dem man come back fuh us,' Orin said gravely.

Mal nodded. 'Let's wing,' he said, turning and striding down the landing, gazing over the balcony all the while. 'Thanks again yout's!'

The kids shouted their goodbyes. The two hopped down the dark and pissy staircase, then headed out of the block, slowly and carefully. When they were sure the coast was clear they hit the road, heading back towards Belsize by unspoken agreement; neither of them wanted to go to Lionel's just then.

'Lissen, thanks again for not runnin' out on me man – I thought I was properly gonna get fucked over,' Malcolm admitted freely.

'Safe man, minor,' Orin replied with a shrug.

They slapped palms, shook hands, then hugged, a light touch of the shoulders, each of them looking out for the black Granada just in case. They continued walking. When they got to Rockwood House again, Mal stopped outside the block.

'You goin' yuh drum?' he asked.

'Yeah yeah.'

'I'll catch you up. I gotta chat to Maverick about summick.'

'Yeah? What?'

'A business ting man, don' worry yuhself . . .' Mal grimaced, as he realised he'd have to say a little more than that to counter Orin's unease. 'We need some protection if we're gonna be walkin' streets wid dem man lookin' for us,' he explained.

'So what, yuh gonna get Maverick to hol' you a bucky?'

Malcolm laughed at that, though he could see where his friend was coming from. Maverick was well known for his interest in guns, and his ability to get hold of one if it was desired. Mal shook his head and jogged on his toes.

'Nah man, who d'you tink I am? I ain' goin' out like certain man aroun' here. We don' *need* no bucky. Jus' trus' me an' wait a while, yeah? I tell you all about my plan later on.'

'You an' yuh fuckin' plans . . .'

Orin gave his friend a measured stare, not believing a word of it. Malcolm was the kind of guy who thought about situations like this a great deal, and often had harebrained schemes to try and counter them. Sometimes he worried that Mal was going to land himself in major trouble one day, but there was nothing he could do as his friend was extremely hard-headed. He would just be there for him.

'All right man. Jus' be careful, an' make sure you come look fuh me when yuh leave Mav's, yeah?'

'Yeh man.' Malcolm smiled off Orin's concern. 'See you in a bit blood.'

'Yeah, later,' Orin replied weakly.

He watched Malcolm bound up the block's stairs, then made for his own, unsure as to whether he'd done the right thing, now, or at any other time during the course of this crazy day.

Eyes pin-balling left and right, Mal returned to Rockwood, his nerves pulsating electricity like a telephone wire. Once again, Beth answered the door.

'Can't get enough of us eh?' she joked letting him inside.

'Yuh know dat innit?'

He walked through to the kitchen, needing no directions. Maverick was still at the counter chopping ash, and two more youths sat at the wooden table. Nazra and Strong, of Asian and West Indian parentage respectively, were familiar faces on the estate. Nazra was a thin, whippet-like wheeler and dealer, full of scams and cockney chatter. Strong was a hefty keep-fit fanatic, with an amiable disposition and a build that grown men craved.

'Whassup boys?' Mal drawled, extending the customary fist. The youths made faces to imply things could be a whole lot better and she had the vibe from Smallie's.

'Cool man,' Nazra mumbled through the chunks of meat. 'Ay, yuh wanna buy a motor?'

'From who?'

'Me innit,' came the sneered reply. 'Who else?'

Malcolm shrugged and crossed the room, reaching for one of the many mugs resting beside the sink. His throat was sandpaper dry. He took it and filled it from the tap, speaking over his shoulder.

'I ain' got no wong to buy a car anyhow.'

'Ride's safe man – 'lectric windows, sunroof, MOT . . .'
Strong intoned, watching Mal's reaction to see if it changed. It
didn't.

'How much d'yuh want?' Maverick queried.

'A gran' an' change.'

'What is it?' Mal cut in.

'Swif', Suzuki Swif'. C reg man, the ride's cold star, trus'
me. I can even get you a tes' run if yuh interested.'

'*Boyyy* . . . No wong, y'nuh.'

Mal emptied the mug and shrugged his apology at the youths,
who murmured but knew the cold sell wasn't working. He
tapped Maverick on the shoulder to get his attention.

'Ay blood, guess what happened to me outta road jus' now.'

'Whassat?'

'Dem fuckin' white brers me an' Orin was tellin' you about
man, fuckin' tried to rush us as we lef' the block. We had to
duss for our lives star, there was nuff ah dem all tryin' t'do us
in an' dat!'

Nazra and Strong had stopped eating and Malcolm knew he
had their full attention. A murderous look came over Maverick's
face, which cheered the youth until he spoke.

'You didn't make 'em see yuh come up 'ere did yuh?'

'Nah man, wha' d'you think I am, barmy? We run all over the
manor tryin' t'lose 'em, then we dussed 'em out down by the
site an' doubled back over here. Don' worry yuhself. Dem man
never saw nuttin'.'

'You wanna hope so,' the young dealer warned. ''Cos if they
come up 'ere it's me an' dem – man's gonna get deaded tonight,
trus' me.'

'They ain' comin' up 'ere man.'

Maverick gave a snort.

'So what Mal, you wanna han' goin' after dem or suttin'?'
Strong offered sincerely, locking eyes with Malcolm to assure he
wasn't kidding. Satisfaction surged through the youth. He knew
his friends would back him up, and he was extremely grateful
for Strong's words.

'Yeah man, I wouldn't min' y'nuh spee, true I don't really feel safe boppin' street wi' dem man lookin' for us. I dunno what they're gonna come wid nex',' he told them in a resigned tone.

'So what, wha' yuh done dem man?' Nazra piped up.

'Ah don' worry about it, it's long to try an' explain the whole ku, y'unnerstan'? They jus' wanna do me suttin', dat's the main ting.'

Strong rubbed his thighs and pushed out his chest like a Sumo. 'All right den, come we go an' hol' our tings an' go look f'dem star,' he said decisively. He was almost out of his seat already.

Mal thought that now was the time to unleash his plan.

'Nah man, hol' up a secon',' he spluttered quickly, gesturing at Strong to sit back down. 'We affa be smart about dis man, we can't go boppin' aroun' the place wid bucky's an' bad looks; we're jus' gonna en' up in Scrubbs like dat. We affa be smart about it, innit Mav?'

'Go on,' the dealer growled stonily, forgetting his work and crossing his arms while turning to face the youth. Malcolm had centre stage.

'All right, 'ear dis – me an' Orin owe dem man money, so I wanna play like we're gonna give it dem back. I'll go look for dem man an' tell 'em we'll meet somewhere aroun' 'ere. I'll phone Mav an' tell 'im when. We give dem man the wong, then we let 'em leave . . .'

'If they duss widout killin' the both ah you firs',' Nazra pointed out wisely.

Mal waved a dismissive hand. 'Let us man worry 'bout dat. Anyway, we make dem leave, den you man can rush the fuckin' ride, make out like yuh stingin' 'em. Get the money back an' get our revenge. Simple as dat.'

'For you maybe,' Maverick snorted. 'All the heat's off you an' on us innit?'

'An' it's fuckin' bait,' Nazra added, skinning up in obvious displeasure.

Malcolm looked at their faces and felt his plan slipping through his fingers. Even Strong looked a little dubious. His friends were his only means of getting out of this. He had to make them see things his way.

'Not as bait as trampin' around wid guns lookin' for dem man,' he argued desperately. 'At least dis way the ball's in our court, an' we ain' relying on chance to sort us out. I'm tellin' you it's simple. Look, me an' Orin are in the most danger yuh nuh. Dis way dere's nex' to no chance of any of you gettin' hurt.

'Yeah right,' Nazra said glumly, but Mal could see his argument was winning them over. That and their expectation that he would do the same for them. Which he probably would.

'Where yuh gonna meet?' Strong asked out of the blue.

Good question. He hadn't even thought about that, he'd been so busy wondering how he could get them to say yes. His mind clutched and fumbled for an answer, then sought his own question to stall them.

'You gonna help me den?'

No one spoke.

'Well . . . ?'

He could say no more, afraid of the answer. They looked at each other silently. Then nodded.

'Where yuh gonna meet den?' Strong repeated. He was ready for action now. Mal had time to think how glad he was that the heavyweight was on his side.

'Uhh . . . the site man, I reckon dat's the bes' place. In about an hour. I'll bell you man though an' let yuh know.'

'All right, the site in an hour,' Nazra agreed, also looking eager.

'Sure you don't wan' us to come wid you?' Maverick said. Now that everything had been decided, Mal knew the dealer could be trusted and relied upon. Still, he had to shake his head at the offer. After all, it wasn't in the plan.

'I don't think it's a good idea yuh nuh blood. If they see me wid someone other than Orry they might get suspicious.'

The youths saw the logic in that, and seemed content to

entrust the whole scenario to Malcolm. After talking over the plan a little longer, he said he was going to go back out and look for the Granada. The others wished him luck. He smiled and took a couple of cigarettes from Maverick's pack of twenty for the road, then went for the front door. 'See yuh later Beth!'

Maverick's girl was watching TV with one eye and scribbling in a notepad. She smiled and continued.

'See yuh!'

He walked down the passage and reached for the latch to the front door. Then he stopped. He stood there for almost half a minute, turning things over in his mind. If Orin could've seen him, he wouldn't have liked the expression on Mal's face one little bit.

He wouldn't have liked what happened next either.

Mal began to smile. He turned back down the passage and entered the living room once more, surprising Beth with his appearance.

'I thought I never heard the door go,' she frowned. 'Can't get rid ah yuh today can we?'

'Yuh know what they say about bad pennies,' Mal grinned, feeling in good spirits. He pushed through the kitchen door to find the scene pretty much the same as when he'd left. Strong hailed him through the thick cloud of ash smoke.

'What, yuh back already blood?' he shouted, while the others grinned but looked slightly confused. 'Yuh get 'fraid or suttin'?'

'Nah man,' Mal replied, his crocodile grin firmly fixed in place 'I was jus' duckin' out when I got a sudden thought. Believe me when I tell yuh, I got a dett idea . . .'

Shannon was in the living room when Orin got back. His sister was sitting on a hard-backed chair in the centre of the room while Carolyn lazed on the couch looking bored. Clive was gone.

The gorgeous hairdresser fussed around Sissy expertly. Orin greeted Shannon in a polite but detached way. His mind was on the streets; looking down on Malcolm being dragged towards the black Granada, hearing the raw screams of the kids burning in his ears, his fear and exhilaration as he'd thrown his own rocks. Now it was all over he felt weak, and his mind refused to accept what had happened – he felt as if he was an actor playing a part, and he'd just stepped off-camera. A lot of things that happened to him on this estate gave him that kind of feeling. He supposed it was his way of dealing with things that most people only saw on a cinema or TV screen.

Shannon smiled back at him and winked, looking tired and drained herself. Orin knew she had a few problems of her own, so he spared the girls his tale, and retreated to the quiet solitude of his bedroom. Once inside, he put on a Hip Hop tape, reflecting his mood, and unlocked his cupboard doors. He stared at the block of ash, knowing the money it represented couldn't be lost. They had to sell to Maverick; but how could they do that without starting some kind of war with these unknown men?

He lay on his bed, ruminating about the problem, his thoughts running along with the pace of the music. An hour passed. Just as he was starting to get worried about Mal, he heard the front door go. Seconds later someone knocked on his bedroom door.

'Come,' he yelled.

'Yes bredrin,' Malcolm said loudly, as he crossed the threshold into the room.

When he'd shut the door behind him he fell into a crouch, still holding the door handle, as if his knees had given way and were too weak to hold his body. Orin got up from the bed urgently, thinking he was hurt. Mal let out a moan.

'Fuckin' 'ell Orin, yuh see how tick Shannon's lookin' blood? Now dat's a woman! I'd gi' dat some serious wuk man!' He gave a mock shiver. '*Damn!*'

Orin laughed. 'Fuckin' e-dyat, man 'ad me all paro yuh nuh! I thought you'd bucked up wi' dem white brers again.'

A strange look came into Mal's eyes, which Orin noticed but dismissed.

'I wish I did,' Malcolm muttered, in a way that chilled his friend. 'Anyway, one ah dem man was black.'

'Who cares?' Orin responded bluntly.

'Innit. Lissen anyway – we got a change ah plans star. Maverick wants dat ki now, he's got the wong together.'

Orin looked puzzled. 'Yeah? How the fuck d'he manage dat?'

'Someone bought dat Henna innit.' Malcolm's eyes were shinning brightly. 'He wants to meet us in five minutes on the buildin' site at the new en' ah the estate. We gotta leave now man.'

Orin scowled and groaned loudly. 'Aah, what's wrong wid the brer? Why's he wanna meet dere? It's full ah site workers an' shit.'

Mal looked at his watch. 'Nah . . . dem man wen' home long time. It'll be deserted now. The place's perfec'!'

'You sure?'

'Yeh man. Come we go star, I waan mek some wong!'

Orin looked at the kilo contemplatively, then went over to the cupboard and picked it up.

'All right den, let's duss,' he growled, making for the door.

Malcolm held his hands up. 'No, no, no yuh don't. Gi' it to me.'

'What?'

'The pox. Gi' it to me man. I'll hol' it.'

Orin scowled again, looking hard at his friend. 'Wha' the fuck for? What difference does it make who carries the ash?'

'It makes every difference,' Malcolm said evenly. 'You're on probation in case you forgot. I ain'. If you get caught wi' dat thcy'll come down a lot harder on you than me innit? So I might as well hol' it for yuh?'

'Don' be stoopid,' the youth shot back. 'If we get caught we're both nicked, no matter who's holdin'.'

Mal sighed. 'Lissen. Gimme the pox, an' if we do get nicked I'll say you didn't know nothin' about it. Trus' me man, I'm lookin' out for yuh blood! Wha' d'you think I'm gonna do, run away?'

Orin grunted then reluctantly handed the block over. 'You ac'
like you know suttin',' he muttered in a low voice.

The other youth shrugged as he slipped the Tesco's bag into
his winter jacket, which had large holes in the lining of both
pockets.

'I only know two things about roun' here,' he replied soberly.
'Number one. If life ever gets a chance to be a bitch, it'll take
every opportunity possible . . .'

'Isit?'

'Yep.' Malcolm went for the door, looking over his shoulder
at Orin. 'An' number two, anythin' can happen round dese
sides star. Anythin'.'

'I can believe dat . . .'

The empty site was desolate and cold. It was filled with station-
ary yellow vehicles, looking like huge creatures from another
planet in the fading light of the evening. The youths marched
across the mounds of dry and not-so-dry earth, eventually taking
shelter behind a metal tool shed in the middle of the site, from
which they could survey as far as they liked. Mal dug around in
his pocket and produced one of Maverick's Silk Cuts, which he
offered to Orin. They lit up and waited in silence.

They didn't have to wait long before a bright light washed
over the area, bouncing and jiggling over the thick mounds of
earth. Orin heard the growl of a car engine – he rubbed his
hands together, then shot a look at his friend. Malcolm had his
eyes closed tight, taking no notice of the arrival of the vehicle.
Giving him a disdainful glare, Orin stood up, peeking around
the corner of the corrugated shed.

At the sight of the battered windscreen and one headlight he
froze, then tugged at Mal's jacket in a panic.

'Mal, it's dem fuckin' white brers man! Wha' the fuck's goin'
on?'

Malcolm opened his eyes. They were distant and vague.
'Leave it to me Orry, it's all sorted. I tol' 'em to come here man.
'ot a plan.'

'Fuck yuh plans!' Orin hissed at him, his fury bubbling over with amazing speed. 'What's wrong wid you, yuh lookin' to get us murdered or summick star? *Shit!*'

He looked around, searching for somewhere to run, but when he saw the vast emptiness around them he realised the uselessness of such a move. Instead, he glared at Malcolm, wanting to do him violent damage for the first time in his life. Mal was breathing heavily; Orin got even more wound up as he realised his friend was scared shitless. He felt trapped and betrayed, and his heart was beating frantically in his chest, though he couldn't tell if it was through anger or fear.

Fuckin' e-dyat! Orin thought bitterly.

'Don' worry, I know what I'm doin' blood,' Mal was saying. 'Jus' trus' me star – an' let me do the talkin', please Orin.'

'You're a fuckin' fool Mal—'

'*Please!*'

The car slowed to a halt and the engine was switched off, though the light remained on, casting its long shadow behind them. Orin slammed his fist against the metal wall of the shed, making it clang loudly.

'Shit!' He breathed deeply, attempting to calm himself. There was nothing else they could do but go through with Malcolm's plan, whatever it entailed. They had no choice. 'OK – all right man, it's on you. But if anythin' happens . . .'

'It won't, it won't,' Malcolm said, getting to his feet. 'Remember, I'll do the talkin'.'

'Yeah yeah . . .'

They stepped into the light. The Granada was parked fifty metres from the shed. All that could be seen of the men were dark shadows in the unlit interior. They moved forwards. The car's door sprang open.

'Stay dere!' Orin heard one of the men call. They stopped dead. The two men slammed the doors and walked over. They stopped ten metres from the youths. The older guy stared at Orin.

'Well, well, well, we meet again,' he said coldly, in his coarse gravelly tone. 'Enjoy ya day in the park did ya?'

Orin cleared his throat and shuffled his feet, but held the man's stare. Mal shrugged.

'Wha' d'you expect a man to do when he sees sumthin' like dat? Let it go? Dis is Greenside, we don' han' things like dat into the local police, y'get me? Anyhow, like I said before, I didn't know nuffin' about dat ki when I see you earlier – my friend an' me talked it over now, an' we realised we're way over our heads. We're tryin' to do summick about it.'

Al grinned over at them, his hands behind his back. Malcolm knew he had a weapon of some kind there.

'Wise boys,' he said in a playful sing-song that was meant to be patronising. Orin began to fume.

The old guy spat on the earth. 'Much as we'd love to chat, we ain' got all day, so've ya got dat thing we 'ad words about?'

'Yeh man,' Malcolm said, pulling out the Tesco's bag. Orin stared in disbelief for a moment, then went mad.

'Nah Mal, wha' you doin'?'

He rushed his friend, trying to grab the bag from him. The men in the back seat of the Granada got out, sensing trouble, but Malcolm pushed Orin away, his face contorted into a cold scowl.

'Leave off Orin, yuh said you'd let me deal wid it!' he yelled. 'Shut yuh fuckin' mout' an' trus' me! It's the bes' way!'

Orin stood with his hands clenched by his sides, glaring at his friend and kicking loose dirt wildly, feeling helpless. The four men watched him, not sure of how to handle this situation – he wasn't attacking them, so there was no real need to hurt him. Orin continued to glare at Malcolm fearfully, before turning his back on the boy, dismissing him. The old guy stepped closer to Mal, reaching for the bag. After shooting a sad look at Orin, Mal sighed and handed it over.

'Dere, dat weren't so hard was it?' Al sneered, looking from face to face. Neither youth said a word. The old guy gave the bag to Al, who grabbed it one-handed, took a quick look, then nodded and passed it to one of the other men, who put it in the car. After that, the burly men stepped into the gathering. The old guy manoeuvred his way into Mal's sightline.

'You're a smart lad,' he whispered slowly. 'But ya friend isn't as blessed. Still, dis time I'll let both ah ya off wid a warnin'. If you ever get the chance to steal from me again, an' *take* it . . . Well, you can guess what'd happen can't ya?'

Mal kept his head and eyes military straight. The men laughed.

'Boys?' the old guy said in a soft voice.

Al moved fast, trotting towards Mal and raising his arm. There was a baseball bat in his hand. Mal raised his arms to ward off the blow, then felt the bat crack against his side. He yelled and collapsed in pain, feeling more blows lash his body as he hit the dirt.

Orin watched this rapid change of events with shocked eyes, then roared and ran straight at Al; he was stopped by the old guy, who grabbed him by the arm and twirled him into the path of the two burly men as gracefully as a ballerina. Orin fell into their arms and found himself powerless to fight; he struggled in vain, while they punched him in his kidneys until he could resist no more. Then they made him watch Mal's beating.

It didn't last long, but to Orin it felt like for ever. When Al was done, the two men let him go and ran towards the Granada. He saw the old guy's face as he gasped in the dirt, and heard him mutter, '*Remember dis*.' Orin tried to spit in his face, but his mouth was too dry to even wet his lips. He heard the car start and roar away. When he worked his way over to Mal, the youth was struggling to his feet.

'Mal . . . You all right man?'

His friend had blood on his lips and his eyes were wide, but he looked OK. He nodded shakily.

'Yeh man – come on, we gotta run, we gotta catch dem man up!'

'What the fuck for?' Now Orin looked furious.

'Never min' man, jus' trus' me! Tings ain' done yet, come on!'

Malcolm got to his feet and started running back towards the estate, though he was obviously in pain and was limping on his right leg. Orin was exasperated. His friend was behaving like a child, and seemed intent on getting them badly hurt. He hated Mal at that moment, but knew he had to look out for him and sprinted in an attempt to catch him up, cursing the pain in his side all the way.

As they ran, Orin and Mal noticed the flashing blue lights coming from the driveway and garages just by the back of Bartholomew House. When they eventually got to the edge of the site, they saw the police vehicles. The youths crept behind some huge rusty dustbins and peered around the metal sides at the scene being played out before them.

The Granada was surrounded. All the men were on the pavement, being intimidated by a vanload of police. Orin recognised the policeman that'd stopped the two men earlier, before spotting their panda parked up too. A number of Rads were searching the inside of the car and one already had the bat Al had used on Malcolm. All four men looked sick at being pulled. Their expressions were heaven to the boys.

Orin looked at Mal, who was smiling broadly. He managed the teeniest of grins.

'Dis is better than I thought!' Mal said happily, rubbing his hands together.

Orin nodded. 'Tellin' me . . . Raa . . .'

They looked up just in time to see one of the policeman back out of the car, loosely holding the Tesco's bag. Judging by his face he'd already looked inside. He walked over to a man both youths assumed was his superior officer and opened the bag to show him.

The men yelled and pointed back towards the site.

'Cunts! They're blamin' us,' Orin spat.

Mal laughed. 'Good fuh dem! See if the Rads believe dat!'

They didn't. In no time, all four men were read their rights and bundled into the TSG; two minutes later, the vehicles started up and drove away, a smug-looking officer driving the Granada. Orin looked up at the tower block beside them, and saw faces at hundreds of windows, looking down curiously on the drama. Mal laughed joyously.

'Better than *The Bill*,' he grinned, following Orin's gaze.

'Yeah? You're a lucky fucker man,' Orin shot back, his anger finally returning. 'I can't believe yuh fucked wid me like dat, Malcolm! We're supposed t'be fuckin' bredrins, then as soon as you get one ah your stoopid "plans" in yuh head you're treatin' me like some servant. Sometimes I feel like whupsin' you wid a bat myself!'

Mal opened his mouth to answer, his eyes bright with glee, but then his phone began to ring. He laughed, unphased by Orin's fury. 'Lucky dat never wen' off earlier! Hol' up a sec'!'

Orin kissed his teeth and shook his head. Malcolm was a joker with a death wish, he was sure of it. He was just glad the whole thing was over, though he was gutted about losing the kilo, and the fact that he wouldn't be rich.

But then, so what? he told himself soberly. If they'd left with the pox in their possession, they might be the ones in the TSG. Maybe it was better this way.

He heard Mal chatting excitedly to the voice on the other end of the phone, and at once felt tired beyond belief. Slowly, Orin began walking towards his house, while Mal followed behind yapping all the way. Soon the youth caught him up.

'Dat was Maverick,' he said happily. 'He reckons one ah dem nosy neighbours musta called the Rads, blatant. We're lucky we live with such hones' people innit!'

Orin turned to him with strained-looking eyes. 'What's goin' on Mal?' he muttered thickly. 'Bit of a coincidence innit, Mav phonin' us right after everyting's done. Wha' you bin up to?'

Malcolm gave an embarrassed little grin before putting a brotherly hand on Orin's shoulder. 'Lissen – when we get to your drum, I'll tell yuh exactly what's bin goin' on. Exactly.'

'You fuckin' better,' the youth snapped back. Mal just smiled.

Back in Orin's bedroom with Hip Hop playing once more, Malcolm told his freind what he'd been up to.

'So what,' Orin started, attempting to get the gist of the story. 'You got Mav an' his boys to try rob the white brers, right?'

'Right!' Malcolm replied, glad his friend was following. 'They was meant to rush dem as they passed Barts – but of course, when they got dere, bere Rads was on the scene. My plan was they'd rob the brers an' dat would be the en' of it. I suppose tings worked out a little better than dat.'

'You reckon,' Orin sneered, reaching for the Rizla. 'We're right back where we started man – no wong, no ash, nothin'! I bet dem Rads'll at leas' get a dett smoke outta dat pox, if they don' sell it to some other fuckin' dealer. I'm proper gutted man.'

Mal's huge grin got even wider at Orin's words, if that was possible.

'I doubt if dem man'll be smokin' *or* sellin',' he said confidently. 'I doubt dat very much!'

'How yuh mean?'

Mal reached into his pocket and pulled out a Tesco's bag, throwing it over to Orin. Open-mouthed, the youth caught it and looked inside. There was a large block of ash. He dipped his face into the bag and smelt. Then he looked up at Malcolm, surprise written on his face.

'What's dis?'

'The pox innit,' Mal replied eagerly. 'When I wen' over to Maverick's girl's the second time, I remembered the Henna. I tol' him I'd tick it, then put it in another Tesco's bag an' brought it to the site. We'll only make profit an' dat, but Mav'll give us some time to work the ki, an' we still got enough wong to play wid when we sell it an' gi' him his cut! We're fat man!'

Orin began to laugh, before walking over to Mal and touching fists; then they hugged tight – the joy at coming out on top taking over.

'I tol' you before blood, you're a crazy brer but yuh come t'rough sometimes man. Yuh come t'rough,' Orin told his friend happily.

'Fuck dat,' Mal replied. 'I'm a *smart* brer – an' nex' time summick like dis happens, I reckon you should trus' me, ah lie?'

'Nah man,' Orin replied, getting up and heading towards the bed. With his back turned to Malcolm, his friend couldn't see the deep and painful wince that crossed his face. Orin vowed to himself there would never be a 'nex' time'. He sat on his mattress and immediately began spending all the money he'd make.

Elisha (II)

Elisha couldn't believe it. She'd been here exactly one night and the beginning of a day. Less than twenty-four hours in her new estate, and she was bored.

She was sprawled on the sofa, her cereal bowl at her feet, watching Richard and Judy on TV with dull dislike. The remains of several cigarettes were in an ashtray on the floor. She was dressed in long shorts and a tiny unironed T-shirt that accentuated her curvy frame. Her hair hadn't been touched yet, even though she'd already bathed and creamed; it was one of those days. She just couldn't be bothered.

She hadn't always been like this. Last year she'd been a girl with a mission – a woman with a purpose. She'd been attending Hammersmith and West London college, studying English, maths, law and politics. The only trouble was, she had the kind of character that was easily led astray, or so her mother always said. Elisha started off with the best intentions, and at the start of the course she'd known no one in any of her classes. By the end of the second month she had friends all over college, notoriety in the staff room, and people knew her name wherever she went.

She began missing lessons to smoke weed with good-looking guys; raving with the girls during the week, then waking up the next morning knowing she had to hand in an assignment, but going back to sleep anyway. Pretty soon her tutors were calling her in to say she'd missed over a month's worth of lessons. By then it was impossible to catch up. She dropped out three weeks later, much to her mother's dismay and Tawanda's very obvious disdain.

There was no one else in the house. Her mum was at work, and Tawanda was over at the East London university, where she was studying a degree in pharmacy. Although part of her was glad her sister wasn't in, her lonely side missed even the insults. *Anything* that could break the monotony was good.

The telephone range, surprising her out of her depression. She jumped up, wondering who it could be; no one around here had her number, and she'd never had a chance to give it to anyone from her old manor. She lifted the receiver to her ear quickly.

'Hello?'

'Yes sexy, wha' yuh ah say?'

She frowned. '*Carl?*'

There was a pause.

'Yeah man . . .' Her ex-boyfriend sounded a little put out, as if he could hear the uncertainty in her voice. 'Whassup wid you anyhow? You soun' all stressed out an' shit.'

Elisha shrugged and pulled the telephone over to the sofa, throwing herself on to the cushions in a dead weight.

'Nuttin's up. I'm jus' in the house on my own an' I'm bored silly y'get me?'

She could almost see his sneer.

'Well dat's Greenside for yuh star. I tol' yuh dem sides was rubbish innit?'

Elisha managed to laugh at that. She couldn't kid herself – it felt damn good to re-tie the ribbon of her old life, although she would've preferred to talk to one of her girls.

'How d'you get my new number anyway? You tryin' t'stalk me or suttin'?'

Now Carl was laughing too.

'Nah man, I seen yuh sister on her way to college, lookin' fine as usual. She gimme the digits man.'

'Huh, yuh better know you ain' gettin' no points talkin' 'bout my older sister like dat,' Elisha said grumpily, feeling a surge of jealousy. She tried to frustrate the bitter, dirty emotion, to no avail.

'I's only jokin', yuh know dat,' he was saying in her ear, his voice lowering a register. 'Suh tell me suttin' – if yuh indoors on yuh own yuh mus' need some company to come cheer you up innit?'

Her lips pouted instantly.

'Who tol' yuh dat?'

'You did innit. *You* said yuh was bored. I could come over, gi' yuh a massage, we could talk . . .'

Elisha couldn't keep the smile from her face, but she was shaking her head and spluttering laughter in reply to his words.

'Yeah yeah, I know yuh idea of talkin' . . . I found dat out the other day when I come to yuh yard innit. Furthermore, I found out the first time I ever come to yuh yard. We was supposed to jus' talk den if yuh remember. Talkin's about the only damn thing we *didn't* do.'

They laughed at the shared memory, which still managed to stir up longing in Elisha, although it had been a while ago. She lay back on the sofa with an arm behind her head. There was a knock at the front door.

'Oh *shit* – the door jus' went Carlos. I gotta go.'

'Ignore it man, whassup? Don't yuh wanna chat?'

'I can't ignore it; anyway, we ain' supposed to be talkin' like dis are we? We're done.'

There was another knock, then the bell. Carlos was trying to talk fast, but the spell had been broken. Somehow, she sensed that he knew it.

'All right, answer the door man, but gimme a bell later on right?'

'I will . . .'

'Seriously, Elisha. Or I'll stalk you fuh real star.'

'All right I said I will! Now I gotta get the door!'

'Later on babes . . .'

She slammed down the phone, then ran to the door and wrenched it open. Valerie and Leonora were standing on the other side. Val was sucking on some kind of fruit-flavoured lollypop, while Leonora was chewing on a pack of roast chicken crisps. Elisha smiled and opened the door wider.

'Hi you lot!'

'Hi,' Val said casually. She turned to Leonora. 'I tol' you she'd be in. Where the fuck's she gonna go aroun' here – she don't *know* no one but us.'

'Hi 'Lisha,' Leonora waved. 'Wanna crip?'

She offered the open packet but Elisha shook her head.

'No thanks.' She suddenly realised she had them standing on the doorstep. 'Come in den . . .'

They wandered in behind her, huddled close together, looking around at the flat and her family's possessions. Elisha pointed at the chairs.

'Take a seat where yuh can find it, we still ain' completely settled in yet,' she mumbled apologetically. She watched them fumble and grasp for seats, then flopped back down on the sofa. 'So what's goin' on?'

Leonora held up her hands and shook her head. 'Tell me nuh . . .'

'How can I tell you, I only jus' moved here girl?'

Valerie nodded slowly. 'Yeah – well dat's probably the mos' exciting ting dat's happened 'ere so far.'

They gave a group sigh and watched TV for a moment. Elisha was playing idly with her hair, twisting it around her finger and checking the ends to see if they'd split. She sat up.

'Hey, what about all dem police downstairs las' night? D'you find out what dat was about?'

'What police?'

Both girls were trying hard to remember, scrunching up their faces and giving each other odd looks.

'You lot bun too much green,' Elisha complained with a grin. 'You know, the ones dat arrested dem white guys. Remember, we was in your yard Val, we was lookin' out the window an' everythin'!'

'Oh yeah,' Val said a little dubiously.

Elisha got up and went into the kitchen. 'D'you wanna juice?'

Both girls did. She poured the orange while listening to them talk in low voices, then went back and handed them the glasses.

'*So?*'

'So what?' Leonora replied between sips.

'So, d'you know what all dem Rads was on the scene fuh?'

'*Oh* – nah man . . .'

Elisha looked at Val.

'Nah man, I don't know nuffin' yet,' Valerie told her lightly.

Elisha crash-dived on to the sofa again, puffing loudly in exasperation.

'*God* man, you lot are deadstock.'

They laughed. Val threw her cushion at Elisha, narrowly missing her head. When Elisha threw the cushion back, she caught it, placing it daintily beneath her bottom.

'Where's Lilliane?' Elisha wanted to know.

'Workin',' Leonora answered, before she threw her head back and tipped the remainder of the crisps down her throat.

'Come fatty, you affa get up anyway, yuh can't stay indoors all day,' Val told Elisha as she relaxed. 'Dere's crap on the telly, crap on the radio, so yuh might as well come out wiv us, innit Lee?'

'Fuh real!'

Elisha showed the girls her middle finger. 'You mus' be crazy man, what am I comin' out for if dere ain' nuthin' goin' on anyway? Might as well stay indoors innit?'

Val and Leonora rolled their eyes.

'What, yuh jus' gonna stay inside like an old aged pensioner den? Don't yuh wanna do *nuttin*'?' Leonora exclaimed.

'Like *what*?'

Val threw up her hands. 'All right I tell yuh what – whatever

you wanna do today, we'll do. Look *man*, look *garms*, hang
out . . . Whatever yuh wanna do, me an' Leonora—'

'—As yuh official Greenside welcomin' committee . . .'
Leonora added.

'. . . Will do our bes' to provide it for yuh. Suh come on den,
tell us wha' yuh want!'

Elisha was cracking up behind her hand all the way through
their little speech. When she realised they weren't laughing
with her, she winced.

'So you lot are serious?'

'Deadly,' Leonora said.

Elisha felt herself smile.

'All right den. The ting I need to do right about now, way
before I bovva lookin' man or garms, is get a fuckin' job y'get
me. Dis time now I'm bruk an' bwoy . . .'

She trailed off as she caught their faces. The girls were grinning at each other in delight.

'Whassup?'

'We can find you a job, easy,' Leonora was saying excitedly.
'Yuh shoulda said ages ago. Dere's a job goin' down at Smallie's
innit? Can you cook?'

'Sure bloody!'

'Well yuh set den,' Val said, rubbing her hands together.
'Jeannie down at Smallie's wanned a extra cook. She offered me
the job the other day.'

'Why didn't yuh take it?'

Val looked embarrassed. 'Well . . . I got bigger plans than
bein' a cook. No offence. Anyway, if I worked dere it'd fuck wid
my plans. But if yuh ain' got nuffin' better to do . . .'

'I ain',' Elisha admitted gamely.

Leonora downed her drink. 'Well yuh better get dressed so
we can go down dere innit?' she ordered. 'I'm sure Jeannie said
she was putting a advert over at the Job Centre.'

'I'm gone!' Elisha yelled, running for her bedroom, glad for
something to do at last.

The door to Smallie's was closed and the inside dark when they got there. Val rapped her knuckles against the glass until a young man emerged from the back. He unlocked the door with a large, heavy-looking set of keys, then nodded at Valerie when it was open.

'Y'all right Val?'

'Yes Stevie . . . Is Jeannie dere yet?'

The light-skinned teenager rubbed his freckled face, stretching and yawning. 'Yeah man, she's upstairs in the office. D'yuh know the way, I could show yuh . . .'

'Nah, dat's all right.' She smiled up at Stevie. 'I think I bin up dere enough times to make my own way, y'get me?'

'Oh, all right den.'

He moved out of the way and held the door open for them. Elisha and Leonora smirked at each other, then followed Val through into the shop. Leonora couldn't resist pulling the young man's leg.

'I could show yuh . . .' she mocked, trying to imitate Stevie's deep voice. He pushed her and she hit his arm in return. He locked the door, then they continued to fight all the way to the stairs that led to the flat and office above.

Elisha caught up with Val, who was tramping boldly upwards. 'Looks like yuh got an' admirer!' she joked.

'Tell me about it,' Val moaned painfully. 'I wouldn't mind but he's only fifteen!'

'What!'

'Don't you say a word either!'

Elisha's mouth hung open. She started to laugh. Val cut her eye at her, but turned away with a smile on her face. They reached a half-open door at the end of a passage. Val waited for Leonora to join them, then she knocked.

'Who is it?'

'It's me Auntie!'

There was a loud exclamation of joy.

'Well come in darlin' . . .'

They entered the tidy room, which was small and carpeted. A

desk was pushed beneath a window, and a PC sat upon it, a Microsoft Excel spreadsheet on the monitor. The woman who had served Elisha the day before spun away from the computer so she could face the youths that were cramming their way into the room.

'Hello luv, how are you?'

'Fine Auntie.'

They hugged and kissed. Leonora waved her hand.

'Hey Jeannie.'

'Hello Leonora.'

Leonora winced but said nothing. She hated her full name, preferring to be called Lee. Jeannie smiled at Elisha in recognition, then turned a questioning glance Val's way.

'Suh what can I do fuh yuh Valerie? It's not often I see yuh dis early in the mornin'.'

Val was doing her best to act coy.

'Well, yuh know dat job dat was goin' the other week . . . I was wonderin' if you found anyone, 'cos if you ain', Elisha needs some work, an' she'd be very grateful if you could help her out . . .'

Jeannie was shaking her head, looking at Elisha sadly. 'Sorry darlin' but when Val say she never want it me did offer Mrs Roper's grandchile de work, an' she tek it willingly. She start las' Tuesday.'

'Damn,' Valerie said. Elisha and Leonora looked forlorn. 'Oh well, it was worth a try I suppose.'

'Yuh shoulda come by me from long time if yuh know yuh frien' did ah look some work. Look how long me did tell yuh from.'

Elisha was stepping from foot to foot, uncomfortable at being talked about like this.

'Well me wish me coulda help . . .' Jeannie sighed.

Elisha decided it was time she spoke up for herself. 'It's OK, I'll be able to fin' summick else. But if anythin' comes up, could yuh let Val know as soon as possible.'

'No problem me dear.'

Elisha smiled. 'Thank you.'

The girls stood around while Val and her auntie chatted routine family talk, then they left the office and got Stevie to unlock the front door, leaving Val to say her goodbyes alone. She joined them outside a few minutes later.

'Sorry 'bout dat 'Lisha,' she said quickly, as they walked past the block of shops. 'I tried speechin' Jeannie some more when you lot dussed, but she wouldn't budge. The bes' ting I could get outta her was firs' refusal if someone leaves, which doesn't happen often.'

'We should get one ah the other cooks the sack – all put a hair in the food or suttin'.' Leonora was grinning.

Val gave her a hard glare.

'More like get my auntie's shop closed down by health inspectors!'

'Tell me about it,' Elisha grumbled. 'Nah, it's all right you lot, yuh tried, I can't say fairer than dat can I? I'll jus' afta go down the Job Centre, or look in the paper or suttin'.'

She pushed her hands into her pockets morosely. Val and Leonora swapped worried looks.

'Don't worry 'Lisha, we'll find yuh somethin',' Val told the girl, putting a consoling arm around her shoulder. 'We won't give up until we got you a decent job. Innit Lee?'

'Fuh real!'

Elisha gave the girls a tiny smile; just enough to show she appreciated the effort they were making.

'Hey, d'yuh wanna go down by the club?' Leonora asked. 'It's all boarded up an' dat, but sometimes people hang about outside it, or by the football pitches inside the park. Lots of men dere too 'Lisha . . .'

Elisha pulled another makeshift grin. 'Ain' got much choice 'ave we?' she grumbled, her low tone causing Val to shake her head.

Leonora prodded at her shoulder. 'Dat's the spirit girl! Carry on like dat an' you'll get into livin' aroun' 'ere sooner than yuh think!' she told her brightly. 'Come, we go youth club man, we mus' fin' suttin' dat can cheer dis girl up.'

They walked in the direction of the park. All the way there Leonora was the brightest and liveliest member of the group. She told jokes, made wisecracks, and even cussed the other youths so imaginatively that they had to laugh at what she was saying. When they got past the park gates, however, Leonora's good cheer clogged in her throat. She watched in disbelief as workmen moved around the youth club, smashing windows, removing chairs, tables and desks from inside, then throwing them in a sprawling heap on the grass. No other youths were in sight. Beside Leonora, Val was equally speechless. Elisha didn't know what to make of the situation.

'What the fuck's goin' on?' Leonora breathed.

No one knew.

'We should ask one of the workmen . . .' Elisha suggested quietly.

Before she could say another word, Leonora was making a beeline for the nearest, a middle-aged guy who was throwing a table on to a pile outside the club. When she was standing directly in front of the man, she put her hands on her hips and launched her tirade.

'Excuse me – what's goin' on?'

'*Eh?*'

The man responded with a dumb look. Leonora sighed. Elisha and Val joined her.

'She said, "What's goin' on?"' Val joined in without hesitation. 'An' she means what's goin' on wiv our club? We wanna know why you're mashin' in our windows an' throwin' all our tables an' chairs outside y'get me?'

For some reason, the three angry-looking black women intimidated the workman no end. He held his hands up high and immediately took the defensive.

'I dunno nuffin' about yuh yoof club, I jus' thought it was a run-down old buildin',' the man was saying, backing away. 'We've bin contracted to knock it down by the end ah the week though luv, an' dat's all I know, straight up.'

'*Knock it down?*' Leonora whispered, her eyes glazed with

shock, not hearing the workman after his admission. He took that as his cue, and disappeared into the club. Val was shaking her head; she too was unable to grasp what was happening.

'We should go an' see Lacey,' she told Leonora seriously. 'Get him to stop dem mashin' up our club.'

Leonora shook herself back to life. 'Yeah we should . . .' She smiled dispiritedly at the girls, then started walking. 'We better go right now man, dere ain' even no time to mess about.'

Moving quickly, they left the park and headed for the block where Lacey, the head youth worker, lived. They gave his door several swift knocks. After the third attempt it was obvious he wasn't in, or wasn't up yet. The girls leaned over the landing wall, spitting and cussing loudly.

'So what, wha' you up to now?' Elisha wanted to know.

Val shrugged, but Leonora was looking confident.

'*Trisha*,' she said crisply, giving the hint of a smile.

'Yuh know dat innit!' Val exclaimed all at once.

Leonora was nodding. 'Yeah man – Trisha's one of the other yout' workers man an' she's safe, she always caters fuh us! We should give her a call, she'll be able to sort out all dis mess, trus' me. I dunno why I never thought earlier.'

Elisha was already making her way down the landing, towards the concrete staircase.

'Suh wha' we waitin' for man, come we phone her innit?'

'Yeah man, the quicker we phone her, the quicker she'll come,' Val added, following Elisha's lead. 'Come nuh Lee, let's duss!'

'Yeah, I'm comin'!' Leonora shouted, turning back to Lacey's door for one last try. She lifted the letterbox, gave it one almighty slam, and waited.

Nothing.

'All right, wait up you lot, I soon come!' Leonora yelled, before she ran down the stairs and into the comparative brightness of the streets below.

The Club

The bus was packed and the traffic stretched as far as she could see. There was no doubt about it, she was going to be late, today of all days – the one day when it really mattered.

She hadn't realised how scared and worried she'd been until the 220 turned the corner on to Shepherd's Bush Road. The bus had come to a slow halt amongst the rush-hour traffic, and Trisha swore it hadn't moved more than thirty metres at any onc time after that. She played with her key ring impatiently, trying to ignore the symphony of horns. Her heart was beating rapidly, so she closed her eyes and prayed that whatever was stopping them moving would just go away.

She revelled in her own personal darkness, at once feeling more relaxed, despite her lack of vision. With her eyes closed it seemed she could hear the muttered conversations around her that much better. She listened for a moment, eavesdropping on other people's lives, hoping their everyday troubles would take her mind off her own.

A mother and child were talking about the Spice Girls movie. The child wanted to see the film, and the mother was weakly protesting, knowing she was merely postponing the inevitable. Two schoolgirls were looking out of the bus windows, pointing at all the boys they fancied and cackling loudly in a way Trisha recognised from her own school days. Two seats behind them, three smartly dressed black women were complaining about the traffic, and wishing they had a car of their own. Everyone else was silent. None of the conversations held her interest. Trisha opened her eyes and sighed deeply for the umpteenth time, knowing she had to leave the bus before the waiting drove her mad.

The minute hand on her Seiko moved steadily along. The bus didn't move at all. After five more minutes Trisha got up, swinging her Kookai bag on to her shoulder and striding towards the stairs that led to the lower deck. Several people followed her lead, including the mother and child and the three black women. She pressed the bell when she reached the bus doors and they hissed open. She stepped on to the pavement, despair washing over her. She snatched a look at her watch. Ten minutes to eleven. There was no way she'd get there in time, especially walking. But there was no way she was going back home. She owed it to her kids to be there.

Almost trotting along the road, Trisha headed towards Greenside. She was oblivious to the people around her, dodging without really seeing them, nodding at their muttered 'Excuse me's without really hearing them, her mind focused on what lay ahead. At the bottom of Shepherd's Bush Road, at the junction where it met the Green, she saw a mini-cab pulling out of StarWash. She waved frantically at the driver to get his attention, and was relieved when he pulled up, looking questioningly at her.

'Are you workin' mate?'

The Somalian-looking driver squinted at her, then rolled down his window. 'Pardon?'

'Are you workin'? I need to get somewhere in a hurry.'

'Well . . .' the man stalled. 'I just finished my shift.'

'Aw go on mate, I don't even wanna go far. C'mon, I really need to get somewhere fast.'

He thought about it. 'Where are you goin'?'

'Greenside.'

The man groaned.

'Aw come on, I ain' gonna do a runner, I'll even pay you up front. It won't take five minutes.'

He thought some more, then shrugged.

'Come on, get in.'

She jumped into the back seat without another word, grateful for the warm blast of air coming from the car heater, digging in her purse for the cab fare.

'How much is that?'

'T'ree fifty.'

'Three pounds bloody fifty!'

She squeezed herself between the front and passenger seat and glared at him.

'Minimum fare, minimum fare!' the man replied quickly.

She tutted and passed over the exact money, feeling stung, but knowing the cab driver was in control. He smiled as he took it, turning the car around and heading back the way he'd come.

'I take back way,' he told her confidently. 'Be there in no time.'

'Thanks a lot,' Trisha replied, sitting back in her seat. She felt drained and she hadn't even got there yet. She crossed her fingers, hoping she wasn't too late.

Soon they were easing their way through Greenside's blocks. She made the cabbie drop her off by the park fence, then stepped briskly towards the gates, biting her lip nervously. As she walked, she saw three small figures coming her way. She squinted until she realised who they were, then smiled in recognition.

They were three designer-clad schoolboys – Stacey Collins, Benji Tremaine and Robby Emerson – *three of my kids*, Trisha thought proudly, feeling warm pleasure at the sight of them. Between them they managed to be the cutest and baddest little group of kids she'd come across on the estate, yet so full of untapped potential that they gave her joy and heartache at the same time.

Trisha had been working with the three of them since they

were eleven, so she knew the ins and outs of their home and street lives as intimately as they knew each other's. She prided herself on being able to talk on a level with them, and although they'd hurt her emotionally in the past, the satisfaction she got from seeing them use their brains every once in a while made it well worth the pain.

An old white woman was heading the youths' way, shuffling at a snail's pace, shopping bags in hand, head down. The youths were laughing, shouting and play fighting with each other uproariously, oblivious to her presence. The old woman didn't see them until they were almost on top of her; when she did, she jumped halfway out of her skin, almost dropped her bags, and shakily crossed the road as quick as her skinny legs would carry her.

Responding in kind, the three youths instantly turned nasty. The began shouting insults at the woman, which scared her even more. When Robby tugged on the others' sleeves and went to cross the road to harass the woman further, Trisha thought she'd better intervene.

'*Oi*, Oi, you lot!'

They turned venomously, screwing up their faces, fully prepared to fight – then they saw her. Their hard expressions instantly became sheepish. Stacey dug his hands in his pockets and casually bounced her way, his pose such a caricature of nonchalance that Trish almost expected him to whistle. Robby kicked a crushed can sitting by the kerb, then rejoined his friends slowly, as if a game of kick-the-can was all he'd been after. Benji, ever the cool one, continued as if nothing had happened, his face blank, his whole manner saying, 'It's a fair cop'.

Trisha approached them rapidly, watching the woman disappearing over their shoulders, trying not to smile at their old-yet-young faces.

'Wha' you guys up to, eh?'

Stacey reached Trisha and blessed her with a wide and completely false smile. The others weren't far behind.

'Nuttin'.'

'Nuttin'.'

'Nuttin' man.'

'Don't tell me "nuttin'"', what was you shoutin' at that ol' woman?'

There was a loud kissing of teeth in reply.

'Fuck 'er man, she was goin' on stoopid,' Stacey blasted, scowling even harder with the words. 'Goin' on like man wanned to rob 'er or suttin' . . .'

'Like say she 'ad anyting fuh us,' Benji joined in, his head down, unable to look at Trisha. She put her hands on her hips and engaged the three with an icy stare.

'Look, I've told you guys a million times before, you don't have to take on everyone else's problems all the time. You could've ignored her or suttin' . . . or *something*,' she corrected. The kids smiled at her bad English. Trisha was from an estate background too, which was probably why she got on so well with the youths. Still, it didn't mean she was going to let herself get away with things she would have chastised them for. 'Instead of her feelin' guilty about the way she was actin' towards you lot, I bet she feels justified now. Every time somethin' like that happens you got the chance to change someone's mind, an' every time you do what you did you throw that chance away.'

'It's easy for you to talk about ignorin' tings,' Robby commented as he joined them. 'You're white innit?'

Everybody looked pained, as though Robby had touched on a sore subject. He started speaking quickly to cover himself.

'Not dat you're *her* type of white person, but you can't understand how it feels to be in our shoes, I don't see how you can. Every day we affa see dat shit man, an' it's all right sympathisin' an' dat, but there's no way you can know how it *feels* y'get me?'

'I know, I know,' Trisha said, trying to disguise the hurt she felt, but doing a very bad job. Stacey was looking at her sadly, while Benji pointedly avoided eye contact, though she could feel his embarrassment from where she stood. She shrugged and continued. 'Listen, you guys are right. I can't understand how you're feelin' – but I do know what's goin' through *their* heads.

Right? An' I know you can't change everybody's mind, but if you tried—'

'Fuck dat star, I ain' tryin' t'change no racis' brers mind,' Benji suddenly spat viciously, looking as though he'd had enough of the conversation. 'Far as I'm concerned dere's two sets ah white people in dis worl' – the safe ones an' the racis' ones. You're one ah the safe ones Trish, but I'm sorry to say it, the racis' ones outweigh the safe ones by nuff, y'get me?'

Trisha sighed and ran an agitated hand through her hair. 'Well, I'm really sorry you feel that way Benji, though I am glad I'm not included in your majority.'

'Safe man,' he said, beaming his handsome smile at her, making her feel a little better about her sermon.

'Anyway, where you goin' at this time of the mornin'? I thought you's supposed to be in school?' she asked, thinking she better get back on safer ground.

'Teacher's strike innit?' Robby answered. 'So we said we'd go up Wes', do some window shoppin' an' dat. We'll probably be off fuh the nex' t'ree days as well.'

They all looked very happy at the prospect.

Trisha knew they were probably lying, but let it pass, as there was no time to argue.

'Good!' she said brightly. 'You can use them free days to get on wid your writin' can't you Robby?'

Robby groaned, while the others smiled and winked at her encouragingly.

'He wrote a *bad* story the other day y'nuh. Proper gangsta lick, y'get me?' Stacey enthused, while Robby blushed, something Trisha had rarely seen.

She smiled at him. 'Well you'll have to come club an' show me sometime . . .'

In her enthusiasm she'd forgotten about the club. Stacey opened his mouth to tell her, then glanced at her face and realised she already knew. He shuffled about, his turn to look embarrassed.

'You bin over?' he asked painfully.

'Nah. I was jus' on my way now. Leonora called me this mornin'.'

No one knew what to say. Trisha decided she better get on with it.

'All right, I'm gonna go an' check things out over there, OK?'

'All right,' the three replied, moving away from her.

'An' don't get up to no badness up Wes' End!'

'Yeah yeah,' they returned cockily, before turning their backs on her and heading out of the estate.

Trisha watched them go, thinking that no matter how close she got to them, she'd always be an outsider. Her age, her way of life and her skin colour practically guaranteed that. Even though the youth club was being demolished, they still had their own little club, although theirs was mental rather than physical. Now, after six years of working on the estate and being part of over a hundred loving families, Trisha felt lost at the thought of having to give it all up. Having to get another job. Not seeing the Greenside kids on a daily basis.

It seemed silly, but Trisha felt as though she'd been expelled from the club. She found it a very lonely feeling.

She strode into the park with a renewed sense of determination, boosted by her encounter with the three boys. As soon as she reached the black tarmac path that led to the club's entrance, she saw the numerous workmen around the building. An intense bolt of rage shot through her. From what she could see, they were removing anything of value they could find and leaving it on the grass in an untidy heap, *where they'd more than likely pick over it like vultures*, she thought to herself unfavourably.

Among the items on the grass was the green felt display board she'd bought with her own money, to showcase the kids' drawings, short stories and poetry. Most of their work was gone, while the rest flapped pitifully in the breeze. A number of office chairs were also in the pile. From the metallic hammering inside the club, Trisha thought she could safely assume that the radiators and any surplus copper they found would probably go too. It burned her to think of them earning off the back of other people's misfortune.

When she saw Valerie, Leonora and another girl she didn't know standing in front of the club watching the men hatefully, she calmed down a little.

I better set a good example, she thought; it'd probably be her last opportunity. She approached them with a tiny smile, which none returned. They simply looked at her with a sombre gaze she'd been used to receiving when she first came to work on Greenside.

'Hey you guys,' she called out as cheerfully as she could. She nodded at the open club doors. 'I see someone's bin busy then . . .'

'Innit,' Valerie said mournfully, her expression never changing. Each girl had a pile of books, files and folders in her hands. Leonora took a couple of steps her way.

'Trisha man, what's goin' on wid the club? I thought they was supposed to be fixin' it *up*, not knockin' the fuckin' ting down. See what I'm sayin' about these people man, they're always takin' the piss outta us, an' what we think don't matter to dem! I'm sick of it! What's the point of me bein' on the fuckin' yout' council if—'

'Hold up, hold up, hold up,' Trisha said quickly, putting up her hands, unable to deal with the torrent of words. 'I'm in the dark just as much as you guys. I don't know anything either.'

'Well dat's friggin' *marvellous*,' Leonora snapped, hands on her hips, looking as angry as Trish had felt coming up the path.

Despite herself, Trish managed to contain her own rage and place a consoling hand on the girl's shoulder. Leonora looked livid. She'd taken her voluntary job on the youth council very seriously, and Trisha knew some of the kids on the estate would blame her for what had happened here. The trouble was, Leonora hadn't even wanted the job; it had been *her* who persuaded Leonora she could make changes, and now all that was being thrown back in her face. Every time Trisha looked into the young woman's eyes, she could see these thoughts running through her head. And although she knew it wasn't intentional, it was logical the girl would at least partly blame her for what had happened.

'What's all that?' Trisha asked them, noticing what they were holding for the first time.

'Oh, jus' your files an' diaries an' shit. Dem workmen was gonna chuck 'em away,' Val told her, handing the things over. Trisha dumped them in her bag without a glance; it'd hurt too much to see all the work she'd done here. She could very easily have burst into tears right where she stood.

The girl she didn't know dumped the files and folders into her arms with a tiny smile of sympathy. *Very pretty*, Trisha noted, smiling back at her.

'This your cousin then?' she asked Val, knowing she'd never seen the girl before.

'Nah, dis's Elisha, Elisha dis's Trish. She moved into Bart yesterday,' Val explained.

'Quite a welcome eh?' Trisha said, nodding at the club.

Elisha shrugged. 'We din't even have a club in Winton, so I ain' missin' nuthin',' she replied resignedly.

Trisha mentally shook her head at the attitude these kids were forced to take, then decided she better get down to business.

'All right,' she began, shaking off the cobwebs woven by her tiredness and shock. 'Have you seen Lacey?'

Leonora and Val shook their heads rapidly.

'Does he know what's goin' on?'

'I dunno,' Val said. 'No one ain' seen him for a while. We knocked at his house, but there was no answer.'

'When did you knock?'

'Dis mornin'.'

'Shit.' She thought for a bit, then decided to have a word with one of the workmen. 'Wait here you guys, I'll be out in a bit.'

'Cool.'

She entered the youth club slowly, looking around and shaking her head every now and then. Everywhere was empty and bare – all the furniture had been removed and everything had been taken from the walls, leaving large plasterless areas that made the rooms look ugly and cold. She saw two workmen tugging away at one of the radiators, just as she had suspected. She approached them, reminding herself that nothing going on here was their fault.

They didn't see or hear her coming as their work was noisy, and they were intent on what they were doing. She stood over them, watching for a moment before deciding to speak.

'Excuse me.'

They continued banging and pulling, unaware of her presence.

'*Excuse me!*' she said again, a little louder. One of the men, a blond-haired spotty youth who looked no older than twenty-one, regarded her speculatively.

'Yes luv?'

'Yes, hello. My name's Trisha Macfarlane. I'm one of the youth workers that work . . .' She looked around the empty room and decided to correct herself. '. . . *Used* to work in this club. The thing is, last I heard this building was supposed to be refurbished, not pulled down. I had a phone call from one of the girls that attended the club this morning, and that was the first I knew about all this. I mean, I hadn't been informed at all. I was wondering if you had any idea what was going on, or who I should talk to . . .'

The youth was regarding her blankly, as if regretting even looking in her direction. However, his colleague, an older man in his early thirties who reminded Trisha of an uncle she had, stood up and engaged her with a saddened expression, empathising with her plight.

'Sorry luv, we was employed by Hammersmith and Fulham council to pull this building down, an' that's all they told us. We're just the hired hands 'ere darlin'.'

Trisha sighed and rubbed her head agitatedly.

'Well, have you seen or heard from a guy called Jonathan Lacey? He's the head youth worker here.'

'Jonathan Lacey . . .' the older man was saying, while the younger shook his head at once. 'Nah sorry luv, never 'eard of the bloke I'm afraid. In fact, you're the first youth worker I've seen 'ere. No one else bothered turnin' up.'

'*Fuck*,' Trisha muttered under her breath, biting her lip once more, feeling her anger return. Both workmen were giving her curious looks. There were five youth workers, including herself, employed at the club, and although she'd known most didn't really give a damn about the kids, she'd thought that Lacey (who'd been brought up on Greenside and still lived in Caldervale House) would at least have made an appearance. She was disappointed in him. Her feelings see-sawed between anger and her latent attraction to the man, which she'd been trying to combat since the first day she set eyes on him.

'All right, thank you very much,' she said off-handedly, walking slowly out of the club, back to where the girls were standing. They looked at her expectantly, and she felt annoyed that everything rested on her, as usual.

Leonora went for her straight away. 'Wha'd they say den?' she asked quickly.

'Ah, the usual, you know. They don't know nothin', they were employed by the council . . .'

Their faces fell.

'*Oh*,' Leonora said, looking crushed, while Val groaned and shook her head. Trisha felt bad for a while, then decided she had one card left to play, if only for Leonora's sake.

'I think I'm gonna go by Lacey's, see what he's gotta say about the matter. I can't believe no one's seen him,' she told them, her voice filled with more confidence than she felt. The girls nodded.

'Good idea,' Val said. 'An' when you see him, tell him to get his arse over here an' deal wid dis shit, pronto. He's supposed to be doin' the runnin' about, not you, y'get me?'

'All right,' Trish grinned, even managing a little chuckle.

Leonora smiled back. 'It'll be cool, don't you worry,' she crooned eagerly.

'Yeah, well the same goes for you guys,' Trish replied seriously. 'Anyhow, I better go an' sort all this out. I'll see you all later.'

'Good luck!' Val said, giving her a little wave and a rarely seen half-smile. Trisha waved back, then turned and took the path out of the park.

Yeah, well I'm bloody well gonna need it, she told herself, as she stepped on to the streets and took a right towards Caldervale House.

Her infatuation with Jonathan Lacey had been going on for nigh on three years now – the whole time he'd been at the Greenside youth club. He'd previously been working on the other side of London, in a Hackney detox centre for under twenty-ones, but when the job for youth leader came up here, he'd jumped at the chance to work with kids he'd known his entire life. She found him a warm and pleasant person to work with, full of laughs, and a great role model for the kids under his wing. They all loved Lacey, as they knew he was one of them.

She found herself beginning to feel the same way about him. Pretty soon he was returning the smiles and lustful looks she'd been giving, even though she'd been in a relationship at the time. She just couldn't help it. They'd never discussed their feelings for each other, so she wasn't even sure if there *were* any from his point of view. Until now they'd been content to work together side by side, in a mutual friendship that had seen them through plenty of bad and lean times, but thankfully a great deal of good ones too.

Sometimes she felt content to let their friendship stay as it was – after all, there were a lot of complications to think about. They worked together, they lived far apart from each other, he was black and she was white . . . if she really thought about it, the whole thing was crazy.

But other times she'd seen him working with the kids, or

talking on the phone, or simply going over the accounts, his head in his hands, full lips moving silently, and she'd have to leave the room, such was the strength of her attraction. She wasn't sure about it, but she thought he felt the same way. She'd caught him staring at her when he thought she wasn't looking, and each time she'd been filled with a pride and confidence that usually lasted her a whole day.

She struggled up Caldervale's stairs to the second floor, then knocked on Lacey's door loudly and rapidly, looking out over the estate when she was done. There was no answer. Feeling her anger surge, she tried again, this time knocking louder and longer. Still no answer. Instead the next-door neighbour, an elderly white woman, opened her door.

''Ello love.'

'Hi there,' she sang, masking her exasperation.

'He's not there ya know. I ain' seen 'im in a while.'

'Are you sure?'

'Well, I go to bed very early in the evenin', so if he came in or out after nine I would've missed 'earing 'im—'

The locks on Lacey's front door clicked, making both women jump. His voice came from behind the door.

'Who's dat?'

'Trisha!' she called hopefully.

There was a silence, then: '*Trish?* How come you reach up 'ere man?'

'I need to talk to you. It's about the club.'

Another silence.

'Oh. All right, gimme a sec.'

Further locks clicked, then the door eased open revealing Lacey, clad in a navy blue towelling dressing gown. She smiled at him, looking the youth leader up and down.

'*Very* nice – the new look suits you Lace!'

'Yeah, yeah, ha ha,' he replied, flashing the grin that first attracted her to him. 'Go through to the living room, I'll be with yuh in a bit.'

She followed his directions and sat down in the nicely

decorated yet small living room, easing her coat from her shoulders, as it was much warmer than outside. A radio could be heard from a room towards the back. Loud bumps and the sound of an adult shouting at their child could be heard from the flat above. Lacey padded into the room, clutching at his dressing gown.

'Shit, it's freezin' out dere.'

'Tell me about it.'

'D'wanna drink of anythin'?' he asked, standing by the kitchen door. 'I got coffee, tea, but no cold drinks. Only water.'

'I'm fine thanks.'

'You sure?'

'Yeah honestly, I'm all right. I—' After all her enraged thoughts, she had no idea how to approach this matter. 'I wanned to talk to you about the club really. I don't understand what's goin' on.'

'Wid what?'

'Well – they're knockin' the fuckin' thing down Lacey!'

'I know.'

'You *know?*'

She was looking at him with a penetrating glare. Lacey looked slightly ashamed.

'Why, don't tell me yuh didn't.'

'That's exactly what I'm tellin' you. I didn't have a clue mate. Last I knew, we were due for "complete refurbishment and a removal of the asbestos in the buildin'"',' she told him, quoting the letter she'd received the previous summer. 'So what happened to change all that?'

He shrugged and pulled a face. 'Well, after goin' through the buildin' an' removin' all dat asbestos they found, I suppose they kep' goin' and found more. The more they found, the more it cost dem to refurbish the buildin' if they wanned too, an' pretty soon the overall cost musta got too high, so they fucked the whole thing off. An' fucked us in the process.'

'Jesus . . .'

Trisha looked at Lacey, finally realising how glum he was

under his general mask of levity. He looked up at her and shook his head.

'They sent me a letter about it four weeks ago. I thought they woulda sent yuh one too.'

'They didn't send me fuck all.'

Trisha sat motionless, staring at her hands. She honestly hadn't expected to hear this. She thought there'd been some mistake.

'So that's it?' she said bitterly. 'We're out of a job now?'

'Well, they did say they'd find us guaranteed work in any youth centres wiv available vacancies—'

'I don't wanna work at any "available vacancies"! I was perfectly all right here!' she blasted, her outrage taking firm root. Lacey looked at her reproachfully then nodded, as if her outburst had merely proven what he already knew.

'I'm sorry Trish, but dere's nothin' we can do about it; they're gonna knock it down by the end of the week,' he said, his strong features outlining his sympathy. 'D'yuh wanna see the letter?'

'Yeah, I suppose . . .'

He left the room. She continued to stare at her hands in disbelief, unable to comprehend the destruction of something she'd thought would last forever. She'd seen it happen to other youth clubs, but there'd never been one moment when she'd thought *her* club would get the axe. What could she do now? She was out of work – worse still, she'd probably never get the chance to see any of her kids again.

How can they do this to me? a voice inside her head wailed, as she fought the tears welling in her eyes. She gulped them back, looking around the room almost frantically, searching for something, *anything*, to take her mind away from her problem and reduce the chance of her breaking down in front of Lacey.

Her first tear-blurred scan of the room revealed nothing. Still blinking and breathing in painful little hiccups, she grabbed blindly at a red and white carrier bag sitting on the sofa next to her thigh. Catching only a glimpse of its contents, she lifted the bag up. Four black balaclavas fell into her lap.

She studied the masks with a frown on her face, then grabbed at one to confirm what she saw. Three empty holes forming two eyes and a mouth punctuated her find like a trio of full stops. She wondered what Lacey could want with balaclavas, besides the obvious . . . Her frown deepened, her mind racing; *What the fuck's Lacey up to?* She felt emotionally unable to deal with the shock of this further oddity, in a day that had been filled with strange occurrences.

Footsteps sounded from the back of the flat. She hastily stuffed the masks into their bag, then sat back as casually as she could, slouching down low to add to the effect. Lacey came back, dressed in jeans and a T-shirt. Trisha eyed him suspiciously, wondering if she should mention what she'd seen. After some thought she decided to say nothing. For the moment.

'Here yuh are,' Lacey muttered, giving her the paper and avoiding her eyes.

She took it and scanned the words, rather than reading with any real interest. The letter basically confirmed everything Lacey had already said. It was stiff and informal, expressing no sympathy, giving no thanks for the years of work they'd put into the club. She scanned it once, looked it over again, then passed it back with a dainty little sniff, her face hardened by the realisation that there was no going back. It was over.

'Well, that's that I suppose . . .'

'Yeah.'

Lacey looked unsure of himself, an expression she wasn't used to.

'What are you gonna do wiv yuhself?'

He shrugged, stalling, unsure of how to answer her question.

'I dunno, hang around. Sign on for a bit. I don't really fell like goin' straight into another job, so I'll wait until my money gets low, den I suppose I'll take whatever post they offer me, wherever it is. I could try writing a book, like my bredrin Mikey . . .' He laughed joylessly, then shook his head. 'What about you?'

She sighed. 'God alone knows Lacey, I really couldn't tell yuh. I still can't believe this is happening.'

'Yeah I know, the whole ting's mad up.'

They sat in silence, neither of them knowing what to say next. Trisha was struck by the strong sudden feeling that this was where they'd part company – this was the point where they'd never see one another again, *if* she let it happen. She couldn't walk out the door without knowing whether there was some kind of future for the two of them; it would leave her tormented, full of '*I should've*s' and '*We could've*s', when she was really clueless about the whole situation. She leaned forwards in her chair.

'So Lacey . . . Lacey, what are we gonna do about *us?*'

There. She'd said it. The thought had transformed itself into hard, solid reality. Lacey looked a little perplexed. It was not the look she'd expected or hoped for.

'*Eh?*'

'I said what are we gonna—'

A figure entered the room. Trisha was so intent on what she'd been saying she hadn't even heard footsteps. Now, as she looked up, she felt the words freeze in her throat. A chill ran through her body, and her feeling of dread grew as the figure came further into the room.

It was a woman, a beautiful black woman, dark-skinned and tall, wrapped in the dressing gown that Lacey had just been wearing. The woman nodded at her; all at once Trisha knew the sentence she'd just uttered had been heard. The youth worker felt shame rushing to her face. Lacey looked very uncomfortable. The woman sat herself on his lap, throwing her arms lightly around his shoulders like the cat that had got the cream.

'Uhh . . . Trisha dis is Shanice, Shanice, Trisha,' Lacey said tightly.

'Hi,' Shanice purred.

'Hi,' Trisha replied, getting to her feet. 'Well, I think I've taken up enough of your time Lace – call me if you need any help findin' work, or if you get anythin' I might be interested in myself, OK?'

'Sure,' he replied. 'I'll see yuh out yeah?'

'Cheers. Nice meetin' yuh,' she called over to Shanice, who nodded, a look of victory all over her face.

'Bye darlin',' she returned huskily.

At the front door they looked at each other with regret.

'Lissen Trish—'

'It's OK Lacey, forget it all right. I will.'

'Nah but—'

'Forget it! Please.'

His eyebrows furrowed, but he nodded.

'All right man, whatever. You gonna be OK?'

'I'll be fine babes, honestly I will. Jus' . . . Jus' gimme me a call from time to time yeah? Jus' to let me know you're well.'

'Course man.'

Trisha almost mentioned the masks, but she couldn't spend another moment beneath the grey and miserable aura hovering above them like a cloud. She began walking down the landing, unable to bear the thought of hugging him, or any other kind of goodbye.

'I'll see you around yeah,' she called softly, her back turned, the silent tears only now beginning to flow.

'Take care,' she heard him say, then a moment later his door closed, and that was it – the end, finito; it was all over.

She walked out of the block and on to the street. Then she left the estate behind her and made her way home.

Valerie's Stolen Soul

Valerie, Elisha and Leonora watched, hands in their pockets and bored expressions on their faces, as Trisha left the park in search of Lacey. Workmen bustled around the youth club, ignoring the lavishly dressed teenagers, their eyes and minds busy on their work. Silence reigned. Leonora took a pack of Embassy from her pocket and handed the cigarettes out. The girls lit up and sat on the nearest park bench.

'Trisha look distressed innit?' Leonora queried, not looking at the others.

'She's got a right to be distressed,' Valerie returned in a dead voice, waving her free hand at the club. 'She's back on the dole now int she? Poor cow.'

'Dat's such a liberty,' Elisha said softly. 'She seems OK as well.'

Valerie shrugged. 'Yeah man, Trisha's cool. She's not like ordinary youth workers – she really cares, an' it shows. Las' year – when the club had a bit more money – we all used to go ice skatin' . . .'

'. . . An' Lacey used to take us theatre. We saw *Smallie*,' Leonora broke in.

'The boys used to do up bangers an' go stock car racin',' Valerie continued. 'Trisha even used to come ravin' wid us star – we wen' a wicked Nasty Love dance one time. You shoulda seen my gyal shuckin' out t'some Studio One bwoy . . .'

The two friends laughed at the memory. Elisha smiled around her cigarette.

'She sounds proper nice,' she told them truthfully.

Leonora shot her a smile tinged with sadness. 'She *is* proper nice. When she firs' come you could see she was kinna narrow, but she didn't let dat stop her bein' able to relate to any one of us.'

'Done know,' Valerie agreed.

'Council's goin' on proper shabby.' Leonora threw her cigarette into the bushes and let the smoke trickle from her mouth. 'Dis cut, dat cut . . . Everythin' for poor people's bein' cut these days man, they don' leave nothin' fuh us . . .'

Another mournful silence overtook the trio. Valerie glanced at Elisha with a vague amount of sympathy.

'Welcome to Greenside,' she said with a sarcastic smile. 'Sorry yuh firs' real day had to be so shit.'

''S' OK, it's not your fault is it?' Elisha replied honestly. 'Dis ain' no different to my ol' estate anyway. In fac', it's pretty much the same.'

The figure of a young man appeared on the other side of the park, coming through the gates with a smaller youth; both were furtively looking around. The young man was tall and stocky, his complexion a rich pine colour. The smaller, darker youth had a head full of plaits, and was walking briskly alongside his friend. As the girls watched, the darker youth pushed his hand into the young man's jacket pocket, then just as quickly pulled it out. When this was done, the two stopped walking and began to chat. After another half-minute they shook hands formally, before the smaller youth wheeled around and left the park.

The young man turned towards the youth club, then spied the girls and waved. Leonora and Valerie waved back and he began to come over.

'*Mmmm-mmmm* . . .' Elisha murmured under her breath. 'Who's dat?'

The girls laughed.

'Watch Elisha though,' Leonora giggled. 'She 'ave an eye for the man dem don't it!'

'Yuh know dat!'

Elisha turned and saw Valerie grinning broadly, which made her smile, despite her mild embarrassment. It was the first time Valerie had looked really happy since they'd met. And even when her new friend laughed, the humour never reached her eyes, which seemed to take in the world around her with a cold, heart-felt kind of anger.

'At leas' yuh 'ave good *taste*,' Val whispered, just before the young man reached them.

He was dressed in a brown knitted D&G jumper, black jeans, and Reebok Classics. His eyes were bright, hazel, and lit with a warmth that made his round face even more handsome.

'Yes you lot,' he muttered, smiling down on them while they watched him eagerly. 'Wha' gwaan?'

'Same ol' shit,' Valerie intoned lifelessly. 'Garvey, I'd like you to meet my frien' Elisha. Elisha meet Garvey.'

'Hello.'

'Hey Elisha.'

They smiled at each other.

'Elisha moved in Bart's yesterday,' Valerie informed him. 'We're lookin' after her, gettin' her to meet people in the manor an' dat.'

Garvey nodded, looking at Elisha with a little more interest.

'Yeah, where you from?'

'Fulham sides – you know Winton Estate?'

He nodded again.

'Yeah man, I know dem sides. So what, yuh know a brer called Rusty, Rusty Dewitt. I think he lives dere.'

'Yeah man, I know Rusty – poor guy, his sister's off it on the crack int she?'

'Suttin' chronic,' Garvey agreed. 'Las' I heard though, she was s'posed to be in rehab.'

Elisha laughed a scornful cackle. 'Not no more she ain' – I

saw her the night before I lef', out dere wid all dem cats from by my way. I dunno if she even lasted t'ree days.'

Leonora plucked a piece of wood from the bench and threw it at Garvey.

'You're so bait,' she told him critically.

'Wha' yuh mean?'

'It's obvious what you an' Jarvis was on man, you shouldn't be baitin' yuhself up like dat, 'specially not here.'

'I don' gi' a fuck,' Garvey shot back, without any obvious venom. 'Money affa make, y'get me? Man affa eat.'

'Yeah yeah, you jus' min' yuhself, yuh hear? Yuh don' see how dere was nuff police over the site las' night?'

'Yea, I heard about it.'

'Well min' out, y'get me? We got enough black man from roun' 'ere in jail star, I don't wanna see you added to dat lis'.'

'Yeah yeah . . .'

Garvey winked at Elisha, who shrugged helplessly. He bounced on his toes and dug his hands in his pockets.

'Anyway, I gotta duck out man,' he told them apologetically, moving away.

Valerie squinted up at him. 'You jugglin' man,' she sneered jokily. 'So busy makin' money you ain' got time for yuh bredrins innit?'

'Nah man,' Garvey returned with a straight face. 'I gotta go see Sean innit. Gi' 'im some green to plug.'

Sean Bradley was one of Garvey's closest friends, imprisoned for his role in an armed robbery the summer before. He'd got fourteen years, of which he'd probably serve nine and a half. No one on Greenside could believe it had happened to such a straight and honest guy.

'Yuk,' Leonora winced in response to Garvey's words. 'Dat's disgustin' man.'

'Gotta be done though.'

'I know. How's he takin' things?'

'Bes' as he can,' Garvey replied solemnly. 'Lissen star, I gotta duss out.' He waved at Elisha. 'Nice meetin' you – I'll see you about I s'pose.'

'All right, take care,' the girls called in reply. They watched as he left, taking the same route as Trisha.

'My baby,' Valerie crooned proudly, wrapping her arms around herself.

'He's cute,' Elisha added. 'But I wanna know wha' we gonna do from here. We can't be sittin' by dis mash up ol' club for the res' ah the day innit?'

Leonora sighed. 'I s'pose we could go to my drum if we have to. I got some green an' a dett R 'n' B tape from my brudda's soun'.'

Elisha cheered up considerably at this prospect.

'Wha d'yuh reckon Val?'

'Yeah man, come we go,' the pretty girl mumbled, her stony gaze looking around the empty park and battered youth club listlessly. Her face was flat and expressionless, and her brown eyes took in her surroundings with a grim disdain that very nearly bordered on hate.

Aimlessly and lazily the three girls walked the short streets towards Leonora's block with the minimum amount of chatter, relaxed in the company of their peers. A steady hum of daytime activity buzzed around the estate – cars roared, children screamed, and older residents called down from balconies to their neighbours on the streets below but each girl was oblivious to the noise, locked in the complexities of their own lives.

Valerie sensed a movement behind her. Looking around, she noticed Trisha walking the straight road that led from Caldervale House, past the park and out of the estate; she was stumbling and lurching as she walked, her movements casting an aura of distress all around her.

Val called to the others. 'Oi – oi Lee, ain' dat Trish?'

Leonora stopped in her tracks, then turned and squinted back down the road. Elisha joined her, also looking that way. After a minute more, Leonora nodded.

'Yeah man, it looks like her. Is she all right or what?'

Val was frowning. 'How'd I know? I'm stanin' right here wid you. Shall I call her?'

'I'll whistle,' Elisha said decisively, putting her fingers in her mouth and letting off a long shrill blast. Trisha's shoulders twitched a little but she kept going. Elisha tried again, longer and louder. This time Trisha stopped and turned, looking up, down and around to see where the whistling was coming from.

'*Trish! Over 'ere!*' Leonora called at the top of her voice. The youth worker didn't move. Val's frown was still etched into her forehead.

'Wha's her problem?'

Trisha was standing with her body turned their way, a trembling hand rubbing at her head. All at once, she turned on her heel and continued to walk out of the estate. The trio of young women swapped perplexed glances.

'*Trish!*' Leonora bawled once more, but Trisha never even slowed. The girls watched her until she was gone.

'I think she was *cryin*' . . .' Elisha said softly.

Just at that moment, Johnny Winsome, Arthur Lyne and Ray Miles appeared from the shadowy staircase of Devonshire House. Valerie's look, unseen by Elisha or Leonora, darkened in a millisecond. Both were watching the young men with just the right measure of disinterest.

All thoughts of Trisha's possible dilemma were instantly and irrevocably erased as Valerie felt her pulse rate soar and the air around her become harder to breathe. Her head felt light and confused, her stomach queasy with fear. Her lips and throat were desert dry and sweat broke out on her forehead, making her scalp itch.

'*Hiii,*' Leonora crooned, adopting her ladylike walk. 'How you lot keepin'?'

'Safe man,' Art replied roughly, his flat, snake-like eyes roaming over Leonora with next to no interest. They rested on Elisha a moment, with interest but no desire.

'Yes new gyal – wha' yuh ah say?' he questioned. 'Yuh cool?'

'Uh huh . . .' She looked away from him, intimidated by his stare, but adopting an unruffled pose so he wouldn't guess how he made her feel. Now the youths were close, she could clearly see them for what they were worth and she wasn't impressed in the slightest. *Cats.* Elisha mentally kissed her teeth. Young men like these turned some girls on, but she'd had enough dealings with them on Winton to know she didn't need to meet more.

'Baybi girl!'

Ray had caught sight of Valerie and was bouncing towards her with Johnny in tow. Val felt herself go ice cold, and her limbs stiffened so that she couldn't have taken a step away, even if she'd wanted to.

Now she understood why the field mouse froze when it realised the hawk was hunting him, why the deer froze in car headlights, its wide eyes filled with the reflection of the car, nothing but the car . . .

It was fear. The same fear that allowed Raymond and Johnny to get close to her again. The fear that stole her soul.

She saw Elisha and Leonora look her way, smiling until they saw the look on her face, and realised she was less than pleased to see the young men. Ray had stepped in front of her and was giving her a cheeky gold-toothed grin.

'Whassup girl? Yuh look good today y'nuh.'

Valerie stared at Ray, a dead expression on her face. Her deep eyes were cemented to his, ignoring the quizzical smile on his face. There was no anger in her eyes; the panic that was plaguing her went unnoticed by everyone. Elisha and Leonora looked at her worriedly, but the overriding thought in both their minds was that Val was simply blanking him. Elisha nudged the other girl.

'I think we should leave . . .' she murmured, unhappy with the vibes she was getting from this scene.

Then Ray reached out to touch Valerie.

She saw his arm stretching her way, but the fear had her locked down so completely that it meant nothing. As soon as she felt his fingers around her left wrist, however, a shot like pure electricity powered through her body. She looked into Ray and Johnny's smiling mouths with a gasp, and saw their jaws moving in slow motion, the words coming in real time . . . '*Come nuh . . . Come nuh . . . Come nuh . . .*'

. . . Then she was back – back in that room where the ceiling was the floor and the floor was the ceiling, and twin voices merged into one overpowering tone that laughed and panted and swore . . . Where fingers wriggled over her like filthy insects, squeezing her breasts like putty, pushing past her knickers, pinching painfully at her clitoris; then letting go and delivering blows which made her reel and spin and lose her sense of reality, of right, of *herself* – where silhouettes roared at her tears and ripped at her clothes, breathing torrid carbon dioxide into her face and cursing her loudly. Every single solitary sound in that room was loud, every noise an unforgettable memory, especially the voice . . . '*Come nuh . . . Come nuh . . . Come nuh . . .*'

She threw Ray's arm from her wrist with a cry, and used her right hand to push him backwards. Shock flashed across his face, and very quickly turned to anger. This made her own rage rise, and gave her the strength to scream at the youth.

'*Fuck off an' leave me alone!*' she roared in a voice that chilled Elisha and Leonora no end. 'Why you always troublin' me? Jus' fuck off, all right?'

Raymond's face was hostile. By his side, Johnny was roaring with laughter. Even moody Art was smiling. Ray bounced back over to Valerie, pushing close to her face and gesturing with his hands.

'Hear what now – wha' you goin' on stush fuh star, yuh shouldn't chat t'yuh man like dat y'nuh.'

'Fuck off, *bastard*!' was all Val could say in reply.

Leonora ran to her friend's side, while Elisha stood a few paces away from the scene, confused, and not knowing what she should do.

'Leave her Raymond, can't you see she ain' inna wha' you gotta say,' Leonora shouted.

'Keep out of it!' Raymond blazed. 'What, you tink yuh nice now Val, my touch not good enough fuh you . . .'

He made to grab her arm again, but Valerie snatched her hand away and only just held back from slapping him across the face.

'I'm warnin' you. Leave me, yuh fuckin' wretch,' she threatened boldly.

Johnny cracked up even more, making the situation worse. Ray stepped forwards, an evil set to his face, his fists bunched tightly by his side.

'All right man, I had enough ah yuh mout' now,' he told the girl menacingly. 'Playtime done, y'get—'

Art appeared from behind Ray, grabbing him around the shoulders in a tight hug, then moving him away from the girls step by step. He looked towards them, his lean face serious now.

'Don' watch my man, he's cluckin',' he told the girls, his tone apologetic. 'Forget it happened, all right?'

Art leaned over Ray and whispered something in his friend's ear. Ray shouted and cursed. The girls watched, hard-eyed.

'OK,' Leonora said hesitantly, watching Art move away, her lip pushed out stiffly, as though anger still had her in its hold. Valerie was wiping her eyes and staring defiantly in the grappling youths' direction. Elisha joined the two girls, feeling useless and strange after Valerie's seemingly irrational behaviour.

Ray tried to struggle, but he wasn't strong enough to break free from Art's grip, so he settled for cursing everyone in the vicinity instead. Johnny cackled, then winked at Valerie before moving to join his friends. Val spat Johnny's way, then wiped her mouth and eyes again, sniffling as though she had hayfever or the flu. The three girls watched the crack-heads leave, before Leonora turned to Val and threw her arms around her, stroking her hair while the girl sobbed silently on her shoulder. Elisha came closer, feeling a little like a fifth wheel.

'Cats,' she said disgustedly. 'They're all the same, don't change wherever they are.'

'Innit,' Leonora muttered, patting Valerie's back and looking up at the block standing over them. Elisha also looked, but there was no one there. Leonora went back to comforting Val. 'It's OK . . . it's OK babes, he's gone now. He's missin' man. Come on, yuh all right now . . .'

Valerie raised her head to reveal red eyes, a red nose, and smudged eyeliner. 'I know . . . I know . . . I'll be safe, jus' gimme a secon' yeah?'

'Yeah.'

'I *really* hate him.'

'OK, OK, I understand.'

'Do you?' The look Val gave Leonora suggested she didn't.

'Course I do. I know what a bastard Raymond Miles is. He's lucky Lilliane ain' here, I know say my girl woulda wanna bore 'im up.'

'Fuh real.'

Val wiped her eyes again, and twitched the corner of her lips in a way that faintly resembled a smile. Then she sighed.

'All right – I'm OK now. I jus' needed to get it out my system,' Valerie told them in a high voice. She gave a shaky kind of grin and shrugged her shoulders loosely. 'I think I'll jus' go to my yard man, 'stead ah comin' yours Lee. I don' really feel like it at the moment.'

'You sure?' Leonora replied, looking infinitely worried about her friend's state of mind. 'We could come over to yours if you want some company or suttin', jus' in case ah Vas. We don' have to go mines.'

'Innit,' Elisha agreed, fully aware she'd go along with anything that was said at that moment. Valerie screwed up her face and shook her head.

'Thanks darlin', I know yuh bein' kind an' dat, but I kinna feel like bein' on my own for a while. I'll gi' you a ring later OK, when I'm feelin' a little bit better. Don't worry about me, I'll be safe man.'

'All right babes. Bell me when you feel better.' Leonora instructed.

'You know where we are,' Elisha added, before the two of

them took the left towards Woodcroft House. They walked down the road side by side, looking like old friends.

Val stared after the girls, then closed her eyes as tight as she could, as if the pictures in her mind were too much for her to bear. When she opened them, Elisha and Leonora were gone from sight. She sighed, took a number of deep, calming breaths, then made her way home.

Valerie Parker lived with her mother and stepfather on the twelfth floor of Bartholomew House on the estate's east side, and had done so for the full eighteen years of her life. She'd followed the usual route taken by the majority of Greenside girls – went to Greenside High, passed a reasonable number of exams (five – maths, English, design and technology, biology and art), then found herself at a loss to what to do next.

Despite her qualifications, intelligence and stunning good looks, the only work she seemed able to find was in retail – usually in places like Argos, Sainsbury's or Tesco. Try as she might (and she had tried very hard), she couldn't stick at a job like that for much longer than a week, two at the most. Valerie had a very active mind, and sitting beside a till for seven and a half hours a day was enough to drive her crazy. Resigning herself to the inevitable, she signed on, and had been for the last year or so while she decided what to do next.

Last week she'd seen something that made her believe she might have found the answer.

It was a course in desktop publishing. She'd seen it advertised on a flier at the Job Centre in Bush Green – *Unemployed for six months or more? Learn DTP free of charge at the Parkhill youth centre. See reception for details.*

She'd picked up the A5 sheet of paper and almost run to the reception with it, such was her eagerness to start. Valerie was a natural born artist – her bedroom was filled with pictures she'd painted and clay pots she'd fashioned while in school, so she felt more than ready to take on the challenge of designing via computer. Five minutes later, she was signed up to start the first run of her course, in two weeks' time. Each time she though about it, Val felt warm inside; she had a good vibe about things – doing this was her little achievement, the light at the end of a pitch black tunnel.

She let herself in and eased through the front door as quietly as she could, hoping against hope Vas wasn't in. She cocked her ear towards the living room, glad when she heard nothing, and closed the door with the minimum amount of noise, just in case he was sleeping on the sofa. Edging her way down the passage, she stopped on the threshold of the room, smiling in relief when she saw the dark, blank screen of the TV. She straightened up, still grinning, then . . .

'What'm sugah!'

She whirled around, shocked at the sound of his voice, then saw his huge bulk emerging from the toilet at the end of the passage; he was doing up his flies, a gap-toothed grin on his face. Repulsed, Valerie looked away, but the image of her mother's boyfriend stuck in her mind – tall and unbelievably fat, with greying hair, yellowy eyes, and razor bumps all over his face. She walked through the living room in the direction of the kitchen. Vas followed, his loud rattling gasps of breath filling the flat.

'So what'm, yuh cyaan speak? Me know yuh moomy teach yuh better dan dat.'

She went into the fridge for some orange juice, feeling the large man's eyes on her arse as she bent over. Shutting the fridge door, she turned to face him with what she hoped was an evil stare.

'*Hello* Vas. OK now?' she growled, before reaching into a cupboard above her head where the glasses and tumblers were kept. Vas laughed as she poured, laughter that rapidly turned into harsh chesty coughs. Wincing, Val turned her head and drank, wanting to get out of the man's vicinity and to the safety of her bedroom as quickly as she could.

'But, is why yuh affe gwaan so?' Vas was now saying, his vocal chords still affected by the strain of his coughing. 'Me ongle try fe mek frien' wid yuh, is no need fe treat me like leper y'nuh? Me care fe yuh sugah, dat is all, an me nuh like see yuh look distress like how yuh lookin' these days . . .'

'I wouldn't *be* distressed if people like you din't keep botherin' me!' she roared all at once, the heat rising in her again.

She threw her tumbler into the sink, then made to leave the kitchen. Vas stood in her way. She sighed and crossed her arms, her lips twisted into a pout of barely held anger.

'Where yuh ah go? Me waan talk t'yuh still, yuh nuh see dat?'

'Lissen man, I don' care wha' you wanna do. I wanna go to my bedroom. So can you get outta the way please. Now!'

'Bwoy, yuh feis'y yuh see!'

Vas reached for Valerie's elbow, grabbing her and trying to bring her closer to his own body, a very unappealing prospect for her. He was wearing an off-white vest, the colour due to the tapestry of stains covering the garment – sweat, oil, Encona hot pepper sauce; as he grabbed her wrists and pulled her towards his blubbery body, Valerie smelt the aroma of all these things and more, which made her want to scream. The only thing stopping her being the realisation that screaming wouldn't help. There was no one to hear.

'Leave me will yuh . . .'

'Stop yuh noise. You ah big gyal now. Me know yuh like men, ain't it?'

She snorted at this and tried stepping on his corns, but he moved his feet before she could.

'Vas, will you 'llow me! Dis ain' funny no more man. I'm gonna tell my mum wha' you bin goin' on wid if you don' lemme go, I swear to God.'

The smell of the man's BO was stifling. He let go of one wrist and slid his hand across her thigh and around to her bum, rubbing her gently. Bright star-like tears formed in Valerie's eyes. Vas smiled down on her, unaware of the anguish he was causing.

'She won' believe yuh. Especially affa she ketch yuh ah wuk wid bwoy inna yuh bedroom while she ah watch TV! Jus' come nuh, me know yuh waan it sugah . . .'

She punched him hard in the chest, twice. At once he began to wheeze and cough, causing his grip on her to relax, and enabling Valerie to snake her arm away from him, sidestepping his body as he folded. She stood over him as he shook, resisting the urge to deliver a kick to his stomach as well for good measure.

'Yuh bitch yuh . . .' Vas wheezed, holding on to the Formica counter with a death-like grip. 'Watch me, me aggo bury yuh! Watch!'

'Shut yuh mout' man,' Valerie snapped stepping out of the room. 'You ain' buryin' nuttin' wid yuh fat ol' asthma-ridden self, an' you ain' getting' no young pum pum either, all coughin' like yuh got HIV! Jus' cool an' be glad my mum'll even have you about star! An' I tell yuh suttin',' Valerie shouted at the top of her voice. 'If you try anythin' like dat again, I'll fuckin' bury *you*, y'unnerstan'! I'll bury you, yuh stinkin' fat raas yuh.'

Vas roared with indignation and tried to make a grab for Valerie, but she dodged easily and ran into her bedroom as fast as she could. She turned the lock, pushed her desk up against the door, then waited. Sure enough, after a minute, the door rattled violently.

'Val! Val, come out nuh gyal, me ongle joke, nuh gwaan suh! Valerie – ay Val, come out nuh!'

'Fuck you man, I ain' comin' out until my mum gets back!'

Silence. Val walked over to her bed, sat down, then patted her pockets for cigarettes before realising Leonora had been the one with the Embassys. She sighed, cupped her head in her hands. The door rattled again.

'Val! Val!'

She went over to her set – a Kenwood stack system Raymond had brought round about six months ago, when things had still been on a getting-to-know-you vibe. She'd known it was stolen, but her old set had been a rusting collection of silver Phillips separates, and she hadn't been about to turn down a grand's worth of hi-fi for any reason. She pressed a button and the system lit up. Another push caused her CD player to whine, before Kelly Price boomed from her speakers. She turned it up as high as she could take. Vas's blows at the door turned into inaudible thumps, before stopping altogether.

Valerie smiled and sat back on the bed, then leaned over, searching for and finding a chip of cigarette in her dresser. She lit it carefully, singing along with the tune until the CD was finished, and replaying the disc after it got to the end. She smoked as close to the butt as she possibly could, then put it out.

The second time the song faded into silence, she slipped her Nikes off and swung her feet up on to her bed.

It had been a cold morning four weeks previously when Valerie bumped into Raymond and Johnny exiting the Sunshine Fruit and Veg store. Ray was laden with carrier bags. She'd been wearing her skin-tight orange Versace jeans, Raymond's purple Ben Sherman shirt and a white Adidas puffer that ensured she looked the lick.

She hailed her boyfriend. Johnny turned and saw her first, then Ray came over, clutching her hand tight, kissing her soulfully and complimenting her on her new Kickers. She took his sunglasses from his head and deposited them on her own.

'Wha' you lot doin'?' she asked, smiling up at him in the way she knew he loved.

'Shoppin' f'Mummy,' he answered easily, looking down at the bags. 'Follow me up dere nuh – she'd be glad t'see yuh face.'

'OK,' she replied simply. She'd been planning to buy some Rizla and go see her friend Cassie, who'd had a baby boy just last week, but meeting with her man had been on the agenda after that. She decided to buy the Rizla anyway, and pass Cassie's on the rebound. She told Ray this, so he accompanied her to the shop before they headed for Belsize House, where both he and Johnny lived.

She chatted amiably with Ray's mother for a while, a skinny half-Asian woman from St Lucia, then sat in his bedroom, joking good-naturedly with Johnny and listening to a Garage tape. Ray had seemed restless, his body filled with jitters, his fingers and limbs unable to keep still, even at rest. Val wrapped her arms around him, wanting his closeness, his warmth, near her. She looked over at Johnny and saw him regarding her with a strange expression – as if he was looking at her intently, while in reality his mind was elsewhere. She smiled a little nervously. His eyes blinked, fluttered, and then left hers entirely – he didn't smile back. His look chilled her. Feeling uneasy, she turned back to her man, though Johnny's expression remained in her mind's eye.

'Ain' you got nuttin' to bun den?' she asked Ray, stroking his leg with a light finger.

He shook his head. 'Nah man, I'm bruk star. You got any money?'

'A fiver, dat's all,' Val replied, looking crestfallen.

'I know where we c'n get a little summick t'smoke den,' Johnny drawled. 'Kenny's got summa dat skunk, we should go an' check him.'

Ray scowled. 'I owe my man a nifty y'nuh—' he started.

Johnny cut him off insistently. 'It don't matter man, he ain' gonna screw about dat is he? An' he's the only man dat's gonna bother wid a jacks right about now, yuh know dat innit?'

Ray said nothing. Valerie kept quiet as well, simply turning her head every time someone said something new. She couldn't understand why Johnny was being so full on about going to the Beechwood crackhouse for weed and she knew his last sentence was wildly off the mark, but he'd always been a strange character so she let it go. Now, four weeks later, she wished she'd seen the signs of what was to come, though part of her thought *fuck it*; she had seen – she'd just been unable to understand what they'd meant.

The skinny white man known only as Spider opened the door to 42 Beechwood House very cautiously. He was unshaven. His sunken eyes bore the mark of too many late nights, and way too many crack pipes. When he saw who was knocking, he nodded grimly and let the young men in. Valerie gave Spider a token nod, and squeezed through into the passage, trying to stay as far away from the man as she could.

'Wha' you after chaps?' Spider muttered, following behind them, wasting no time.

'Got any ah dat punk?' Ray queried immediately, going into the back room instinctively. Spider shook his head sadly as they stood in various positions around the room.

'Nah mate, all out. Ken's gone to see if he can look up some more, but I dunno when he'll be back – you know the score innit? He lef' hours ago, so he could be back any minute. You can wait if you want.'

'Shall we wait den?' Johnny asked straight away.

'We could go Lionel's—' Val started.

'Wha' for?' Johnny countered. 'We're here now innit? Besides, Lionel's got a whole heap ah pox man.'

'I don't mind pox—' Valerie began again.

Ray spoke up. 'We'll wait,' he said, with a finality that made Val frown questioningly, but he was already continuing his conversation, aiming his talk at Spider. 'So what, you got anythin' for us to draw on while we wait?'

'Depends on wha' you want,' Spider replied, giving a bruk-teeth grin.

'I feel fuh some shit . . .'

In the background, Val rolled her eyes but said nothing. It would be useless – she'd said it all before. Johnny winked at her. Val looked away. He moved past her, inclining his head back down the passage in the direction of the crack room. Ray and Spider were already heading that way. She sighed, then shuffled reluctantly behind them, watching as they headed for the kitchen area of the flat. Just before they got there, Ray turned to her, a look of shock on his face; Val swore he'd only just remembered she was with him, which made her own face harden. He gave her a sour look, then pointed at the closed door of the crack room.

'Wait fuh me in dere, yeah?'

'*What?*' Her mouth dropped open and she stared at him in disbelief. Ray's face twisted in anger. His words came at her louder now, his arms moving around in the air with the speed and agility of a predatory bird.

'Jus' fuh a second man, you'll be all right . . . Dere ain' even no one dere all dese times, since all dat drama. Unless yuh wanna wait in the fuckin' passage . . .'

'Wha' you swearin' at me for Raymond?'

He realised he was shouting and walked over to her, arms dropping to his sides, his look softer and more appealing. He touched her shoulder with his hand.

'Jus' gimme two seconds an' I'll be back babes − come on man, I won't be long.'

'I thought you was gonna give dat shit up.'

Val's face was hard, and resolute in its expression.

Ray shrugged. 'It's only one bone man, jus' to tide us over till the green comes. Come on man, I bin doin' well up to now ain' I?'

'All the more reason why you should 'llow it now,' she fumed, not looking at him. 'D'you really need to smoke dat right now? We only have to wait around ten minutes.'

Ray sighed idly, a thin smile spreading across his lips, his head to one side in a nonchalant pose.

'Wait nuttin' man, I waan smoke suttin' star, y'get me . . .'

She stared at him, reaching for him with her eyes, hoping he'd realise she was being adamant about the subject for his own good. In the three months they'd been seeing each other Val had gradually managed to wean Ray away from the crack-heads he'd been moving with for most of his adult life, and get him into staying at home with her. This began to occur a couple of weeks after their fourth outing to the cinema, when they'd come back to Greenside and ended up in this very flat − where she'd watched her man and his friends smoke over four hundred pounds worth of shit. That was when she realised he had a problem.

Since then she'd been imploring him to give up the pipe on a 24-7 basis, something that had burned him until he realised just how serious she was. One day Val had gone over to Ray's house when he wasn't in. His mother had no qualms about letting her wait in his bedroom. Charlotte believed she was the best thing to happen to her son since nursery school, so Val was ushered upstairs with no delay, a glass of cold lemonade in one hand, a plate of bun and cheese in the other. After a full half-hour of watching TV and chewing on her snack, she got restless. She started looking around his room to see what she could see. Valerie had always had a curious nature, though in the back of her mind she knew what she'd been looking for – and she knew that it was more than plain old curiosity driving her.

She found his old school pictures (which made her smile); she found Valentine's Day cards from years gone by (which made her slightly jealous, even though they looked quite old); she also found a number of flyers promoting a crack detox programme in Portobello Road. That made her smile again, until eventually, inevitably, she found a number of his pipes (and yes – she had gone through his drawers and cupboards, but she'd been doing it for his own good, hadn't she?).

Val had confronted him when he'd got back, and a fearful argument had blown up, with Ray reacting angrily, pointing out that he had been enquiring about detox, hadn't he? Valerie responded by yelling that keeping a selection of pipes in your bedroom while giving up crack was like going on a diet and surrounding yourself with cream cakes. By that time Charlotte had heard the shouting and came running upstairs, thinking Ray might be beating his girlfriend. After Val explained her position, she yelled at Ray a little more, then departed, telling him it was either the crack or her.

Two tense and anxious days later, he turned up on her doorstep looking weary and forlorn – she'd taken him back in, and things had been great between them ever since.

Until this day, when Ray was obviously in urgent need of a lick of the pipe, regardless of the consequences. Val watched him jittering restlessly, and could almost feel the anticipation coming off him in foul-smelling waves, wafting into her nostrils, making her instantly ill. The sickly churning in her belly caused anger to rise like bile in her throat. She glared even harder at her man, as the urge to thump him became an unbearable desire she could barely resist.

'Go on den, fuck off an' smoke yuh shit if it makes you happy – I dunno why I bovva try tell you any different,' she snarled, tearing into him as only she could. Usually, she could affect Ray with words, make him feel bad, even if he didn't entirely agree with the things she was coming out with. Val had been using this method of dealing with him for the last couple of weeks, but gradually felt her faith in the tactic ebbing as he got more and more fed up with her bullying. This time he simply looked at her, smiled, then nodded his head as if he'd expected no better, and had known she wouldn't understand his point of view. He turned away.

'Jus' wait in the back man – I soon come all right?'

Then he rejoined Johnny and Spider and was gone, leaving Valerie steaming in fury and frustration behind him.

Exasperated, she looked at the crack-room door and felt tiny shivers of fear go through her. There were thousands upon thousands of rumours concerning this infamous flat, but the gossip surrounding the room behind that particular door ran into tens of thousands. Knifings. Overdoses. Drug raids. She'd never actually seen these things happen, but she'd heard. She *believed*. After all, she knew most of the main players in the local tales, so she took it for granted that the stories in which she didn't know the players were true as well. Now she was being made to go inside the room that she'd feared for most of her teenage life (and fearing anything wasn't something she admitted lightly). She felt betrayed by Raymond. Part of her wished she'd told him that a minute ago.

She looked down the corridor at the room into which he'd gone with his friends, tempted to follow and give him a piece of her mind. She took a few steps that way. Laughter floated from behind the door, stinging her pride like the prick of a sharp thorn. The sound erased her fear and replaced it with the rage that had burned in her moments before.

She kissed her teeth, more at herself than him, then let her stubborn side take over. She didn't need *any* man, especially not any crack-head. She was intelligent, good-looking, and sick to death of having to watch over Ray and his fucked-up habit. It wasn't fair on her, not when she could be doing things with her life, excelling in something that could benefit her future. It was *his* fault she wasn't following a career in art, or design and tech, or any other field in which she was talented. Her mother kept telling her she was crazy going out with 'one of the most thievingist boys on Greenside'. At this stage Valerie whole-heartedly agreed that life with a cat was no kind of life at all. Her mother also said that a man who had no respect for his own family, or even his own body, could never have respect for her. Val thought she was right – and decided she'd tell him so when he came back.

But for now, she grudgingly admitted she'd wait in that damned room.

An' dis is the last fuckin' time I wait for him to pipe dat shit up, she promised herself sternly. *The very las' time . . .*

She pushed her ear against the door to see if there were any sounds of movement. Nothing. She clutched the door handle tight, then pulled downwards with baited breath, almost closing her eyes as she walked inside the room, not wanting to see what it contained.

When she looked through her squint she was surprised to see the room was completely empty. Either all the cats had gone home or most of the people who formerly visited Beechwood for bone went elsewhere these days. Val suspected the latter was true. Although the crackhouse had been prolific years ago, events on the estate had slowly and inevitably led to its demise. She went deeper into the room, casting her eyes left and right, shaking her head in disbelief and fascination at the way people chose to conduct their lives.

The room was the most sordid display of squalor and degra-dation she'd seen in her eighteen years on Greenside. The walls had been white, but the steady accumulation of grime and smoke had turned them a dusky grey. The stench of urine mixed with

a pervading smell of months-old crack smoke, and, Val suspected, human faeces, which was not seen, but could certainly
be smelt. Areas of the wall were lined with dried blood. The top
pane of the one window was shattered, the bottom boarded
with cardboard.

There were no chairs in the small room. Val looked about her,
an expression of disgust frozen all over her pretty features and
a hard glare in her eyes. She stood by the window, breathing in
and out with shallow sips, hating every second she spent in this
place, where people had lost their self-respect, dignity and sometimes even their lives. The ghosts of past events seemed to
whirl around her head, haunting her imagination with vivid,
shocking images. Her heart thumped in irregular blasts. Her
palms felt clammy and cold to the touch.

The wait seemed to take forever, but eventually the door
squeaked open. Ray wandered into the room with Johnny trailing behind. Both clutched personal pipes. Ray grinned in a
sloppy manner that spoke volumes, and approached Val with a
lustful gleam in his eyes.

'Wha' yuh ah say, sexy?' he drawled, oozing his way over to
her and rubbing his body close. This was another reason Val
hated it when Ray smoked. He always got unbearably horny and
annoying, and the thought of having some drugged-up sex fiend
drooling all over her did nothing for her libido, regardless of
who he was. She screwed up her face in frustration, and pushed
him away with one hand.

'Get off me Raymond, I ain' in the fuckin' mood all right?'

'What's your problem?'

'If you can't guess, I don't see why I should tell yuh.'

'Cha man, yuh too miserable star – fix up yuh face nuh gyal!'

Ray and Johnny laughed loudly, then Ray crossed the room to
sit in the middle of the floor, his pipe posed dramatically by his
lips. Johnny was already there. Val knew she should drop it, but
she couldn't stop her mind working and her mouth forcing the
words from her brain into the musty air.

'Lissen man, don' start wid me y'nuh – I ain' got time for

yuh foolishness right about now. I can't believe you're goin' ahead an' smokin' after all we talked about Ray, an' I'm bloody disappointed in you.'

'Yah, yah, yah . . .' her man replied, his attention fully and completely on the pipe. Valerie crossed her arms and bit her tongue, knowing that if she didn't she and Ray would have the biggest fight in their history, and this room would have yet another tale to tell.

Half an hour later Val was bubbling and steaming like a volcano set to erupt. She was sitting in a corner of the room, wanting to leave, but not wanting to go without Ray. She knew he'd definitely smoke himself stupid without her presence. He and his friend were semi-comatosed on the floor, where they'd sprawled after relighting their respective pipes for the second time running. The effects of the drug were taking full control. She gazed at cracks in the walls that meandered and spread like black veins, lost in her own thoughts and scared about the amount of rock Spider seemed to have ticked the young men.

Ray suddenly stirred, leaning over and grabbing for his pipe and lighter once more. His movements were fuddled and he seemed unaware of the cold look his girl was giving him. At the sight of him lighting up again, Valerie realised she'd had enough. She jumped to her feet and marched towards the pipe room door, determined to leave now, knowing she could no longer take the sight of Ray smoking himself into oblivion.

'Ay, ay, where yuh ah go star?'

Clumsily, but as urgently as he could, Ray got to his feet and staggered over to Val. Johnny stirred as well, looking up at them through his crack haze, a tiny smile on his youthful face. Ray tried to grab his girl by the hand. She snatched it away and gave him a disdainful sneer.

'I'm goin' home Raymond. I've had enough of yuh shit for one day.'

She opened the door. He slammed it shut with the palm of his hand. A wriggle of fear squirmed through her. She let it go and forgot about it, wanting anger as her primary emotion.

'Nah man, you ain' goin' home star. I ain' ready to leave yet. Lemme jus' bun dis ting 'ere an'—'

'Fuck dat, I ain' waitin' for you to bun nuttin', I wanna go home now! I can't believe you're even tellin' me dat, after you done know how I feel about you smokin'! Cha man, I don' even want no more argument wid you, I'm goin'! Bye.'

Another grab for the door. Ray pushed again, harder this time, so the slam echoed through the flat. He squeezed his body between Val and the door handle, his brow frowned and his lips twisted in rage.

'I said, *you ain' goin' nowhere*. Sit yuh arse down where you was an' cool yuhself, yuh 'ear me? Tryin' t'go on like you run tings . . .'

'*What*? Who the fuck d'you think yuh chattin' to?'

'You man!'

Before she could reply, or even react to his words, Val felt the vicious backhand across the side of her face. The world went bright for a second, before multi-coloured spots appeared in front of her eyes, dazzling in their sharpness and intensity. She took a step towards the wall, more shocked than hurt, looking up at Raymond with defiant anger. He moved closer, his face contorted and his eyes unblinking.

Despite her high emotions, his manner scared Valerie. He didn't look like someone you could reason with. Ray moved closer still, a pulse in his neck beating madly, his hands murderously squeezing the pipe he held.

'I'm chattin' t'you. So what? *So what, eh?* Wha' you gonna do?'

'Fuck you, you bastard!'

Valerie stood up to her full height and choked back the angry tears. She still found the fact that Raymond had the audacity to hit her hard to believe – he'd never raised a hand to her in the past, and even though she knew he was a violent kind of guy, she never imagined he'd use that violence against her. Ray pushed her shoulder, making her stumble and almost hit the wall again. Behind them, Johnny was getting to his feet with great difficulty.

'Fuck *me*? Don't even try chuck it y'nuh.'

He raised his hand again, bringing it halfway, but not follow-ing through. Val still flinched. She was incensed by her own fright, enough to make her want to hit back. She couldn't curb the desire and threw a strike to his face with her left hand, then pushed his chest as hard as she could with her right. Ray stum-bled backwards in his drugged-up stupor, tripping and falling against the wall behind him. Johnny started to laugh in thick bellows, pointing at his friend and bending at the waist.

'Raa blood, yuh get man-handle like dat? I know who wears the pants in dis ting 'ere, y'get me . . .'

Val rounded on him like a predator catching first sight of its prey. She was livid, wishing she'd followed her instincts earlier and left when she'd felt like it. Slapping the pipe from Johnny's hand, she pushed him away too, meaning to turn around and make a run for the door before both youths switched on her. She got a brief glance at Johnny's face as she knocked the pipe away; he didn't look happy and she knew there was no way on earth Ray would let what she'd done to him slide. She'd embar-rassed him in front of his friend. Hey boyfriend's reputation was very important in his own eyes, so it was better she left now before any more of a scene could erupt. She'd avoid him for a while, then link him up again when he'd calmed down.

When Val turned she saw Ray had got to his feet and was standing in front of the door with his back to her, fiddling. She heard the sound of a key in a lock. Her anger fled her body in two seconds flat, leaving her cold and apprehensive. Ray turned around, showed her the key, then put it in his inside pocket.

'Wha' you doin' Raymond?'

She tried to keep the tremor from her voice but it was impos-sible. She was scared. Ray's face was remorseless.

'Gonna teach yuh some manners star. Show yuh how to humble yuhself wid yuh man.'

'Wha' you talkin' about? I ain' jokin' wid you y'nuh—'

'Hol' 'er Jay.'

Johnny's hands grabbed her from behind, pinning her arms

behind her back, making her yelp with pain and renewed anger. She struggled, but she wasn't big built, or big boned, or big any- thing – she was skinny and Johnny was way too strong for her, even though he was a crack-head. She tried to stamp on his toes and kick between his legs, but he moved his feet away and jerked at her arms until she cried out. She yelled and screamed, recalling Johnny's leering face earlier at Ray's house; suddenly she knew what was coming.

Ray came closer. It seemed as though he was enjoying seeing Val in this position, though she hoped – prayed – it was only the crack making him like this. She also hoped his good sense would prevail and he would let her go.

'Don't do dis Ray. I swear to God I'll kill yuh if you touch me.'

He stood in front of her. She was still, wanting to cry, but gulping back the tears, telling herself, *You won't bawl, you fuckin' won't* . . .

He slapped her, hard. She struggled some more, desperate to escape the madness that had overtaken them, but Johnny's grip was iron strong and it seemed the more she moved, the worse it made things. The stench of her fear saturated the room; she was sure Raymond smelt it, and sure the odour compelled the youths to further acts of violence. Ray hit her in the stomach, telling her to keep still and to 'learn to take licks if she knew how to give dem out'. That blow knocked the wind from her. Her knees buckled and she would have fallen to the floor if it weren't for Johnny holding her up.

'*Leave* me . . .' she managed to gasp, when she'd found her breath.

Ray gave her yet another slap. She screamed loud and fought like a wildcat, freeing one hand and flinging her fist against his face in desperation. She aimed a kick at his balls, but he simply laughed and got out of the way while Johnny grabbed her hand again, twisting until she screamed even louder.

'Hol' her man, whassup?' Ray growled.

Johnny tried, but Valerie continued to wriggle. Raymond

reached for the Ben Sherman shirt, grabbed it and pulled, splitting the garment down the front and exposing Val's bare flat stomach and black lace bra. Buttons popped, bouncing on the carpet. Val was stunned and kicked out even harder.

'Fuck off—' she roared in a heart-felt plea.

Johnny threw his arm around her throat so the crook of his elbow was underneath her chin. He squeezed. She tried to scream again but her voice was gone. Raw panic trapped her in its embrace. She thought she was about to die, yet could only feel outrage – the fear was way, way back in a distant corner of her mind. Her head went fuzzy and the scant light in the room began to fade.

'Let her go man. Let her go . . .'

Her boyfriend's voice came from somewhere above the haze that surrounded her. The arm was gone, but for a while it didn't make any difference. She coughed and spluttered, hands on her knees, while the youths talked excitedly over her – then amazingly another blow landed on her cheek, sending her reeling into the corner of the room, unable to fight back any more. Her nose was buried in the carpet, immersed in the smells of vomit, shit and semen embedded there. She was on all fours. Above her, the sound of zippers brought fresh panic to her gut, as she heaved thick strands of phlegm from her throat. She felt rough fingers on her arse and inner thighs, pulling at her jeans, attempting to tug them from her waist. That must have been Johnny, because Ray was in front of her, tugging at the shirt, the shirt *he'd* lent her, saying, *'Come nuh . . . Come nuh . . . Come nuh . . .'*

She wanted to fight but all her strength was gone. They'd talked about this kind of thing before, she and her friends, and they'd all been sure of what they'd do if anyone even considered trying to rape them.

They'd kick them in the balls. They'd scream for help. They'd *kill* the motherfuckers if they had to – but there was no way anyone would get the chance to take that kind of liberty with them, of that they were all sure.

So Val refused to believe she was having her jeans pulled from her legs and coarse fingers pushed between them . . . Couldn't believe she was being turned over, limbs spread in all directions, her man encouraging his best friend to rip the knickers from her and push his face down *there*. She went limp, disassociating herself from their actions, feeling profound guilt for her wetness, unable to take the whole thing in as reality. When the first one entered her she managed a weak gasp, not knowing which of them it was. She closed her eyes and cried, wishing she could make herself fight, but feeling, knowing, she was powerless.

She prayed so long and so hard for it to be over, that when it eventually was she continued praying – eyes closed, lips moving silently, body deathly still, chest hardly moving. She could feel their hands and their penises inside her like phantoms, destined to haunt her for eternity. When she eventually found the courage to open her eyes and face the room, she was appalled (but not surprised) to see them laid out in the centre, pipes in hand, their eyes as spaced out and dreamy looking as before.

Tearfully, Val picked up her clothes and banged on the door until Spider came with the spare key. When he repeatedly asked if she was OK, she burst into tears again and fled the flat as fast as she could, knowing the man had heard every second of her ordeal.

She shook her head to banish the spectres of her memories and rubbed her eyes tiredly, sitting upon her small single bed. Although only four weeks had passed since the rape, she'd stopped crying well within the first, though she still wouldn't allow anyone to touch her – the very thought made her shiver. She didn't know if she was coping all that well. When women were raped on TV, they had breakdowns that lasted for months, their men felt outrage, then they poured the gory details out to a sympathetic policeman or woman. None of these things had happened to Val.

Instead of a breakdown, her emotional response to all that had happened was revenge. It had been growing and festering in her brain ever since that day. She'd managed to stay away from Raymond until now – she wouldn't answer his phone calls and told her mother they'd had an argument and split up, so she certainly didn't mind telling him to get lost on Val's behalf. Valerie's first sight of him had been yesterday, walking back from Smallie's with Elisha.

Sure, to see Ray brought back all the hurt, anguish and fear that had controlled her in that tiny room a month ago. But she also felt her wild temper igniting in a way she felt strangely comfortable with – it was as though she'd grabbed the emotion she felt more accustomed to, rather than the one every other woman seemed to feel. Or believed they should feel. Laying back on her bed and thinking about it, she decided she had to find a way to strike back in order to make her able to cope (though she wasn't sure that it would, or even *could*). She had to find a way to make Ray go through the same shit he'd put her through.

She couldn't tell the police. Grassing was something that just wasn't tolerated on the estate. She could imagine how miserable her life would become if she took that route. Having to deal with Ray and Johnny's hundreds of friends. Having to deal with *her* friends, especially those close to the youths. Having to deal with medical examinations, courtrooms, and the chance that they could both be acquitted, leaving her in an even worse situation than before.

She couldn't even tell her mother what Vas had been doing to her over the last two years, so how was she meant to tell some stony-faced policewoman about Ray?

No, there was no chance of Valerie even approaching a police station – everyone in the area knew she and Ray had been involved in a steamy relationship. And what about the other boyfriends she'd had sexual relations with before Ray, especially the ones that knew him. Was there any chance they might be brought into the picture?

But besides all that, what about the biggest and most important question of all in Val's eyes – the question that irrefutably cemented her decision to remain silent, and ensured she never told anyone what had happened, even the people dearest and closest to her heart: who would possibly believe her own man could rape her?

Later that day, the three Greenside girls loafed in Elisha's bedroom, listening to the steady *thump, thump* of Tawanda's set through the walls, Leonora wiggling her shoulders and bottom to the Ragga beats. Lillianne was smoking a cigarette and idly examining the paint-job she'd done on her nails. Valerie was standing by the window, looking out wistfully and tapping her foot against the skirting board. Elisha came in with a tray of drinks and placed it on the floor. She sat on the bed next to Leonora, then slapped her shoulder as she noticed her movements.

'Oi you, stop wipin' yuh big arse on my duvet!'

Leonora gasped, while the others laughed.

'*Feis'y*, I don't like yuh mout' y'nuh gyal,' Leonora intoned in a deep voice. 'Bes' min' I don't gi' yuh two bitch licks and sen' yuh raas out to yuh mudda bawlin'.'

'Eh eh, watch my girl though . . . Yuh arse big yes. You know I ain' lyin'.'

Val leaned her head against the cold glass of the window and closed her eyes, unable to join in with her friends' playful banter. She just wasn't in the mood. After more of their back and forth arguing, Elisha noticed Val had separated herself from the group. She called her, looking at the young woman's back with concern.

'Val, dere's juice 'ere if yuh wannit y'nuh.'

Valerie looked around thoughtfully, then came and sat down in an empty chair.

'Ta.'

'S'all right. Lilly wassup man, gimme a twos nuh! Smokin' dat all the B&H's t'yuhself!'

'My girl's mout' can run innit? Don't you regret talkin' to her

in Smallie's? I do. Fuckin' 'ell,' Lillianne teased, passing the cigarettes over with a grin.

'Run like river,' Leonora agreed, winking at Val. 'Still, we
shoulda known she was feis'y when we laid eyes on 'er innit?
She's got a cheeky kinda cute look to her face, like a . . . a . . .
a rat, or somethin'.'

'A *rat*!' Elisha screamed. 'You reckon I look like a rat? Oh my
God . . .'

'You think rats are cute?' Val spluttered.

'Not as cute as hamsters – but cute still, gi' a damn.'

'Bloody Nora,' was all Elisha could see fit to reply. They all
found that funny, though none of them knew why.

There was a knock on the door.

'Come!' Elisha shouted.

Veronica poked her head in.

'Jus' goin' over Linton's cousin's,' she said cheerily, looking
relaxed and a little less harassed than she had the previous day.
'D'want anythin' to eat out the road or can you get yuhself
somethin'?'

'What, you rich or suttin' Mum?'

'No – Linton's payin',' Veronica giggled girlishly. 'So what
d'you want den?'

'Ken*fucky*!' Elisha shouted, throwing her arms out wide and
shouting her reply at the ceiling.

'*Elisha!*' Veronica gasped, more for show than anything else.
She looked mortified, though there was a hint of a smile on her
lips. Her daughter subsided and withered into the duvet, face
red, fully aware she may have gone too far. Her friends were
rolling with glee from various positions of the room, trying to
contain their laughter.

'I'll be back later with the food,' Veronica finished, giving the
young woman a stern yet understanding eye, before leaving the
girls to their own devices. Valerie smiled at her friend.

'Yuh mum's safe. Min' woulda gone ballistic if I dropped
suttin' like dat on 'er,' she admitted.

'Yeah, my mum's all right,' Elisha agreed. 'I know it soun's corny, but she's more like my sister than my mum – which makes a strange kinna sense I suppose, seein' as my sister come like my fuckin' mother.'

'Why, what's she like?' Leonora wanted to know.

'Ah, she's OK. She's jus' miserable and moany and hard to live wid—'

'In other words, she's a typical older sister. Soun's jus' like mine,' Lilliane told her, not without a small amount of sympathy.

Elisha shrugged in acceptance. 'Yeah, I suppose. What about you Lee, got any sisters or brothers?'

'Two,' the girl replied in a bored tone. 'Two older brothers. Made my life fuckin' hell when I was in school. Not one guy wanned to chirp me – they was too scared ah gettin' t'ump up if they tried it on too heavy. Even when my brothers left, brers was paro to go out wid me. I had to literally force them to stick their tongues down my throat. It was bloody embarrassin'.'

'An' nuttin' ain' changed to dis day – Lee's still forcin' brers to stick their tongues down 'er throat,' Valerie laughed, ignoring Leonora's rude gestures. 'Spare us yuh life story, my girl only asked if you had any sisters or brothers,' she continued, picking up a juice and taking the smallest of sips. Elisha gulped hers and looked straight at the dark-skinned girl.

'What about you Val?'

Valerie put her glass down.

'I got a half-brother in Birmingham. He's only five, and he's really cute.'

'He is as well. Musta bin from the mudda's side ah tings,' Leonora added.

Val gave her a mock smile, feeling a little better now. That was the good thing about being around her friends. They couldn't erase the hurt, but they could make it easier to handle, or help put it to the back of her mind. Without Lillianne, Leonora and her new friend Elisha, she'd probably want to curl up and die.

'I should go up dere and see 'im really,' Val continued,

contemplating the idea as she spoke. 'Me dad's up dere as well, an' I ain' seen my man in ages. I reckon I need to get away from these sides for a while.'

'Don't say dat, I only jus' got 'ere,' Elisha moaned.

The others gave her pitiful glances.

A few uneventful days later, Val watched Ricki Lake while stretched on her mother's sofa smoking a weed spliff. She wasn't meant to smoke in the house. Whenever her mum came home and complained about the smell she always got out of it by laying the blame on Vas – and today wasn't likely to be any different.

The show was a lively one; Ricki's discussion was about gun crime. She had a crew of ex-gangster girls on one side of the studio and a girl who'd been paralysed by a gun on the other. Heated arguments flew back and forth. Val watched eagerly, half hoping some kind of fight would break out, though she did feel sorry for the crippled girl. She bent down to reach for the ash-tray, then sparked the spliff up again, every movement idle and slow.

Just as the zook touched her lips, Val paused, as if an invisible light bulb had switched itself on over her head. Her eyes widened and her mouth dropped open. Staring at the TV screen an idea of the purest simplicity shot through her as the voices ranted, and Ricki tried her best to calm them down.

Val had a solution. She knew what to do about Ray. She was amazed she hadn't thought of it before.

Her mother's boyfriend Vas owned a gun.

She'd come across it around two years ago, when she'd been in her mother's room looking for some Always pads, as she'd run out. The house had been empty – both her mother and Vas had been at work. Searching through drawers, she'd been amazed to find the weapon pushed to the back of the cupboard, covered with a pile of her mother's clean knickers. She pulled it from its hiding place and looked it over with childish glee; it was a Taurus, a make she'd never heard of before, though she'd seen enough films to know it was a nine millimetre. Val dug some more and found a box of ammunition, pushed even further back than the pistol. That evening she'd taken the gun out on the block with her. All her friends were impressed, and Val had felt like a hardcore rude gyal – until she got home and had to face her mother and stepfather's angry faces.

That's the problem, she mused to herself. Since that day the gun had been locked away in her mum's filing cabinet. Only she and Vas had the keys. Getting hold of it would require complex deviousness and ingenuity – both of which she was more than capable of – but it would also take some time. The more Val considered, the more committed she felt. As Ricki Lake came to a close and the credits began to roll, Valerie smiled. She sparked the spliff and put it to her lips, this time drawing the smoke in deeply. She closed her eyes, not concentrating, but allowing thoughts to flow, knowing the remaining part of the idea would come if she just let it happen. She didn't have to wait long.

From then on Vas and her mother began to notice a change in Valerie that was amazing to behold. It began when she came into the kitchen one morning just as Felicia, her mum, was getting ready to leave for work. Vas sat at the kitchen table dressed in his usual attire – a string vest and tracksuit bottoms. He was eating cornmeal porridge and watching Felicia with a look that plainly wanted her back in bed. Val strolled into this scene like a skinny little ray of sunshine, determined to bring joy to the world.

'Hey Mum. Hi Vas. Any lef' fuh me?'

She went over to the cupboard where the cereal bowls were kept, knowing their eyes were on her, feeling their wonder tickling her spine and the back of her thighs. She held down a smile and headed towards the pot of porridge on the cooker.

'Mornin' . . .' her mum began, unsure of what to make of her daughter's actions. Valerie was a terror in the mornings – a grunt was all Felicia usually got from her, and Vas could hardly raise a bad look. She frowned at her partner, who shrugged in return, just as perplexed as she.

'Mornin' . . .' he said hesitantly. The word almost never left his mouth.

Valerie ladled thick globs of cornmeal into her bowl and turned to her mother. 'Ain' it a bit early for work? You don't usually leave before ten,' she asked, putting the lid on the pot and the spoon in the sink. Felicia's confusion remained on her face.

'Well, I thought I'd do a little shoppin' beforehand . . .'

Her words trailed away. She found herself caught completely off guard by Val's remarkable character change. The daughter she knew was sullen, quiet and introspective at best, moody and argumentative at worst. It wasn't that Val couldn't be kind – it was just that her kindness became apparent in ways far removed from the manner she was currently displaying.

Like when Felicia's common-law husband left her. She'd remember that time forever. Valerie had been asking for her daddy all day. Felicia couldn't bring herself to say he'd left a note two days earlier saying he'd met someone else and was getting married in the summer, and don't try to look for him because it was over. She didn't have the courage to speak of what she couldn't even think about.

So she remained silent, and went about the business of living as normal. Felicia was a strong, beautiful woman who'd been brought up to believe that no matter how bad things got, she should never bow, never falter. But it was hard to live up to her mother's standards – *damn* hard – and all through Valerie's desperate, selfish-sounding ranting, the pain got worse and harder to bear, until a line deep within her soul was crossed.

'Mum, where's Daddy? Where's Daddy? *Muuumm* . . .'

She pushed the child away from her and rose in the blink of an eye.

'You stupid, selfish little child, your father's gone, d'you hear me? He's gone an' he's not comin' back.'

Her daughter was eight years old. Felicia broke down and fell on to the sofa, hating herself for doing this, but compelled to expel her deep grief. Her tears were loud – her body shook with their force. She beat the cushions, unable to stop the actions that she knew bordered on hysterical.

Eventually the well within her ran dry. She coughed and spluttered her last dregs of emotion, lifting her head to gaze around the room.

Then she saw Valerie. Standing there, staring. Fists clenched, eyes hard, but no expression on her face. Unconcerned by her mother's gaze, nothing moved but her eyelids when she blinked. Felicia was chilled; at first for herself, but then for her child's state of mind.

'Valerie are you OK . . .'

The little girl turned and went to her bedroom without a word. Felicia heard the door shut and considered going after her. She eventually balked – she was in no state to comfort anyone. *She* needed comfort. But her mother was dead, her daughter was a child, and she had nobody. Felicia went to her room to cry some more.

She woke the next morning with her eyelids stuck together, her nose blocked and her muscles stiff and aching. Dragging herself from the bed, she trundled to her door, opening it to find the most extraordinary bunch of flowers she'd ever laid eyes on. Someone later told her they were Dahlias, with petals that looked as light as butterfly wings and a scent that filled her mind with blissful images. Beside them was a home-made card with one word – *sorry* – inscribed along the top. Underneath was a picture of a brown-skinned woman drawn in crayon, thick teardrops dripping down her cheeks. Beside the card was a box of All Gold, and everything was presumably bought with Val's pocket money.

Felicia at once felt ashamed and distraught. She carefully picked up her gifts and went to her daughter's room to find her sitting on her tiny bed with Sonia Chamberlain, the quiet little girl who lived three floors down. Obliviously, Felicia smothered Val with hugs and kisses, rocking her from side to side and telling her how sorry she was. Sonia watched the proceedings with wide eyes, a slight smile at the corner of her lips, wondering if the whole thing was a joke.

After a while, Val began to hug her mother back. It wasn't long until tears began to flow.

That was what Val was like.

Felicia had to admit that she'd never seen her this cheerful in the morning since the age of twelve – after that, the dreaded teenage years had sunk their claws into her and turned her into someone completely different. She strained to understand what could have produced such a radical about-face, while appearing not to probe. Vas himself was so perplexed he'd stopped the routine ladling and lifting of his spoon and was now staring at the young woman mutely, dry lips trembling as he breathed.

'Why d'you ask?' Felicia continued the conversation, finding her feet like a toddler taking first practice steps.

Val shrugged, her face as deadpan as it had been all those years ago. She took a huge gulp of porridge and swallowed nonchalantly. She coughed a little, then held her face straight.

Shit! Her mind screamed. *Dis fuckin' ting's burnin' hot!*

The lump scorched its way down. Val went red. Sweat appeared on her forehead. Her mother stepped forwards, deeply concerned. Valerie was attempting to remain as normal as possible by digging around in her bowl and finding a sizeable enough scoop to replace the one roasting her insides. Her mother reached her and grabbed at her arm.

'Valerie, you're chokin' . . .'

Her daughter coughed again loudly, twice, her head down. Cornmeal splattered the bowl.

Vas chuckled until Felicia shot him an angry glare.

'Shit,' Val managed weakly.

'Valerie . . .'

'I'm safe Mum, don' worry.'

A little embarrassed, she went over to the bin, spooned her breakfast out, then went back to the sink and dumped the bowl inside. Not stopping for one moment, head straight, she marched past her mother and Vas, saying, 'I'll wash dat up later, all right?'

'But you haven't 'ad breakfast . . .' Felicia started.

'I ain' 'ungry. I'll eat later,' Valerie sang, hastening to her room and cursing her stupidity all the way.

Felicia stared at Vas, unable to understand one solitary part of the scene. She could've just forgotten about the whole thing if nothing else had happened.

But things got stranger. Valerie and Vas began to get on.

Although Valerie's venture hadn't started very well, she'd accepted this and decided to continue as planned, but with an added twist. *Go for the weak link in the chain*, a little voice inside her whispered. She'd laid herself down on the bed, the thick sugary taste of cornmeal filling her mouth. Her mother had decided to leave Val to her own devices. The young woman pondered her next move, then decided the weak link in the chain was her mother's boyfriend; the tool she'd use to break the chain would be infatuation.

She began paying Vas special attention, smiling secretly when Felicia wasn't looking, steeling herself and talking to him at close range when she was at work. Valerie knew the game she was playing was dangerous, but consoled herself with the thought that he'd be pawing after her regardless of the moves she made. He treated her suspiciously at first, but within a week or so began to mellow enough to smile and even start winking back.

A few days later she bought the first bottle of rum.

Vas was what Leonora had often called a 'habitual drinker' – which in practical terms meant he liked to get pissed. Whisky, brandy, or most often Jamaican white rum usually accompanied his long days in front of the TV. Sometimes Felicia would come home to find him sprawled on the sofa snoring, the last dregs of alcohol resting placidly in the bottom of a Wray and Nephew bottle. The small flat would resound with her loud cussing for hours.

Valerie knew that Yard rum was one sure-fire way of keeping Vas out of the picture for as long as it took to acquire what she needed.

It took three bottles and a good portion of her giro to achieve the desired effect. The first two had only made the man horny – she'd run around the flat for half an hour before she'd had enough, made some lame excuse, and escaped to the comparative utopia of her friend Cassie's home. She knew of Valerie's scheme – Val had blurted everything out to her over brandy and spliffs one night when Cassie's boyfriend had gone raving and her baby was enjoying a rare snooze. Strangely enough, the young mum thought it was a marvellous idea. Cassie was the only person on the estate who hated Ray as much as Val – he'd made her cousin pregnant sometime last year and ignored the baby's existence to this day.

Two days later she gave Vas the third bottle.

This time Val retired to her room while Vas loafed on the sofa. She then timed him – she'd given him the rum at midday, and so spent the next three hours listening to *Choice*, reading a little J. California Cooper and waiting. At half past three she emerged from her self-imposed isolation.

The bottle was half-full. Vas was asleep, his head thrown back far enough to see his oversized tonsils if you cared to look. Which she didn't.

For a moment she couldn't believe it had worked. She stared at him, fully expecting him to jump up and begin fondling her any second. Vas stayed motionless. She went over and grabbed his legs, lifting them on to the sofa so he could lie straight. While she did this, she managed to feel at his tracksuit pockets, searching for the keys to the filing cabinet. Vas moaned and snorted, but settled down once she left him alone. The keys weren't there. Her face bore some regret, but mostly relief. Part of her thought there must be a God.

Her mother's bedroom was the next stop. She peered about the room, looking for Vas's outdoor jacket, which she eventually found hanging on a hook behind the door. Frantically she plunged her arm into the left pocket, then the right, smiling when she heard the metallic jangle. She retrieved the keys and lifted them slowly from the jacket, real pleasure all over her face.

Her ears were attuned to the slightest sound, but the living room was quiet.

It worked! she cheered brightly to herself. *It fuckin' worked man!*

Unlocking the cabinet was no problem. When the gun was free she held it to her breast like a magic talisman. It was cold, but the warmth it gave her was almost real. The strength she felt was unimaginable. Val reached further back inside for the ammunition when she heard the bedroom door behind her move with a small creak. The image of Vas filled her mind and the warmth fled her body. She jumped and turned . . .

. . . To see the door swinging shut of its own accord. Which meant Vas was still asleep on the sofa. Which meant her plan had worked.

She grabbed the box of shells quickly, then hurried from the room before fate decided she'd tempted him enough.

Valerie scurried through the streets of Greenside eagerly, the hefty weight of the gun in her pocket, eyes peeled for any sign of Ray and Johnny. Her first stop was Beechwood House, the most logical place to start looking. After knocking on the door of the crackhouse for at least five minutes it became apparent that no one was there, so she trotted back downstairs and continued her search.

She decided to make for Belsize House to see if the youths were hanging around outside their home block. She was nervous, but grappled with her feelings until they were fully subdued deep inside her. The funny thing about the whole situation was that she really didn't have a clue what she was going to do when she found them; all she knew was that she wanted to transfer her anger and grief back to their source – where they would hopefully stay forever.

She kept seeing Ray's face in her mind as she walked. The images caused her eyes to blur with tears that refused to fall. Not for the first time she felt the familiar ache deep in her body every time she imagined his gold-toothed smile. Not for the first time she felt pangs of that emotion called love surging through her as she recalled situations when they'd been a couple – when they'd been happy.

Bastard! She seethed, her jaws clenching in pent-up rage, her mind uncomfortable with the conflicting thoughts going through her head. She was so intent on her destination that she didn't see the middle-aged Asian woman crossing the road in front of her, heading in the same direction. Val walked on oblivious, then heard the woman shouting her name. She shook herself back to the present and turned around.

'Oh hi Mrs Pitt, how are you, I din't see yuh dere. Y'all right?'

The woman stared at Valerie intensely, looking deep into her eyes and shaking her head, clearly not liking what she saw. She was a tall, proud woman, with deep dark-rimmed eyes and thin lipstick-coated lips. Kindly, the woman touched Valerie's arm in a gesture of concern. The delicate touch and worried look on her face almost caused the tears to spring into Val's eyes once again. Choked, she gulped them back down and stood firm.

'Yes me darlin', me is fine, but yuh nuh look so fine yuhself, if yuh don't min' me sayin'. Me see yuh walkin' from far, far back down the road yuh see, an' me affe ask meself but wait; is why de gyal look suh vex ee? Now me know yuh nevah bin de mos' happiest chile in de worl', but bwoy . . . Today yuh look real h'upset fe true. Suh come nuh darlin', tell Auntie Gladys wha' wrong.'

Valerie stepped from foot to foot, arms limp by her sides, not knowing what to say. Mrs Pitt was an ex-dinner lady from Greenside High and she'd known Val for as long as the young woman could remember. They'd always loved one another. Valerie even used to visit Gladys at her house, although she hated her son Martin, and was only on nodding terms with her daughter, Sheron.

'I'm OK Auntie, jus' a little under the weather dat's all. You know. Stress an' all dat. An' it's my time ah the month too.' She gave the woman a half-hearted smile that quickly faded; she just wasn't in the mood for good cheer. 'I wouldn't worry about me if I was you. I was jus' daydreamin'.'

'Yuh sure darlin'?'

Mrs Pitt seemed unconvinced. Valerie squeezed her facial muscles into the nearest reproduction of a smile she could muster, and lightly clutched the woman's arm in return.

'Yeah I'm fine, really I am. How's things with you anyway, Martin and Sheron OK?'

Mrs Pitt shrugged. 'Well, Martin is Martin, y'nuh . . . Always up to no good yuh see? Sheron is workin' hard an' doin' very well fe 'erself though. She 'ave a lickle job in Vauxhall as a receptionis' in a hotel.'

'Oh, dat's good,' Val returned brightly. She touched Mrs Pitt's arm again then took a step backwards, wanting to continue her journey. 'Lissen, I gotta go, but I'll definitely come an' see yuh dis week, no joke either. It's bin ages since I bin up to see you guys.'

'Well all right,' the woman said, nodding slowly, never letting her eyes leave Val's. To the young woman, it was almost as if Mrs Pitt knew she was lying, and could see past all her excuses, right into the depths of her soul. Feeling a little subdued by the thought, she waved, then turned and walked away, taking a left into Belsize House and trotting up the stairs, quick as she could.

She knocked on the door. Ray's mother answered. He wasn't there. She talked to Charlotte for a little while, feeling guilty about her plans for her son, but she buried the thought, said goodbye, and headed one floor up to Johnny's flat. There was no answer there either. Exasperated, Val left the block and walked aimlessly in the direction of the park, which was devoid of people.

A stray dog ran up and began sniffing at her ankles. At first she waved it away, but when it refused to move she felt sorry for it, and began to stroke it absently. When she headed for the park bench the dog followed, looking at her mournfully. She sat down. The dog pushed itself against her, moving her hand with its nose, wanting more affection.

'Hey doggy dog, how yuh doin'? Whassup?' she whispered sadly.

The dog stared, its mouth hanging open, sniffing at the scent of unseen dog urine which lingered by the bench. It then left to go wandering off towards the opposite side of the park. She watched it running and searching for other scents with a faint smile.

What the fuck are you doin' Val? she wondered inwardly, doubt flooding her being, washing away her rage. In the cold light of day her plan seemed kind of ridiculous to say the least – and pretty unfeasible. After all, what was she going to do when she found the youths? Make a citizen's arrest and march the pair to Shepherd's Bush police station? Shoot them in broad daylight with her stepfather's gun?

Of course not, she told herself with a sigh, getting up from the bench and brushing herself down, looking for her stray friend.

It was gone. She sighed and left the park.

She was walking past Caldervale House when she saw them. Ray and Johnny walking with a few of the younger Greenside girls, some of whom were dressed in school uniform. Val felt a pang of hurt at seeing Ray bouncing along with the teenagers, cracking jokes like he was still in school himself. She knew what he was after even if the younger girls didn't. She sincerely hoped none of them had slept with either of the youths, for their sakes more than anything else.

They were five girls Val didn't know very well, though she recognised their faces. They were all baby lotion and hair grease, short skirts, mature bodies and innocent faces. She ducked back into the shadows of the block, not knowing how to take their sudden appearance. No one had seen her. They strolled past her meagre hiding place without even knowing she was there.

Watching them walk away from her towards the other end of the estate as though they didn't have a care in the world, Val felt her anger build again. Eyes narrowed, she saw Ray touch the cutest girl's arm, and heard the light tinkle of her laughter as she looked up at him, swinging her school bag at his legs. Seething, she fingered the gun again.

On an impulse she reached for the band which pulled her hair into a tight ponytail, then released it so her long locks fell to her shoulders. She couldn't do much about her clothes, but she quickly pulled and tugged at her T-shirt so the hem hung around her waist like a skirt, then ran after Ray and the others until she was just behind them. On another whim, she lit up a cigarette to add to the effect, then stood in the middle of the road and called as loud as she could.

'Ray! Oi Ray, wha' yuh sayin' babes!'

He turned and looked, then visibly gaped as he saw who was calling him. She waved and he squinted even harder. She saw him talking with Johnny and the girls, but she knew there was no way he'd want to hang around with what the youths on the estate called 'young tings' when there was a healthy woman beckoning as a seductive alternative.

She was right. After another moment of indecision, he left Johnny to continue the conversation and sauntered her way, his expression a mixture of suspicion and lust.

'What'm girl?' he said when he got close enough to speak.

'Hi,' she said, looking into his eyes without a smile. 'Wha' was you doin' chattin' to all dem lot?'

'Don't worry about it,' Ray shot back, his face emotionless and flat. 'I got some business with Rianna's brudda dat's all.'

'So what's she gotta do wid it?'

He laughed and shook his head, which made Val burn even more, but she buried it deep within her and managed a smile in return.

'I thought you was paro wid me or suttin',' he told her, coming closer, a wary look on his face. 'Las' time I bucked you up you was makin' up a whole 'eap of noise an' callin' me bere bad names. What was dat all about?'

Val shrugged uncaringly, as if the incident meant nothing to her now, shooting Ray deep and meaningful looks all the while.

'I'm jus' fed up wid you smokin' all the time Raymond man – you know I don't like it. I can't deal wid you all fucked up. I needed some time wid my girls to sort my head out. I'm sorry I lashed out at you, but I wasn't in the mood to see you cluckin' for crack again.'

He had no reply to that but stood with his hands in his pockets, looking subdued. Behind him, Johnny had finished his conversation with the girls and was approaching, a moody aura about him. The former couple looked at one another balefully. Val felt a strange air flowing between them. She couldn't put her finger on what was weird about it, but it chilled her nonetheless. Ray shuffled uncomfortably.

'I jus' thought . . . After what happened an' dat . . .'

No, don't talk about it! Her mind screamed. Val's face remained expressionless, though she hadn't expected her ex to talk about her rape so readily, even if it was only in a round-about way.

'I thought you'd be mad about how I went on, y'get me? I know wha' you mean about the bone Val, an' it was dat I was under dem times dere . . .'

He wasn't looking at her. Johnny was about fifty metres from where they stood, coming up at a steady pace. Val willed Ray to shut up before she went crazy with indecision, and sincerely hoped he wouldn't apologise. She steeled herself to remain strong, vigilant, and most of all committed to her course of action. It was too late for apologies. And no amount of kind words would stop the feeling she'd been harbouring ever since that day.

Suppressing her hate, she reached for his hand and held it lightly, hoping the look she was giving him was forgiving. He'd given her an inkling of how she could control this situation, and although it meant going for broke, she was pretty sure she was a good enough actress to pull it off.

'I know you can't help the things you do when you're on dat shit,' she whispered to him slowly. 'Which is why I want you to stop. The *only* reason I want you to stop. I can help you if you let me Raymond, I really can. But the thing is . . . apart from you lot slappin' an' kickin' me, I liked what you did dat day. I mean it, it felt kinda nice . . .'

The look Ray gave her was incredulous – almost as if he wanted to believe her words, but didn't quite dare. Johnny was nearly upon them and she knew that if she got Ray on her side, his best friend was sure to follow. They were like that.

'So how come you was screamin' an' fightin' us off like dat?' Ray muttered, the shock sinking in and spreading across his features.

'I was scared,' Val returned quickly. 'You was hurtin' me as well – both of you were.'

She dug down deep in her psyche for her next sentence, hating herself even as she said it. But she had to follow through completely.

'I . . . I had a multiple orgasm for the firs' time,' she told him stiltedly. 'I wanna do it again Ray. Wiv both of you . . .'

Johnny joined them. Ray watched his former girl while Val tried not to look physically sickened by the words she'd uttered. Her body felt weak and drained, but her mind was spinning with thoughts that all ended in violence. Still, they gave her the time to be grateful for one thing. Having to sink so low secured her feelings of vengeance towards the young men.

There was no question of her backtracking now. She was going to make sure they knew exactly how she felt, in no uncertain terms.

'Yes Val,' Johnny said, grinning all over his face in a manner that had always made him look foolish.

Fully committed now, Val grinned back. 'Hey Johnny.'

'Lookin' kinna ruff today innit?' he informed, staring at her in his cold and unflinching way; the kind of stare a scientist might give a lab rat. She shook off his comment and smiled in reply.

'I don't look dat bad do I?'

Johnny was acting a little flustered. 'Nah . . . Nah, I weren't saying dat man. I's jus' sayin' yuh don't look as good as you usually do. Yuh nuh . . .'

Ray gave him an evil glare, then turned to Val, the look of an annoyed child plastered across his face.

'So wha' you sayin'?'

She screwed up her own features. 'About what?'

Ray stepped forwards. She steeled herself for his touch, but thanked the Lord when he settled for simply looking her dead in the eyes and smiling easily.

'About wha' you jus' said . . .'

Johnny was looking at both of them, confused by the turn of conversation. Neither Ray nor Val paid him any mind.

'Where can we go?' Val said. 'I don't wanna go by your mum's, an' we can't go by mines while Vas is dere.'

Ray waved a hand.

'Fuck it man, we can go to our little hideout, remember the place – up the way deh?'

She thought about it a little, scratching her head and frowning; then she remembered.

'Let's go . . . '

She fingered the gun once more, then clutched at it until it was safe in her palm. She kicked the door shut behind her, relishing the finality of the loud slam. Ray and Johnny were talking loudly amongst themselves.

'Fuckin' place stinks man,' Ray was saying as he kicked a lone sofa cushion halfway across the room. It bounced against the blackened wall, then rolled in a lazy circle before falling to the floor like a tired old man. Johnny had his hands in his pockets and was squinting at the clutter.

'Yeh man, I swear they practise devil worship in 'ere yuh nuh. One time I come in an' find a dead crow in the middle of the room. You know dere's gotta be some Satanism in dat.'

'Proper off-key people come in 'ere star . . .' Ray was breathing, unaware of the irony of his words. He walked over to the large sliding windows on the other side of the room and pulled the upper section open. 'Dis come like society within society, y'get me? A world inside another world, operatin' with its own rules and regulations, its own terms and understandin's.'

Ray turned around to look at Val as he was speaking – then stopped in mid-flow as he noticed what she was holding. Johnny followed his gaze; when he saw her, his mouth fell open. He too realised things were not going as they'd planned.

'Val? Wha' the fuck's goin' on? Wha' you think you're playin' at?'

Ray's voice was high like a child's and owed more to fear than the aggression he was so desperately trying to maintain. Valerie pointed the pistol steadily in his direction, her aura calm and full of quiet anger. She was breathing deeply; her heart was pumping like a piston, but she wasn't scared. She wasn't scared, and she felt relaxed, at peace, serene.

'What I should've done the same day you two did what you did to me Raymond,' she told him slowly. 'The same day you hurt me worse than I've ever bin hurt before in my life – an' I bin fuckin' *hurt* man – after all, you know about Vas. You of all people should know dat.'

'Wha' the fuck's dis gotta do wid *him*—' Ray started, moving towards Valerie, his intention plain on his anger-filled face.

'You shut yuh fuckin' mout' an' get back over by dat wall!' Val screamed, stepping forwards to intercept the youth, waving the gun at him maniacally as a rush of adrenaline flowed through her veins in a sharp burst. Johnny could do nothing but stare as she forced Ray over to the wall and pressed the weapon hard against his temple. Ray backed off, hit the wall, then slid to the floor in one swift motion. He started to wimper. Val's lips followed him down, then aligned themselves with his ear. She whispered her next words in a deadly hiss.

'I hope you're beginnin' to understand how seriously I feel about dis matter Ray,' she told him softly. She shot a quick look at Johnny to make sure he hadn't moved from his spot in the centre of the room, then focused her attention back on the youth. 'I want you to understan' dat I will *never* be able to look at you again wivout hatin' you from deep down inside my fuckin' heart man. Never stop despisin' you an' your fuckin' friend for what you did to me.

'Every night I have to lie dere and think about it, knowin' I'm gonna dream about it, knowin' I'm gonna wake up fuckin' sweatin' an' knowin' I'm gonna get up an' go the whole day thinkin' about the same damn ting. An' you know what?' She moved her head closer, while Ray trembled and moaned beside her. '*I gotta live wi' dat you fuckin' bastard*. I'll always have to. An' the more I think about you two pussies walkin' about an' livin' life normal while I suffer 'cos ah what you done, the more I feel sick to my stomach, an' know it can't happen like dat! Which is why we're here. 'Cos we're gonna talk about what *can* happen . . .'

Johnny was staring at her, his eyes prominent in his face. His arms were raised to head height, and his hands dangled loosely at the wrist, like a puppet's without the aid of its master.

'Val man, put the gun away an' let's talk about dis . . .'

'We're gonna talk about dis on my terms Johnny.'

Her voice was as cold as ice. She pressed the gun harder against Ray's head.

'But we already cleared all dis up didn't we?' he begged, in a tone she'd never heard before. 'Out dere when we was talkin' jus' now man. I tol' you I didn't mean to act like dat . . .'

She shut her eyes for a second, confident they'd be too scared to try and take the gun, then she began to chuckle to herself. Shaking her head, she opened her eyes and looked straight at him.

'So you think dat wraps up everyting nice an' neat do you? You think dat's it – a few words about how bad you feel about it all an' everyting'll be back to normal?'

'*Valerie* man—' Ray began, but she snarled and pushed the pistol harder for a third time. Johnny lost his temper. He snapped violently at her, lowering his hands as he did.

'Fuckin' hell Val, come off it man, we never done nuttin' dat bad! Fuck it man, you said you enjoyed it an' it sure *sounded* like you enjoyed it the way you was moanin' an' shit, innit Ray?'

'Fuh real,' Ray managed to croak, forcing the words through his drying lips.

Val sighed once, her only outward sign of emotion, then stood up, still aiming the weapon at the youth's head.

'Ay, *fuck* you lot man . . . Johnny, throw me over dat cushion will yuh?'

He was still sneering at her with cruel dislike.

'*What* fuckin' cushion?'

'The one Ray kicked. An' fuckin' move or I blas' up yuh bredrin, yuh 'ear?'

He went for the cushion in a sloth-like manner, but she let it pass, knowing she was the mistress now. He grabbed it, then made to walk over and hand it to her.

'Stay dere. Chuck it over.'

The cushion landed by her foot and she bent down. Staying crouched, she grabbed Ray's arm with her left hand and pushed it against the wall.

'Keep your arm dere.'

She stood up

'Get the cushion and hold it up against your hand.'

'How?' Ray whined.

'*Wiv yuh right hand stoopid.* An' hurry up!'

Ray complied, while Johnny made protesting noises.

'Val, wha' the fuck you on man—'

'Shut it Johnny. But before you do tell me suttin' – what's nex' door to dis room?'

'Wha'?'

She was starting to get angry.

'*I ain' repeatin' myself Johnny!*'

'Uhh . . . A bedroom I tink.' The look of concentration on his face was a picture. He looked vague, but his confirmation was enough for Valerie.

'Good,' she replied quickly.

Without another word, she jammed the gun against the cushion and fired. There was a dull explosion. Her hand jolted, sending a spasm of pain through her arm. Ray screamed and his face went pale. Blood began to drip on to the floor in thick red droplets. He grasped his wrist with his hand.

Val stepped back and let the cushion fall, eyeing his open-mouthed face with cold-eyed satisfaction. Johnny was still standing on his spot, looking sickened.

'All right man – *now* we can talk,' Val said daintily, over the sound of Ray's moans. She sat on the floor, crossed her legs, and pointed the pistol at Johnny.

The day quickly passed. The sun died and the moon came to life, though it only shed flimsy light on that room, where the innocent held trial over the guilty. As the light faded, Val watched their silhouettes in the dark, shivering in the cold of the flat. Whimpering at her every movement. Ray moaning at the hole in his palm, watching his own blood seeping through the piece of curtain they'd used to wrap his hand. And Val talked for what seemed like days.

She wanted to kill them but she couldn't. She *needed* to kill them but it was impossible. Seeing the youths now, weighing everything up in her mind, Val knew she had so much more to live for than the two of them – so much promise; she couldn't risk it all by becoming a murderess. Valerie couldn't let them turn her to that. So she talked to them instead. Made them understand her point of view.

'See, I think I've found somewhere to go,' she told them, looking at the ceiling wistfully. 'I think I've found a place where things can be all right, an' I can live a good life, a *happy* life. I'll have a nice house somewhere on the other side ah town. The suburbs probably, fuck the city. I'll 'ave some cris' lookin' kids wid big innocent-lookin' eyes, an' enough money so I won't have to worry about money, 'cos I'll be workin' . . . At a job I'll *enjoy*, y'get me? I'll 'ave cris' lookin' husband too an' yuh know what? I'll smile a lot more. My mum always says I used to smile more as a kid an' she's right. I'll smile my whole fuckin' face off I'm tellin' yuh star. 'Cos I'll be *happy* y'get me. I'll be happy man . . .'

Val laughed to herself and lowered her head. Part of her

thought she might be going crazy, but deep inside she knew she wasn't. Besides, she'd read in a magazine somewhere that crazy people never thought they were crazy, so she must be sane.

'The only ting dat stands in the way is you two jokers,' she whispered softly. 'You bastards are the only ting in this whole entire planet dat stands between me an' my goal in life, an' I'm not fuckin' gonna let you. I *can't* let you . . .'

She trailed off, only realising she had nothing left to say when she reached the end of her sentence. She wouldn't have believed their demise could've been so swift, even though she'd recognised the scared little boys inside of them, and had done so for longer than she'd even known. She didn't know what would happen after this, and in a way she didn't care. She'd made her point and that was enough. She could get on with the rest of her life. Val stepped backwards out of the room, leaving the two youths whimpering in the darkness.

The counsellor's waiting room was packed, but she didn't mind. She clutched her book, *In Search of Satisfaction*, to her breast, as though there was no one else in the room. She thought about the previous day – her first on her DTP course at Parkhill. She knew she'd like it. She'd used computers in school so she was fairly clued up on the basic operation skills, and she was good at art, so it seemed she would have no problem. Her lecturer was a woman, and she was great; she'd made some new friends . . .

There was even a good-looking boy in the class. Bernie. She wasn't sure if he was husband material . . . but she wasn't looking for a husband right now. She was looking for a friend.

And from the way Bernie looked at her, it seemed like he could do with a friend too. Badly. She'd friend the hell out of him when the time was right.

Well, when I get done wid all dis shit, she told herself, even unfazed by that thought.

Cassie, who was sitting in the seat beside Val with her child made sure that whatever one had – respect, money, clothes, jewellery – the other had too.

They were equal in every way except one.

Girls.

Much to Little Stacey's dismay, Benji was one of those boys every other boy wanted to be – the Don Juan, the Casanova, the guy that girls talked and giggled about in school, and the guy that received Valentine's cards *every* February without fail. No one was quite sure how he did it; yeah, he was handsome, but he was short, skinny as a rake, and dark enough to be cussed by the other youths for being way too black. Plus there were a number of Greenside High kids much nearer the *GQ* ideal than he. Still, girls flocked around Benji like junkies around a dealer, and the Greensider always had at least one on the go – and that was when he was doing badly.

What made it worse was that he never seemed to do all the speeching, arguing and pleading for sex that the other boys were forced to go through. He often talked of getting regular sex and though it pissed people off, they knew he wasn't lying, particularly Little Stacey, who'd once been in a girl's bedroom watching Holyfield v Tyson on video while Benji had been wukking his latest squeeze as quietly as he could, just in case her dad heard and killed the lot of them. It wasn't as though Stacey couldn't get girls; he just couldn't do it with the ease and dexterity his friend displayed. He could get past first, second, and even third base – but he'd never made a home run yet.

Around his manor a guy like him was called a V reg. *Virgins.* Fifteen years old and he hadn't slept with a girl. Little Stacey didn't know how to deal with it, so he lied, even to Benji and Robby, which meant it was his deepest darkest secret ever. He'd fingered girls before (he liked the way they squirmed and panted in his ear), and had even had his dick sucked (which was dett!), but he'd never gone the whole hog.

One day, he couldn't remember when, he'd woken up with a start to find his sheets stained and sticky, the residue of his

in her arms, looked at her, turned away, then looked back, frowning.

'You OK?'

'Yeah man!'

Cassie was grinning.

'Wha' you smilin' at you freak, sittin' dere wid a big ol' grin over yuh little face? You look like a nutter!'

Val shrugged and beamed wider. 'I feel good dat's all. I was thinkin' about my DTP course.'

'An' dat fit tings in yuh class never crossed yuh min' once huh?'

'Shit Cas, my man cross my min' all ten, twenny times already girl, trus' me!'

They laughed to each other sisterly. Val turned to Cassie and clutched her arm.

'I'm really grateful you come wid me today Cas. I needed you man. You're the only one I tol' about all dis – I wouldn't have been able to do it without you.'

Cassie's face crumpled and she looked sad. She squeezed Val's hand, and even though she didn't actually cry, Val was sure she saw her eyes fill with tears.

'Ah man, don't worry about dat yuh nuh Valerie. You're my frien' an' I love you, simple. You can tell me anythin'. I want you to know dat.'

'I do,' Val replied with feeling.

The people in the waiting room were smiling and nudging each other, probably thinking they were having an affair. Valerie still couldn't care less. She almost expected them to clap like they did in the Nice 'n' Easy advert. A bell chimed and seconds later a man walked out of a nearby door, one of five along a corridor at the end of the room.

Val looked expectantly at the receptionist. She had to wait a moment, but she was right. The receptionist smiled at her.

'Valerie Parker.'

'Yes?'

She stood up.

'Doctor Gosling will see you now.'

'Thank you.' She looked down at Cassie. 'See you in about a hour?'

'You sure will. An' remember what we said. Tell your story – but be honest yeah?'

'OK. See yuh later.'

She walked down the corridor, to a door with a bronze plaque that read *Doctor Gosling Ph.D.* She knocked three times. When the woman's voice told her to come in, she opened the door and stepped through, the pretty and expectant smile still on her face.

A Little Bump an' Gri

Little Stacey Collins loved his best friend Benjamin like the twin brother he'd always wished he'd had. Not looked anything alike (which they didn't); and not th didn't already have a brother (which he did – though Nicky like a mortal enemy, always had, always woulc was no one else in his life that knew him as well as Be laughed at the same jokes, reacted to life with the same instincts and had a sense of daring and fun way beyond nary. Benji Tremaine was his partner in crime, brother, his very best friend.

They'd first met aged three in the nursery run by Adventure Playground, and hadn't left each other's They ran amok all over their estate and surround London area for the subsequent twelve years of tl being as bad as they could, along with Robert Emers assortment of other young roughnecks. But through double act of Little Stacey and Benji Tremaine was throughout the streets, youth clubs and schools of and beyond. They gained an infamy that made the cringe. Adults hated them, while other kids feared tl secretly wished they could emulate their exploits. didn't care; they were in their element, and eacl

dreams taunting his head. Ashamed, he lay there, trying not to think about the object of his desire (it had been Jada Pinkett-Smith), and wondering who he could get to remove this stigma from him forever. He felt alone and lonely – there was no one he could think of that would definitely want to fuck, so he put it in the back of his mind and busied himself changing the sheets.

About a week or so after his wet dream, he, Benji and Robby had been sitting outside their Rockwood block when a group of local girls passed by. They were wearing tight stretch jeans, sports sweatshirts and puffers. Benji got the lecherous look that the others were accustomed to seeing and he hopped off the wall, Robby and Stacey not far behind.

'Yuh all right?' Benji drawled, approaching them foxily.

The nearest girl, a studious-looking Oriental called Siân, smiled.

'Hi Benji, how yuh doin'?'

'Cool yuh nuh . . .'

'Y'all right Robby, Stacey?'

'Yeah man, wha' *you* girls sayin' star.'

Benji hugged the girls tightly and extravagantly, making cheeky comments about their physical fitness, eyeing their shapely bottoms shamelessly. The girls were Siân, Lilah, Sophie, Orin's younger sister Sissy and her friend Carolyn. Little Stacey pushed himself forwards amongst the girls, chatting small talk with all, concentrating on none, while his friends did the same beside him. The girls had obviously been bored walking around the estate and they didn't seem to mind the full-on sexual bantering. They gave the boys bright smiles, looks that were unashamed, and threw the sexual jokes straight back at them. Even Benji had to laugh and shake his head at their boldness.

'Ay, I like the way yuh look yuh nuh Siân,' Benji was saying, while Little Stacey made conversation with Carolyn, even though he knew her man Clive. He was also trying to ignore the fact that Robby was talking animatedly with Sissy. It made him feel uncomfortable, as he'd been noticing her for a long time.

'An'?' Siân replied cockily.

'Wha'? How yuh mean "an'"?'

'*An'* innit? An' wha' you wanna do about it?'

'Nah man, it's wha' *you* wanna do about it, dat's the real question, true I ain' got no time t'play.'

'You lot are all the same man, yuh full ah big talk but when it come down to it, you get narrow,' Lilah told him archly. Benji frowned and turned to face the group as a whole. Little Stacey rolled his eyes. He knew what was coming.

'Ay, ay, AY!' Benji roared, adopting his badbwoy pose, but still managing to smile at Siân, who was taking all of him in with interested eyes. 'Yuh know say Benzi never affa talk man, is bere live-o *action* run dis ting 'ere, y'get me—'

'Yeah *yeah*,' Lilah yawned, winking exaggeratedly at Carolyn when she was done. They both grinned, but Benji never let a little thing like disbelief dissuade him, so he dismissed the whole thing, saying, 'So what den Siân, how come you never bell me when yuh say yuh gonna bell me, eh? I ain' the one sellin' it aroun' 'ere.'

'I did ring. It ain' my fault you ain' got no answerphone.'

'Ah, don't try it man,' Benji laughed. 'Wi' dem lame ones dere. Ay you man, yuh 'ear how Siân's tryin' t'style it out? It's you comin' wid all the big talk innit?'

'Yuh hair looks nice y'nuh,' he said quietly. She looked up, a little surprised, and then smiled shyly, which threw him slightly.

'Yuh reckon?'

'Yeah man, I like it when girls layer their hair, it looks dett. Where d'you get it done?'

'Shannon did it . . .' Sissy was visibly preening under his flattery. She hadn't been ready for Stacey's attention, although they'd been giving each other the eye for quite a while now. 'She's really good man. I used to go Grove to get my hair done, but I think I'll let her do it regular.'

'Blatant, you should,' Little Stacey agreed enthusiastically.

That's it, Sissy thought to herself. *Grove gets the chop man.*

She smiled Little Stacey's way. 'So, wha' you bin up to? I ain' seen you about in ages.'

'Dis an' dat y'get me, nuttin' too tuff . . .'

She sighed. 'Wha' the fuck is dat meant t'mean? Bere badness or suttin'?'

'Nah man,' he screwed up his face, knowing she probably heard everything he got up to, so he couldn't really lie. 'Well, y'nuh . . . a little badness maybe, but not *bere* badness.'

She laughed loudly, which *really* threw him, though he managed to join in, liking the feel of the way this was going. Behind him, Benji and Robby were talking with the others and smiling at his back every time there was a break in their conversation.

'Anyway, you don' wanna hear all dat shit,' he told her boldly. 'I seen you in school man, you're one ah dem smart girls, top ah the class an' all dat. I always says to Benzi, "Dat's a positive gyal dere, done know." Serious man, I like the way you drop it.'

'Yuh don' carry yuhself too bad either,' she allowed carefully, not wanting to give the youth too much too soon.

'So where yuh hide yuhself after school den, seein' as I never seen you about. At yuh man's?' he asked her, watching her face.

'Who tol' you I got a man?'

'No one. I jus' thought you did innit.'

'Dat's some deep thinkin' bwoy.'

'Well . . .' he shrugged and smiled. She laughed again.

'Well, for your information Grave Digger Collins, I ain' seein' anyone.'

'Good.'

They gazed at each other openly. Benji nudged Siân and made her look.

'Ay, who's Grave Digger Collins anyhow?' Little Stacey continued, pushing his hands into his pockets.

'Grave Digger Collins is *you*,' Sissy said wisely. 'Seein' as you're such a detective I'd thought I'd name you after Grave Digger Jones.'

'Grave Digger *who*?'

'Jones. He's a detective in a book I read. *The Real Cool Killers*. It's by a guy called Chester Himes. He's dead now. It's good.'

'I don't really read books,' he admitted reluctantly. He didn't want to seem like some kind of dumbo. 'Specially white books.'

She frowned, and he felt his stomach cringe, knowing he'd said something fucked up.

'Chester Himes was black.'

'Oh.'

Little Stacey went quiet. She smiled at him, the most unpatronising smile she could manage, and she could see it made him feel better. Just then, the steady beep of a car horn sounded from a small side road, yards from where they were all standing. The youths looked over. A blue Suzuki had pulled up; inside were Strong, who was driving, as well as Orin, Malcolm and Nazra. Orin was looking at his sister with a hard-eyed glare.

'Wha' you doin' Sis?' he called over stridently.

Sissy's expression was blank and she looked carefully at the others before speaking.

'I was jus' talkin', dat's all,' she said defensively.

'Well yuh know what Dad says about you hangin' aroun' on street – he blatantly don't like it, so don't you think you should go home?'

'I'm goin' to Lilah's to do some homework,' the teenager returned, her tone short and tinged with aggression. 'Dad knows, so you don't afta be goin' on like his deputy do you?'

Orin gave her a dark look and raised his eyebrows. 'Yeah, well jus' make sure yuh go straight dere all right?' he sneered, looking at Little Stacey, his eyes full of deep meaning. The youth returned his gaze with one of nonchalance, hands in his pockets, lip curled unconsciously.

'Doctor Gosling will see you now.'

'Thank you.' She looked down at Cassie. 'See you in about a hour?'

'You sure will. An' remember what we said. Tell your story – but be honest yeah?'

'OK. See yuh later.'

She walked down the corridor, to a door with a bronze plaque that read *Doctor Gosling Ph.D.* She knocked three times. When the woman's voice told her to come in, she opened the door and stepped through, the pretty and expectant smile still on her face.

in her arms, looked at her, turned away, then looked back, frowning.

'You OK?'

'Yeah man!'

Cassie was grinning.

'Wha' you smilin' at you freak, sittin' dere wid a big ol' grin over yuh little face? You look like a nutter!'

Val shrugged and beamed wider. 'I feel good dat's all. I was thinkin' about my DTP course.'

'An' dat fit tings in yuh class never crossed yuh min' once huh?'

'Shit Cas, my man cross my min' all ten, twenny times already girl, trus' me!'

They laughed to each other sisterly. Val turned to Cassie and clutched her arm.

'I'm really grateful you come wid me today Cas. I needed you man. You're the only one I tol' about all dis – I wouldn't have been able to do it without you.'

Cassie's face crumpled and she looked sad. She squeezed Val's hand, and even though she didn't actually cry, Val was sure she saw her eyes fill with tears.

'Ah man, don't worry about dat yuh nuh Valerie. You're my frien' an' I love you, simple. You can tell me anythin'. I want you to know dat.'

'I do,' Val replied with feeling.

The people in the waiting room were smiling and nudging each other, probably thinking they were having an affair. Valerie still couldn't care less. She almost expected them to clap like they did in the Nice 'n' Easy advert. A bell chimed and seconds later a man walked out of a nearby door, one of five along a corridor at the end of the room.

Val looked expectantly at the receptionist. She had to wait a moment, but she was right. The receptionist smiled at her.

'Valerie Parker.'

'Yes?'

She stood up.

Sissy caught their stares and looked at each of them in turn, before giving up the fight.

'OK, I'm goin' all right!' she snapped, but she didn't move. Orin threw a spliff butt out of the window, then nodded at Strong, who floored the accelerator. The Suzuki headed away.

Sissy stepped back towards the group of boys.

'I'll borrow you dat book if you want,' she told Stacey, just as Carolyn tugged at her arm and told her they had better move on.

'You can chat 'er up another day,' Carolyn grinned at him, while behind them Siân and Benji swapped numbers for at least the second time. Little Stacey shrugged and stepped from foot to foot, unable to take his eyes off Sissy. She took a few slow steps away with her friends, before she looked back at him and grinned a full and totally unself-conscious smile.

'See yuh!'

'Yeah man; don't forget dat book y'nuh,' he replied, letting the lust show in his eyes.

The girls wandered away, nattering to themselves and bursting into loud laughter, while the trio of boys walked over to their wall and perched themselves back up. Benji pushed Little Stacey with one hand.

'Wha's dat about books den?'

Stacey put on a hard face. 'Never you min' . . .'

'Since when yuh start pick up book?'

'I ain' man, I was jus' chattin' wid Sissy, what'm? She was the one comin' wid all the book talk, I was jus' ridin' wid it, y'get me?'

'She's on you though blood,' Robby told him without a trace of jealousy.

'I dunno man.'

'*I* know,' Benji said, stabbing at his own chest with a finger. 'I always thought you two would look good togevva. She's buff as well man, got a wicked back off star!'

'An' the titties are *live*,' Robby informed them.

Little Stacey nodded.

'Yeah man, I wouldn't min' gettin' t'rough wid Sissy, but I ain' gonna go mad for it. An' you *know* how Orin stay already. It was a dett vibe between us jus' now though, trus' me. Vibe was all right,' he muttered, almost to himself.

'I *have* to gi' Siân the wuk,' Benji was roaring at them. 'You know how long I bin on dat, an' the gyal nah let off? Watch me star, I ain' havin' no stallin' no longer – I'm gonna make dat pum-pum hotter than 'er mudda's wok two minutes before dinner, trus' me!'

They laughed at that one for a good five minutes.

Sissy walked towards Lilah's flat with her friends, unable to keep the smile from her face, even though she bit her bottom lip to try and stop it. Carolyn skipped along by her side.

'Well,' she grinned at her. 'Wha' did he have to say for himself den?'

'Not a lot really,' Sissy shrugged. 'We was jus' chattin'.'

'You shoulda seen the way he was lookin' at you,' Sophie joined them. 'My man blatantly likes you.'

'I know,' Sissy replied.

'So yuh gonna do it?' Carolyn asked.

'Do what?'

Carolyn turned around and shook her bottom at her friend.

'Da *booty* call girl,' Carolyn enthused, while the others cracked up. 'After all, you haven't had it for ages.'

'Shut up you, jus' 'cos you got yuh regular ting innit? Don't go rubbin' it in my face.'

Carolyn smiled to herself but didn't say anything more.

'I dunno how you can be so casual about sex,' Sophie was telling them in the grown-up tone of voice she always used. 'I'm not a prude or anythin', but I'm gonna wait a little longer before I let off to any boy, I don' business. I *like* bein' a virgin, so the man who wants the job ah takin' my virginity has to be special, trus' me. An' none ah dem lot from round 'ere need to bovva applyin' fuh the position.'

The girls smiled and jostled Sophie good naturedly, but left it at that. Everyone was quite respectful of the girl. She'd always been the most sensible member of their group.

'Well, you should be rubbin' *suttin'* in someone's face girl,' Lilah told Sissy, ignoring Sophie's words. 'It's a shame not to be, 'specially wid someone as cute as Little Stacey after yuh.'

Sissy cackled like a hen. 'Yuh so nasty. I dunno how I stay so pure hangin' around wiv you lot.'

'*Huh?*' They cried in unison.

Sissy batted her eyelids, a picture of innocence.

'Anyway, you gonna do it wid Benji den or what Siân?' she asked the Chinese girl curiously.

They all turned Siân's way. She smiled shyly and blushed.

'More than likely. He's all right man, he makes me laugh, an' I've liked him from way back.'

'You better carry some plastic macs wid yuh if you wanna deal wid *him*,' Lilah told the girl sternly.

'Don' worry I will. I know my man's vibe, he's a proper slag, so I ain' doin' nuffin' widout condoms. It's jus' fun dat's all. I tell yuh suttin' though, if Benji thinks he can get aroun' me easy, he can think again boy. He's gonna hafta *work*.'

'Eh eh,' Sissy laughed, while her friends fell about. Siân wasn't as innocent as she looked.

Sissy waited three days before she made her move. By that time she was back at school and had seen quite a lot of Little Stacey, as they shared a drama class together. They'd talked politely, but although the sexual chemistry was still there, it was nowhere near as strong as it had been a few days before. She still liked him, and was sure he felt the same, but nervousness seemed to stifle the both of them in school, so she decided to see the youth as an out-of-school activity.

On the third day, she came home on her own (Carolyn was stuck in detention again), to hear the sounds of computer games coming from her brother's room. She knocked on the door and waited for a reply.

'Yeah man.'

'It's me Orry.'

'Come nuh.'

She entered the room to see Orin, Malcolm, Ryan Wilson and Jason Taylor, all sprawled in various positions, eyes glued to the portable TV. Ash smoke filled the room. Sissy smiled and waved at the occupants.

'Hiya, hiya,' she muttered casually.

'Whassup?' Orin replied, while the others grunted at her.

'*Pooh*, it stink in 'ere star,' she said, holding her nose dramatically. 'Open a window will yuh?'

'Jus' cool,' Orin told her, then looked around the room. 'Every man's safe innit?' They all nodded, taking no notice of his younger sister. 'See, it's cool,' he finished, winking at her. He seemed in a good mood, so she pressed on.

'Ay Orin, yuh got dat book I borrowed you the other day?'

'What book?' He was more interested in the game than any conversation with her, though she was well used to it.

'Dat Chester Himes, *The Real Cool Killers*.'

'Uhhh . . .'

'Did you even read it?'

'Yeah man—'

'KO!!!!' Malcolm roared, while the others cracked up and pointed at Orin. He pulled a face, then handed the pad over to Jason.

'I'm the bes', the fuckin' bes' man,' Malcolm was jeering.

'See what I'm sayin'?' Orin complained bitterly to his sister. She rolled her eyes. 'It's only a fuckin' game.'

'Dat's what you say. Anyway, wha' you after?'

She put her hands on her hips and glared at him.

'My *book*. *The Real Cool Killers*. Have you got it or what?'

He frowned as he thought.

'Yeah, yeah man, I got it. Somewhere . . .'

Orin got up from the bed and started digging around in a remote corner of his room. Sissy stood, watching and waiting. After five minutes it was apparent he couldn't find it.

'Aw Orry man, I bought dat an' everythin'.'

'It's here man, it's here,' he insisted from somewhere near the floor, while his friends muttered and moved with every computerised blow. 'Tell yuh what, gimme a few minutes an' I'll dig it out.'

'You better not 'ave lost it.'

'It's somewhere about man, serious ting. Jus' gimme a bit, yeah?'

'All right . . . '

She went into her room and sat on the bed. She switched on the radio, which was already tuned to Skyline. They were playing an old Ragga tune she loved called 'Mavis'. She sang along, thinking of Little Stacey, half wondering if she should light a cigarette while she waited, but eventually decided against it. Having Orin as a brother was like living with a prison warder, but when he didn't appear with her book in hand after half an hour, she got bored and headed for her father's room. She left her bedroom door open so she could still hear the music, then she picked up the phone and dialled.

'Hello?' The voice was deep, gruff and male.

'Hey Francis, is Carolyn dere please?'

'Yeah man – 'oos dat? Sissy?'

'Uh huh.'

'Yes gorgeous . . .'

'Hiya.'

The phone went down with a clunk, then there was muffled shouting, followed by heavy footsteps, steadily getting louder. More clunking, then, 'Hello?'

'Hey Cee, it's me Sissy.'

'Hey what's up? Where are yuh?'

'At home.' She grinned into the receiver and lay herself out on the bed with her arms outstretched. 'Guess what? I'm gonna do it.'

'Eh?'

'I'm gonna go see Little Stacey.'

'*Is it?*' Carolyn shrieked in her ear. 'Damn girl, you ain' playin'. So what brought dat on?'

'Do I have to spell it out? Let's jus' say I have needs.'

'Boy. Dat's deep.' Sissy could tell her friend was grinning. 'So when yuh gonna check 'im?'

'Soon as.'

'What if Gayla's there?'

'I'm jus' gonna *talk* to 'im for now Cee, I ain' gonna t'row him down on his doorstep an' start fuckin' 'im right dere an' den!'

They laughed loudly, then Sissy looked at her bedroom door and decided she'd better modify the volume of her words. If her father or brother heard her talking like that, both of them would probably kill her stone dead.

'You better tell me all about it when yuh done,' Caroline was saying excitedly. From outside in the passage, Sissy heard a knock on her bedroom door.

'Sis, where are yuh? I got it!'

Sissy sat up straight, attempting to look prim and proper.

'Course I will, as soon as summick happens. I tell you what, I'll ring you when I get back from his yard, yeah? I gotta go, my brudda wants me.'

'All right safe. An' good luck, hope it all goes well!'

'Thanks babes. Talk soon yeah?'

'See yuh!'

She put the phone down just as Orin entered the room. He looked at her and shook his head.

'Smashin' the phone again are we? Watch when Dad gets the bill.'

'Ah 'llow me man, it ain' as if you don't use it too.'

He dismissed the argument as she'd hoped he would and handed her the book.

'Dere yuh go.'

'What d'yuh think?'

'Yeah man, book was all right star. Certain man was crackin' me up. Thanks Sis.'

'No problem.'

He left the room. Sissy went back to her own and flopped on

the bed. She looked at the book, weighing up what she was about to do and wondering if she should call Stacey before she went over. She decided against that too, then shrugged herself out of her school clothes and into some leggings and a thick jumper. She was going to do her hair but changed her mind and jammed a baseball cap on her head instead. She spent the next ten minutes looking in the mirror and swapping her clothes around – different leggings, different jeans, different jumpers – before finally settling for what she'd put on in the first place. She smiled at herself, then stuck her tongue out at her reflection and left the flat.

Twilight was falling over the estate. Teeth chattering, she fairly ran to Little Stacey's block, then knocked on the door timidly. There was no answer for a long while, before it suddenly swung open to reveal Little Stacey's older brother, Nicky. Sissy gave a mental sigh. Nicky wasn't her favourite person at any time, much less today. He stared at her openly, making her shiver as his eyes roamed from head to foot.

'Hey Nicky, is Little Stacey in please?'

Nicky grunted, then half closed the door so she couldn't see inside, though she could hear him mumbling, '*Little* fuckin' Stacey . . . Wha' kinna foolish name is dat?' all the way to Stacey's room. She stared after him, then kissed her teeth and shook her head.

'*Fuckin' cat,*' she mumbled under her breath, the severity of her words making her feel good. '*Stoopid lickle crack-takin' pussy 'ole—*'

The door flew open. Her breath caught in her throat and her heart joined it in one jump. She felt her stomach tremble and lurch with shock – then she saw it was Little Stacey holding the latch, not his maniac brother. Sissy almost collapsed on the doorstep in her relief, while he watched her, looking amused.

'Yuh lucky,' he told her. 'If my brudda heard dat, dere woulda bin bere alms goin' on.'

She sighed her reply and her voice shook, embarrassment taking over. 'I know man, dat was outta order. I'm sorry Stace.'

The youth shrugged his shoulders, which were quite wide for his size. 'Minor star, you never said nuttin' dat weren't true. So wha' you sayin' anyway?'

'I'm cool, I'm all right.'

It was taking her a while to get herself together again.

'I would invite you in,' Little Stacey was saying, 'but my mum don' like me bringin' girls inta my room, Always thinks mad orgies are goin' on or summick.'

'I don't blame her,' Sissy replied. 'I'd be the same way, knowin' what you an' Benji are like.'

'Is dat wha' you think of me den?'

She smiled. 'I know you ain' no angel if dat's what yuh mean.'

He leaned against the doorframe idly. 'Yeah well, I can't lie – I ain' a angel, blatant. But I ain' *dat* bad. I dunno why everyone keeps goin' on like—'

'S'OK anyway, there ain' much room for angels aroun' about here,' Sissy admitted, cutting him off.

Little Stacey shivered in reply. 'It's fuckin' cuttin' out 'ere man. Ay, yuh got dat book you was talkin' about?'

'Oh yeah!'

Sissy dug the novel out of her puffer jacket, surprised Stacey had remembered. She passed it over, then studied him as he read the cover and the blurb, his eyes squinting in the dull glow from the lights of the block. He nodded sternly when he was done.

'Soun's safe y'nuh. When d'yuh wannit back?'

'Whenever. As long as you take care of it I don't mind. I've read it innit, so it don't bother me.'

'Thanks man.'

'S'OK. It's a pleasure . . .'

'Oh shit!' Little Stacey jumped as if he'd just recalled something of extreme importance. Sissy studied him, wondering what was on his mind.

'Wha' you doin' tomorra?' the youth asked her excitedly.

'Nuttin'. I got biology an' maths homework dat needs to be in Friday, so I gotta get dat done.'

'Nah – I mean tomorra day.'

'I'll be at *school* Stacey.'

She gave him a guarded look. He made a face, looking a little ashamed.

'Oh . . . well . . . You any good at writin' signatures?'

'*What?*'

'Are you any good at signatures? You know, like autographs or suttin'?'

'Yeah . . .' she said, sounding unsure. 'I'm all right. Why?'

Sissy stared at him, wondering what the problem was. Stacey thought about it, then went for broke.

'All right lissen. I got a card to work but it's a girl's. I need someone to sign for me. My friend's a sales assistant in one sports shop up Wes' an' she says it's easy to work cards dere, so I's wonderin' if you wanned to take the day off—'

Sissy gave him an incredulous look.

'You want me to bunk off school to run up a stolen credit card wid you?'

Little Stacey stopped dead in his tracks. He *knew* he shouldn't have said anything about the credit card to Sissy. Her face was as solid and unreadable as a statue's, and he couldn't tell if she thought it was a good, bad, or just plain stupid idea. He shrugged and touched her arm.

'Well, we don't 'ave to do the card ting y'nuh – I wanned to link you up really, dat's what I was really on.'

'Why can't we link after school den?'

'We can – but I gotta work dat card whether I link you or not, so I figured it'd be nice to spend the day together. If you wanna.'

He could see her thinking about it, so he decided to shut his mouth and let her get on with it. She wouldn't look his way and that worried him; he didn't want to get blown out – he could imagine the embarrassment he'd feel having to see the girl day in and day out on the estate. Sissy was chewing on her bottom lip, head down, so all he could see was the little button on top of her baseball cap. He flicked the cap's peak with a finger.

She looked up and he was pleased to see she was smiling.

'So wha' you sayin'?'

She pushed her lip out in a manner he found very sexy, and eyed him up and down.

'Yeah all right, I'll come wid yuh. But I'm tellin' you, anyhow you get me nicked—'

'Safe man, it's all under control. Dere ain' even no cameras in the shop, so we're copa y'get me?'

'All right den . . . I'm trustin' you y'nuh Stacey.'

'Yeh man, it'll be cool believe me. Knock for me tomorra an we'll drop it like we're goin' school like normal. I'll take you for breakfast or summick.'

Sissy nodded slowly, trying to make it look like she was used to this kind of thing.

'You better gimme the card den so I can practise.'

'Oh yeah – one sec'.'

Little Stacey disappeared. Sissy hopped about on his doorstep, wondering why she didn't feel any disquiet. She wasn't a criminal, in fact she'd never taken part in any crimes, besides nicking penny sweets from Kareem's 24-hour food store when she was a kid. She was aware what her brother and his mates got up to, but she'd never considered doing anything that was even vaguely against the law since the days of stuffing her pockets full of lemon sherbets. Still, Sissy was encouraged to see the youth had a gleam in his eye when he looked at her, and that she felt clear desire herself. The thought of spending time with Little Stacey and going mad with someone else's money was enticing too, there was no doubt about that. She found herself looking forward to the next day already.

When he came back, he handed her the card, a serious look on his face. It was a Midland Visa card, which she inspected casually before shoving in her pocket.

'Cheer up,' she beamed shyly.

Stacey responded with a cheeky grin. 'Don't lose it y'nuh,' he warned her.

'I won't.'

'Oh, an' bring a change of clothes wid yuh. An' don't tell no one, not even Carolyn. She can fin' out when she sees you wid a cris' pair ah Nikes yeah?'

'Cool.'

'OK.'

Without another word, he reached for her. She stepped eagerly into his embrace and kissed him hard – quick, short pecks at first, then she opened her mouth and let her tongue roam. His kiss felt quite nice. His hands were rubbing warmly against her arse. She let him move them up to her right breast, playing with her nipple through her bra (which felt nice and tingly), then she stopped him as he started going back down again; Sissy knew the drill, and she wasn't going there just yet.

'Uh uh,' she told him. 'Not out 'ere.'

He nodded. They kissed some more, until they heard his mum screaming at him from somewhere inside the house.

'*What?*' he yelled back, looking vex.

His mother's reply cracked like a whip. 'I beg your pardon?'

Little Stacey sighed.

'Yes Mum?'

Gayla's voice floated outside, only just audible.

'Will you close in the front door, you're lettin' out all the warm air!'

'One sec', I'm comin' in now.'

'Well hurry up!'

He turned to her, a minuscule smile on his face.

'I gotta go.'

She grabbed his hand and entwined her fingers in his.

'OK. An' make sure you're up on time tomorra, I don't wanna hafta pretend we're goin' in late.'

He chuckled. 'Yeah man. Walk careful all right?'

'Thanks. Bye.'

She stepped on to the asphalt and waved his way, before turning and heading back towards Belsize. Her lips felt warm from his. She touched them with a finger, smiled to herself, then hurried a little faster so she could tell all her friends the news.

Little Stacey stumbled his way into the bathroom and heaved himself into the shower bleary-eyed. It normally took him about an hour to actually wake up, but when he was underneath the powerful spray he could usually bring it down to about half an hour, maybe even fifteen minutes. He washed quickly, put on his uniform, then headed for the kitchen where his mother was putting out two cereal bowls. He kissed her and sat at the table.

'So wha' you up to today den?' she asked casually.

Little Stacey studied her, then answered slowly, wondering if her MSP – Mother's Sensory Perception – was at work.

'Nuttin' really – today I got all the borin' lessons, maths, RS, office studies . . .'

'Maths an' office studies are essential skills,' his mother told him. 'Get you a job, those will. I dunno about religious studies though. Unless you wanna be a priest.'

'Yuh never know innit.'

'Yeah *right*,' she snorted.

'It's interestin' though,' he said thoughtfully, between mouthfuls of muesli. 'We're learnin' about Buddhism – dem monks are deep man. I reckon I could get into bein' a Shaolin monk at least, even if I wasn't an ordinary one.'

Gayla gave her son a cynical glance, then waved her spoon at him, letting his words go.

'I'm gonna be out dis evenin',' she told him. 'It's Michelle's birthday, so we're gonna go for a meal an' a drink after work. I probably won't be in until late, so you'll hafta get somethin' out the freezer for yuh dinner.'

'Who's Michelle?'

'You know, dat little black girl from my work. The one you think's cute.'

'Oh *her*,' he answered. 'She is nice too. How old is she den?'

'Too old for you luv. Anyway, I'm gonna take my normal clothes to work an' change there, so I won't even be comin' back. I want you to behave yuhself an' not get into any grief wid yuh brother, all right?'

'Cool,' he replied, thinking he couldn't have had a more perfect opportunity with Sissy if he'd planned it himself. He ate the rest of his cereal, then dumped his bowl in the sink.

'Wash it,' his mother ordered.

'Ah Mum . . .'

'*Wash it*, I said.'

He ran the water and squirted some washing-up liquid on a sponge. 'So where you drinkin' den? Up Bush?'

'Nah, I'll be in the King's Arms as usual.'

Unseen by his mother, Stacey sneered.

'Damn Mum, you call dat goin' out?'

She smiled at his back.

'It ain' dat bad. An' it's cheap.'

'You only get what you pay for,' he replied, placing the bowl in the rack and turning from the sink. Gayla laughed.

'Lissen to you though. My little baby's growin' up,' she teased, while he rolled his eyes and pretended he wasn't proud. There was a knock on the front door.

'Dat must be Benji,' his mother told him. 'Is yuh bag packed?'

'Yeah . . .'

He went for the front door knowing full well it wasn't Benji; he'd called his friend the night before and told him not to bother knocking for him. Sissy was standing there, a full-looking rucksack on her back, golden brown skin gleaming warmly, like honey on hot toast. She kissed him tenderly on the lips and stood back smiling.

'Hiya!'

'Yeah man – come in. I'll jus' get my bag.'

'Cool.'

They went through to the kitchen. Gayla's eyes widened when she saw Sissy. Little Stacey stood awkwardly by the door, watching his mother.

'Mum, dis is Sissy. Sissy dis is my mum Gayla. I won't be a minute, I'm jus' gonna get my bag.'

'OK.'

It wasn't OK at all but there was nothing Sissy could do about it.

'Hi luv!' Gayla trilled, studying the girl with mild amusement. Stacey disappeared. Sissy smiled and almost curtsied, so intent was she on being the embodiment of politeness.

'Mornin'! How are you?'

'Fine, thank you.'

Gayla was still looking at the young girl, her eyes narrowed. Sissy stood in silence. She was normally a mile-a-minute talker, but right now she couldn't think of a damn thing to say. Gayla pointed the spoon at her.

'I *know* you,' she said surely. 'Are you from around here?'

'Yeah, Belsize House. You might've seen me around, or you might know my brother, Orin.'

'Orin . . .' Gayla tapped her chin with the spoon. 'I can't say I do know him. Yuh look familiar though. I know I've seen you about.'

'*Uggh*, don't – the last thing I wanna be known as is an around-the-way girl,' Sissy grumbled, shivering theatrically. Gayla laughed again.

'*So* . . . are you two jus' friends or more than friends?'

'Jus' friends,' Sissy smiled, keeping her voice low.

'Well, here's a word of advice – don't you take any of his shit. If he give you any, chuck it back in his face. I know what Stacey's like, he's a little terror. You keep him under manners an' if he gives yuh any trouble, come an' tell me. I'll soon sort 'im out.'

Sissy was giggling helplessly, amazed at Gayla's frankness. She liked the woman already. Little Stacey came back, looked at their faces, then frowned.

'Whassup? What was you lot sayin'?'

'Nuttin',' Gayla told him innocently. The youth shook his head and gave up.

'Come den or we'll be late.'

'Aren't you waitin' for Benji?' his mother asked.

'Nah, I'll go an' knock fuh him on the way. I ain' able for no detention man.'

'All right den. Have a good day you two. Nice meetin' yuh darlin', an' remember what I said, yeah!'

'OK,' Sissy laughed, following Little Stacey out of the room.

Halfway down the passage he stopped her. 'Wha' was she sayin' den?'

'Never you mind.'

'Nah, go on, wha'd she say?'

'Don't be nosy!'

She wrapped her arms round his waist and pushed her body against his. Before he could say another word, she trapped his questions with a kiss so long and deep that she almost felt dizzy. They both smiled shyly and squeezed each other tightly.

'Come we go,' she told him, and they left the flat.

Sitting in McDonald's at Shepherd's Bush Green, Little Stacey felt intense pride when he saw Sissy come strolling from the Ladies in her out-of-school clothes. She was wearing a wood brown skirt that outlined every womanly curve, sensible black shoes that gave her at least two inches, and a smart-looking blouse a shade darker than the skirt. With the addition of some make-up (a little blusher, eyeliner and lipstick), she looked twenty at a glance, eighteen if you really studied hard. She sat down at the table in front of her Big Breakfast, then smiled at Little Stacey when she saw him staring.

'Do I look OK?'

'You look dett!'

'Thank you.'

'I like the brown lipstick . . .'

'Cheers.'

'. . . Jus' be careful not to get none on your teet' when yuh nyam dat food y'get me?'

'Shut up you!'

She pulled a face at him then started to attack her eggs. Little Stacey lit a cigarette and sipped on orange juice.

'We're lucky anyway, I saw Miss Davison come in 'ere jus' after you left, late as usual.'

Sissy stopped shovelling.

'Serious!'

'Yeah man.'

'Did she see yuh?'

'Nah, she was too busy thinkin' about cussin' the staff 'cos they was takin' so long. She takes liberties anyway, yuh tink if dat was us we could stroll in school any time like 'er? Nah man, it couldn't run.'

'I hope we don't see anyone else from school today.'

'Why?'

'Well . . .' She stopped eating and looked at him. 'I'd kinda like to keep all dis between us for now. Even yuh mum was askin' if anythin' was goin' on between us . . .'

'*And?*' he prompted.

'I said we were good friends.'

Little Stacey didn't know if that was a good or a bad thing, so he decided to play like it was a good thing while he thought about it.

'Safe man. Dat's what we are innit?'

'For real.'

Sissy started on her hash brown. Little Stacey watched her, then took a big puff on his cigarette.

'I hope we can develop from bein' good friends though,' he started casually.

Sissy swallowed a bit of potato along with her smile and looked up. 'Really?'

'Yeah man – I mean, I dunno if I could handle bein' ordinary friends an' all dat. Every time I look at you my dick gets hard an'—'

'I *really* don't need to hear dat Stacey,' the girl said quickly, turning her head away. She wasn't disgusted or anything; she'd just expected a bit more romance from the youth.

Stacey grinned. 'I'm jus' bein' real wid you Sissy, proper. You know I liked you from time man, all dem years we known each other.'

'Yeah, an' I liked you from dem times too,' she responded

truthfully. 'But there's two things I don't want out of all dis – to be treated like a possession, you know, jus' some easy fuck, an' everybody on the estate knowin' our business. Which will only happen if you go runnin' off yuh mout', 'cos I ain' tellin' no one.'

Little Stacey made plain his disbelief.

'What, you ain' gonna say nuttin' to Carolyn an' the res' ah dem lot?'

'Yeah, of course – jus' like I know you will wid Robby an' Benji. But I *know* Carolyn an' dem won't let it go no further. It's up to you to deal with your friends.'

'Dat ain' nuttin' man,' he replied, full of bravado.

She gave him a very unimpressed glance, before finishing her sausage and sitting back in her seat. He offered her a cigarette, which she took and he lit.

'I'm not gonna ask you for much Stacey, but I'm serious about what I jus' said. If my brother or my dad find out, we're both dead.'

Little Stacey nodded, trying to get the whole thing straight in his head. She was saying she wanted to sleep with him, but it seemed too damn easy to be real. If anyone had told him a month ago that he'd be sitting in McDonald's talking about sex with one of the most sought-after teenagers in Greenside, he'd have reacted casually – but with total disbelief. Sissy was so matter-of-fact about the whole thing that it didn't seem right. He almost felt as if he was reading too much into the situation.

They finished their cigarettes in silence then walked outside to the bus stop. They caught a 94 to the West End in no time, talking quietly and seriously on the top deck all the while. Now the games were over, both teenagers relaxed in each other's attention. Sissy felt the buzz of good company flowing through her veins, making her smile at Little Stacey's every word. The small Greensider was visibly bubbling with confidence underneath her gaze, and for the moment it seemed like everything he said was right.

When they reached the West End sports shop, they stood

outside amongst the sober-faced business people and tourists, psyching themselves up. Stacey led Sissy towards the large, brightly lit shop window full of trainers, tracksuits and sweaters. They stood in awe, very much aware of all the things they desired and the shortening distance between themselves and those items.

'Dem Nikes are *cold*,' Sissy whispered in hushed excitement.

'They're yours star. I might even get a pair too.'

'*Look a' dat jacket!* Ah, Stacey man, I'm gonna get wild on dis ting y'nuh!'

He shot her a slightly frightened look.

'Hear what now, don't get too wild, I got work t'do too y'get me? Gotta get some shit on consignment.'

'Can yuh see your frien' den?' the girl asked animatedly, standing on tiptoes and peering past the window dummies and neatly stacked trainers that made up the display.

Little Stacey glared at her. 'C'mon man, don't shout up the place like dat; we affa go on discreet.'

Sissy wilted.

'I ain' gonna distress it.'

'An' we affa talk proper when we go in dere, y'unnerstan'. Can't be goin' on like no bait ghetto yout's.'

'All right,' Sissy conceded, seeing the sense in that. 'Let's go.'

Little Stacey rolled his eyes and sighed. A deep frown spread across his forehead.

'Come nuh,' he motioned. They went inside the shop.

They arrived at Little Stacey's home hours later, all non-stop chatter and loud voices, arms straining with glossy plastic carrier bags. Stacey put a finger to his lips as he opened the front door. Sissy went quiet, thinking something was wrong.

'Jus' gotta check an' see if Nicky's deh 'bout. He'll blatantly try it if he sees us wid all dis.'

She nodded and stood still and silent in the chilly passage. He came back, smiling his even-toothed grin and still holding the bags.

'Yeah it's safe man, he's missin'.'

Sissy was staring at him so hard her eyes could have popped out of her head and rolled their way over to the youth.

'I'm glad. Put down the bags,' she ordered.

Little Stacey did as he was told and stepped her way, noticing the strange look on her face. Faint unease niggled like a troublesome tooth. He forced it down and wrapped his arms around her. She rested her head against his.

'You done well y'nuh,' he mumbled slowly. 'I admit I was a bit worried when we was outside, but from time we wen' in dere you was droppin' it dark! You ain' a bad actress either. Serious man, you done proper well.'

'I know.'

'Almost *too* well. I hope you ain' gonna start gettin' into dis.'

She brushed her lips across his throat delicately and spoke just beneath his ear, feeling his wriggle, loving her power.

'Thanks but no thanks. I ain' like you y'nuh. I ain' *bad*.'

'Well all right. 'Cos I like how you stay already, yuh 'ear me?'

'I like you too Stacey. A lot.'

Their lips sought and found each other. Sissy backed him against the wall slowly, lazily entwining her tongue with his. His belt was hurting her stomach, so she reached down and undid it, putting a warm hand inside his boxers, rubbing and tugging gently, feeling him twitch against her tightening fingers. Little Stacey murmured; he was hard in two seconds flat. She returned to his neck and nibbled lightly, while he lifted and pulled at her skirt. Seconds later, she felt sensation creeping between her legs in pulsing waves of pleasure, making her sigh and flop against his shoulder. He pulled their bodies together as hard as he could manage. She lifted her head and licked his lips sensually, tracing the outline of his mouth with her tongue. It was Little Stacey who broke it off.

'Come we go to my room.'

Stacey pulled up his trousers, then gathered up the bags and headed down the passage.

Sissy smiled as she followed him. The room was small, but

warm and bright, neat and well ordered. His single bed boasted a colourful purple duvet; for music he had a slightly battered 3D cassette player, and for entertainment the obligatory Sony Playstation, complete with a stack of games and tangled game pads. Mighty piles of trainer boxes were pushed in a corner, probably every brand any teenaged Londoner could think of wearing. Posters advocating the legalisation of weed shouted topical information at anyone who cared to read.

'It's *tidy*,' she teased as he put the bags down in the centre of the room. 'I'm shocked.'

Little Stacey sat on the bed proudly, trying to ignore her sassy tone.

'Yeah man, dat's how tings affa run, I can't live in no messy room star.'

'Yeah yeah, don't try it, yuh only tidied up 'cos yuh knew I was comin'.'

He grinned. 'Yeah, whatever yuh say. Come 'ere man, I waan shock yuh some more.'

She approached him knowingly.

'Don't yuh even wanna look at the stuff we got?'

Stacey sneered.

'Nah man, fuck dat, we can look at dem tings later, we got the whole night man. My mum ain' comin' back till late.'

'OK . . . But I'll have to phone my dad at some point though, tell him I'm at one of the girls' flats.'

'When yuh ready phone 'im innit? Dat ain' no worry.'

Sissy sat on his lap. They embraced once more. When they let each other go, Little Stacey's penis was back in Sissy's tightly clenched palm, her skirt around her waist in a creased bunch. She stroked the youth's face, then kissed his nose.

'Condoms,' she said, very firmly and matter-of-factly.

He tapped her shoulder. 'Get up den.'

She moved, then lay back on the bed, arranging herself carefully and watching Stacey's arse as he bent over and dug in a sock-filled chest of drawers. Excitement made her nerve endings crackle like static. Little Stacey turned, three condoms in his hand. She sat up and began unstrapping her bra.

'Yuh don't waste time innit,' he noted, sitting next to her on the bed. He was nervous as fuck and trying not to show it.

'What for?' Sissy replied, as she did away with the wood brown skirt.

Her knickers were black, her thighs and calves slightly muscled and shining from a light sheen of cocoa butter lotion. The faint odour of the cream added to Stacey's arousal. He undressed to his boxer shorts quickly, with Sissy appraising him all the way – his firm chest, defined arms, and legs toned by hours on the football pitch at the centre of Greenside. When he was done, he wriggled next to her and ripped the seal off the condom packet with a great flourish. Sissy sat up like a shot.

'*Oh*,' she said brightly, leaning back on one arm and beaming at him. 'Music. I need my music man.'

'What, you got a tape?' he asked, eyeing her petite yet proportioned body like a hungry dog staring at his master's supper.

She jumped up. 'Yeah. My brudda's got a bad rares tape I nicked off 'im dis mornin'. Hol' up.'

She went over to her jacket and searched. A moment later she slipped the tape into the 3D deck, rewinding then pressing play. Roy Ayres' 'Searching' began. Sissy shimmied her way back to the bed, while Little Stacey nodded in approval.

He took out the condom, turned his back to her, and began fiddling. After a while she frowned. 'Whassup?'

'Nuttin'. Fuckin' ting ain' goin' on, dat's all.'

'You're big, but you ain' *dat* big.'

He craned around, gave her a look, then returned to his fiddling.

'Lemme see . . .'

'Fuck off will yuh?'

'Lemme *see*,' she insisted, peering over his shoulder. There was a moment of silence, then a shrill giggle. 'You got in on the wrong way.'

'Is it?'

'*Yeah* . . .'

She waited while he sorted himself out, watching his back thoughtfully. When he turned to her he had such a proud grin on his face that she burst out laughing at once. Little Stacey looked at her reproachfully.

'Oi you, don't look like dat. You jus' looked so sweet,' she chuckled lovingly.

'Ah, *what?*'

He pushed his lip out, not at all pleased. Sissy grabbed the back of his head and leaned over, sucking amorously on the protruding morsel of flesh. She let him go, then stared.

'Ay Stacey . . . If I ask you summick will you be honest wid me?'

'Huh?'

'I said if I asked you summick would you . . . you know, would you be straight an' honest wid me?'

'Whassat?'

Now he looked worried *and* displeased.

'Ah . . . How can I put dis . . . Lissen right, don't take offence if I'm wrong or nuttin', 'cos I might be, but . . . are you . . . you know . . . are you a virgin Stacey?'

She held her breath and waited for the answer, not knowing which way things would go. There was dead silence. Then he said, 'So what if I am?'

It was enough of an answer for her. He continued harshly. 'Why, does dat bovva you or suttin', 'cos if it does . . .'

The Stacey Collins she'd come to know during the course of the day was scuttling back into his shell. Instead, out came Little Stacey, robber of handbags and stabber of bad yout's; the street persona he wore like an armour that protected him from harm in all formats. Sissy realised she could hurt him quite a lot if she didn't explain herself. She grabbed his arm and locked her almond-shaped eyes with his.

'Nah man. Nah, it don't bovva me. Lissen, to tell you the truth, it makes me feel good. I don't wanna be wid no one who's out dere slammin' every gyal on the estate . . .'

'An' it'll be good ting to tell yuh girls so you can get points innit?' he grumbled morosely, not looking at her.

She puffed a massive sigh and squeezed his hand.

'*No* man, I ain' like dat. I'm serious Stace, I tol' you I like you innit. I don't do tings like dat to people I like. Look – lie back a minute will yuh?'

Eyeing her distrustfully, he grudgingly lay back on his small bed. She got up, hopped over to the tape deck, then rewound and pressed play again. Roy came back from the top. She jumped on the bed, clicking her fingers in time and humming.

'I love dis tune. It always relaxes me.'

Little Stacey's reply was as quick as a mother's slap, and moody as a rainy London morning.

'So how many man you wukked to dis den?'

Sissy frowned at him then let his words go, recognising them for the macho bullshit they were. She tapped her nose.

'Dat ain' your worry.' His look didn't change. She felt a little annoyed at the youth, but held it down. 'Hey, will yuh relax or suttin'? I said it don't matter. Jus' lemme do suttin' for you all right? Trus' me. I trusted you in dat shop din't I?'

'Yeah . . .' She gave him a tiny smile and winked. He smiled back. 'Don't say nuttin' to no one though . . .'

'I *won't*. Now shaddup, my tune's playin'.'

'All right, shit . . .'

He liked the way that whenever he started feeling like a chump Sissy gave him a smile or a few soothing words and he felt a little better about whatever he'd done; although part of him was still berating himself for his brazen display of weakness. The thing was, he really didn't feel like Sissy would hold it against him. Little Stacey was mildly surprised. He truly hadn't expected her to be like that.

She took his limp penis in her hand and kissed his sculpted chest with slightly parted lips; nibbling, probing, licking at his nipples until the youth was breathing heavily and his member was as hard as she liked. She then sat astride him, the only sounds their breathing, the music, and the plastic crackling of the condom as she moved her palm slowly up and down, up and down, up and down . . . She pressed the tip of his penis against the lips of her vagina; touching but not entering. She felt the earlier sensation return, running through her body like electricity. Biting her lip, she eased herself down, closing her eyes tight as he parted then filled her – he *was* big.

She opened her eyes and looked at him. He winked. Sissy giggled and ran her hands up and down his lean body.

'Cool?' she whispered, passion clogging her tongue.

'Sure bloody. Yuh safe?'

'*Mmmm* . . . You feel *good.*'

She let out a small sigh of contentment, while the youth revelled in the moment. Little Stacey found his member enclosed in warmth he'd never guessed at before – warmth he instantly knew he'd be trying to regain the rest of his life. He relished the heat of Sissy's thighs and the sweet smell their actions created . . . The musky scent of a wild flower he'd never picked, a flower he'd only sniffed at from a distance, always wondering what it would be like to hold it to his nose and immerse his nostrils in the soft, bright, wondrous petals.

It hurt him slightly when she wriggled, but even the pain was good. She kissed his lips once more. He found himself responding with a lust that he'd never known he possessed.

They abandoned words as Sissy moved, timing her motions with the tune, hating the loss of feeling due to the condom, but knowing it was absolutely necessary. Stacey was moving with her and pretty soon they knew each other's rhythm and were meeting with smooth thrusts of the hips, causing sweat to line their bodies and their actions to become more frenzied. Sissy knew Little Stacey would come soon – she could feel it in his body and see it on his face. She tried to take it easy, but was enjoying herself too much up there. Putting a hand on either side of his head, she leaned forwards so her face was directly above his and rode him hard until they were both gasping for breath, and the bed was gasping with them. He grabbed her arse, digging his fingers into her flesh, then groaned and closed his eyes. When he relaxed again, she kissed the side of his head and climbed off him.

Stacey just lay there. It was his first real orgasm; or the first he hadn't orchestrated himself. He didn't feel like he'd ever move again.

Sissy lay on her side, propping herself up on an elbow, her breasts heaving and making her thin gold chains move, watching him with a smile of unchecked affection.

'Take dat suttin' off man, I ain' goin' near yuh 'till yuh do.'

'Oh yeah.'

'We'll do it again in a bit if yuh up for it.'

'Damn right I'm up for it man.'

He wrenched the condom from his shrinking penis in no time.

Sissy laughed. 'Jus' cool man, like you said, we got all day. Ay, you got any tissues?'

'Yep.'

'You better wipe yuh hands too den.'

'*Damn.*'

'Yeah, well I bet you wouldn't carry a bambino even if you could. I certainly don't want one, so you bes' wipe dem hands.'

'All right, for fuck's sake . . .'

He grumbled some more, but made sure he did it. After that they lay comfortably naked in each other's arms, talking quietly and smoking weed, feeling pleased with their accomplishments while listening to the music play on Sissy's tape. They talked in earnest about their respective families, Sissy enthusing over her love for her brother and father, but also expressing her resentment at their protective treatment towards her. Little Stacey told her about his pent-up hate of Nicky, which she found a little hard to believe, even though she knew full well what he was like; after all, he was Stacey's brother – there had to be some love embedded in them somewhere.

As the day turned into evening they took out their new clothes and trainers and examined their haul with an almost hysterical glee. When they'd had enough of gloating and Little

Stacey felt ready for action again, they threw the items aside and pounced hungrily on one another.

This time he was much better. Stacey took control and lasted longer, pacing himself. Sissy felt her head buzzing with the rush of it all; she closed her eyes in pleasure, pushing her fingers into his mouth, her whole body went sensitive, becoming wetter and stickier the deeper he slid inside her. After twenty minutes, Stacey was *really* going for it. He moved his hips so he was at a different angle, then pulled his whole body up, looking down on her as she'd done previously. They pounded away for another ten minutes, with Stacey showing no signs of flagging. Goose pimples burst out all over Sissy's body and her golden skin began to flush a dark red, making her look as though she was lit from within.

Sissy could feel herself losing control. She was shocked; part of her screamed alarm, but her body wouldn't stop moving, no matter what her brain was telling her. She opened her legs wider, unheeding of the sounds it caused, passionately urging the youth on between gasps.

'*Fuck* . . . I'm comin' . . . Keep doin' dat . . . Keep doin' dat . . .'

Sissy sank her teeth into his shoulder hard and Little Stacey relished the pain. She let her head fall back on to the pillow. Stacey was puffing with the exertion, while she was moaning softly and involuntarily, powerless to stop the surges of desire coursing through her. She came, grabbing Stacey's head, then came once more, even harder. The youth joined her moments later, holding her tight in his arms as she wrapped her legs around his waist; they were kissing in a frenzy, driven by emotions and lust way behind the realms of previous experience.

Soon, the couple lay in each other's arms, the warmth of their bodies keeping them together. Sissy was stroking the back of Stacey's head tenderly.

'Dat was nice.'

'Fuh real . . .'

Little Stacey's voice was deep and low-pitched.

'Don't forget dat condom.'

'Uh huh.'

He eased out of her quickly. Sissy gasped and closed her eyes again. He took the rubber off and leaned over, dumping it in the bin then wiping his hands with a tissue.

'I better open a window, jus' in case,' he told her.

'Innit.'

She turned on her side and watched his naked body as he jumped from the bed and snaked his hand underneath the net curtains. Deep calm was floating through her. Her legs twitched without warning every now and then, an aftermath of the frantic sex they'd just had. Stacey came back, peering at her curiously; she was starry-eyed, curled in a foetal position, looking warm and extremely inviting. He wriggled under the duvet and reached for her. She moved over to him and put her head against his.

'You OK?'

'Uh huh,' she murmured, smiling at his cheek. 'You didn't do bad for a beginner. I don't always get like dis.'

'Good,' he said, kissing her forehead. 'An . . . Well, I'm jus' glad my firs' time was with you.'

'So am I,' she replied, closing her eyes and resting against his shoulder.

They relaxed in silence and darkness, listening to the shouts of the kids outside, both a part, yet apart from that world for now. By the time Sissy's tape stopped playing, they were asleep, wrapped in a comforting cocoon of serenity.

Little Stacey woke abruptly to hear loud voices. He was instantly aware of who he was, what he'd been doing and what the implications of being caught were. None of that first-five-seconds-of-awakening confusion for him, no way – he knew at once that he was in deep shit.

Sissy was breathing quickly and quietly on the side of the bed nearest the wall, her head almost covered by his duvet. All he could see of her was hair, and he found himself thanking the

Lord they'd let each other go at some point during their sleep. So far it seemed like someone was looking out for him. He craned a glance at his Binatone bedside clock.

12.55 am

Shit, the youth cursed, looking over at the girl once more. They were well and truly fucked.

He got out of bed, remembering they'd never made Sissy's phone call and cursing himself further. She stirred but stayed fast asleep. He put on his new tracksuit bottoms, knowing Nicky would be the only one to notice, then wrestled himself into a T-shirt, sniffing himself quickly to see if he stank of sweat or anything worse. He wasn't at his best, but he seemed OK.

The voices outside his bedroom door came back and he listened closely; he could recognise his mother's voice, but the other one belonged to a man. He was almost certain the voice wasn't Nicky's.

Frowning, he covered Sissy fully then crept for the door, easing himself through. All the way down the passage he could hear laughter and music. His mother had a raw, earthy kind of laugh that had people staring at her whenever he told her a dirty joke on the streets, or the bus on the way home from shopping. That same laugh was filling the flat right now, but Stacey's keen ear detected something different in her tone; her laugh was flavoured by something more than just humour, or even drink and spliffs. Still, the thick smell of weed was drifting from the living room like smoke from a chimney stack . . . Stacey stopped dead by the threshold and sniffed the air, once, twice . . .

Shit, he thought once more – it was *skunk*. His mother was smoking better weed than he was! Confused and still frowning, he shuffled into the living room. He stopped dead by the door, refusing to believe what was going on before his very eyes.

The man he'd heard talking and laughing was looking his way. Stacey recognised him at once. His mother saw the man peering over her shoulder and turned around. She had a sweet smelling spliff in one hand and a glass of what looked like champagne in the other. She beamed a slightly drunken smile at him as he came further into the room, feeling more and more apprehensive the further in he got.

'Hey Stace!' she sang in a strange voice that almost made him cringe. 'I looked in on you earlier an' saw you were sleepin' so I left you alone. Did we wake you up or suttin'? Are we too loud?'

'Nah man . . . I's jus' wonderin' what was goin' on,' Stacey mumbled sleepily, rubbing his eyes. He was more than a little perplexed. 'How long you bin home?'

'A few hours,' Gayla answered. She took a big drag on the zook and exhaled elegantly. The man and Stacey eyed each other like two tomcats circling in a garden, but said nothing. Gayla gave her son a hard glare. 'Don't you speak?'

'We haven't bin introduced innit?' he replied gruffly, pushing his lip out, ready for an argument. Gayla ignored his reaction and swung her head between the two males, looking each in the eye as she spoke their name.

'I'm sure you must've seen each other on the estate anyway,' she began in a girlish tone, hands fluttering like flags in the wind. 'OK . . . Stacey, dis is Lewis . . . An' Lewis, dis is my youngest son Stacey.'

'Yes,' Stacey muttered.

'Yuh all right?' Lewis replied, still eyeing the youth soberly. They touched fists. Lewis knew who Little Stacey was all right. He'd seen him hanging around Belsize on too many occasions not to know.

Stacey needed time to think about the whole thing, so he decided to get out of there as quick as he could, before someone said something that would make matters a whole lot worse.

'I jus' come out for a drink of water anyway,' he said, moving towards the kitchen with no delay. 'I'm goin' back to bed man I'm proper tired.'

'OK . . .'

His mother's focus was back on Lewis again. As he entered the kitchen, grabbed a glass and blasted cold water into it, he could hear the man cracking jokes and his mother giggling as though she had Curtis Walker sitting right there in the living room with her. He banged his fist against his forehead a few times. The pressure woke him up a little, but didn't make him feel any better.

'I can't believe dis is happenin',' he whispered softly. He sipped at the murky grey water without waiting for it to settle, then walked back to his bedroom, trying not to listen to the lively sounding conversation in the next room. Stacey found himself wondering if Lewis knew Nicky was his brother. Not a lot of people did. After all, they didn't exactly look alike.

Sissy was still sleeping. He sat on the bed and sipped some more water, thinking hard in the darkness. When he'd drunk half the glass and come to a sane conclusion about what to do, he leaned over and shook her gently. She moaned, pushed him away, then turned over, clutching at the duvet. He tried again. She swore drowsily, then blinked and lay on her back looking weak. He thrust the water at her. She took it and gulped four times before handing it back. Then she lay back with her arm over her head, heavy eyes looking at him.

'What time's it?'

'You don't wanna know.'

'Oh no . . .'

She was coming to her senses now. He looked at the Binatone again.

'It's one in the mornin'.'

'*Fuck!*' she croaked in a whispery old woman's voice.

'An' dat ain' even the worst ting . . .' he continued, looking grave.

Sissy was staring at him in worry. The vacant look was gone from her face. Dull nerves in his stomach made him feel queasy.

'Go on . . .' she prompted

'Yuh dad has only gone an' picked up my mum, an' now they're sittin' in my livin' room right dis second, drinkin' champagne an' bunnin' greenery,' he fumbled, not knowing any simple, tactful way of telling Sissy the situation.

Her eyes flew wide, then shut tight until she was squeezing the lids together. He watched her, feeling vaguely guilty, although he knew he had nothing to feel guilty about. She sighed and swore, then visibly grabbed hold of her senses and sat up in the bed.

'Does he know I'm here?'

He screwed up his face.

'You must be jokin' innit. If he did yuh think we'd be talkin' here now?'

She pushed him a little.

'Ay, how'd you know he picked her up? She coulda picked him up you know, it does happen.'

'My mum don't pick up men, so he *musta* bin the one on it,' Little Stacey replied quickly, almost glaring at the girl. 'Anyway, who picked up who ain' the problem. Our problem is the fact dat if things go the way they look like they're gonna go, your dad an' my mum are gonna get together, and we'll end up bein' stepbrother and -sister. Dat's a big fuckin' problem!'

'I don't think dat's the problem,' Sissy countered dubiously.

'How yuh mean?'

'Well, don't you think we've got more immediate worries? Like me gettin' back to my house without losin' my fuckin' life an' my dad wantin' to mash your little head in?'

Little Stacey's casual look returned.

'I thought about dat,' he answered confidently. 'You can climb out the window, I done it nuff times. If we ain' too noisy they won't hear a ting. You'll 'ave yuh life an' my little head'll be safe.'

'Oh.' She looked over at the window. It was definitely big enough, and they were on the ground floor. 'OK, dat seems simple enough.'

'All right den.'

She kissed him, then hugged him tight, intensely grateful. He hugged her back and rubbed her shoulder warmly.

'You better get dressed. An' be quiet.'

'Yeah yeah.'

Sissy jumped out of the bed shivering, and put her clothes on as silently as she could. Stacey sat there watching her, rubbing his head, resigned to whatever might come their way. When she was fully clothed she stood in front of him with her bag on her shoulder, giving him a strange look. An unspoken vibe was passing between them. If anyone had been there to see the youths, they would have been amazed at how adult they looked. Sissy reached out and stroked Little Stacey's head, her fingers brushing his temples. He smiled at her, but couldn't hold it for long.

'You know, if they start seein' each other there'll be no way we can keep gettin' together. My dad don't even know I'm havin' sex yet,' Sissy whispered sadly. 'It jus' ain' worth the risk.'

'I thought you was thinkin' suttin' like dat,' he replied soberly. 'It's cool though. I dunno what yuh dad would screw about more – the fact dat you're wukkin', or the fact dat you're wukkin' wid *me*. I know he don't like me much. One time we—'

'*Stacey*,' she said sharply, grabbing his hand and squeezing tight. '*I don't wanna know*. If I hear anythin' like dat I'm gonna hafta take sides, an' neither of us wanna do dat do we?'

'I suppose so.'

'OK. So I better go anyway.'

'Yeah man.'

He went over to the window and opened it for her, feeling faintly sad and vainly attempting to hide it from Sissy. She was doing the same, and as a result they were moving and acting stiffly, mere caricatures of themselves, with no life and emotion to drive them. Cold night air filled the room. She kissed him twice, then opened her mouth for him and for a while they couldn't let each other go. Sissy broke it off this time.

'Gotta go, gotta go,' she whispered throatily, grinning at him, then stepping on a chair beneath the window and pulling herself through. When she was outside he handed her the bag. She blew him a kiss and planted it on his lips.

'Don't be givin' dat ting between yuh legs away too soon,' she told him sassily. 'I might be back for some more sooner than yuh reckon.'

'You remember dat too,' he told her. 'There's plenty of places to hide away around 'ere yuh nuh.'

They chuckled quietly. Sissy waved a tiny shake of her hand, then shouldered her bag and walked back to her block. He watched her for a little, cursing his bad luck, and shut the window. He climbed back into bed. The voices from the living room kept him from sleep for a very long time.

It was barely two days before the following conversation took place.

'Where'd you meet him den?'

'The King's Arms innit.'

'How come you come back here?'

'I invited him! Dis is my house you know Stacey, I can invite who I want when I want. I don't hafta ask you.'

'Do you like 'im?'

'He's OK. Will you stop botherin' me, I'm tryin' t'watch *Brookie*.'

'One more question one more question. Uhh . . . Who approach who?'

'What d'you mean?' She looked at him curiously.

'You know. Who made the first move?'

'Well . . . Yuh know what . . .' She smiled Little Stacey's way, then looked up at the ceiling dreamily. 'I think I did yuh know. In fact . . . Yeah, I'm sure I did.'

'Oh *Mum* man,' Stacey groaned, looking mortified.

He turned on his heel and tramped back to his bedroom dejectedly. Gayla watched him, then shook her head and turned back to the TV.

Two weeks later, a second conversation took place.

'Stacey?'

'Yes Mum?'

They were eating breakfast on either side of the table, looking over their Tupperware cereal bowls at each other.

'I jus' wanned to let you know, you'll be seein' a lot more of Lewis around here. We're officially seein' each other now.'

Stacey's eyes bugged at her. 'What, is it serious or suttin'?'

'Nah . . . We're jus' takin' it as it comes. But we like each other a lot.'

'Oh. Dat's . . . Uhh, dat's good.'

'You're not happy are you?'

'I'm happy if you're happy,' Stacey half-lied. He was happy for his mother because Lewis, unlike his son Orin, was a straightforward, decent and law-abiding soul. He was less happy for himself, as he was none of those things, and the two elements were bound to come into conflict at some stage.

He tried not to think about what it meant for him and Sissy, even though he had a pretty good idea.

'Good,' his mother said in answer, returning to her breakfast heartily. Little Stacey watched her, then got up, dumped his cereal bowl and left the flat to go and call for Benji.

Things didn't get much better. A few days after that, Gayla announced that there was to be a 'melding of the families', as she put it, meaning they were all supposed to get together and have dinner one Sunday. Of course, neither parent was able to enforce attendance on the elders of their respective families; they were both grown men in their own right and came and went as they pleased. So, on the chosen Sunday, Orin sent an apology to Gayla via his father, telling her he had pressing business on the east side of London, while Nicky hadn't been seen in four days anyway, so Gayla had been pretty sure her angel-eyed son wasn't about to turn up.

Which left Little Stacey and Sissy, led to the dinner table like proverbial lambs to the slaughter.

Sissy sat with her head down, her knife and fork resting limply in her fingers, her attention completely focused on the food. Little Stacey was playing cool – leaning back in his seat, stabbing with carefree abandon at the golden slices of plantain his mother had fried, and eyeing Lewis with a look of casual equality. After all, *he* was in control now. Lewis had to prove himself to *him*.

Sissy's father didn't look at all flustered though, Stacey had to give him that. He was the loudest talker, the funniest comedian, the biggest eater – the heaped mound of rice and meat on his plate was testimony to that. Gayla was the polite and cheerful hostess, seeing Sissy as a potential ally in her bid to win favour, pursuing her with relentless questions, as well as anecdotes about her own teenage antics (which had been wild, to say the least). Nothing she said helped her case. Sissy bore the barrage of words in a quiet and dignified manner that her father knew wasn't her. Gayla didn't notice and continued playing surrogate mother to the girl, mistaking her quiet manners for shyness.

'So wha' you studyin' at school darlin'?'

'French, chemistry, art, business studies, drama,' Sissy mumbled without looking up.

'*Really!* I was quite the little actress when I was at school too. Only a few plays, dat was all, but I felt at home on the stage honestly. I was gonna go college to take it further, but den I had Nicky . . .'

'I thought you had an aura about you.' Lewis was musing over his huge bone of lamb. 'You got presence, yuh know dat Gayla. I noticed it right off . . .'

Sissy smiled into her food, then looked up into Stacey's humour-filled eyes. They grinned at each other, then went back to looking at their rice. Lewis was too busy munching to pay the teenagers any mind, but Gayla, who had missed nothing over the course of this dinner, couldn't fail to see what passed between them. She watched them eat for a second, then casually cut at her own piece of lamb.

'It's really good you two know each other already,' she said slyly, looking at neither of them as she spoke. 'Sissy even came callin' for Stacey not too long ago, didn't you darlin'?'

Lewis's head shot up. Little Stacey kept every facial muscle straight, every tendon straining to maintain his casual pose. But Lewis wasn't even seeing him – all his focus was centred on his daughter.

'When was dat?' he spat crudely.

'A couple ah weeks ago.' Sissy's reply was filled with annoyance.

'I thought I tol' yuh to go straight to school in the mornin' Sissy!' he blasted.

'It didn't take long, I wasn't even here five minutes, was I Gayla?'

Stacey's mother nodded mutely, unwilling to be drawn any further into the argument she'd unintentionally started.

'You shouldn't go on at me so much anyway, it's only on my way!'

'On yuh way to where?'

'To *school*!' she gaped in amazement. Little Stacey was smiling again.

'Yuh school's in completely the other direction!' Lewis blazed, his fork clattering on to his food-strewn plate, completely forgotten in his exasperation.

Everyone looked at each other. Then Little Stacey chuckled a little, which made Sissy grin and splutter, unable to hold it back. Lewis put his head in his hands, too slow to hide the broad smile which identically matched Sissy's, shoulders shaking from the laughter that had caught him. Gayla ended it with one of her loud and dirty-sounding belly laughs, then it was all over as they roared and bellowed over their food, slapping the wooden table and rubbing their eyes until the tension was lost under the sounds of hilarity.

After that, everything was OK. The kids willingly washed the dishes, while Lewis and Gayla stood in the kitchen with them. Conversation flowed with little or no effort. When they were finished Stacey asked his mum if he could play Sissy some tapes in his bedroom, and was inwardly amazed when she said yes. Beckoning at her, Little Stacey left the two parents cuddled up on the couch watching *Eastenders*, with Sissy following slowly behind him. Once in his room, she shut the door tight and stood still for a second, breathing deeply. He watched her and said nothing.

'Now *dat* was weird . . .' she began, with a timid little smile. 'I never really believed it till now. I mean, you saw 'em together, I didn't. *Now* I believe it.'

'They look all right togedda though?' he ventured, unable to hide the question in his voice. She nodded and came deeper into the room.

'Yuh know what – I think they do.'

She sat on the bed. Stacey searched through his tapes, then put on some Hip Hop. Sissy was glancing around the room when she noticed her book sitting on the tiny night table beside her. She picked it up as Stacey came back.

'So d'yuh read it?'

He grinned. 'Yeah man, finished dat star, one time. The brudda's bad man, dat book was dark! Hear what now, where you buy dat from?'

'You know the bookshop in Bush, in the precinct?'

'Yeah ycah.'

'They got a worl' ah his books in dere. I tell yuh what though. You can 'ave dis . . .' She passed the book over to him. Stacey took it slowly, but he was frowning all the same. 'Seein' as yuh so inta Chester,' Sissy explained. 'I kinda knew you'd like it, an' when I read it I used to think of you, don't ask me why.'

'You sure?'

Hc was clutching the novel and looking at her with concern.

'Yeah, I'm very sure. An' you can't give a present away, so you hafta keep it. Hopefully it'll remind you of me.'

She lay back on the bed with a tiny sigh. Little Stacey rubbed his chin and looked blindly at the walls of his room, tapping the book's spine with one finger.

'Kinna fucked up all dis is, innit?'

'*Yeah* . . .' she intoned glumly.

'Still, it weren't dat hard was it? I mean, I ain' tryin' t'get deep an' dat, but it weren't bad in dere was it?'

He inclined his head towards the bedroom door as he spoke. Sissy shrugged. 'Nah it weren't. But you gotta understand summick about my dad. He don't trus' me at all. I'm not allowed to see anyone until I'm in college he says, an' even den I know he's gonna go on fuck up. An' as fuh Orin . . .' She snorted and ended her speech at that.

Little Stacey blew out a long puff of air.

'Well, let's see what happens when yuh in college den, simple as dat?' he said with great confidence, looking at her steadily.

Sissy smiled into the silence and gave no further reply.

Little Stacey and Sissy didn't talk much after that. They said hello, but that was the extent of their friendship, while Gayla and Lewis got closer and closer, and began spending more and more time with each other. Almost four weeks after his mother's family dinner, Little Stacey was sitting outside Rockwood with Benji and Robby when the shiny blue Suzuki pulled up by the kerb. Inside the car were Strong, Malcolm, Gavin Hall, and Orin. Strong beeped the horn. Orin waved Little Stacey over.

'Come man,' he called.

Benji nudged Stacey. 'Wha' the fuck does he want?'

'How'd I know?'

'You gonna go over?'

'Yeah man, what can my man do me now?'

'I'm tooled up anyway,' Robby sneered.

'Safe man, it's all right,' Stacey warned, walking over to the car with a forced sense of calm.

Orin was watching him without a smile. So were the others. Apprehensively, he stopped, looked down at the hardened faces and unconsciously adopted the same expression.

'Whassup?' Little Stacey said gruffly.

'Nuttin' man,' Orin replied in a relaxed tone. 'I jus' thought me an' you should 'ave a little chat, what wid all the new developments goin' on in our families an' dat. You get me?'

'Not really,' Little Stacey replied, hands in his pockets, though alert as he could possibly be. 'Wha' d'yuh mean?'

'I mean, if tings run the way I think they will, me an' you'll be practically related innit?'

'Yeah?' Stacey muttered cautiously.

'So if dat's the case, we're gonna hafta start lookin' out for each other. I mean, I know we ain' always bin the best ah bredrins an' all dat, but I reckon we should forget all dem tings an' make a new start, at least for our parents' sakes. Wha d'yuh reckon?'

Little Stacey was smiling broadly.

'Yeah man . . . Yeah man, I can be down wi' dat.'

'So from now on we're brudda's right? No matter what happens.'

'Yeah. All right, dat soun's good.'

Orin was reaching between his legs to the floor of the car. 'Suh all right, seein' as I'm the one makin' dis proposal, here's suttin' to show I ain' rampin' wid you.'

As low and furtively as possible, Orin passed Little Stacey a small block of ash. The youth took it, trying to keep the shock from his face, glancing around to make sure no one could see him, then sliding it inside his jacket. The others were smiling now and nodding in approval. Orin raised a fist to be touched. Stacey complied.

'I'm givin' you dat oz for a edge. Work it an bring me the wong, then we can move on to bigger tings. All right?'

'Yeah man, wicked,' the youth replied easily. 'I'll have the money by the en' ah the week.'

'Ain' no hurry,' Orin told him. 'Lissen man, I gotta splurt anyway, so jus' come an' see me when you done wi' dat.'

'Safe man.'

He stepped back and the car roared away, screeching and blasting out of the estate. Stacey walked back to the others with a smile on his face.

'Ay you man, it's about time we made some money, wha' you sayin'?'

From the way they rushed him, Little Stacey was sure Robby and Benji agreed.

The Art of Long Games with Short Sharp Knives

'You can't come in.'

'Wha' you talkin' about man? Lissen – dis is stoopidness star. I jus' wanna chat t'you, dat's all. I wanna explain what happened—'

'I don't gi' a fuck, dere ain' no one 'ere dat wants to lissen wha' you gotta say so jus' go 'bout yuh business man!'

'I ain' leavin' till I say what I gotta say man, believe me . . .'

'Well you can stay out dere an' freeze for all I fuckin' care! An' if you knock the door again I'm callin' my man fuh you, so you better jus' stay away all right?'

The door slammed shut with a ferocity that gave voice to the slammer's intent, far louder than any words. The young man stared at it forlornly, wanting to punch his fist though the glass, kick the door down, shout profane curses until his throat was raw – any number of things that would express his own fury as venomously and completely as she had.

Instead, he dug his hands in his pockets and looked around to see if their arguing had brought any neighbouring nosy bastards from their holes. All was quiet. The landing looked grey and limitless, a cold construction of concrete, wood and glass forming the walls, doors and windows of this floor. Another nineteen made Denver House a towering monument of post-war architecture.

He stood in front of the door for a while, torn between his determination to say his piece, and his knowledge of the afore-mentioned boyfriend's temper. Eventually, he decided to bide his time and come back when things were less heated. Grim-faced, he stepped towards the swing doors and twin lifts with a heavy yet silent tread. He recalled the waiting lift with a push of a finger, then entered and descended to the ground floor.

Fuck it, dat shit don't matter, he told himself as he felt the lift drop. *Sooner or later I'll tell 'em what happened. I gotta let 'em know man. I gotta let 'em know.*

And with that, Art walked out into the reception area of the building and flipped up his hood against the chilly evening, feeling like a man on the eve of vindication after a lifetime's imprisonment in hell.

He'd been on the edge for a very long while.

Sometimes he pictured everything that had happened almost a year and a half ago like this – he'd been led to the top of a cliff blindfolded, not knowing where he was, or where he was being taken. At the edge, the very edge of this cliff, the blindfold had been whipped away. He'd looked down – hundreds and hundreds of metres down – to see nothing but rocks, dank and acridly smelly green moss, and the sea, crashing and roaring like some unimaginable animal, calling for blood and flesh in a voice that shook the earth. He grabbed for something solid, praying he wouldn't fall, but an unseen force was pulling at him. He couldn't control himself. Pebbles and dry soil began to fall. His feet slipped and scrabbled for a hold . . .

Then another force – as invisible as the first and just as powerful – gave him a tug and told him: *You Have One Last Chance*.

And that's where he found himself now. Here. A year and a half later. With One Last Chance to make things right and to stop playing the game. And he had to a certain degree. But he had one last thing to do.

I have to let them know it wasn't my fault.

He was trying, God knew he was trying, but she wasn't having it, and he really couldn't blame her. So much had happened since then, and he now found it very easy to admit that most of it was down to his own misguided input. His departure from the life he'd once known had made him see that quite clearly. He felt pain, real pain, over everything that had gone on the previous summer, and in order to ease that pain he had to do this one last thing.

He had to talk with Shannon.

Art sat in his grandmother's living room, a cup of hot tea in one hand, a slow smouldering cigarette in the other. His eyes were sparkling and keen, and though his cap-less head was covered in a thick mat of hair, it was clean, healthy-looking and combed. The living room was cluttered with all the possessions his gran had collected since coming to these shores back in the fifties, when the estates were new and London was a bright yet smog-filled magnet for immigrants. She shuffled her large weighty frame into the room, clutching her own cup of tea, before easing herself into a chair opposite him. She sighed a huge puff of breath once she was settled, then beamed a warm and loving smile his way.

'Suh yuh all right darlin'?'

'Yeah, I'm cool Gran. I feel good man.'

'Yuh look a lot better since yuh kick de habit. Well, me glad fe dat fuh true. Yuh even start look handsome again!'

He smiled in acceptance and looked down at his tea, watching the steam twist and curl its way upwards. 'It's early days yet though,' he told her deeply. 'I only been off four months nex' week.'

His gran's smile became even wider. 'Well dat's good don't it? Stop bein' so hard on yuhself all de while, yuh mus' be proud of wha' yuh achieve Arthur. Everybody tek a lickle fall in life from time to time. The good ting is when yuh realise an' start fe do suttin' about it.'

'Thanks Gran. But don't start goin' wild jus' yet. Time'll tell innit.'

She pulled a face at him, kissed her dentures, then struggled to her feet.

'Ay – ay where yuh goin' man?' Art also got up, concern all over his face.

'Cha' man, come mek we celebrate,' she was telling him, as she slid snail-like back towards the kitchen. 'Me 'ave a bockle ah rum Miss Suzy did bring from back 'ome. Me was savin' it fe ah special occasion, an' me feel say dis is special enuff, nuh true?'

Art said nothing for a moment, then shook his head in silent acceptance, grinning to himself. He took a last drag on his cigarette, then stubbed it out and followed her into the other room.

'Yeah all right, go on den. I know I can't stop yuh anyway.'

'Believe dat,' she said confidently over her shoulder, as she reached into a cupboard to retrieve a couple of short glasses. Art leaned up against the cooker, watching her movements with clear and thoughtful eyes. She went for the freezer and pulled out an ice tray and some Coke, humming a hymn under her breath as she attended to her task.

I've put her through so much, he thought to himself sadly, *an' look – she's still so fuckin' strong.*

In the old days, Art hadn't exactly been the ideal grandson. In fact he'd been far from ideal. He'd been the type of grandson that lied to, cursed, and even robbed his grandmother over the years of his crack addiction. He'd brought grief into her home in the form of police officers, debt collectors and other vengeful people he'd crossed along the way. He'd even been violent towards her on more than one occasion; yet she'd survived and bore him no ill will, instead showering him with nothing but love and sympathy for his plight (even though he hadn't realised he had a plight).

Standing in the kitchen now, Art found himself coming to the conclusion that he could never repay the debt he owed his grandmother, even if she lived to be a hundred years old. He closed his eyes to stay the emotion he felt when thinking about things that way. It would make what he had to tell her that much harder.

'Thanks.'

Taking the proffered glass, he went back into the living room and sat in the easy chair, which was still warm from moments before. When his gran was seated comfortably, she raised her glass in his direction. He got up, crossed the room, and let his glass clink against hers.

'To yuh continuin' recovery, an' may de Lord be wid yuh in yuh struggle. Cheers me darlin' . . .'

'Cheers Gran.'

He returned to his place and sipped at the rum and Coke, feeling a kick despite the dilution. The TV adverts went unseen by the Lynes, who were both savouring the flavour of Yard rum appreciatively. Art listened to his grandmother smacking her lips together happily for a while, before finally plucking up the courage to say what he'd come to say. He put his glass down by his feet and looked steadily at her.

'Gran . . .'

'Hmmm?'

She was sitting back in her seat gazing at the ceiling, the taste on her tongue perhaps filling her mind with memories of sun and sand, and a life far away from this silent flat, where she seemed destined to end her days. He shook the thoughts from his brain and continued.

'I didn't jus' come 'ere fuh a social call yuh nuh. I mean I had suttin' to tell yuh dat's all, not dat I don't enjoy yuh company . . .'

'*Yesss . . .*'

The look she was giving him was making it very hard for him to speak.

'In a way what I'm gonna say has a lot to do wid everyting we was talkin' about a minute ago. About me kickin' the bone an' all dat. See, in order fuh me to really go t'rough an' get rid ah dis weight around my throat, dere's one more ting I gotta do

Gran. An' it's gonna be the hardest ting I ever done in my life. But if I don't I'll start smokin' again, I know I will, an' I can't go back to bein' the brer I was before – it jus' ain' happenin' man. So . . . I wrote to Uncle Will over in South Carolina, told him everyting dat had been goin' on. He was proper supportive yuh nuh. Wrote back within a month an' everythin' . . .'

Art was watching his gran closely, but she was holding her body rigid and still, as though waiting for the firing squad to pull the trigger.

'He's got dat little hardware store out dere, so he's got work an' more than enough space to put me up. He . . . Uhhh, he offered to let me stay out there for at least six months, maybe indefinitely. I . . . I wrote back an' tol' him indefinitely sounded a lot better. He sent me back a ticket las' week. I'm gonna go live in America, Gran.'

She said nothing in reply, simply staring at the TV, which now had her full attention. For a while he thought he'd got away with telling her without causing too much pain. But suddenly she couldn't keep her emotion in check any longer. Her hand flew to her mouth, though it was unable to stifle the moan of agony that echoed into the room.

'Gran, man . . .'

He was up and over to her in a second, kneeling by the side of her chair and clutching her hand, feeling bad for hurting her once more, after he'd promised it would never happen again. His grandmother shook her free hand, though the one he was holding squeezed his own tightly, as if he was preparing to leave the country that second. Tears rolled down her weathered brown cheeks, tracing the contours of her features like rainfall down a mountain face.

'Nuh worry wid me man, nuh worry yuhself,' she cried stiltedly, dragging the remains of her self-respect around her like a worn shawl. 'You is a big man now, yuh mus' go an' do yuh own ting. Live yuh life, nuh bodda wid my crocodile tears. Dem come from me own selfishness, dat's all.'

'Don't be silly,' he told her, in a voice softer than he'd ever managed before. 'You don't know how much you mean to me Gran – you're the only one dat stood by me when I decided to kick. You *made* me kick. You're the one dat's taken more of my shit than anyone ah dem fools out dere . . .'

He waved a hand at the window, which looked out over the estate he'd once loved so much, and now hated with a passion that supplemented his desire to leave.

'. . . So if you tell me yuh want me to stay, I'm stayin'. I'm dere fuh you now, as long as yuh need me. An' I'll stay if yuh tell me to.'

She looked at him through misty eyes, desperately trying to pull herself together. 'But yuh cyaan stay! Me know why yuh feel say yuh mus' go, an' part ah me agree it is de bes' ting fe yuh to do.'

'So why d'yuh reckon I wanna go?'

She stared him straight in the eye as she replied. Once again, Art found himself amazed by her strength of character.

'Yuh 'fraid de crack ketch yuh again if yuh stay, don't it? Yuh believe yuh nah 'ave de strengt' fe fight yuh addiction. Ah lie me ah tell?'

'No Gran,' Art said, gently letting go of her hand. His head fell. He found he couldn't confess his weakness and look her in the eye at the same time – that was impossible after seeing how she'd regained her own faltering steps. At that moment he decided he couldn't tell her the whole truth.

'I was out dere wid Johnny an' Ray the other day man. Both ah dem was goin' mad fuh bone, an' I was tryin' to talk dem out of it. The way they was actin' an' dat – it jus' reminded me of how I used to be, an' for a moment—'

'Yuh smoke wid dem?' Gran asked out of the blue, in a no-nonsense tone that told him exactly how she felt.

'No Gran . . .'

He looked her in the eye as he said it. It was the truth, but he knew what she was asking, and he knew he was lying, just as he'd done so many times in the past. He hadn't smoked with Ray and Johnny, but she was asking a deeper, more probing question. A question he couldn't bear to answer. And all the while his conscience burned and screamed at him to tell the *real* truth, just this once . . . But he couldn't. He couldn't let her down again, not this last time.

'I never smoked wi' dem, but I really think I need to get away from here before the temptation gets to me. It's dat serious.'

She said nothing in reply. He knocked back the remainder of his glass and consciously kept his gaze away from her, fearful of a simple look persuading him not to leave. For although he'd lied about the pipe, he'd been nothing but truthful about wanting to stay for his gran's sake. And he would if she asked. Even if it meant he'd spend the rest of his days as a crack fiend.

'Suh when yuh gaan leave?' she said finally, when the silence had gone on for as long as both of them could take.

He shrugged. 'Nex' week, Thursday. The flight's at half two. You don't hafta come if you can't make it, it don't bovva me . . .'

'But of course me affe see yuh off,' she squealed stridently. 'Me nuh care wha' yuh say, me at least affe see yuh off. Me might never see yuh again.'

'You'll definitely see me again Gran, even if I do stay out dere.'

She moved around in her chair, her face expressionless but her body language speaking for her.

'Well – we will see. We will see,' she returned heavily, sitting back in her chair, her glass in one tightly clenched hand.

Shannon slammed the door in Art's face as hard as she could, then stormed back down the passage in a fit of rage and fury. Her full lips moved with unspoken profanities, and her dark eyes bore hate that transformed her beautiful features into a horrid mask of taut muscles and frown lines. Storming into her bedroom like the Tasmanian Devil on speed, it took her sister-in-law Sonia just once glance to guess who their unwanted visitor had been. Eight-month-old Vawn was wailing loudly in response to the shouting, her tiny face red with the strain of her efforts. Sonia made settling noises and rocked her back and forth absently, staring at Shannon as she paced and fumed and muttered.

'Dat was dat fuckin' Art innit?' she sneered between coos.

Shannon could only nod curtly in reply. Sonia kissed her teeth and shook her head, then shot a glance at her baby daughter and returned to her crooning. Shannon's blood was boiling, and the power of speech evaded her as her emotions were churning full throttle. She just couldn't believe Art's nerve. She went over to her set, which was playing a Garage tape, and turned it up loud. Sonia looked at Shannon as she returned to the bed; she was biting her lip, but her jaw was set like concrete.

'Wha' d'he want den?'

'I dunno. It's not like I stood dere passin' the time ah day wi' the fucker.'

'Ssssh baby, I know, I know . . .' Sonia rocked Vawn's tiny form some more. 'But I don't get it Shannon, really I don't. D'yuh know what my man's on?'

'Nah man. But I'm gettin' sick of him comin' aroun' here causin' bere grief. An' you check how he always turns up when Mum's at work? He knows what she'd do if she ever set eyes on the bastard.'

'I know what *I'd* do,' Sonia returned seriously, her expression equally as unforgiving.

Shannon drew her knees up and rested her chin against them. She closed her eyes, as if to ward off this latest chapter of a tale that never seemed to end. Her blood, red-hot moments ago, turned to ice, as she remembered the fear she would never forget. She lived with it every day.

'You stay away from 'im if you see 'im,' she muttered to Sonia, her voice a grim echo of the past, then fright claimed her and she had to swallow hard, gasping to stop the tears overflowing from her eyes. She clenched her teeth and forced the salty wetness back down her throat in one deep swallow. Sonia's lip was still pushed out in subborn defiance.

'I don't care though, he mus' feel say he's got some reason to be knockin' yuh door. I mean, 'as he bin up 'ere since las' year?'

'Nope. Not dat I know of anyway.'

Sonia's mind was back on Vawn for a minute, as she was screaming even louder, annoyed that her cries were not bringing the attention she felt she deserved. Shannon watched her, finally taking notice of her niece's discomfort – she'd been too wrapped up in murderous thoughts about Art to hear her. Letting go of her knees so her legs could hang over the edge of the bed, she reached for Vawn with concern.

'Give 'er over here a sec, she usually settles down fuh me,' she told Sonia. The teenager handed her child to Shannon with a grateful look.

'Gonna go wiv auntie den Vawnie?'

Sonia smiled at her daughter, then sat back on the bed and watched in amazement as Vawn stared into Shannon's delicately etched face in wonder, then moaned and cried a little more, before completely giving up.

'Yuh so fuckin' jammy! Yuh know you're the only person beside me an' Sean who can do dat? Even my mum can't get her to shut up dat quick!'

Shannon winked at Sonnie, though her face was still humourless and stern. 'You either got it or yuh ain'!'

'She loves her auntie man, dat's what it is. Can't bear to be away from her!'

'Yeah . . . An' she woulda loved her uncle too, if it weren't fuh dat fuckin' bastard. An' her dad . . .'

Sonnie's face crumpled in a second. She rubbed her nose, then fiddled with her rings, looking very uncomfortable. Shannon sighed and rolled her eyes, kicking herself for her lack of tact.

'I'm sorry Sonnie. Me an' my big mout' . . .'

'It's OK man. Anyway, I thought you'd credit me wid a thicker skin than dat after all these years.'

They laughed, then reached for each other's hand simultaneously. Shannon squeezed hard, needing the touch of someone who understood.

'It was still pretty insensitive,' she admitted as she let go.

'Fuck it innit. I don't have the monopoly on hurt around here you know.'

'Oh, I know dat,' Shannon sighed. 'Hol' on a sec'.'

She passed Vawn to Sonnie and went back to her set, turning the knob until the music was at a bearable level. When she turned to the mother and child once more, Sonia was lifting Vawn high in the air, then bringing her down to deposit kisses on her tiny lips. She paused for a second.

'So yuh gonna tell Emmanuel about Art?' she asked the young woman as she returned.

'Oh Jesus no. If Manny found out it'd be like world war t'ree on dis estate, an' I ain' able for his drama. Nah, it can't be done like dat. I think I'm gonna hafta deal wi' dis one myself.'

'Wha' d'you mean?'

'I mean I have to go an' see what Art wants before he comes around when Manny's here.'

'Yeah, I suppose.' A thoughtful look came over Sonnie's face, which had become chubbier since the birth of her baby daughter. 'I should come wid yuh innit Shan?'

Shannon shook her head. 'No you shouldn't,' she told the girl firmly. 'I said myself, which means *by* myself. I don't want you anywhere near Art at any time. You're not exactly known for great control of your temper.'

Sonnie had to smile at that. 'Yeah, you're right as usual,' she mused. 'But I honestly don't like the idea of you meetin' up wid Art on your own. He's dangerous man, I've seen my man do some fucked-up tings in his time.'

'He wouldn't dare try it wid *me*.'

'Can't you give Garvey a call an' get him to come wid yuh?'

Shannon thought about it. She wouldn't have minded some company, but the truth of the matter was, the people she trusted were the very people she wanted to keep out of this business, for fear of them doing something unimaginable to Art. Manny, her boyfriend, would fly off the handle at the slightest provocation. Sonnie was the same, and as for Garvey – well, he'd already had one serious set-to with the crack-head back when the problem had originally begun, and the pair of them had almost beaten each other unconscious. Which left things clearly and squarely in her lap.

'Nah Sonnie, look what happened las' time. It has to be me man; after all it's me he keeps knockin' round to see. I'll go over dere bright an' early, wake the fucker up, yuh know dem way dere? He knows Manny very well, so he knows what'll happen if he tries get bright.'

'Whatever you say,' Sonia said doubtfully. 'But if I don't hear from you by midday I'm tellin' Garvey an' we're both comin' over dere, I don't care.'

Shannon was smiling.

'Thanks babes,' she beamed gratefully. The young women hugged lightly, trying not to squash Vawn, who was stuck in the middle and staring at her relatives with a bemused expression. Sonnie got to her feet when they were done, looking around for Vawn's jacket and Baby Gap shoes.

'I better go – my sister's comin' to stay over around nine, so I better do some tidyin' up. Have you seen Vawnie's shoes?'

'Yeah, they're dere behind the bed. I'll get 'em.'

'Cheers.'

When Vawn was fully dressed and Sonnie had found her jacket, they trooped to the front door. Out on the landing, Shannon held the baby while Sonia unfolded the pram and slid the child in, making monster faces and talking in a funny voice.

'Well I'll speak to you tomorra babes, yeah?' Shannon was saying over Vawn's squeals of laughter.

'Make sure yuh do,' Sonia replied absently. 'Anyway, you should come *over* sometime. Help me decorate. I could do wid a helpin' han' an' you ain' even seen my flat properly yet.'

'Sure. I'm a demon wid a roller, I'm tellin' yuh. Jus' lemme know when yuh need me.'

'All right den, but whatever happens, don't make me worry about you tomorra OK.'

'OK. Bye Vawnie!'

She waved at her niece, who skinned gums back. Sonnie pushed the pram down the corridor. Shannon watched them, feeling slightly melancholy at the lonely picture they presented, then shut the door before the image made her change her mind about seeing Art.

THE ART OF LONG GAMES WITH SHORT SHARP KNIVES

The words leapt from the page at him. They had been an expression and compression of his angst during the long and turbulent period when he'd still been playing the game; the period when he'd been someone other than himself, held sway by the very drug he'd once controlled. One page of a book that lasted a lifetime; a torrent of words that outlined the nature of the beast the drug had created within him.

Yet whatever happened in his life – whatever he'd become or whoever he'd meet – he'd make sure he never lost that single creased sheet of paper. It was a reminder of everything he'd believed, and yet a warning, both at the same time. That was why it had to be kept and locked away, its painful connotations always in his memory, like a scar reminded a child of the wrong he'd done to gain the wound.

Written while he'd been force-fed soup and denied crack by his grandmother, this crumpled sheet had received his words during a lucid moment in the madness that had raged in his mind, body and spirit during withdrawal. Even now, he could still see the splashes of sweat that stained the sheet and blurred the lines as he wrote. He could still feel the pains that had racked his bones, and see his shaking hand baring his soul in a manner he knew he'd never regain. The Art (as he'd named his one-page journal) both excited and frightened him, sustained and condemned him. Inspired by the novel *Iced*, which Raymond had lent him and Art had devoured mercilessly, these scribblings were as close to a diary as he'd ever come. Only his grandmother had read them – and only his grandmother ever would.

He smoothed out the paper with his callused hands and stared at it, ate it up with his eyes, took in every word so they were forever burned in his mind. He laid the paper on his lap while the *Big Breakfast* played on his tiny portable black and white TV – he'd had numerous wide-screen TVs in his time, but they were always the first to go whenever his flat got raided by the Met. Ignoring the programme, he found himself transported back in time, far away from the possessions he'd been packing away for the last week, back to the spare room in his grandmother's flat that he'd inhabited months ago. He held the reflection of himself between his fingers and read:

I rekon I new about The Art a long time before I even realised it. I feel say I was playing the game without even nowing. Fuck nows why its taken me so long to get to the state where I even start thinking about this shit but I do now the time is well overdue and I woud've done it a hell of a lot sooner if it wasn't for the outside cuming in If you get what I mean. See I was playing the game almost my whole fucking life man, from the age of eight until now, and it hasn't brougt me any good Once I thougt it did, but I'm lying hear now an I'm thinking to myself if the things it brougt me was so good how cum I'm so fucked up now? And I am fucked man. I lived twenty fucking three years on this earth an what have I got to show for all that time? Fuck all that's what. Cos I spent all my time playing the game. the long game with the short sharp knives. The game that slicis you like razor blades and stings like paper cuts, but you keep playing until one day the cuts get too much to tak and you have to stop and just screem at the shear agony of it all. Or one of the knives cuts a major vein or arteray and you bleed to deat rite there an then. Or they all bleed at once and flo lik a raging river, drowing everyone in its path, including people that have never played or even heard of the game—

The letterbox rattled harshly. Art blinked and sat up, then

tucked the paper underneath his thigh, as though banishing it from sight and mind. He waited. The letterbox went again.

Art made no move to answer the door, simply sitting on his bed with his mouth open, hoping the person, whoever they were, would piss off and leave him alone. He had no such luck. There was another knock, louder and slower this time, then a voice, almost making him jump with the suddenness of its arrival.

'Art! Art open the door man I know yuh dere! It's Shannon! We need to talk!'

He frowned deeply for a moment, then hid his writings, before jumping up and walking from his bedroom to the front door, disengaging the myriad of locks with no hurry. He was about to face the inevitable, and now that Shannon had come to him, he knew it was the beginning of the end of his life on Greenside. When the bigger locks were dealt with, he unlatched the Chubb and opened his door. Shannon was standing on the landing wearing a sour expression and looking like one of the models from the Black Hair and Beauty Fair. He was thrown by how good she looked, but not enough to force his tongue into forming any kind of niceties.

'Yeah, wha' gwaan?'

The dragon put her hands on curving hips and cut her eyes. She waited a moment before breathing fire.

'Don't be playing the arse Art, you know full fuckin' well why I come 'ere. After you bin bangin' down my door every day the past few weeks.'

Art scowled, refusing to back down.

'Hear what now, I don't hafta take you chattin' to mans like they ain' nuttin', y'get me? It'll make tings much easier if yuh jus' cool an' act civil, 'cos you ain' helpin' tings.'

'Lissen you,' the young woman sneered between her teeth, her voice fierce. 'I ain' got one solitary reason to be easy wid you star. I jus' want you to tell me wha' you been bustin' to say all dis time, den I'm leavin' fuck bein' easy. You want civil rights, go see Darcus Howe.'

The former crack-head was shaking his head, his lips twisted in anger. 'Bwoy, you ain' changed man. Still the same ol' Shannon, still walkin' around droppin' it like yuh too nice fuh the res' ah us. When you gonna learn *we're one an' the same man*. When yuh gonna see you ain' no better than us?'

There was a moment of silence while Shannon digested Art's words. It wasn't the first time such a claim had been levelled against her, and yet she truly believed she never behaved that way.

'I dunno who tol' you I thought I was better than you, but it certainly wasn't me.'

'You don't affa say it man, you jus' act it star, act it all the while . . .'

Shannon kissed her teeth. 'Anyway I ain' even goin' dere, I ain' able for all dat noise. Let's talk inside man, unless yuh inna us chattin' our business out 'ere on the landin'.'

He stepped back and swung the door open, gazing at her flatly. 'Come nuh,' he said simply, looking bored.

She breezed past him regally, making him laugh to himself and shake his head once again, even as he noted the sweet yet musky smell of her perfume. One push was enough to slam the door shut, and he followed at a casual pace, talking at her back, marvelling at the slow flow of her buttocks from left to right and back again. They were as hypnotising as a mesmerist's watch.

'Go right t'rough to the bedroom man, it's tidy,' he guided.

Shannon stopped dead.

'No thanks. Where's yuh livin' room?'

'Bus' a right man,' he replied without missing a beat.

She took his instructions and entered a room devoid of wallpaper and paint; the seating consisted only of a torn and beaten sofa, and an equally decrepit easy chair of the same material. Tatty-looking boxes took up most of the floor space. Shannon perched gingerly on the edge of the sofa, while Art took the easy chair. Both sat uncomfortably in their respective places, each waiting for the other to start. Art coughed.

'Goin' somewhere?' She gestured at the packed boxes.

He shrugged. 'If I can. Ay . . . D'yuh wanna cold drink or summick?'

'No I bloody well don't! I want you to tell me why yuh bin botherin' me, an dat's all I want.'

'For *fuck's* sake—' Art spat dangerously.

He clenched his fists then looked at the floor, as if it was the only barrier between harsh words and the pretty hairdresser sitting across the room. Shannon watched. There wasn't an iota of forgiveness in her gaze. She waited a while, then got fed up.

'Well?'

He rubbed his head roughly. 'All right man, stop goin' on at me will yuh? Dis ain' a easy ting to talk about man, 'specially since it's my talk dat caused most of dis . . .'

'Well yuh got *dat* right.'

He managed to ignore her.

'Most of it, but not all,' he continued doggedly. 'An dat's the main ting I wanned to say to you man. I wanned to explain it weren't all my fault.'

'You don't hafta explain nuffin',' Shannon blazed, her features contorting with her words. 'I *know* what you did. Your talk put my brudda in prison an' made my cousin inta some kinda fugitive. It took my niece's daddy away an' broke my mum's fuckin' heart man. You destroyed my family! I don't see how you can sit dere an' expect me to treat you like my bes' mate wid all the shit you caused!'

'Yeah, but you can't blame the whole ting on me man,' Art shot back. 'I know I had a big part to play an' all dat, but I never went out dere wid a bucky an' started blazin' man up did I? If yuh gonna blame me you might as well blame Cory, or Craig, or Rosie, who knew about the whole ting but din't say fuck all to no one. Why stop wid me?'

Shannon huffed loudly. 'Dat's bullshit an' you know it Art. Cory ain' here to be blamed, an' at least Rosie an' Craig come over to show they was sorry about what happened. You jus' went on like everyting was normal, life was fine fuh Art, fuck everyone else! You was s'pposed to be my cousin's bredrin man—'

'Which is why I had to *say* somethin' to him,' the young man returned exasperatedly.

Shannon gave a bitter little laugh.

'Yeah, well it was the wrong fuckin' ting, we know dat much don't we?'

They sat in a conversational void; there was nowhere further they could go. Art stared at his trainers while Shannon rubbed tiredly at the aching muscles in her neck, massaging the painful spots until she suddenly remembered why she'd come.

'So what did you wanna tell me den?'

He lifted his head and eyeballed her with a dignity she'd never seen in him before. He looked unafraid of what she might say or do.

'I bin goin' through some ruff shit lately, shit dat made me realise what you said is right – I was fucked up fuh what I did las' year—'

He waited to see if she'd say anything about that, but she didn't. He continued.

'Not dat it was intentional an' dat . . . But it was fucked all the same, an' I shoulda come an' explained myself a long time ago.'

'I tol' you Art – you don't hafta explain. I know what happened. I've heard it a million different times from a zillion different people, so I beg you don't repeat it again. I'm tired of hearin' it man.'

'Well, will yuh lemme tell yuh I'm sorry?' Art implored, sitting forwards in his seat earnestly. 'Can I tell you how it feels to see Sonnie pushin' dat pram, an' see the way she looks at me every time I see her on road? To 'ave yuh man blatantly tell me he waan do me suttin'? Tell me he's gonna tek 'way my life . . . 'Cos I might've licked the pipe an' dat, but I got feelin's man, I'm a fuckin' human bein', flesh an' blood like everybody else on dis fuckin' estate y'get me? I ain' no evil brer or nuttin', you know dat innit Shannon, we grew up together. You of all people should know dat.'

Her hands were still locked on the sore spot at the base of her neck, but her fingers had stopped their movements as she listened to Art's words.

'So how come you never wen' on like you was feelin' nuttin'? Remember dat time I saw you in Caesar's wid all dem 'Bridge man, chattin' 'bout "part-time criminals" an' how "people can't handle their time"? You wasn't sorry about tings when you was biggin' up yuh ches' wi' dem crack-heads was you? An' what about what you did to Garvey . . .'

'Nah, nah, nah man,' Art shouted at once, getting to his feet. Shannon looked surprised, but nothing more. 'Garvey's bin on my case from day one star, yuh don't know. Man was constantly chuckin' it . . .'

''Cos you told him his bredrin was a fool an' you hoped he'd get caught an' slung inside till he *rots*,' Shannon roared feverishly. 'How can you sit dere an' tell me you give a damn when all you done is show everyone how much you don't! How can you expect people not to wanna t'ump you down as soon as they see yuh, when yuh actin' like a complete an' utter bastard!'

Art sat back in his seat at that, having no reply. When the young woman looked at him, his expression was sombre and ashamed. 'Yeah – well dat was bone innit . . .'

Shannon rolled her eyes.

'Nah man it was blatant; dat an' my whole fucked-up lifestyle Shannon, you know it's the truth. But now I give up—'

Shannon's mouth fell open. She stopped him with an open-palmed hand and gave him such a direct look of bemusement he had to laugh.

'Uh – I beg your pardon?'

'I give up the bone innit. My gran got so worried about me she locked me in her back room one day an' wouldn't lemme out fuh fuckin' ages. I dunno how she put up wid me man. I even tried climb out the window one time.'

'Jesus . . .' She was giving him a strange stare, as if he'd had two heads and one of them had just dropped off right there in front of her. 'So how long since you packed it in?'

'Four mont's nex' week.'

'*Wow* Art.'

'But it's early days man. I had a little slip on the firs' month or so, but I sorted it all out now man, an' I'm flyin' straight as a bird.'

He shrugged a little and looked bashful, like an infant child.

'Dis is really weird,' the hairdresser was saying, shaking her head. 'You know I never thought I'd ever hear those words from your lips.'

He smiled. 'Yeah, well I told you man, I wasn't born like how I was, it jus' happened. C'mon man, you musta thought I was all right, we went out togevva in school innit?'

'I know.' Shannon was smiling a little, looking uneasy, but smiling nonetheless. 'Dat was so long ago I can't even remember what you was like den . . .'

'Yeah? I remember everythin' man,' Art recalled proudly. 'Adrienne was goin' on at me, "Art, she likes you man, ask her out, she likes you".'

Shannon made an ugly face. 'I remember dat diamond ring you got me, dat's what I remember! All Adrienne an' dem lot was proper jealous until we got stopped by casians an' they tol' me the ring was stolen! I was in dat cell twelve hours man, had to tell my mum I los' it when I came home without it.'

Art winced painfully. 'Serious?'

'Yeah man – don't tell me yuh don't remember?'

'I fuckin' well don't. Anyhow, I think I was jus' gettin' inta the wash dem times dere. Jus' started blingin' man an' dat.'

'Well dat don't surprise me,' Shannon said without rancour. 'Though I gotta admit, I did have quite a ting fuh yuh dem times.'

Art nodded and held her gaze. 'Yeah, an' look at yuh. I blatantly fucked myself up innit?'

Shannon sighed, the smile still lingering on her lips, before she looked down at her feet, avoiding his eyes. Art bit his lip and rubbed his chin, surveying his full-to-the-brim boxes. The void had returned.

'Lissen, d'yuh wanna cup ah tea or suttin'?'

'*Noo*. I should be goin' – if you done wid wha' yuh gotta say dat is?'

'Yeah. I reckon I 'ave man.'

He stepped from foot to foot. She got up, unsure of what to do or say. Tension had filled the room, a mixture of their harsh words and recollections of the past.

'I'm glad you tol' me you apologise Art. It means a lot man, believe me it does, an' I know my mum an' Sonnie'll feel the same way too. Jus' to know yuh thinkin' about it helps.'

He nodded solemnly. 'Well dat's good. 'Cos I am.'

She stepped across the room and he let her pass, once again taking in the deep-scented smell of her – something else to remind him of the life he could have lived, the person he might've been. At the front door they stopped and looked everywhere but at each other, Art with his hand on the latch, Shannon's hands stuck in her coat pockets. She laughed to herself under her breath, then smiled and raised her eyes.

'Bloody well shocked me tellin' me yuh give up! I din't know whether to believe it or not at firs'!'

'Well it's the truth, so help me God. An' I ain' goin' back to it again.'

'I'll be watchin', but try an' stay straight please. I haven't heard you chat dis much sense since before yuh started smokin'.'

He smiled but said nothing, knowing she spoke the truth. She touched his hand lightly.

'No more slips right?' she whispered.

'Eh?'

'Wid the bone I mean. No more slips.'

'Oh. Yeah. It's jus' dat when I'm roastin', some other part of me takes over man, makes me do things I wouldn't do otherwise. When I had my slip it was nearly like las' summer all over again.'

A chill shot through her. She frowned and looked at Art harder, taking a step towards him.

'Wha' d'you mean?'

'By what?'

He was returning her frown, but Shannon was sure she could see something beyond that – some fear or misgiving about the sentence he'd so thoughtlessly uttered. She pressed further.

'By what you jus' said – dat it was like las' summer again.'

'*Almost* like las' summer.'

'Meanin' what?'

'I dunno . . .' His brain was whirling, his mouth stuttering on every word as he thought. 'The bone, my state of mind, my money problems . . . An' dat brudda Lacey always up in my face like I got summick fuh him . . .'

Shannon was looking even more confused, while Art cursed his loose tongue for the second time.

'Lacey?' she frowned, still scrutinising him with those wide, all-seeing eyes. 'What's Lacey got to do wid Cory an' Sean?'

Art winced inwardly, thinking *I gotta put a stop to dis shit, quick*. He forced himself to take a step closer to Shannon, placing a consoling hand on her upper arm.

'Damn, you gotta stop thinkin' everythin's about Cory an' Sean man, life goes on innit? An' I don't mean to dismiss 'em by dat, but it ain' healthy to keep thinkin' on it, thinkin' on it, thinkin' on it all while. You'll drive yuhself crazy dat way, blatant.'

Shannon gave a lifeless laugh. Had she really witnessed fear in his eyes? Now it was very hard to tell.

'Sometimes I feel like I'm already dere,' she allowed, her confusion making the words all the more vulnerable. The about-turn chilled her, but it also felt good. She'd been playing strong for such a long time . . .

'See what I'm sayin'?' Art continued, finally feeling the truth behind his own words. 'Let it go Shannon, it'll be good fuh you. Dat's what I had to go t'rough.'

'*Yeah*,' she huffed loudly, before staring at him with heart-felt brown eyes. The look of plain sorrow shook him to the bone, and he had to look away. 'Why did dis shit have to happen man, *why*? An' how come I can't find someone to blame?'

He shrugged helplessly, then opened the door, providing the young woman's escape route. She pulled herself together admirably and went outside. Art poked his head around the door as though it was a warrior's shield. The sight of her pain was too much for him on top of his own troubles.

'All righty den,' Shannon said, her voice regaining its usual strong tone. 'I suppose I'll see you about.'

'I suppose,' he agreed slowly, from behind the door.

'See yuh Art.'

'See yuh. Look after yuhself girl.'

'You too,' she threw back.

He went inside the flat and retrieved The Art. Skipping the majority of his words, he focused on the last lines – the ones that meant more than any of the others – and read them, feeling energised by the familiar tones resonating from the paper.

. . . an the crasiest ting about all shit is dat only now – literily this minute – right hear an now I realise I can't go bak. Bak to everybody looking at me lik I'm shit an no one trusting me an leading people I grow with into the guter with me? Nah man. so that's it – I'll never be that breer again fuck that shit

Never be that breer again!!!!!!

'Which means I ain' comin' back, ever – fuck dis place anyway,' Art said aloud to the empty room. And he meant it.

He'd lied to his gran twice over. But the second lie was even worse than the first, for it was about his flight to America.

He couldn't bear to say goodbye, and the actual date of his flight was the Saturday after Shannon came to his flat – not the Thursday as he'd told his gran. He knew she'd be devastated, but he could already see her face on the journey towards Heathrow, already feel her hot tears on his neck and her snug embrace that reluctantly let him leave, though it ached to make him stay. The cab came to his flat around twelve (at least he'd been truthful about the time of the flight) and between him and the cabbie, they made short work of his herd of suitcases and bags, loading them into the estate car in no time.

Jacqui, the girl who was renting his flat, waved at him from his former landing, then complained profusely about the cold before going inside. Art looked around for bit, heading for the passenger door of the car. A loud shout pulled him up before could enter.

'Art! *Art* man! Wait up blood, one second!'

He turned, looked, then cursed as much as he could without his lips moving. It was Lacey, the local youth worker. He shouted some more, then trotted to a stop beside the car.

'Wha' you ah say?' The tall man enthused, punching him playfully on his arm.

'Nuttin' man. I gotta bus' some movements though, now now,' Art replied quickly.

'Ah what, I was jus' comin' over to chat t'you man, I ain' seen yuh arse in ages! It's serious business blood, believe me.'

'It'll hafta wait Lace. I gotta duss man, look the cabbie's waitin' an' shit. We can chat when I get back. Wha'—' He stopped for a second, knowing the answer before he said it, but tried again. 'Wha' d'you wanna talk about?'

Lacey looked him straight in the eye. 'You know man. Wha' we chatted about in the pub dat night. Wha' I bought yuh dat bone fuh.' The youth worker looked at the cabbie, who was sitting silently in the car, then lowered his voice to a barely perceptible level.

'*The Beechwood ting man*—'

Art waved a frantic hand. 'Yeah all right blood, I get you, I get you. Lissen – I'm dussin' up Sout' fuh a bit, but I'll check you as soon as I lan', hear?'

'All right super, an' if I'm not in ding me yeah?'

'Yeah yeah,' Art said, getting into the motor. 'Soon come!'

'Yes bredrin,' Lacey replied, banging a hand on the roof. As soon as Art shut the door, he turned to the cabbie and nodded.

'Come man, let's get outta here,' he told him quickly. 'The sooner I see the back of dis place the better.'

The Iranian-looking driver swung the car out of the block, his thin lips pursed, his deep dark eyes sweeping the estate roads with distaste.

'My friend, I always find trouble when I come to this place. No offence—' he added rapidly, while Art shrugged and shook his pack of Benson & Hedges at him. The man waved a hand and continued as Art eagerly lit up. 'But it's true. I would hate to live in a place like this. Truthfully I would.'

'Yeah mate, yuh damn right you would,' Art puffed, relaxing as much as his body would allow. He leaned back in his seat, took a deep drag, and closed his weary eyes to it all.

Elisha (III)

Elisha busied herself rolling the dough she'd made into thin circles, just the right size for fresh, tasty rotis. She was placing them on a roti pan – a large metal skillet that looked like a flattened frying pan – when a hot and sweaty Boozy Roper came into the kitchen area.

'Jesus Chris', you should see the amount ah people waitin' on rotis out dere! Are the corn on the cobs done yet?'

She was opening the large industrial oven before Elisha could even reply. She nodded, then realised the tall girl was bent over, her head almost immersed in the cooker's mighty depths.

'Yeah, they should be done by now, they bin in fuh ages.'

Jeannie came into the kitchen clutching a handful of orders. *'Two chicken curries, rice an' peas, an' three beef rotis!'* she yelled, giving the slips of paper to Elisha before disappearing back into the shop.

'*Man*, gi' us a break!' Boozy moaned under her breath, taking out the hot baking tray as fast as she could, then going for the gigantic pot of beef curry.

'Don' they hear 'bout BSE or suttin'? How many beef rotis again 'Lisha?'

'Three,' Elisha said helpfully. 'If yuh want, I can do the chicken curries before I deal with these roti skins innit?'

'Yeah, dat'd be safe y'nuh,' Boozy gushed gratefully, ladling the curry on to the skins. She wrapped them up quickly, pushed them in a paper bag and smiled.

'Back in a bit!' she gasped, before she also ran out into the shop.

Elisha continued her work while humming along to the radio, which was blasting a Shepherd's Bush-based pirate station as loud as Jeannie would allow. She got out two aluminium containers, spooned the chicken, rice and peas inside, then crammed a cardboard cover on top. Stevie came into the kitchen from upstairs. He checked to see how much curry was left, then winked at Elisha.

'Copin' all right yeah?' he smiled easily.

'Yeah man I'm safe,' Elisha replied quickly. 'Do us a favour – pass these over to Jeannie while I put the roti skins in the oven yeah?'

Stevie was grinning all over his freckled face. 'Anythin' for such a gorgeous young lady,' he told her smoothly.

Elisha laughed and pushed him out of the room, then shook her head and went back towards the oven. Stevie not only had a crush on Valerie, he also fancied himself as some kind of junior playboy, with a line for every good-looking girl he saw. Elisha thought he'd be quite nice when he got older, but she had no intention of possessing a toy boy.

Boozy came back, Stevie close in tow. 'Leave me alone Stevie man – don' make me hafta get my husband fuh you,' she was telling him, running behind Elisha and using her body as a shield. 'Elisha, I beg you tell my man to stop troublin' me.'

'Yeah Stevie, you should leave the woman alone man! Don't you know yuh too young to be tryin' to mess wiv what yuh can't handle!'

Stevie kissed his teeth and made a noisy protest to the contrary. Boozy laughed, placing another roti skin on a skillet. Elisha looked at the girl, wonder written all over her features. Boozy didn't notice at first, but then felt the stare. She glanced up, then smiled.

'Whassup 'Lisha – yuh cool?'

'Yeah man,' Elisha caught herself, then looked down. 'I was jus' thinkin' man. About you I mean . . . Uhh . . . Tell me suttin' – how does it feel to be married?'

Boozy laughed. 'You still on dat girl?'

Elisha shrugged helplessly.

'Well . . . It doesn't feel like *not* bein' married, I can tell yuh dat right away.'

'Dat makes sense . . .' Elisha murmured, resting against one of the cabinets. Boozy was only a year older than herself, yet the addition of a child and husband made her almost an entirely different breed of woman.

'An' sometimes it's tough yuh know,' Boozy continued. 'Really tough, 'cos we both gotta work an' look after the baby, so we're always tired man. But it feels good to have my man stand by me yuh know. I suppose dat's why I said yes when he proposed. I was too shocked to say anythin' else. Shit, I was five months pregnant, still livin' at home man. I was all set to be a single mum, blatant!'

Elisha was looking at the ceiling, a dreamy look in her eyes. 'Gosh man, I think dat's so romantic,' she told the girl quietly. Stevie laughed. They frowned at him until he went silent.

'Well, I can tell you fuh sure, the reality's *nothin'* like any of your dreams,' Boozy returned cheerfully. 'We're still livin' wiv my mum an' everythin' – I'm on the council waitin' list an' they're supposed to be givin' me a flat aroun' here any day now, but *bwoy* . . .'

She sneered and went back to work. They lit up the gas and began frying the roti skins. Half an hour later, after an abundance of hi-speed cooking, Jeannie came through into the kitchen, looking and sounding a great deal more relaxed. The queue was down to a pleasant minimum and Elisha, Boozy and Stevie were talking quietly.

'All right Elisha, how yuh doin'?'

Elisha beamed. 'Fine thanks Jeannie, I'm kinna enjoyin' myself yuh nuh! I know I tol' yuh dis already, but I definitely think I can get inta workin' 'ere!'

The older woman came closer and clutched her hand. 'Well, I'm glad to hear dat fuh true – lissen, yuh min' tekin' over de till fuh about a hour, while me go to de cash an' carry? Yuh feel yuh can remember how to work it?'

'I'll give it a go man,' Elisha told her casually.

Jeannie thanked her quickly, winked, and hurried off upstairs. Elisha went into the shop, then stopped and burst into a wide grin as she saw who was in the queue. *Now* she understood what Jeannie's wink had meant.

'*Ay*, it's my girls dem star! Wha' you lot sayin'?'

She leaned over the counter and gave Val and Leonora tight hugs, genuinely glad to see them. They were the only people in the shop apart from two nurses who'd made the long walk from the local Hammersmith Hospital. Elisha saw them clutching their slips, so she knew they'd already ordered. She mentally thanked Jeannie, then turned her attention back to the girls.

'Safe man,' Val beamed, bouncing on her toes and dancing along to the radio, her whole body a live wire.

'How's the job treatin' yuh. Still like it?' Leonora asked, her inquisitive eyes searching Elisha's face.

'Yeah man, I still like it,' she told her friends contentedly. Jeannie passed them. They smiled, let her by, then continued. 'I'm proper glad you got me dis work, both ah yuh man – an' I won't forget it either.'

A fortnight after Jeannie had turned down Elisha's initial request for work, one of her regular cooks had a near fatal sickle-cell attack, and was hospitalised for an indefinite period. It wasn't the best situation to find a job under, but guilt had no chance of causing Elisha to pass up the opportunity of a regular wage. Today was her third full day.

'Yuh know say yuh safe man,' Val enthused, waving a hand of dismissal. 'How's Stevie goin' on anyway?'

'Ah, Stevie's no trouble. Actually he's a real sweetheart,' Elisha admitted. 'An' dat girl Boozy's proper safe . . . Ay she's married an' dat, yuh know dat Lee?'

'Yeah man, done know,' Leonora responded. 'We was all at the weddin' an' everythin'. My girl's got some *fit* cousins star, blatant.'

'Yeah man – yuh know her cousins was runnin' tings in dat reception dance,' Valerie chipped in loudly.

Elisha looked at the girl with a furrowed brow, even though she was grinning in delight. Something had changed. She couldn't put her finger on it as she hadn't known the girl that long, but there was no doubt about it – she was suddenly very, very different.

'Suh you gettin' on well in yuh DTP course den Val?'

Leonora coughed and spluttered.

'Yuh should be askin' is she gettin' on wid the mans dem, dat's wha' you should be askin'.'

'Shut up you,' Val spat sharply. 'It's goin' really well 'Lisha, don' watch her. I'm properly gettin' into it too, jus' like you. It's hard work, but it's hard work I like doin', you wid me?'

'I know exactly wha' yuh mean,' Elisha told her with a smile.

Boozy came out from the back with the nurses' food.

'Hey Val. Hi Lee.'

'Hi Boozy,' the girls greeted her.

Boozy handed the packages over, and watched as the nurses left the shop. She leaned up against the counter when they were gone, ready and willing to gossip with her peers. The door jangled open again. Orin and Malcolm came in.

'Yes people!' Malcolm shouted as he saw them. 'Look like Greenside's sexiest women are all in 'ere at one time innit Orry!'

'Blatant, come like we get lucky today!' Orin agreed, equally loud.

He greeted the girls, then stepped up to Elisha and the counter with a speculative expression. Elisha covered herself with a casual pose – she hadn't seen him around since her moving day, and was unprepared for seeing him now. She didn't want him to know how good-looking she thought he was just yet, or that she'd been hoping to bump into him. She eyed him emotionlessly, as if nothing he could say would move her. It failed to wipe the knowing, but definitely cute smile from his face.

'How are you new gyal? Yuh keepin' all right?' he asked, while the others watched curiously, and Malcolm chatted to Boozy.

'Yeah I ain' bad. Yuhself?'

'Yeah, I'm all right . . .' He was playing with a set of car keys as he spoke. 'So what, ain' yuh gonna gimme the pleasure of knowin' yuh name den?'

She was laughing. 'Yuh don't afta chat like dat man.'

He grinned with her, a good sign; she liked a man who didn't take himself too seriously.

'Jus' bein' polite man, suh yuh know I was brought up, not dragged up y'get me. Suh tell me yuh name nuh.'

'Elisha,' she said, holding out her hand for him to shake. He took it and kissed the back. Val and Leonora fell about laughing, while Malcolm and Boozy smiled.

'Suh don' yuh wanna know mine den?'

'I know it,' she said smugly, deciding to bring him in just a little. 'It's Orin ain' it?'

He was smiling. 'Yeah man, dat's right – you bin doin' yuh homework den Elisha! Don't lissen what dem lot say about me yuh nuh . . .' He pointed to Val and Leonora. Val winked. Leonora kissed her teeth and looked away.

'All right I won't den,' she said quickly. 'Pity, they tol' me you was a OK guy . . .'

He laughed and held his hands up, conceding the point.

Elisha went on. 'But anyway, I think you better order suttin' before Jeannie comes back an' starts goin' on about dis place comin' like a doss house, 'cos I ain' able to lose the job I jus' got. So what can I get yuh?'

'Safe man, I know Jeannie yuh nuh, she ain' gonna say nuttin' t'me.'

'What can I get yuh anyway? I'm workin' jus' in case yuh ain' noticed.'

Orin looked into the glass display cabinet. 'All right, can I 'ave . . . what Mal, yuh wanna couple saltfish dumplin'?'

'Nah man, get me two dumplin' an' two piece ah fry chicken man.'

'All right,' he motioned at Elisha, who dealt with Mal's order. 'An' two saltfish dumplin'.'

'Anythin' else?' Elisha asked, as she boxed and bagged the food, pushing it over the counter.

'Two can ah Ting please.'

She rang it all up on the till, haltingly but successfully. Orin gave her the money, looking hard into her face, but she took it and handed him back his change without returning his gaze. He stuffed it into a bulging wallet that she couldn't fail to notice, as Mal came over and tapped him on the shoulder.

'Come man, we affa duss, we're late as it is,' he told him, shrugging at Elisha. Orin smiled her way.

'Yuh workin' 'ere every day now?'

'Yeah, mos' probably,' she replied, returning his smile.

'I know where to fin' yuh den innit?'

'I do have a lunch break yuh nuh, so come an' see me den – don't be baitin' me up comin' in an' loungin' all over the counter y'get me?' she told him encouragingly.

'Yeah?'

'Yeah man,' she wiped the counter with a dishcloth. 'I'll see yuh later OK?'

'Yuh definitely will,' he told her before they left.

Val and Leonora were staring open-mouthed.

'Someone in 'ere ain' *rampin*' star . . .' Leonora said excitedly. Elisha was doing her best to remain calm, though she knew she wasn't fooling anyone, especially Val. Her friend had heard her talk of Orin on many occasions and had an all-knowing look on her face, even though she didn't say a word.

'Mek 'im stay dere man – we'll see if he comes back innit,' Elisha said, knowing full well that the intense look of longing he'd given her before he left meant he would.

Small-Island Mindedness

Clive Hanson bounced the tennis ball against the secondary school's tall black gates, bored, tired, and sick to death of waiting. His aim was quite good; nine times out of ten the ball would strike the thin lengths of metal and bounce back to his waiting hand, no problem. He'd been doing it for twenty minutes now, back and forth, back and forth, bounce, bounce, bounce. It was a repetitive game, but Clive couldn't take anything too complicated the way he was feeling right now. Of course, the one in ten had to come along some time. The teenager felt only mild surprise when he saw the ball squeeze through a tight gap in the railings, roll over a patch of fallen yellow leaves, and settle gently by a car's back tyre. *Great,* he thought. Just what he needed.

His lack of surprise didn't stop him swearing at the ball with venom. He stared across the school car park, then looked up at a large rectangle sign painted a weather-beaten sky blue that peeled from the wood like dry make-up on old skin. His face was round and his complexion a rich dark brown colour, like chocolate melting in a hot pan. Heavy lidded dark eyes turned upwards towards the sign. His mouth hung open as he read the information silently, as if for the first time.

There was a crest and some Latin words that looked like

nonsense to him, although he supposed *somebody* must understand them. Between the crest and the Latin, the sign proclaimed:

GREENSIDE HIGH

SECONDARY SCHOOL

HEADTEACHER: MR A.E. DOYLE
DEPUTY HEAD: MS B. LORAN

Clive gazed at the sign a moment longer then looked towards his ball. This wasn't his school. He went to Avery Park, which was a fifteen-minute walk from the institution of learning he was currently standing before.

In actual fact, Clive had been banned from Greenside High premises because of a fight he'd had with one of the Greenside kids. His year-head had told him that if he was ever seen on the school grounds again, the headmaster would send for the police and have him arrested for trespassing. Upon his return to his own school he would face suspension, then his headmaster would contact the school governors to discuss expulsion.

Funny word, *ex-pul-sion*. A scary word, so teachers thought. They didn't understand that the idea of no school was heaven to a kid. Expulsion was a word he'd also have to repeat to his dad, however, and that was a lot more like hell.

He'd stuck to hanging around outside the school gates waiting for Carolyn since then. Greenside teachers had spotted him on many occasions, though they usually left him alone. Until today he'd kept his word to stay off the premises, but there was no way he was leaving without his ball. Clive sighed, glanced at the sign once more (for luck, he told himself), then walked through the gates and down the driveway into Greenside High.

Hundreds of classroom windows looked down on him. Clive walked slowly, hoping that if anyone saw him they'd think he was a Greensider. Though he knew the building was occupied, it seemed perfectly still, as if solemnly watching him cross the car park, waiting to pounce. The hairs on the back of his neck rose. He snapped his head around to look at the multiple panes of glass, each one reflecting red light from a sinking autumn sun.

No one was there. He hurried as he took the last steps to his ball, snatching it from the ground and stuffing it into his pocket as quick as he could. *Made it!* He grinned down at the asphalt, preparing to get the fuck out of the school. Then he heard it.

'*You!* You boy!'.

The voice was posh, male, and unmistakably a teacher's. He was nicked. He heard his knees crack like twigs as he stood up and prepared to defend himself, though he doubted if talk would do him any good. Clive reached into his pocket for the ball as he turned to face the caller, glad that he had it as solid evidence that his intentions were harmless.

When he saw the owner of the voice, his face contorted with anger.

'I shoulda known it was you, fuckin' speng! Only you could be so stoopid!'

'Who's the stoopid one?' one of the two schoolboys coming towards him spluttered. He had a vague West Indian accent, though it was hard to hear in amongst his laughter and London slang. 'We're not the man dat fell for it, y'get me!'

'Done know!' his friend cackled. They slapped palms and touched each other energetically, much to Clive's annoyance. He turned away and tried to ignore them.

'Wha' you doin' down dese sides Avery bwoy?' the second kid sneered, bouncing his way over to the gate. The other youth walked by his friend's side and answered for Clive.

'He's waitin' for dat big batty African girl ah his innit?! Y'know, Carolyn . . .'

The second boy opened his mouth and looked up at his friend, about to laugh, but his expression turned to shock as Clive crossed the space between them in two large steps, grabbing the first boy by his regulation black tie. He rammed his fist into the youth's throat and pushed his face close to the Greensider's.

'Min' me y'nuh,' he growled dangerously. 'Don't dis my girl in my face star, or me an' you'll hafta start rowin', blatant. You wanna talk dem talks, go somewhere else an' do it, 'ear me?'

'All right, all right, leggo my tie man, I was jokin'!' the boy yelled. His friend stood on the sidelines, a concerned but uninvolved spectator. 'Ease me up nuh! Clive, cool man!'

Clive shook the boy once more then let him go, looking fearfully at the building as he stepped back.

'Jus' as long as you remember. I ain' 'avin' man chattin' 'bout my girl like dat. Besides, she ain' even African, she's from Jamaica. Jus' talkin' shit man.'

He cut his eye at the two boys.

'Jamaican!' the first boy spat, regaining his confidence. 'They ain' much better! Mos' ignorant people on the Islands! My mum says—'

'Shut yuh mout' Sammy!' Clive snapped, looking set to lose his temper again. The second boy looked at his friend reproachfully, his face a twisted mask of confusion.

'Hey Sammy. I'm Jamaican man.'

'You ain' bin Jamaica in yuh life!'

'My parents are Jamaican den!'

'Yeah they are . . .' Sammy pondered this carefully, then smiled. 'Yuh see! I'm right!'

'Yuh takin' the piss?'

The second boy was now looking venomously at him, as Clive had been moments before. He now clutched his tennis ball and watched with a smile.

'Nah man, nah!' Sammy was shouting. 'You have to be honest wid yourself though, an' accep' the truth! They're an ignorant people! Ask Clive, he'll tell you!'

'Don't bring me in dis,' Clive warned, stepping away again. 'I don't even know why you're comin' wid all dis bullshit! Don't you feel say we shoulda lef' all dat wid our parents? We're stuck on dis one island now, all goin' through the same shit no matter where we come from. You think *they* give a fuck which island, which country we're from?' He kissed his teeth. 'You're 'avin' a laugh mate.'

No one said anything. Clive looked around, exasperated. The second boy looked shame-faced, even though he wasn't the guilty party. Sammy just beamed his foolish grin and wafted his words away like a foul smell.

'Ah, wha' d'you know, you're a Bajan,' he muttered dismissively, walking past Clive and towards the school gate.

Clive stared at the darkening sky and counted to ten. When he looked back down Sammy and his friend were gone, though he could hear a voice complaining, 'Why didn't you jump 'im! We're supposed to be bredrins!'

Clive chuckled, then realised where he was and walked back outside the gates. He bounced his ball a little, but his heart wasn't in it any more. His phone rang. He unclipped it and fumbled it to his ear.

'Huh. . . Hello?'

'Yes Clive, what'm?'

'Who's dis?'

'Gary man, from club.'

'Oh yeah, y'all right?'

'Yeah yeah. I's jus' wondrin' if yuh comin' club tonight?'

Clive was pacing about on the pavement, trying to make passing motorists see him talking on the phone, until a police car drove past and he had to force himself to act normal.

'Yeah, I'm comin' club. Tell dem man to 'ave their money ready,' he told the youth.

Gary sounded relieved.

'Will do man, hol' a Henry for me, yeah?'

'Safe.'

'Later.'

Clive pressed 'End', pushed the phone into his pocket and smiled. There was no sign of the police car. The phone was in his older brother's name, but he paid the bills, something he was very proud of. Since he'd begun flexing at his local youth club, life was flowing as smooth as silk. Nowadays his wardrobe was full of Versace and Armani, Nike and Karl Kani, and his bedroom sported a serious Technics stack system, complete with multi-play CD. He was fourteen years old and his existence was nothing but fun. He even sold spliffs at school during breaks, one pound fifty a go. Right about now he was raking money in.

Even though he'd dealt with drugs some adults had only read about, Clive kept a straight head and only smoked cigarettes. He didn't like the way people acted when they were messed up, and he didn't want anyone to see him looking that way either. His friends said he'd change his mind one day, but personally he thought the whole thing was a waste of money. He was saving his money for the big surprise . . . and getting closer to it every month. Someday soon he'd go to his brother and collect all the cash, then he'd go to his mum and say . . .

'Hey stranger!'

Carolyn was coming up the driveway, pushing her hair from her eyes. A gust of wind blew leaves around her. Clive didn't know whether to feel proud or angry at her appearance – she was late, and her school skirt was short, showing plenty of her shapely legs. The fight he'd had at the school had had a lot to do with her skirts, that and his temper. Basically, a boy had been teasing him about how Carolyn dressed and he'd hit him. And broken his nose. Carolyn had been upset, but Clive thought it served the fool right and would do the same thing again if he had to.

'Yes, wha' gwaan?' he called, burying his anger like a stinking corpse. 'How was detention?'

'Borin'. They made me write a hundred times – *I will not scream in the school corridors again.*'

'Damn.'

'How'd you know 'bout my detention anyhow? I was surprised to see you, thought you'd gone home from time.'

'One ah yuh girlfriends tol' me. Nanette or Nancy or summick . . .'

'Oh, Nancy. She's safe man, she cracks me up.'

They kissed and hugged a little stiffly, due more to the cold than lack of emotion. He pulled her woolly Chicago Bulls hat down over her eyes. She giggled and slapped his hand. She was wearing a pair of black gloves, and she reached out and rubbed his knuckles and fingers, smiling. They stood still for a moment, looking hungrily at each other, then she tugged his hand and pulled him down the road.

She was small and supermodel pretty – not that there was a supermodel alive with a body like hers, but her face . . . her face was perfect in every way. Clive had once believed she only got together with him because he had a bit of a reputation, but now he was confident she saw a lot more in him. She had a bit of rep too – not for slackness or anything, but just as a girl who wasn't afraid of trouble. She dressed loud out of school and was known for being incredibly stush. Clive thought that despite her mother, they were quite well suited.

Carolyn glided along the street, Clive bouncing by her side, still watching out for the police car he'd seen. The girl's school bag jerked rhythmically by her hip, but she never once broke her stride. She glanced at him, then looked harder, as if she'd seen something in his face.

'You nervous?' she asked.

'Nah man, I ain' nervous. S'only yuh mum man, I met mum's before . . .'

'You know she don't really cater fuh you innit?'

'Ycah I know.' Clive looked at the pavement carefully. 'I wish she never seen all dat.'

'It's jus' one ah dem things.' She smiled at him, her face glowing despite the cold wind gusting around them. She linked her arm into his. 'Don't take it personal.'

He grinned and burrowed his head into his jacket. Carolyn's mum worked at an old folk's home in Westbourne Park. A couple of times after he'd been to the house (his one and only visit), she'd seen him on the streets around his estate, smoking, play fighting and selling the occasional draw. Since then, she'd repeatedly told her daughter to stay away from him. Or so his girl said.

Clive thought that was just Carolyn's story. In his eyes, Carolyn's mother had been biased against him from the day she'd asked where his parents were from, in an offhand, unprobing way. Unknown to him, Carolyn had always insisted his family were Jamaican.

His girl claimed it was an oversight on her part, and that she'd misunderstood or misheard when he'd said his parents were Bajan. He didn't see what difference it made, but in the last three months he'd realised some people took their roots very seriously; even if they weren't actually born there. Today he was meant to be making amends with his girl's mother, making a brand new start for Carolyn's sake. Clive didn't think they had a chance in hell, but he was still going to test the water.

'Listen 'Lyn, I ain' got nuffin' agains' yuh mum, I mean it y'nuh. She gave birt' t'you man, how c'n I have suttin' agains' the woman!'

Carolyn beamed at him, delighted.

'I jus' want you two to get on. I love you both, an' I'm caught in the middle of all this. It ain' fair.' She paused. 'Hey, you got a browns? I'll twos you if yuh want.'

Clive nodded. He opened a brand new packet of Benson & Hedges, pocketed the Gratis point, then gave his girl a cigarette. She lit it, took a few puffs and continued.

'She's jus' bein' over protective, dat's all. I'm the only girl in the family, her only daughter, and she's really picky about who I go out wid. No one's good enough for me, accordin' to her. Once she sees your face on a regular basis, she'll soon change her mind, you watch.'

'Boy . . .' Clive muttered, looking unconvinced.

Carolyn puffed out a cloud of smoke and warm breath. 'Wha' d'you mean, "*boy*"? You *are* nervous ain' you?'

The teenager kissed his teeth and shook his head.

'Nah man. It's jus' I ain't sure about the reasons you're givin' for yuh mudda not likin' me, simple. You and I know the real reason she's goin' on so dark.'

'I dunno what yuh talkin' about.'

Carolyn was holding her pretty face straight, betraying nothing. Clive sighed and beckoned for the cigarette.

'Yes you do man, you jus' won't admit it.'

Carolyn's expression softened. 'Dat's crazy,' she complained. 'No one gives a damn about what island you're from any more. I know my mum goes on about Yard, but she'd never hold anythin' against you jus' cause yuh parents are Barbadian . . .'

'Bajan,' Clive puffed. 'An' you tell dat "no one gives a damn" stuff to yuh frien' Sammy. I nearly had a fight wid him, true he was tryin' to dis you sayin' yuh African an' shit!'

Carolyn raised an eyebrow.

'Not *again*. Ain' you sick ah fightin' wid brers from my school by now? Anyway, he's a fool, I wouldn't follow what he says.'

Clive stayed silent, smoking rapidly while surveying the passing cars and buses.

'What's wrong wid Africans anyway?' his girl continued. 'We're all African when it comes down to it, ain' nuttin' to fight about. For all you know, yuh descendants are Nigerian or summick, y'get me?'

Clive made a face, but changed the subject.

'I dunno why yuh tellin' me yuh mum would never say dem tings anyway, she already has. If she's not bothered about where I'm from, why'd she tell me she'd thought her daughter was wid a intelligent Jamaican yout', an' she always imagined you settlin' wid a nex' Yardie? If she don' really business, wha's she sayin' dat for?'

'I dunno, jus' give her a chance will you? She ain' dat bad. She'll soon change her mind when she gets to know you, I know she will.'

Clive put an arm around her shoulders, squeezing her close to him. 'Boy, I hope so, serious ting. I'm doin' dis for you man. I hope you know dat.'

Carolyn smiled up at him, an adoring look in her eyes.

His girl lived in Devonshire House. The area was packed with school kids and parents, even though it was over an hour since most schools had finished. Greenside blazers were everywhere. Clive felt a little uncomfortable, his burgundy Avery Park blazer like a spotlight, constantly following him around. He did see some other Avery kids, but they were all first and second years – pupils he only knew by face. Despite his discomfort (the boy he'd fought lived in one of the surrounding blocks), he liked Greenside; he usually ended up making some money when he passed through.

After stopping at Kareem's 24-hour store for munchies, he and Carolyn headed for Devonshire, both trying to hide the tension they were feeling. A group of older boys were loafing outside Carolyn's ground-floor flat, smoking and holding bottles of 20/20 grape wine. A few of them sighted Clive and Carolyn and someone whistled sarcastically until Carolyn's older brother Francis put a rapid stop to it. At six foot five he was awesomely large, and the muscles on his chest and arms bulged through his shirt. He wore brand new tracksuit bottoms that looked as though they could hold two average-size men. His hands and arms were covered in gold.

A youth from Grove recognised Clive and called jeeringly, 'What'm my drugs yout', wha' yuh 'ave fuh me today?' He motioned at the others to look. 'See dis yout' y'asso? Dis yout' sell *everyting* y'nuh, wash, ash, green . . .'

'All right Ramsey, why not tell the whole world?' Carolyn snapped, cutting her eye at the older boy.

Francis tipped his drink back with a massive fist and smacked his lips as he spoke.

'Innit man.' He glared at Ramsey. 'My mudda's inside the yard man, so keep yuh big talk t'yuhself.'

'All right man, I's jus' sayin' . . .' Ramsey spluttered, not wanting Clive to see him get handled so easily, but knowing he could do nothing.

'Well don't,' Francis told him sternly. The young man shut up.

'Yes Clivey! What'm sis?' her brother called, switching on good cheer with the ease of someone switching on a bedside lamp.

'Safe man,' Carolyn replied. 'Is Mum in a good mood?'

Francis scowled. 'Would I be out here if she was?'

She turned to Clive and pulled an apologetic face, then they walked into the front garden where her brother was perched. Clive felt Francis staring at him as his sister fumbled with her keys, but he was determined not to show any fear. Carolyn's brother had a rep all right – he was known as a local nutter and it was rumoured that he'd killed someone, though this was never proven in court. Clive often told people he wasn't scared of anything that breathed air and shat, and for the most part it was true, so he concentrated on keeping cool. Besides, as long as he stayed tight with Francis's sister, he was safe – the older youth treated Carolyn as if she were the Crown Jewels and he'd been personally appointed to take them back to Africa.

Francis continued staring at him, then as Carolyn opened the door, he said, 'What'm Clivey, yuh c'n do me a John ah greenery?'

Clive hesitated and looked at his girl. She nodded and pulled the door to, stepping back outside. The youth sat down on a wall, looked about, then went to the inner pair of his two socks, opening a tiny safety pin. Attached to the pin were four self-seal, bags of weed; he'd gone to school that morning with eight. He gave Francis the draw, watched as the older youth smelled and inspected it, then smiled as he handed over an orange ten-pound note. After checking it, he pinned the draws back to his inside sock and pushed the tenner into his pocket with the others.

'Cheers mate,' Francis nodded.

'Any time,' Clive replied.

Carolyn studied them both, then took Clive by the hand and led him into the flat. There was a strong smell of cooking, coupled with a deeper, stronger smell of old plaster. The walls of the flat were wallpapered and rag-rolled in shades of blue, purple and green, but paint couldn't brighten the permanent darkness that seemed to invade every room. They peeked in the kitchen, but there was nothing in there but bubbling pans and a large colourful poster of Yard. Carolyn buried her head in the fridge, and emerged with a carton of orange juice. She poured two glasses then put it back.

'*Muuuum!*' she yelled.

'Carolyn?'

Oh man, Clive thought. The nervousness he'd been denying suddenly rushed him like a rugby player and tried to grapple him to the floor. He swayed, light-headed, but managed to remain standing.

'Where are yuh?' Carolyn yelled again.

'In de front room. Come see me nuh.'

Clive looked at Carolyn, a little perplexed. Something wasn't adding up.

'Does she know I'm comin'?' he asked.

'Well . . .' She looked at her feet and pouted.

'Fuckin' hell 'Lyn!' he hissed, quiet as he could. 'All dat speechin' yuh gimme an' you ain' even tol' her yet! I shoulda known you was up to summick man, yuh takin' berties . . .'

'I'm sorry,' she whispered in a small voice.

Clive looked at the plaster cracking on the ceiling, asking God for strength. He could never hold his temper with his girl for long.

'Carolyn? You got someone in de kitchen?' the voice from the living room enquired.

'Yes Mummy, I'm comin' now anyway,' her daughter yelled back. She turned to Clive, a forlorn expression on her face. He gazed back feeling trapped. 'Ready?' she asked.

'I s'pose,' he grumbled. They put their glasses in the sink and walked into the living room.

A few paces behind his girl, Clive caught only a fleeting glance of the room before his attention was fully focused on her mother. It was quite a small room, filled to the brim with all the mod-cons a person could want – Nicam TV and video, cable . . . Clive frowned as he glanced at three Sony Playstation boxes pushed behind the TV cabinet. *Three!* He was dying to have one and there was a fourth unboxed by the cable receiver. He'd have to talk to Francis.

In the centre of the room stood a black marble table, with a small flowerpot and some dried flowers among the items on its surface. Along the walls were more pictures of Yard, and some black and whites of Carolyn, Francis and a grinning man Clive assumed was their father, though he'd never seen or spoken to him. A small armchair and a sofa filled the other side of the room, and a large figure was sitting in the armchair. He flicked his gaze over everything again, not wanting to look at the chair. Carolyn moved from in front of him.

He noted the look of shock and distrust on the woman's face as she looked his way.

'Mum,' Carolyn said quickly. 'You remember Clive don't you, he came round not long ago. I thought it'd be good if you two got to know each other, innit?'

'Good evenin',' Clive muttered, waving a little and standing self-consciously by the door. Carolyn's mum looked at him as though he was something her daughter had brought in on her heel.

'It afternoon,' she informed him uncharitably.

'*Mum!*'

'Wha' wrong wid yuh?'

'Don' be like dat, dat's what. Clive's makin' a effort. You could *try* an' do the same.'

His girl looked at him. 'Siddown man.'

Clive sat on the sofa opposite her mum, the only available seat in the room. He looked at the TV. *Trisha* was on, but as it was almost five o'clock he guessed it was a video from earlier in the day. He looked at Carolyn. She'd been making faces at her mum when his head was turned, but stopped quickly and smiled at him. No one spoke. Her mum sat in sullen silence, pointedly ignoring him, her daughter and even the TV. There was shouted laughter from outside. No one took any notice. Embarrassed, Clive looked at the marble table. There was a pack of small blues sitting by some cigarettes. He picked them up and pushed them towards the silent woman. Carolyn's face registered shock and horror in equal measures.

Her mum stared at the Rizla, then at his face.

'Wha'?'

'Buil' a spliff man,' Clive urged.

The woman's face turned as dark as a storm cloud pregnant

with rain. She knocked the Rizla from the table with one swift
movement and glared at him. Her daughter put her head in her
hands.

'Is who tell yuh me smoke?'

Clive managed not to look at Carolyn.

'I saw the Rizla on the table an' I guessed.'

'So becausin' yuh see papers on de table, yuh feel say yuh c'n
smoke wid me? Yuh a yout', is what'm? Who yuh tink I am?'

Clive shrugged, fed up by now.

'Buil' it if yuh wanna buil' it, don't if yuh don't innit. No skin
off my nose.' He sat back. 'What, c'n I buil' it fuh Carolyn den?'

The woman snorted. 'Yuh musse mad.'

Clive sighed and sat back. He looked at Carolyn, but she
refused to hold his eye. No one said a word. He looked at the
pictures, the TV. The marble table. The dried flowers. Carolyn.
Still no one said a word.

After five minutes, Clive got up.

'Yeah well, I gotta go now, yout' club's on. It was nice
meetin' you an' all dat.'

Carolyn's mum snorted again. Clive opened his mouth, but
remembered Francis outside and held his tongue.

'I'll see you out,' Carolyn whispered. They made their way to
the front door, then stood in the hallway morosely.

'Dat was good fun,' Clive sniffed.

'I'm sorry. She's in a bad mood. Come back another time.'

'Yeah right.'

'Seriously. She'll have to face fac's someday innit?'

'Mmm.'

They stared at each other, both a little pissed off. They
embraced, then kissed until they heard laughter and shouting
from outside, echoing in the hallway. They let each other go
quickly, wiping their mouths. Clive opened the door and
stepped outside. Carolyn watched him walk through her
brother's crowd of friends, then push his hands into his pockets
and disappear around a corner. She gazed at her brother, then
closed the door on his questioning face. Her own face was full

of rage, and by the time she'd stomped back down the corridor into the living room, she was willing and able to rumble. She blasted the door open to find her mother building a spliff on the marble table. Her mum jumped in shock.

'Thanks a lot for being so nice!'

Her mother wore her ashamed expression like a Hallowe'en mask, strapped on for the occasion.

'How yuh mean?'

'Yuh coulda treated Clive a bit better! Dat was downright rude what you jus' did!'

Her mother kissed her teeth.

'Cha, yuh tink me ah watch dat? Bring a decent bwoy inna dis 'ouse an' I will treat 'im like gold, yuh 'ear me? Solid gold! But you keep bringin' dem bruk down, good fe nuttin' bwoy here, an' me will treat dem like what dem is! Dut, Carolyn, nuttin' but dut!'

'But he ain' done nuttin' to you!' Carolyn whined. 'So you see 'im jugglin' weed . . . Your own son's bin jugglin' worse than dat for years, an' you never tell 'im jack.'

'Yuh cyann choose family! Yuh can choose yuh bwoyfrien'.'

'But look at dis house!' The girl pointed at the various items scattered around the room – the very things Clive had been studying from the sofa. 'Don't you think Clive sees us as a bit hypocritical? I mean, you won't chat to him 'cos he juggles, yet the house if full up wid stolen goods! D'yuh think dat's right?'

'Me nuh care what 'im tink.'

'Mum what's wrong wid you? You're actin' crazy!'

'You crazy. Arguin' wid me over some fool bwoy who don't gi' ah damn about you – mek de yout' tun yuh stupid! Yuh never act dis way before yuh meet dat rebel. It won't las' long, I'm tellin' you!'

'I can't believe I'm hearin' dis. You don't even know the boy, how'd you know he don't give a damn about me? If you'd jus' give him a chance . . .'

'Chance wha'? Listen Carolyn, dis de trut' me ah tell. Fin' yuhself a Jamaican bwoy . . .'

'*Mum*,' she growled.

'Yuh cyaan get nowhere wi' dem small–island people. Jamaican an' Barbadian . . . Dem jus' not compatible.'

'Bajan Mum, they're called Bajans,' Carolyn told her mother. The woman wasn't listening.

'You'll go away from me, an' de nex' ting yuh know, 'im 'ave yuh eatin' monkey-brain an' blue rice . . .'

Carolyn gazed at her mother in disbelief, eyes wide with anger. The woman stopped talking, realising she'd gone a touch too far in condemning her daughter's boyfriend, flinching slightly as the girl shot vexed looks her way. Carolyn zipped up her jacket and glared.

'You know what you sound like?' Her voice was thick with emotion, and she was frowning fiercely, an expression that made her look a lot like her brother. 'You sound like dem racist white people dat stick leaflets through people's doors. I think dat's kinna sad, don't you?'

Her mother looked away, the mask slipping from her face to reveal real, undisguised shame. Carolyn kissed her teeth, then left the room, wrapping her scarf around her neck.

'Carolyn! *Carolyn, come back here!*' Her mother yelled. She ignored her and walked straight out the door, slamming it with all her might to the surprise of the people sitting outside. Francis, looking more than a little charged by now, passed her a zook.

'What'm sis?'

The others stared at her curiously, but kept out of her way.

'Nuttin' man. Mum's jus' goin' inta one about Clive.'

She took three deep pulls on the zook, then went to pass it back. Francis shook his head.

'Kill it. I know what it's like when Mum's in bitch mode.'

Carolyn smiled and kissed her brother on the cheek. 'Ta. I'll be back later.'

'Safe sis.'

She walked to the end of her block, still puffing on the spliff, until she arrived at an open-air phone. She put in a fifty pence piece and dialled Clive's number from memory. He answered almost straight away.

'Yush.'

'Hey, it's me.'

'Who's dis?'

'Who the fuck yuh think?' she almost yelled.

'All right all right, I was jokin'. What's up wid you?'

She played with the coiled metal protruding from the receiver and pouted.

'Argument. Mum. Nuttin' new.'

'About what?'

She sighed. 'Guess.'

'Ah shit. So wha' you on?'

'I wanned to stay at your house tonight. I can't take my drum no more man.'

'*Serious?*'

Clive sounded both excited and fearful. Carolyn smiled.

'Yeah, I think it's about time don't you? We've bin goin' out four months, an' I'm ready. Mind you, would yuh mum 'llow it?'

'Never min' her, we'll jus' go club an' come back when she's in bed, simple. They won't catch us.'

The pips went, loud in her ears. Carolyn stopped smiling.

'Anyway I gotta go, my money's run out. Where shall I meet you?'

'Up my yout' club, innit? I . . .'

Dial tone.

Carolyn replaced the receiver, then walked over to her house, shivering slightly. The lights had come on along her block, illuminating her brother's friends like actors in an open-air theatre. She joined them and held out her hand.

'Anyone got change? I need bus fare to Grove.'

Her brother nodded and dug in his deep pockets. She saw the living-room curtains twitch as he gave her the money. From the corner of her eye, Carolyn could see her mother standing by the window, but she ignored her presence, quickly pocketing the pound coin her brother handed over. Her mother's silhouette was imprinted on her memory as she left the block and headed for the bus stop.

Rejection

He was at the door before the postman reached his next-door neighbour – as he bent to pick the envelope up, he heard Mr Hillman's letterbox flap, then clicking steps heading away, further down the block. Soon afterwards, Mr Hillman's Labrador Rusty began the frenzied barking that accompanied the postman's arrival every morning. Michael cussed. Rusty could bark for up to fifteen minutes at a time, which drove him insane when he was trying to concentrate on his writing. Today it seemed as though she was content to bring it down to around fifteen seconds. He sighed in relief, and looked closely at the envelope.

He turned it over, frowning. When he saw who the sender was, hope and good cheer tentatively settled on his face. His eyes virtually caressed the name stamped in ink next to the Queen's head – *Armstrong Publications*; they were one of the many companies he'd sent his manuscript to nearly three months before. This was the last of the replies. All the others had said the same . . .

. . . *After careful consideration, we feel that the novel does not fit into our list . . . May I wish you success in placing your ideas elsewhere . . . We regret to inform you that your manuscript is not representative of the work we are currently seeking to publish.*

Which were basically three different ways of saying the same thing – fuck off, we don't want you.

Michael didn't hold it against the publishers; he knew they worked hard, forever searching for a new writer, the gamble that would really pay off. It was just . . . half the time, he was sure the person sending the letter hadn't even bothered to read his hard work. The work he'd spent hours typing on to a computer screen with one hand and had had to beg Lynette to type for him, when he eventually developed a very sore finger.

The envelope felt light and thin; sometimes when his book was rejected, they'd send back everything he'd posted – he usually knew the answer the moment he squeezed the package. He felt his stomach churn in anticipation and almost danced his way into the living room, where Lynette was watching the TV. She turned her head in his direction, startled by his joyful manner.

'Look what come t'rough the door,' he grinned, waving the envelope at her. She was wrapped in a thick blanket – the heating in the flat had packed up again, and the council couldn't get to them before Monday. A small fan heater they'd borrowed from Mr Hillman kept them reasonably warm, but they only had the one, carting it from room to room as they moved. The couple had only been up for five minutes, hence the freezing temperature and Lynette's blankets.

'Whassat?' she mumbled, pushing her lip out and shuddering as though having a fit.

'Armstrong Publications man,' he said, flopping down beside her. 'They sent me a reply at last.'

Lynette smiled at him, and he grinned back. She had a little gap in her front teeth that he loved. She moved closer to him, pushing her arm through his, and ignoring the noise of the television set.

'*Really?*' Lynette's chubby face was genuinely pleased. 'At last. We bin waitin' ages for dat! Wha' did they say?'

'I ain' opened it yet, but . . .' Michael glanced at her with a grin, then noticed her expression and stopped. His single spoken word was harsh, making him gag as though his food had gone down the wrong way. '*What?*'

As soon as she heard the envelope was still sealed, her face became drawn and grave.

'Oh babes, I thought they said yes . . .'

'Wha' d'you mean?' he snarled. 'I ain' opened it yet I said. Dat means they could still say yes. Innit?'

'Yeah. But . . .'

'But what?'

He was holding the manila envelope tight in his hands, staring at her with hard furious eyes. Treading carefully, the brown-skinned girl tried to warn him.

'I'm jus' sayin' don't get yuh hopes up babes, dat's all. After what happened las' time . . .'

Michael's whole body was rigid, anger coursing over his face. Lynette flinched in her seat – fright had taken over, and it made her look as fragile as a porcelain doll.

'I knew it wouldn't take you long to come back to dat,' he roared at her. 'I said I was sorry, but you keep on about it, nag, nag, nag, like an old fuckin' woman.'

He stopped his tirade as soon as he realised he was making a mountain out of a molehill once again. He looked around the room, sickened by his actions of three weeks before. When the last rejection note came through, he'd smashed the flat to bits – all their ornaments, their CD and record collection, their pictures, plates, stereo system . . . When he looked at the room, shame threatened to boil his brain so hard he felt like it would explode.

The remains of the stereo had been put out front for the bin men to collect. It'd taken him a whole day to tidy the mess of crushed plates and broken glass from the shattered TV screen. Lynette had refused to help; she'd been at work at the time of his destructive spree, and when she came in and saw the mess she stopped speaking to him for a week.

The TV blaring in front of them now was on loan from Lynette's mother – a woman as thin and stern as her daughter was chubby and kind. She'd handed it over very grudgingly.

Lynette's mother had never approved of him, as he'd often made it plain he had no intention of working – at least not for anybody else. Michael looked at his girl's expression and at once felt her hurt at his harsh words. He leaned over and took her hand, noting the way her eyes watched his fingers, waiting to see if they would form a fist.

'I apologise,' he said humbly. 'All dis frustration's killin' me Lyn. What's so wrong about wantin' to be successful?'

Her dark eyes were full of sorrow and forgiveness.

'Open the letter. You never know, yuh luck might've changed.'

Michael nodded.

'OK.'

He tore the envelope open with eager fingers and pulled out a solitary sheet of paper. They smiled at one another. He read the letter as fast as he could.

Dear Michael Weathers,

Thank you for your recent letter and proposal.

I regret to say that we do not feel it is a project we would be able to market effectively as part of our publishing programme here at Armstrong.

Thank you for giving us the chance to consider the idea, and I trust you will have every success in placing it with the right publisher.

Yours sincerely,

Andrea Clark
Editor

He read it twice while Lynette watched, unable to believe what it was saying. The third time he read it, he did so aloud; only then did the words sink in and take on meaning. Another rejection. Another letter saying that *Darkest Berries in the Bush* wasn't up to scratch. This had been the last letter he was expecting. What could he possibly do now?

Lynette saw a trace of all these questions and more flickering over his face; as she watched, she felt a mild unease. Michael didn't look angry now, he looked lost, as though he'd given up completely.

Her throat ached to say something to soothe his hurt feelings . . . to say he wouldn't have to worry about the bills, or the heating, that he wouldn't have to sign on, or eat baked beans and fish fingers for dinner every day because it was cheaper than meat. She opened her mouth, wanting to say those things so much – but she couldn't, of course. None of them was true.

'*Someone*'ll be interested soon, jus' you wait—' she started consolingly.

Before she could finish, Michael pushed her away from him, ripped the letter in half, then got up and marched for the door.

'Yeah, when?' he growled back at her. 'When I'm *dead*? Fat lot ah good it'll do me den innit?'

Lynette looked at him, speechless, as he stomped into the bedroom, slamming the door behind him hard enough to send a shower of plaster on to the carpet. She covered her eyes and leaned her head back, wishing things were different.

'Please God, don't let him smash up the place,' she muttered under her breath. After looking fearfully at the bedroom door again, torn between going after him and ignoring him, she decided to play a waiting game. She turned her attention back to the TV.

Michael emerged from the bedroom at the sound of the doorbell. It was Lacey.

'Yes blood,' Lacey greeted, as he sauntered past him towards the living room. *He was a lanky fucker*, Michael often thought, tall and light-skinned, with arms and legs like a praying mantis. He was also his best friend.

'How's the writin' goin' Nig-Nog?' he enquired with his usual brutal charm.

'Don't ask,' Michael replied, following with his head down.

Lacey laughed. 'Like dat is it? I tol' you man – they ain' givin' nuttin' to a black man. You affa *take* it.' Lacey seized the air between his fingers with a grim smile, turning to face his friend. 'Yuh get what I'm sayin'?'

'Yeah man . . .'

They entered the living room. Lynette was still there, now fully dressed. She smiled at their visitor and the sight of her beautiful grin made Michael feel selfish and cruel – she was only nineteen, and already living a nobody's life. She should have been sitting on a leather sofa, her arms draped with jewellery, her skin smelling of expensive perfume. She should've been wearing Donna Karan and Versace dresses instead of Bleu Bolt jeans and T-shirts. He shook his head as he realised how beautiful she was – and how much he couldn't give her.

Lacey sat down and hugged Lynette. Michael took in his friend's Armani jeans, Nike Triax trainers and black leather jacket. Not to mention his gold.

'Wha' gwaan?' Lacey grinned at Lynette.

'Nuttin'.' She hugged him back sisterly. 'How's you?'

'Safe y'nuh.' He looked up at Michael questioningly. 'I ain' even stoppin' anyway. I'm on a pass t'rough vibe dat's all. I was wonderin' if you change yuh mind spee . . .'

There was a hefty silence; it could have been ominous if the insane chatter of the TV hadn't whispered underneath all the while. Michael sighed, fidgeted and looked at Lynette. She was watching him, but refused to say a word.

'Mikey, it'll be fuckin' simple man,' Lacey cajoled in a relaxed manner. His face was deadly serious. 'Five of us can deal wid dem bwoys, yuh know dat innit? Lynette, tell him . . .'

She shook her head and shifted towards the other end of the sofa.

'Uh uh, I ain' sayin' nothin'. He knows how I feel. It's entirely up to Michael.'

The man in question stood by the living-room door, also keeping quiet, watching his girl. He knew how she felt all right. They'd practically screamed the flat down over it when Lacey had first come up with his plan. He was sure her point of view hadn't changed. His hadn't either; he knew it could easily be done, as things had changed over the past few months. The balance of power had shifted, and everything was there for the taking.

Lacey scrutinised him, then reached into his jacket and pulled out an automatic handgun.

'Look a' dis man, Look a' dis an' tell me we ain' ready!'

'*Lacey!*' Lynette screeched stridently, as she caught sight of the gun. Michael smiled.

'Jus' cool man,' he replied. He took the pistol from Lacey and checked the safety. It was already on. 'We ain' little kids messin' around wid tings we don' unnerstan', y'get me?'

'Yeah, well I don't want dat thing in my house Michael.'

He glared at her. Lacey noticed, and hopped up, quick as a dog stepping on broken glass. 'Listen, I 'ad a feelin' yuh still wasn't sure, so I writ down Timmy's number. Dis time now, if you change yuh min', jus' call 'im – but make it before four, OK?'

Michael didn't answer, but handed back the gun. Lacey wanted to exchange the pistol for the number, but Michael wasn't having it. In the end, Lacey put the piece of paper on top of the TV, then waved at Lynette.

'I'll leave you law-abidin' folks alone now!' he yelled as he left. Michael saw him out, then came back into the living room wearing a worried frown. Lynette looked as frightened as a rabbit shivering under the claws of a hungry eagle.

'Well?' she grumbled. 'You're thinkin' about it ain' yuh?'

Her eyes turned to meet his; at once he felt like they were all-knowing brown pools, staring into his very brain, reading his thoughts as easily as a comic strip. He felt as though she could see exactly how much he wanted to pick up the phone and *dial* that fucker – how much he wanted to make the money everybody else was making. For a moment he wanted to scream denial, to stamp across the room, look into her face and yell it at her, to roar at the top of his lungs, no, *No* . . .

'Nah,' he said, forcing himself to stroll over to where she was sitting. Every casual step was as painful as walking on hot coals. Lynette was still watching, and as her eyes followed him, he knew that casual walk or no casual walk, he hadn't fooled her.

'Michael, don't do anything stupid, please. We can survive a little longer, and something'll come up, it's got to. Don't do somethin' so hasty you'll jus' regret it in a couple of months. I need you to promise me that. Jus' think of all you got to look forward to . . .'

Yeah jus' think, he told himself. *All the good things I got to look forward to . . .*

A new house, with electricity that worked, far away from the others so he could blast his music whenever he wanted; a chance to think about kids – he and Lynette were so paranoid she might fall unexpectedly pregnant that she always took the pill and he always used condoms. Yet they both loved kids; they were just dead-set against bringing them up in a flat that felt like a fridge.

Michael dismissed his girlfriend's voice, and, not for the first time, wondered if the life he was living was so right.

Look at me, he chided himself. *I swore to the others that I'd be successful. I told them to keep their short-term money, their gold and fancy rides. I'd wait around to collect the larger dividends. I'd invest and sacrifice for myself. And what happened?*

What happened was he waited, and waited, and waited. *The Darkest Berries in the Bush* was his fourth novel, and none of the others had fared any better. His friends were sympathetic at his first rejection, encouraging at his second, then slightly sarcastic at the third (he'd heard the phrase 'third time unlucky' a million times). When the rejections started coming in for his latest novel, they hid their smiles and looked the other way, but he began to notice the odd glances they swapped when they thought he wasn't looking. He started to wonder if they thought they were better than him, or if they were simply cracking up behind his back. He sank into an inner depression, cursing his lack of money and contacts, cursing his parents, who'd been born poor, and cursing everything and everyone that entered his realm of misery. Then Lacey had come along.

'Hear what now Mikey,' he had said one cold and frosty evening only two nights ago. Once again Michael had been complaining about how broke they were. Lacey nodded in sympathy, then spoke up.

'I got a very simple way for you to earn some wong, so lissen up. Yuh know the crackhouse on Beechwood – used to be run by dat Dredd?'

'Yeah, I know who you mean,' Lynette whispered, her voice light and airy, as if she was afraid of speaking the name aloud.

'Yeah, I thought you might,' Lacey replied sombrely. His eyes had the kind of look typical of police photo-fit pictures. He drew on his zook and went on.

'I know for a fact tings 'ave got sloppy round dere,' he told them confidently. 'His partners are tryin' t'run tings, but all the guys who were jugglin' fuh him are gettin' jerked like no one's business, y'get me? Since all dem tings went on, every brer wid a bucky's game for a try. I heard mos' ah the big boys ain' even givin' the partners no more drugs, 'cos they ain' got no money – the Rads took the fuckin' lot after they raided the place.

'So Spider an' Kenny – dat's the partners – they pulled some money together, fuck knows where from. Maybe they robbed someone. Or maybe the Dredd's women had some tucked away, though I dunno why'd they'd give it to them . . .'

Who tol' you all dis?' Michael asked stonily.

'Art, the fuckin' cat,' Lacey grinned. 'All it cost was one bone.'

Lynette shook her head in disbelief. Lacey moved on.

'Lissen anyhow. Spider an' Kenny pulled the money together and held about half a ki—'

'—of bone?!' Lynette squealed.

'Nah, powder innit. They washed it all up then they started jugglin' again, yeah? Now the ting is, Art's tellin' me the fools

are keepin' all that wong right dere in the squat – they mus' feel
say they're too bad to get robbed or summick. I was chattin' to
my brother an' a couple ah his boys, an' dem man are up for
stingin' the drum, blatant. Even if we don't fin' no wong, dere'll
be enough bone for all of us to juggle innit? My brother can get
'matics off his bredrin, so all we have to do is go in dere mob-
handed, y'unnerstan'.' Lacey pulled a tight, frustrated face.
'The way I see it, I got no job, no money, bere bills . . . I got
nothin' to lose man, an' you ain' too. It's all dere for the takin'
blood.'

Lacey got up from his seat and aimed an imaginary weapon.
Michael watched him, amused, while Lynette watched *him*, her
expression far from humorous.

'So wha' you sayin' Mikey?' Lacey was asking, from where he
was still standing. 'Dere'll be four man – me, my brother, my
brother's spar Reggie, an' hopefully you.' He cuffed Michael's
knee enthusiastically. 'So wha' you ah say blood?'

He shrugged limply. 'Where's the wong gonna be?'

Lacey smiled. 'I can't tell you *dat*.'

'Why not?'

'Trade secret,' he said, tapping his nose. 'Nex' question!'

'Supposin' they got buckies demselves,' Lynette stated in a
hard tone of voice that made her point of view very clear.

'Dat's the beauty of it!' Lacey exclaimed. 'When the crackhouse got raided, the Rads were lookin' for a whole case ah the
fuckin' guns my man was jugglin'. Yuh tink they fin' anythin'?'

Michael frowned critically. 'Don't you think dat might mean
the partners got it?'

Lacey shook his head, clearly knowing more. 'Nah star!
Kenny an' dem lot ain' got ah clue where it is. Art reckons the
case went missin' star – nobody knows where it is!'

'Bullshit,' Lynette sneered. '*Somebody* mus' know.'

'I reckon dat Sean Bradley yout' knows sumthin',' Michael
said slowly, making the others turn and look at him searchingly.
His face had taken on a thoughtful set and his hand rubbed his
chin lazily. 'Even if he didn't pull the trigger, they reckon he

was still kinna tight wid the Dredd for a couple mont's. He *mus'* know sumthin'.'

'Fuck dat,' Lacey growled. 'We'll never know the full story.'

He went over to the living-room window, looking out, studying the block opposite. The broad bulk of Beechwood loomed, each of its five landings bright despite the gloom. Lacey pointed at it and turned back to the couple.

'Dere's wong in dat dere block!' he joked, trying to sound like a cowboy from the Wild West. 'Are you in or not Mikey?'

That was the big question.

Michael was jolted back to the present to find the TV going in one ear and Lynette sounding off in the other. He blinked and gazed at her. She hadn't even noticed his daydreaming, so intent was she on persuading him not to take part in the sting, her hands hopping and fluttering like sparrows in the air, her voice thin and filled with panic.

She really doesn't understand, he thought to himself coldly. *She really doesn't understand the pressure I'm under.*

She kept talking, but he couldn't hear over the rage in his head. He felt harassed, browbeaten, harangued from all sides – and accompanying it all was the steady thump of his anger in his head. Boom. BOOM. *BOOM*.

Lynette's voice was flowing back into his ears.

'. . . An' you don't have to prove anythin' to *anyone*, least of all Lacey,' she was saying, unaware he'd only just started listening. 'What you need to concentrate on is *writing* . . . Because I know yuh good. Remember what you said when I firs' met you? Can you remember dat? You said, "Some writers go for five to ten years without being published". You've only been at it for four, so dat means you got plenty ah time to write new things. An' if you go wid Lacey an' you get caught, dat'll be it – you'll have gambled everythin' for the same amount of money you could make wid yuh novel. Y'get me?'

And all the time, the telephone number beckoned from the top of the TV set, luring him with thoughts of money and crack (which was worth more than gold on his estate), tempting him with the chance of a new life for himself and Lynette. Her voice and the telephone number taunted him mercilessly until he couldn't take any more.

He got up, cutting her off in mid-sentence. Lynette watched him, flinching as he marched over to the TV and picked up the number. After holding the paper for at least ten seconds, he whirled to face Lynette – then tore it into little shreds that tumbled and swooped gracefully to the floor.

'Now you can shut up, can't you?' he seethed, only just managing to hold back his real feelings.

Lynette said nothing, staring at the walls until he sat down. They watched the TV in silence.

Michael couldn't sleep. When he looked at the clock on his bedside cabinet it was midnight. He lay awake until quarter to one, then eased out of bed, feeling goosebumps prickle into life on his arms and chest. He left the slumbering Lynette and tiptoed along to the living room.

He headed straight for the window that looked out on to Beechwood; from there he had an unobstructed view of the house opposite. He went into the kitchen for a while, and came back with a mug of tea and some chocolate digestives, then stood by the window and sipped, waiting.

For fifteen minutes nothing happened. Then, as the clock in the living room eased towards twenty past one, a battered black car passed slowly between the concrete walls marking the block's entrance. The windows were clear. Michael recognised the driver right away. He stepped back from the window a little and watched as the car pulled into the first available space.

Four men dressed in black from head to foot exited. All wore balaclavas. Two of them looked around, clocking the area, while the other two opened the boot. Michael didn't see what they went for, but when the boot was closed the men were pulling at their long leather jackets, and he guessed sawn-offs.

Their preparation dealt with, the four men headed towards Beechwood's concrete stairs. The lookouts still cast wary glances at the surrounding windows. One of the figures stopped at the bottom of the stairs for a moment, looking up intently. Michael could swear the man was staring right into his eyes. He stopped breathing, willing his body not to move . . .

Then the moment was gone, and the figure disappeared into the dark cover of the stairs. Michael breathed a slow puff of air, thinking *Lacey*, and edged back towards the window. A noise came from behind him. He turned to see Lynette.

'Wha' you doin' awake?' she pouted sleepily.

A little annoyed, but determined to treat his woman like a princess, he wrapped an arm around her and drew her close. 'Ssssh – it's about to go off at the squat,' he whispered.

Her brown eyes widened a little, then she leaned against him, frowning deeply. 'I'm not sure I wanna see dis . . .' she muttered.

'Well go back to bed.'

She glared at him. He smiled and kissed her forehead.

'All right, don't,' he whispered. 'But don't blame me if yuh see somethin' yuh don't like.'

'All right, shut up . . .'

The four men suddenly appeared on the third-floor landing, walking stiffly but confidently towards the crackhouse. Once outside, they wasted no time, drawing their guns, blasting open the door and storming into the flat. The light in the one visible window went out. Short bright flashes like sheet lightning replaced it. Soon there was nothing but the sound of screams and random gunshots, rebounding and echoing between the blocks.

'*Oh my god* . . .' Lynette started.

There was a deep boom – Michael presumed a sawn-off had been fired – then there was a sound that surprised both him and Lynette. Above the wailing, the shouting, and the cursing, the sound of random gunshots got faster, and more erratic. After a minute of this, an eerie silence emanated onto the concrete landing between shots. The pace of the shooting was just as rapid.

Somebody was beginning to fire back.

For the next five minutes, shots rang out like harsh words –
there were blasts that were aggressive and fierce, screaming to
their victims to bow down – then came the return fire, that spat
a homicidal reply of 'no surrender'. Michael and Lynette
clutched each other like kids afraid of the dark. Then the looming figure of a black man stepped out of the squat, backing
down the landing, his gun still blazing at the front door. He was
bleeding from a multitude of wounds. His face was scared and
his aim was bad because of his injuries.

Michael only just had time to whisper the name '*Kenny!*'
before the balaclava'd figure he'd taken to be Lacey also stepped
out the door, his pistol raised. Kenny rained three shots at him.
Two hit – one in the shoulder, the other in the chest. Lacey
remained standing. Kenny tried to fire again, but his gun
seemed to be jammed. Lacey blasted at the man with no
remorse; long after he'd fallen, he kept firing. When he was
done, he turned and went back inside the squat.

Lights were coming on all over the block, but not a soul ventured out. Lacey returned two minutes later, dragging his
brother's limp body after him. Michael watched as Lacey disappeared, bundling his brother into the lift, before throwing
himself inside and starting their descent. From far away, sirens
could be heard.

'Oh God . . .' Lynette was crying uncontrollably on his
shoulder, her tears tearing at Michael's heart. 'Dat was Richard.
he looked *dead* . . .'

Michael could say nothing – he only had breath enough to
quiet her softly. Police Armed Response Vehicles crowded the
area like insects on a summer's night. Men and women clad in
bullet-proof vests ran around the block, while residents came out
of their flats, pointing at the lift, feeling safe in the Met's presence. The police urged them to step back, and then waited. A
man with an electronic megaphone appeared.

'*You're completely surrounded,*' he yelled at the lift doors. '*Give
yourselves . . .*'

The steel doors opened with a shriek of rusting metal. Lacey was slumped against his brother, their blood mingled and pooled on the lift floor in a thick curd. Richard never moved; bullets had taken him in the neck and head – unknown to Lacey, he'd died while still inside the squat.

As soon as he saw the gathering of armed police standing like mannequins, Lacey dropped his gun and held his hands high in the air.

Michael and Lynette covered their eyes, expecting the police to open fire.

A lone marksman detached himself from the crowd of snipers, carefully making his way over to Lacey. His weapon was pointed straight at the youth worker's head. Shadowed by a colleague, he eased into the lift, then made Lacey stand up and turn his face to the wall, while another policeman ran over and handcuffed him. He was led roughly towards a waiting TSG and in minutes the vehicle was speeding away. Paramedics swarmed the lift in a matter of seconds, feeling at Richard's corpse for any sign of a pulse; they touched his wrist and his bloody neck before shaking their heads in confirmation of his death.

For half an hour Michael and Lynette wept. When the knock on their door finally came, they dried their eyes and held each other's hands. Lynette led Michael to his computer table and made him sit down, flicking switches that turned on the word processor.

'Now do you see?' she told him, her vocal chords straining at the words. She turned her head to the window, now flooded with blue light, and raised a hand in that direction while repeating her words. 'Do you see?'

Michael sat gazing at the monitor for a long time, finally nodding his head and starting to type. Lynette watched him for a moment longer – then slowly headed for the front door to greet the police.

Midnight on Greenside

It was cold out, but Nathan Walters was oblivious to the frosty bite of the air, and the icy wind that blew across his face, making his eyes tear and his lips go numb within minutes. The streets were empty, which meant he wasn't the only one feeling the cold. He crossed the Greenside cul de sacs, side streets and car parks with enthusiastic urgency, glad there was no one about to stall his progress or side-track him from his mission.

Grimy-faced kids were shouting at each other and leaping against the high linked fence that surrounded Greenside primary, but apart from them, the park and adventure playground were empty. He cut through the park when he reached the south entrance, then marched across the grass, glancing quickly at the site of the old youth club that had been the centre of activities for Greenside kids such as himself. Sometime over the course of the last few days a wrecking ball had been taken to the building. Although the foundations still looked strong, the walls had fallen in on themselves, forming a pile of smashed bricks and rubble that stood at least one storey high.

Nathan shook his head but kept moving; there was no time to dwell on ghosts of the past, when the future held so much in store.

He reached Oakhill House and bounded up the steps, knowing it was quicker than waiting for the lift. He knocked on the relevant door hurriedly, a half-smile on his small face, stepping from foot to foot and bouncing on his toes, full of nervous energy. The door opened. It was Jake.

'What'm suh?' the Rastafarian said amiably. He was dressed impeccably as usual, in army fatigues, new Nikes and a Russell Athletic sweatshirt that failed to hide his wide shoulders and large frame. Nathan looked him up and down admiringly, then grinned at the man and raised his fist.

'Yes Jake.' Their fists knocked together. 'Garvey deh 'bout?'

'Yeah man; me tink him 'ave a visitor though.'

'What, is it safe fuh me to knock on 'is door den?' the young man asked.

'Gwaan nuh,' Jake replied, swinging the front door open and stepping aside. 'Yuh 'ear from yuh mudda yet?'

Nathan nodded as he walked through, looking over his shoulder as he spoke. 'Yeah I did man, she wrote me las' week sayin' she was lovin' it out dere. She's dyin' fuh me to come an' join 'er, but I need to save some spendin' money firs', y'get me?'

'Fuh real. Where she ah go?'

'Guyana,' Nathan said proudly. 'Dat's where my people are from man, Guyana.'

Jake grinned. 'Yeh man, me 'ear it all right out dere fuh real, but me never did go,' he told the youth, following him into the living room, where he sat down and continued watching TV. Nathan padded towards Garvey's bedroom door and saw it was closed tight. He listened. There were faint voices, and also sounds of movement, which were loud and frequent. He knocked on the door. The voices and movement stopped.

'Who is it?' Garvey asked after a moment.

'Nathan man.'

'One sec' blood, hol' up yeah?'

'Yeah yeah.'

He waited. Seconds later the door opened. Tara Wilson, a pretty Beechwood House girl, sauntered out of the room with all the grace and pose of a Siamese cat. She looked Nathan straight in the eye without smiling and didn't pause for a second.

'Hi Nay. How yuh keepin'?'

'I'm cool Tara, wha' gwaan?' Nathan grinned.

'Nuttin'. I gotta go anyway. I'm late fuh work.'

'All right, safe. Say hello to Rosie fuh me will yuh?'

'Yeh man.'

He went into the room while Tara said her goodbyes to Jake. The curtains were drawn and weed was strong in the air. Garvey was lying on his unmade bed exhaling smoke lazily. He was dressed only in a pair of tracksuit bottoms, and his stack system was playing KCi & Jo Jo. Nathan smiled at his prone form and approached the bed.

'Yeah yeah . . .'

They touched.

'Blood . . .' Garvey took three quick puffs, then passed the zook. 'Yuh up early innit? I don't usually see yuh arse before two.'

'Yeah well, yuh can't live like dat all yuh life can yuh? Yuh affa get on the ball sometime innit?'

Nathan took the spliff and puffed, watching the half-caste youth to see what his reaction would be. To his satisfaction, Garvey was nodding slowly.

'Fuh real . . .'

He leaned back and closed his eyes. Nathan laughed.

'So what blood, wha' gwaan wid Tara, I din't know you was throwin' dat down.'

Garvey opened his hazel eyes and shrugged.

'Yeah well dat's a low P ting, so don't be showin' no one yuh see 'er in my gates blood. She jus' comes an' sees me every so often y'get me?'

'Ain' she dealin' wid Ronnie?' his friend queried.

'Yeah, but she ain' in love or nuttin' – *can't* be anyway,' Garvey responded.

Nathan sat on the nearest available chair and passed the zook back.

'What about Sandi den?'

Garvey walked to his cupboard, picking out a T-shirt and jumper he could throw on his wide frame. He disappeared beneath his clothes, then his head popped through the hole at the top.

'Sandi's my bona fide. Dat's a different ting altogether.'

'Fuh real,' Nathan allowed easily, leaving the subject there.

Garvey came back to the bed and lazily flopped down. 'So wha' you on?'

The black youth shrugged and smiled. Garvey gave him a stern look, then groaned and covered his eyes with an arm.

'Ah man; you ain' gonna start goin' on about dat record label again are you?'

Nathan looked offended.

'Well, yeah, I was as it goes. An' it ain' a record label. It's a radio station man. An' it can work.'

Garvey was shaking his head in disagreement, while his toes tapped to the music from his stereo. 'Lissen Nay, I ain' gonna lie to yuh, the idea soun's good, blatant. But tings ain' gonna run widout co-operation, an' you ain' gettin' no co-operation from no man aroun' here. Everyone's on their owna ting star.'

Nathan was getting heated.

'Nah man, dat ain' true. I already spoke to Paulo, Omar an' Jarvis, an' they was down fuh it.'

Garvey scowled.

'Yeah, an' wha' dem man gonna do? Which one ah dem got money? An' wha' do they know about runnin' a radio station?'

Silence. Nathan fidgeted and stared at the carpet.

'*See?*' Garvey said in a soft, fatherly manner. 'We don't need more unable bodies man. If yuh gonna do dis ting seriously, yuh gonna hafta have man wid brains an' a business plan. Money fuh a transmitter, turntables, a mixer, mics . . . I mean, d'you even know where yuh gonna base dis station?'

'I gotta idea,' Nathan started cagily. 'It ain' definite, but I think it'll work. I jus' need to know dat if tings do get off the groun', certain man'll be prepared to come in wiv me, dat's all at dis stage. Dat's where you come in Garv's. I need to know I got DJs man.'

The youth waved a casual hand at Nathan's words. 'Yeah,

you know I'll come an' play fuh you Nay, dat ain' no trouble.
But you can't use my decks, an' tings need to be more sorted
than how you got 'em now man. I ain' able fuh comin' inta no
joke ting, it needs to be serious.'

Nathan was nodding vehemently. 'All right, so supposin' I
can show you a decent business plan. Will you get involved on
a bigger level than jus' DJing?'

'What d'you mean?'

'Well, you was talkin' about man wid brains an' dat, an'
you're a man wid brains,' Nathan said in earnest. 'Look, yuh the
firs' man I spoke to about dis idea dat even mentioned all the
tings you jus' did. If dat don't prove you know wha' you're
talkin' about, nothin' else will.'

Garvey rubbed his chin slowly, massaged his beard. 'I dunno
man . . .'

'C'mon Garv's, I need yuh – help a bredrin out . . .'

The youth was smiling at his friend.

'All right – come wid the business plan an' I'll think about it
blood, dat's all I can say fuh now,' he mumbled resolutely, in a
way that told Nathan the conversation was over. Garvey punctuated his sentence by throwing over the Rizla packet. Nathan
slid a sheet out and tore one side while his friend busied himself changing the selection on his CD player.

'How's Tasha anyway?' Garvey threw over his shoulder.

'She's OK . . .'

Nathan was concentrating intensely on the sheet of Rizla.
Garvey turned and looked at him with a knowing smile.

'When you two gonna get it togevva star? The girl's the lick
man. You two are always wid one another too, so wha' gwaan?
It's like you're on the low profile tip as well blood, ah lie?'

'Nah I ain',' Nathan said, embarrassed. His face felt hot, and he
was glad he was as dark-skinned as he was, or his discomfort
would have been instantly apparent. 'She's jus' a platonic girlfrien'
man, you know dem ones? Come on, look how long I bin movin'
wid the girl star. We gone past dem stages from way back.'

'Wha'?' Garvey's face was a picture of real and unmistakable disbelief. 'Lissen man, I know you lot bin frien's since firs' year an all dat shit, but yuh seriously tryin' to tell me yuh never noticed the way Tasha looks at you, wi' dem big soppy green eyes ah hers? Or you never noticed how tick she looks in the summer, wi' dem bad little shorts she always bus'—'

Nathan had his eyes firmly closed, the sheet of Rizla held tight in his hand, as if the image Garvey was recalling was too much for him to bear. When he opened them, he was laughing good-naturedly.

'Yeah, I can't lie, sometimes some low down thoughts cross my mind blood, fuh true,' he told Garvey.

Garvey shrugged in reply. 'It's human nature blood, she's blatantly cris',' he admitted with no qualms. 'But I know it's more than a flesh ting wid you lot man. I don't see why yuh don't jus' tell each other how yuh feel. Everyone's wondering what's takin' yuh so long.'

Nathan made a casual face.

'Yeah man, maybe I will,' he said confidently, knowing his words were a lie.

Putting the latter half of Garvey's speech to the back of his mind, Nathan concentrated on the former and proceeded to do exactly what he was asked. He was a deep and determined young man, always positive in his attitude; the word procrastination wasn't in Nathan's vocabulary. As soon as he left Garvey's flat, he went back to his own and phoned Natasha, begging the use of her word processor for his business plan. She said it was no problem. After scribbling vague thoughts on what he wanted to achieve from Midnight FM, he rushed over to Tasha's hostel in Ladbroke Grove, where she spent the rest of the day helping him with a budget and a business description. Three hours later she'd had enough of him slowing her down, and told him to go home while she typed the information on to the computer. Pleased with their work, he agreed and went back to Greenside, thinking hard about Garvey's encouraging comments.

Two days later Tasha phoned him to say the plan was ready,

and suggested they should meet on the football pitch in Greenside. Nathan arrived feeling excited and scared in equal measure. There was a large group of Greensiders hanging out, kicking around a Mitre football and swapping the latest gossip. R 'n' B blared from an unseen source. The general atmosphere was one of togetherness, joy and fun.

Nathan raised a fist as he saw Garvey passing the football around with Maverick, Gavin, Omar, Paulo and Jarvis, as well as boys from various other blocks. Garvey thumped his chest and held his fist against his body solemnly. Tara and her boyfriend Ronnie were sitting on the grass on the other side of the pitch, arms wrapped around each other. With them was Garvey's girl Sandi, plus Mav's girl Beth and her son Neil, as well as Rosie Joseph, Cassie, Valerie, Leonora and Elisha.

Nathan spotted Tasha sitting a little further away with a crew of girls from the area. He passed the others and quickly headed her way.

Natasha Kindersly was a former Greenside resident who'd left the estate when she left home, opting for hostel life over living with her parents. She was bubbly and full of sarcastic charm. Men couldn't fail to notice her more obvious attributes – her long legs, curly ginger hair, green eyes and creamy tanned skin, precious gifts from her Spanish mother and half-caste father. Natasha was mature and strong-willed, which earned the respect of the other youths. She carried herself like a queen – there was even a group of twelve-year-old girls on the north side of the estate who dressed like her, and had even dyed their hair ginger.

Tasha hung around with the Fidelea twins, Justine and Tianna, two average-looking fair-skinned girls, who made up for their lack of personality by wearing the shortest, most revealing items of clothing they could manage. The three girls had been inseparable, both at primary school and Greenside High, until Justine and Tianna's parents decided to finish their education in Barbados. Four years later the twins were back, boasting ten GCSE passes each, strange English/Bajan accents and personalities that had become louder and more outgoing. The three girls got on as if the twins had never left.

Nodding, winking and saying hello as he passed the varied groups, Nathan finally reached Tasha. Justine tapped Tasha's shoulder to let her know he was coming.

'Hi Nay,' Justine said, looking at the youth with flat dark eyes that scrutinised him emotionlessly. They'd never got on, but Nathan made sure contact between them was kept to a minimum so she never knew of his dislike. He nodded.

'Yes Justine. Wha' you sayin' Tianna?'

'I'm cool.'

Tianna was all right as far as Nathan was concerned. He'd always felt she was smarter and prettier than her sister, even though people often asked how he worked the latter out, seeing as they were identical twins.

'Hi Nay!'

Tasha's smile instantly made him forget Justine and Tianna Fidelea.

'Yeah, yuh cool Tasha?'

'I'm all *right*, I'm all *right* . . .' she crooned, screwing up her face as she pulled on the spliff she was smoking. 'Jus' out 'ere chillin' innit.'

'Yuh got dat suttin' fuh me den?'

'Eh, eh, but look 'ow de bwoy eager yuh see,' Tasha mocked in a Jamaican accent. 'I can't believe 'ow you bin sweatin' me about dis radio station ting . . .'

'*Sssh!*' Nathan hissed, looking around to see if anyone had heard. No one beside the Fideleas had. Tasha simply blinked, then looked amused. 'Not so loud Tash. Anyway, what, you was sayin' I need to do suttin' positive wid myself innit? At least I'm tryin'.'

'Fuh real . . .' Tasha was smiling as she looked at him. 'I jus' can't believe yuh makin' all dis effort all of a sudden. Dis is the firs' time I see you carry suttin' through more than a mont'!'

'So did you deal wi' the ku den?'

'Of course. Step into my office . . .'

She led him towards a chain-linked fence under the watchful eye of the twins. She dug in her bag and pulled out a neat little blue folder with a few sheets of A4 inside.

'Here yuh go,' she said as she passed the folder over. He took it, then opened it up, scanning the words and nodding every now and then. There were only four pages, but they were four very good pages. Everything seemed to be covered. Tasha watched and waited for his approval.

'Yeah . . . Dis soun's good y'nuh Tash. Thanks man, thanks a lot . . .'

''S OK. Jus' gimme a spliff for my troubles an' we're squared up innit?'

'Yeh man . . .'

Maverick and Beth were leaving the pitch and waving at the others. The girls 'ahhed' and giggled at Neil's squeaky goodbyes. Nathan frowned.

'Ay lissen, hol' up a minute Tash I jus' gotta talk to Maverick man . . .'

'Go on den.'

He ran after them and caught them up outside the park, just as they were piling into the Escort convertible Maverick was driving. Nathan called out and ran up to the driver's side of the car. Maverick started the vehicle up but let it idle, waiting for the youth to reach him. Behind the car, four black guys entered the park, each strutting with the confidence of youth. Neither Maverick nor Nathan noticed.

'Whassup bro'?' the dealer asked. Beth smiled at Nathan while Neil kept his attention firmly focused on the red Gameboy he held in his little hands.

'Safe blood, everyting's cris', y'get me? I wanned to talk t'yuh about dat business proposition I hinted at when we spoke the other day. Remember?'

Maverick laughed.

'I remember you wouldn't let off about wha' dis' "proposition" was,' the young man said with humour.

Nathan grinned. 'Yeah, well I gotta business plan an everyting now, true I know you're serious about making money man. I wanned to 'ave a meetin' between me an' some other people I had in min' fuh dis ting, like dis Wednesday or suttin' like dat. Den I can show yuh exactly what I'm talkin' 'bout.'

Excitement was flavouring Nathan's words. He could see Beth giving him looks of encouragement, making him feel good about what he was saying. Maverick looked at the blue folder.

'So what, is dat the business plan?'

'Sure is.'

'Can't I jus' take it an' read it tonight blood? It won't take me long; dere ain' exactly a lot dere is it?'

Nathan shook his head.

'Nah man, I jus' got dis copy, an' dis the only one I got too. If you can make it on Wednesday I'll have some photocopied so everyone'll get one.'

'What time den?'

'About four, five, you know dem way deh? As it goes, make it five innit?'

Maverick thought about it.

'Yeh man dat should be safe. Yuh got my number innit?'

'No . . .'

The dealer mumbled something to Beth. She opened the glove compartment and gave Maverick a pack of business cards wrapped in rubber bands. Maverick passed a card to Nathan. It read:

HARVEY'S WALLBANGERS

QUALITY HOME-MADE SPEAKER
BOXES FOR ANY OCCASION
(RENTAL OR PURCHASE)

CONTACT: M. Harvey
0973 861 333

'Gwaan,' Nathan breathed in honest admiration. 'I din't know you could make speaker boxes.'

'Not as good as you blood, but I can do it if I set my min' to it. Mostly it's jus' a cover fuh the shit, y'get me?'

'Done know,' the young man replied, pushing the card into his shirt pocket. There was no doubt in his mind; Maverick was a man to have on his team. 'I'll gi' you a call Tuesday evenin' to remind you blood.'

'Yeah, do dat.'

'All right, I'll let yuh get on. See yuh Beth, later on Neil.'

'Lickle . . .' Maverick muttered. The others waved. Maverick gunned the engine and executed an ear-piercing wheel-spin before disappearing around the corner.

Nathan turned to go back into the park, then looked through the chain-link fence and saw what was occurring inside the confines of the football pitch. He groaned, feeling displeasure and jealousy, even though he knew he had no right.

The four boys who had walked into the park were standing taking to Natasha, the twins and their friends, and were producing a great deal of laughter. They came from Goldsmith House, and were tall, bad-minded and strong, all draped in gold and fashionable garments. Nathan knew for sure that one of them, a light-skinned guy called Alfie Richardson, had a thing for Natasha; and she liked him too, she'd told Nathan as much. The thing was, until Garvey had doled out his little sermon three days before, Nathan hadn't allowed himself to analyse his feelings for his long-time friend. Now that he'd allowed those feelings to surface, he felt like it was way too late to try anything.

The football players had stopped kicking the ball around following Maverick's departure. Nathan entered the park slowly, hands in pockets, face glum, and headed towards Garvey, Sandi and the others. Sandi was a beautiful half-caste girl who always looked more like a skinny school kid than the mature woman she really was – she was also one of the kindest people Nathan had ever met. He sat down amongst the group of teenagers, everyone looking at him knowingly.

'*Alfie* bwoy,' Paulo, the Spanish youth from Bartholomew

House, said. His friend Omar smiled, while Garvey shook his head.

'Wha' d'I say Nathan man, certain man ain' gonna let opportunities pass, yuh know dat innit?'

'Safe man, safe,' Nathan grumbled, not wanting to talk around such a gossip-hungry crowd. He changed the subject. 'Anyway, I wanned to ask if you lot'd be available fuh a meetin' on Wednesday t'talk about our business. I got the plan sorted an' everyting. You up fuh it?'

'Yeah man, what time?' Garvey asked with no delay.

''Bout five at my drum.'

The youth nodded.

'Yeh man, dat can run. I'll be dere.'

'So will I,' Sandi smiled prettily, her head in her man's lap.

'What Nay, are us man invited den or what?' Omar was asking insistently. 'You was chattin' to us about dat radio ting too y'nuh, don't forget.'

'Yeah man, you know yuh safe,' Nathan replied, ignoring the look that Garvey was giving him. 'An' Ronnie – if you wanna come to a meetin' about startin' up a pirate station on dis estate, yuh welcome,' he called over to Tara's man. Ronnie shrugged his huge shoulders.

'What, you said five innit?'

'Yeh man.'

'Yeh, I might pass t'rough if I ain' busy . . .'

'Yuh know yuh welcome.'

Natasha and the Fidelea twins walked past the group, with Alfie and his friends close behind them. Tasha saw Nathan on the grass and blew a kiss his way.

'I'll see yuh later Nay. Call me if yuh need anyting else all right?'

'Yeah . . .' Nathan said hesitantly, not sure if he should tell her. He decided he should. 'Ay, we're 'avin' a meetin' on Wednesday t'talk about dis whole ting – it'd be nice if you could show yuh face, seein' as yuh know so much about what we need.'

'Yeah?' Tasha's green eyes sparkled like emeralds and were locked on to Nathan's. 'I'd love t'come an' help yuh out man. Gimme a call to remind me an' I'll definitely be dere OK?'

'OK. Where yuh goin' anyway?'

Natasha smiled at that; Nathan was sure she was glad he was asking, though he couldn't see why.

Or he could, but he didn't want to believe it.

'I'm goin' Smallie's, den home. You welcome t'come if yuh want.'

Nathan looked at her crowd as she said it. Justine very obviously didn't want him to join them; she was looking in the other direction, screwing up her face, and the youth could feel her displeasure from where he sat. Tianna looked indifferent; her gaze was focused on Andrew Wheelock – a broad-chested, dark-skinned friend of Alfie's. Alfie himself was looking at Nathan quizzically, though without malice. They knew each other from the manor, but Nathan guessed Alfie wasn't sure of his position in Tasha's life, so he didn't know how to act. Everybody else looked like they didn't give a fuck. Alfie and Nathan caught each other's eye.

'Yes blood . . .'

'Yeah yeah . . .'

Tasha was hopping idly on one foot.

'You comin' den?' she urged.

'Nah man, if anyting I'll bell you or see yuh Wednesday all right?'

'OK. Take care you guys. I'll see yuh later Nay . . .'

'Hol' it up Tash,' Nathan called to the girl.

Nathan had to force himself not to watch as the group left the park. He looked straight into Sandi's large brown eyes.

'I don't gi' a fuck – dat girl's on you star,' Sandi said seriously, her expression sympathising with Nathan's dilemma. 'Trus' me Nath, I'm a woman, I know,' she finished confidently.

Garvey showed no such remorse.

'Not as much as she's on Alfie Richardson y'get me?' he laughed, cackling and throwing his head back in glee. Everyone chuckled, hid their smiles, or blatantly grinned in the youth's face, not caring whether he witnessed their mirth.

Nathan held his tongue and said nothing, though at that point he could easily have strangled Garvey with one hand tied behind his back.

On the day of the meeting, Nathan pottered around his place, trying to make it as tidy as possible. The two-bedroom flat had formerly belonged to his parents. When they returned to Guyana four months ago, Nathan opted to stay behind and look after the place. At first it'd been hard, even with housing benefit and the cash-in-hand work he'd found, but after the third month he took on an African lodger, and after that he could just about manage. His mother sent long letters, pleading him to join them, but perversely (in his eyes), Nathan felt England was his home, though he did intend to take yearly holidays.

He went out on to the balcony to wait for his friends, anticipation making him unable to keep still for a second. He lived on the top floor of Mackenzie House, so he had a panoramic view of Greenside from his landing – the cars, people and the crisscross of streets formed an ever-changing tableau that always provided entertainment.

He leaned over the wall and lit a Silk Cut, watching the smoke float lazily, like a miniature cloud. The door next to his rattled and a short black youth wearing an Adidas tracksuit came out.

'Wha' gwaan?'

'Yes blood.'

His neighbour obviously wasn't stopping.

'Later boss.'

Weed smoke hovered over the youth. He slammed the door, then walked off down the landing. Nathan watched.

'Ay Ant'ny!'

'Yeah yeah?'

Anthony had turned around and was frowning back at Nathan.

'Wha' you up to right about now?'

'Nuttin' . . .' The youth came closer. 'Jus' goin' shop man. What'm?'

'I's jus' wonderin' . . . You can hook up soun' systems innit?'

Anthony shrugged and spun his house keys around his index finger. 'Well . . . Yeh man, me hook up a few. Nuttin' too big, but me know de fundamentals y'get me?'

'*Dett!*' Nathan yelped, ignoring his neighbour's look of surprise. 'Lissen man, I'm tryin' t'set up a radio station. I need a man like you around me to help us hook up the equipment. I could prob'ly do it, but at the end of the day I'm gonna be dealin' wid a worl' ah problems, so if a nex' man could run tings . . .'

Anthony's mouth was wide open now. 'Wha', you ah set up radio station inna yuh yard?'

'Nah man, you mus' be crazy! It'll be somewhere on dis estate, but I ain' sayin' where fuh now. I'll let yuh know when it's settled – if yuh interested?'

'Yeh man, me interested, fe real. When tings kick off?'

'Well, we're about to 'ave a meetin' in . . .' Nathan looked at his watch. '. . . five minutes time.'

Anthony was already backing away down the corridor, trails of smoke all around him. 'All right blood, me ah go shop, an' me come right back to yuh meetin'. Don' start widout me!'

'Well be quick!' Nathan yelled, wincing as his shout caused a dog to start barking two doors from his. He turned to look over the balcony again and took a satisfied drag on his cigarette. He smiled to himself. Maverick's Escort was pulling into the car park below.

By the time Anthony came back from the shops, everyone who needed to be in Nathan's flat had arrived. Garvey and Sandi were whispering to one another, while Paulo, Omar and Jarvis (a sixteen-year-old rudebwoy/comedian) compared bags of weed and argued over what tasted best, Skunk or Sensi. Maverick was helping Nathan pour the drinks (Coca-Cola or Holsten Pils). Tasha sat on the other side of the room with

Ramona Willerton, a well-built black girl, and another of the many cronies Tasha hung out with. Ronnie and Tara hadn't made it but Nathan hadn't really expected them to come.

Garvey waved a hand at Nathan.

'Ay Nath. Where's the other DJs man? I hope you ain' expectin' me to play no twenty-four-hour set. I'm out the door if you are, trus' me!'

Nathan mimed silent laughter, then rolled his eyes in mock exasperation. 'I tol' yuh man, I want yuh to DJ an' dat, but everyone who's here tonight are the brains ah dis operation. Once we sorted out the head, the body – meanin' the DJs – will be ready to come and link us!'

'*Eh eh*, watch Nathan though,' Sandi teased.

Garvey was grinning. 'Yeah man, yuh know my man's makin' sense,' he complimented easily.

Nathan took a deep breath, then looked at each face in turn, before deciding he should get the ball rolling right away.

'All right people. Firs' ting I'm gonna do is gi' you one ah dese business plans dat Tasha very kindly printed out fuh us.' He nodded at the girl, who beamed in reply as he handed the plans around. 'As you can see by the title, I'm lookin' t'call the station Midnight FM—'

'Midnight FM? Why you wanna call it dat?' Maverick sneered.

'I like it,' Sandi said primly.

Nathan shrugged at the group.

'It explains it in the plan, but basically we're gonna broadcast from midnight Friday till midnight Sunday night. Less chance ah gettin' caught innit? Dat's what I reckon anyway.'

The others were quiet, still scanning the plans busily, each with a stern look of concentration. Garvey had flipped the paper over and was studying the budget with a grim little smile.

'I tol' you we needed nuff tings man.'

'Yeah, but look 'ow much the total comes to. We don't even need no great amount ah money.' Nathan looked at Maverick. 'I mean, does dat look like an unreasonable amount to you blood?'

The dealer looked at the sheet of paper, cleared his throat, then scratched his head a number of times before replying.

'Nah. Fuh wha' you got dere yuh costs don't seem too unreasonable. What I wanna know is how you gonna get all dis shit so cheap? An' whether I'm gonna be the only funder in dis ting 'ere?'

Nathan was on the end of another group stare. He sat down.

'Well, I was thinkin' of gettin' our equipment an' shit from the Ol' Man . . .'

This brought an immediate response from the youths; all loud, but also varied. Some simply nodded or grumbled their agreement, others (like Garvey) thought the idea was stupid.

'C'mon man, how's an ol' brer like dat gonna kit us out wid equipment fuh a pirate? All my man does is sell knocked-off garms an' shit – dat ain' helpin' us,' he argued casually.

Nathan's reply was swift – the last thing he needed was a negative response from that corner.

'He sells more than knocked-off garms, believe me . . .' he started.

'All right, so he sol' my mum a fridge freezer years ago,' Ramona snapped at Nathan from where she sat with Tasha. 'Dat hardly makes him able to supply what you want does it?'

Nathan sighed. 'His son owns an electrical shop,' he countered, ignoring the harshness of Ramona's voice. 'I was talkin' to him a while ago an' he reckons dere's some gear floatin' about, so he quoted me the price I got in the business plan. It'd make sense to buy the stuff off someone we know innit?'

'Yuh see de stuff?' Anthony wanted to know.

'Not yet, but providin' Mav comes t'rough before someone else comes along, it's ours,' Nathan told them, his insides urging them to go for it. 'Me an' you'll look it over an' make sure everythin's working', then we're live.'

They thought about that for a minute.

'I gotta question,' Tasha said, raising a hand slightly, as though she was back in school. Nathan gave her his full attention. 'Uh, what music you gonna play?'

'Garage man!' Paulo said passionately. 'Has to be, yuh know say Garage's mashin' tings up right about now!'

'Some Hip Hop man, I don' business!' Maverick mumbled, sipping at his cup of Pils. 'Bring in some ah the local rappers an' ting . . .'

'Ay Nath, yuh affa drop some Soul as well yuh nuh, fuh the girls dem,' Sandi told him brightly.

Nathan nodded at them all. 'Yeah man, we'll 'ave all ah dat, as well as Drum 'n' Bass, Rares, a little Reggae – even some Soca if we can fin' a Soca DJ . . .'

'*Bere* Soca dances goin' on dese days! They're live too!' Jarvis shouted enthusiastically.

'As long as the music's good, Midnight'll play it,' Nathan replied keenly. 'If you got any ideas of summick we should cover dat we don't, an' you know a DJ, let me know. Even if it's not right now OK?'

'Yeah man,' came the group reply.

It all seemed pretty feasible, so no one had any further negative thoughts. Or if they did they kept them to themselves.

'So what about dis wong Nay?' Maverick asked suddenly.

Nathan blinked, not knowing what he meant, until he realised he was talking about the funding.

'Well, I ain' really sure if dis'll work, but I wanna talk to Lionel downstairs about puttin' in some wong.'

'How much is some?' Maverick asked straight away.

'Maybe half . . .' Nathan muttered, unable to disguise the hope in his voice.

Garvey laughed. 'You ain' spoke to him 'ave yuh?'

'Not yet,' Nathan admitted. 'I was waitin' on you lot. I'm tellin' yuh man, wivout you lot I got nuttin'. All it takes is a simple yes or no from each of you.'

He waited. Eventually Paulo took the hint.

'Yeah, well yuh know say I'm in,' he said in his forceful, confident manner.

'An' us!' Jarvis and Omar shouted.

'Ain' no way dis is goin' on widout me,' Anthony smiled at his neighbour.

Nathan grinned back in relief. 'What about you Garvey?' He held his breath.

'Yeah man,' the DJ shrugged. 'The plan looks good. I'm involved.'

Nathan had saved the worst – or best – for last. He turned to Maverick, who was still scanning the plan with thoughtful eyes. 'Mav?'

The youth looked at the paper for a long time, avoiding Nathan's eyes. His phone rang, and when he pulled it from his pocket Nathan thought he was going to prolong his agony and answer it, so he was grateful when Maverick turned it off.

'Yeah, I'm in – I mean I'm in if you can get Lionel to supply the other half ah wha' you want. If you do dat I guarantee to match it.'

Nathan felt joy surge through his body, making him tingle from head to foot. With some effort he held everything back, even the smile that threatened to split his face in two if he let it loose. He looked Maverick dead in the eye.

'Mav man, I appreciate dat a way, yuh don't know,' he said, even as he wondered how he'd get Lionel, the pimp who ran a 'massage and aromatherapy parlour' on the ground floor, interested in his own little business venture. Maverick was taking his grateful words calmly.

'Safe man, you know I like seein' constructiveness goin' on aroun' me star,' he said, waving his friend's words away.

Nathan looked Natasha's way and saw that the girl was watching him intently, a slight smile touching the corner of her lips.

'Ay Nay, you thought about advertisin'? You know, gettin' local businesses to promote demselves on the air. Like Smallie's fuh instance?'

'*Ay!*' Nathan blurted in surprise, while the others looked at Tasha and smiled. 'Ay, dat's a fuckin' good idea! I didn't even think about dat!'

'So how was you plannin' to make money?' Garvey said wryly.

'I wasn't even thinkin' on dem levels man . . . I jus' wanned to occupy my mind,' Nathan said, holding Natasha's eye.

Maverick kissed his teeth. 'Lissen man, you *need* a fuckin' businessman in dis ting 'ere,' he sneered at Nathan.

The youth waved a dismissive hand his way.

'I can deal wi' bookin' the business people for yuh Nath,' Tasha said, her head lowered. She looked flushed and she couldn't hold Nathan's eye – a rarity in their friendship. Nathan looked away from her, feeling strange, and inwardly cursing Garvey.

'Yeah man, deal wi' dat if you wanna Tash,' he said quickly, before he regained his composure and decided it was time to bring things to close. He clapped his hand together and grinned at everyone. 'All right people, I think dat's it fuh now. I'll chat to Lionel, then I'll call everyone an' let 'em know the nex' move, OK?'

They all nodded their agreement, then got up and began filing out of the house, chatting and cracking personal jokes back and forth. Ramona and Tasha were the last to leave. When they reached the landing, Ramona stopped Nathan with a serious expression.

'I beg you think about buyin' dat equipment from the Ol' Man. Dat fridge freezer he sold my mum bruk down within a mont'.'

'Yeah, well it's the Ol' Man's son I'm getting the tings off, not the Ol' Man himself. An' even if the tings are bruk down, fuh the price we're gettin' the package, we could still hol' 'em an' it would jus' be a simple case ah me an Ant'ny fixin' everythin' up, yuh nuh?'

'Make sure the stuff's workin' man, never mind about fixin' nuttin',' Tasha said lazily. 'Anyway . . .' She kissed him on the cheek and hugged him grandly. 'I'll see yuh tommora after college OK? D'yuh want us to see if I can get any shops interested in advertisin'?'

'You could. We ain' got nuthin' to lose at dis stage.'

'All right den. I'll see yuh tommora, yeah?'

'Yeah, later Tash. See yuh later Ramona.'

'Bye Nathan.'

He watched them leave, then shut the front door and jumped up and down in glee.

'*Yes!*'

He'd got them together, and they'd agreed his plan was a good one. For some reason, Nathan didn't want things to go any further. He'd achieved something, and part of him didn't want anything else that might happen from now on to detract from the warm feeling of accomplishment this gave him.

Amazingly enough, Lionel said yes. Between them, Garvey and Nathan phoned everybody (including Maverick), and told them things were on. After that, the only thing left to do was call the Old Man's son, Ganemede. Nathan confessed he'd written the number down on a piece of paper and subsequently lost it, so on a rainy Monday morning, he and his friend tramped over to Belsize House to see if the Old Man would give them the number once more.

They knocked and waited, knowing they had to be patient due to his advanced age. Nathan heard shuffling slippers. He waggled his eyebrows at Garvey, then stood straight as the locks clicked and the door swung open. Nathan went straight into action.

'Hey Ol' Man I—'

He stopped dead. The person in front of him was not the Old Man. The person in front of him was far from old, and she certainly wasn't a man, he was pretty sure of that. Beside him, Garvey was appraising her intently. The girl smiled.

''Allo. Who are you?'

'Uh . . . My name's Nathan man. Dis is my bredrin Garvey . . .'

Garvey adopted a casual expression and nodded at the girl, who was dressed in morning wear – towelling dressing gown and big fluffy slippers – and was still smiling. She was fresh-faced and cute looking, with olive skin, Chinese eyes and long black hair. A glorious smell of frying food was coming from inside the flat, a pleasant addition to the girl's appearance.

'Y'all right princess?' Garvey crooned.

'Hello,' she murmured demurely.

'So 'oo are you den?' Nathan muttered, gaining momentum and confidence under the girl's cheerful gaze, like a flower blooming beneath a summer sun. She let her eyes fall, looking shy and slightly embarrassed, and though both youths could tell it was an act, they still liked it.

'Melanie,' she said bashfully, aiming her smile at the floor. Nathan scratched his head, maintaining his casual pose.

'Is the Ol' Man about?'

The girl frowned, then looked up and grinned again, squinting into the sun.

'Granddad yuh mean?'

'Yeah, I suppose . . .'

Melanie opened the door for them and stood back. 'Come in. He's in the kitchen.'

'Cheers, yeah?'

They walked into the flat, Garvey first. Inside it was dark, but filled with the scent of the West Indies, as well as seventies wallpaper and pictures of beaches, palm trees and bronze-skinned women. All the pictures had the title 'St Vincent' underneath. Boxes of miscellaneous goods lined the passage and could be seen in rooms where the doors had been left open.

Garvey nodded and breathed deeply, his eyes closed, making Nathan laugh. Melanie followed behind, watching in approval.

'Where yuh people from?' she asked.

'Yard,' Garvey beamed. 'Yeh man, but my mum's from Staffordshire y'get me.'

'What about you?' Nathan asked the girl, looking back.

'Uhh . . . Well me dad's from St Vincent innit? His name's Cassius, d'yuh know 'im?'

'Yeah man,' both youths replied, while Nathan tried not to

show his embarrassment for asking such a stupid question. Melanie seemed not to notice.

'I din't know Cassius 'ad a daughter your age,' Garvey was telling the girl in surprise.

She shrugged. 'I live wid me mum. She's English too . . . Well, Brummie anyway.'

They piled into the kitchen, where the Old Man was standing over a sizzling Dutch pot, watching a number of dumplings fry. Piles of golden balls were stacked on a large dish, which was balanced on the grille above his head. Along the Formica counter lay plates bearing plantain, sliced home-cooked ham, piles of hard dough bread and tasty looking fried fish. Garvey entered the heat-filled room, a broad smile on his face.

'Yes man, ah cook you ah cook!' he yelled brightly. The Old Man looked up, then flashed gold teeth as he saw who his visitors were.

'Yes yout's! Bear wid me one moment and me ah deal wid yuh promptly. Melanie, tek de bwoy dem inna de sittin' room nuh . . .'

'All right . . .'

They turned and followed Melanie back the way they'd come and into the living room, which looked like the aftermath of a bring-and-buy sale. More boxes were in view, filled with tracksuits and Armani shirts. Melanie threw piles of clothes from the sofa on to the floor, then gestured at the seat she'd made.

'Tek a seat, do,' she told the youths, her accent a mixture of Birmingham and St Vincent. The young men did as they were told. When they were seated, Melanie sat next to Nathan very deliberately. She turned to him, hands on her knees and a smile on her face. Nathan was surprised, though he tried not to let it show.

'So where yuh people from den?'

'Guyana – they're over dere at the moment still yuh nuh.'

The young woman smiled and nodded. 'Really? So wha' you doin' still in England den, yuh mus' like the cold weather or suttin'?'

They laughed dutifully.

'Nah man,' Nathan told her. 'It's jus' a money ting keepin' me here; dat an' the fac' dat I ain' done certain tings I wanna do in dis country. I wanna make suttin' of myself man, den go an' res' up back home. You can't make no money on the Islands man – not like here anyway. Why yuh reckon our parents come over innit?'

He took a look at the girl, liking her features and feeling the first stirrings of desire. Melanie was nodding as if she was listening, but although she was staring him in the face, she seemed to be unaware that he'd stopped speaking. He frowned at her. She realised what she was doing and giggled, looking at her hands.

'*Sorry*,' she muttered, while Garvey grinned at his friend behind her back and gave Nathan the thumbs up.

'S'all right . . .' he was saying, as he heard footsteps. The Old Man entered the room, balancing a tray bearing a pile of plates, some dumplings and some ham. He stopped in the doorway and stared at his granddaughter.

'Go put some clothes on, wha' do yuh?' he stormed as he put the tray down on the nearest table he could find.

Melanie's face set like stone, but she got up without a word and left the room. The Old Man passed the plates to the youths and followed her out. Garvey and Nathan gave each other hang-dog glances.

'What, can we eat or suttin'?' Garvey said hungrily.

'I reckon so.'

'*Bwoy*, I 'ad breakfast, but – yuh nuh . . .'

Garvey reached for the dumplings, prompting Nathan to stab at some ham with a fork the Old Man had provided. By the time he came back, the Greensiders were sitting back on the sofa, jaws moving in unison, and identical looks of complete and utter bliss on their faces. The Old Man carried the plates of fish and plantain. He rested them on the table, before taking his own plate and selecting the choicest slabs of ham, fish and dumplings. No one said a word, too busy concentrating on the food. They ate in silence for a long time, before Nathan swallowed hard and looked up from his plate.

'Bwoy . . . Ol' Man, I come to beg a favour off you yuh nuh . . .' he began.

The man had got up from his seat and was shuffling towards the door again. Garvey was watching him, but was more interested in the spicy piece of fish he was chewing on, plucking the bones from his mouth with unconcerned joy.

'Yuh want a col' drink?' he asked them.

'Safe man,' the boys replied.

'One moment, me beg yuh . . .'

He left the room once more. The youths looked at each other, shrugged, then continued eating. The door eased open. Melanie returned dressed in tracksuit bottoms and a little white T-shirt. She beamed Nathan's way and took her former seat, going for a plate right away.

'Oh *yummy*, I'm starved me. Dis smells so good . . .'

'It's the lick,' Garvey said, his words muffled by the food in his mouth. The others laughed as he covered his lips with an arm and looked contrite. The aged fence returned with a jug of fruit juice and some glasses on another tray. He gave Melanie a look, which she pointedly ignored, then set the tray down and took his seat again.

'Eat firs', talk later,' he said as he grasped his plate.

Nathan made a face, but tended to his food without another word. Garvey and Melanie needed no such encouragement; they were already tucking into their breakfast with a zeal that was humorous to watch. When they'd finished, the Old Man handed out some napkins and sat back, looking sleepy and full. Nathan watched him worriedly, wondering if he'd nod off before he could ask him for the number.

He was a thin yet tall figure of a man, his dark black skin as leathery as an old wallet, sagging from his chin and neck, giving his face a dour expression of displeasure. In actual fact, the fence was the most youthful and cheerful pensioner Garvey or Nathan had met. He dressed in the clothes he sold, which meant he was also the most fashionable. Greenside gossip said that he'd been a violent gangster in the fifties, but such tales only served to draw youths to his one-bedroom flat, and helped him sell the stolen goods his two sons off-loaded on a regular basis.

'So – yuh belly feel nice?' he asked the trio, who all nodded, the greasy smiles lighting up their faces.

Nathan began again. 'Yeah man, I really appreciate you feedin' us like dat yuh nuh.'

'It all right – food was dere, so yuh musse eat, yes?'

'Well, thanks again,' Garvey said sincerely.

The Old Man nodded. 'Suh why yuh pass?'

Nathan sat forward on the chair, aware of Melanie watching him. He made a solemn promise to himself to obtain her number before he left the flat.

'You know I was talkin' about settin' up dat pirate radio station? Yeah, well Ganemede tol' me he had some aerials and other equipment on the go, an' I've raised the money, so I wanned to look over the stuff. Only trouble is, he gimme his number like las' year sometime, an' I lost dat long ago. Could you gimme it again please?'

'Yes man, dat is simple!' he said at once, getting up from his seat. 'Hol' on one second, me will carry it fe yuh.'

'Thanks,' the young men chimed, as he slow-stepped out of the room for the umpteenth time. Melanie turned to Nathan as soon as he was out the door. It seemed she knew she had a limited time to speak her mind.

'D'yuh live aroun' here den?'

Nathan was nodding. 'Yeh man, Mackenzie House, over by the tower block on the west side? Denver?'

Melanie leaned forward eagerly. 'Yeah, I don't know the name, but I think I know the block yuh mean. If yuh gimme yuh number I might be able to come over an' see yuh before I go back up North. Dat's if you wanna.'

The youth was already digging for his pen and his diary, retrieving both in haste, as he didn't want the Old Man to have the slightest inclination of the plans he had for his grand-daughter. He scribbled down his mobile number, then tore off the sheet and handed it to the girl, who was smiling shyly once more. She hid the sheet of paper with similar haste.

'I would give you the number here, but . . .'

She inclined her head at the living-room door and Nathan nodded in understanding. Two minutes later the Old Man came back into the room with a worn and battered-looking diary in his hand. Nathan already sat with his pen poised, an inquiring look on his face. The Old Man read out the number in a slow and halting voice. When he was finished, he gave the youths a satisfied grin.

'Thanks Ol' Man, dat's well appreciated,' Garvey told him as they got to their feet, preparing to leave.

The fence shrugged. 'Anyting me can do to help, yuh jus' affe ask,' he replied seriously. 'Me nuh like de thievin' yout's aroun' 'ere, but me love see de yout's dat try start suttin' good, yuh hear?'

'Yeah man, thanks again,' Nathan said.

They left the room behind the Old Man, who was talking and showing them the door. Melanie was staring at Nathan with plain lust. When he caught her eye, she waved, then put her thumb and little finger next to her ear and lips respectively, mouthing the word 'tomorrow'. Nathan winked at her, feeling his excitement rise. He knew tomorrow would be worth looking forward to.

They said their goodbyes, then found themselves outside on the landing again, the Old Man's door firmly shut behind them. Neither of them spoke until they were on the ground floor, walking across the car park and away from the block.

'Bwoy, talk about lust at firs' sight!' Garvey commented, slapping his friend's back good-naturedly. 'Yuh lucky I was dere to help you out man, otherwise you woulda had the clothes torn off yuh back . . .'

'. . . Nipples sucked by dem juicy lookin' lips . . .' Nathan added dreamily.

'A instant shine, while the Ol' Man's in the kitchen fryin' dumplings . . .'

'How yuh mean, I'd be *wukkin*' dat suttin' hard blood, all on the sly, don't even gi' a damn if I bus' quick either. Save the long shit fuh when she comes to my yard star, done know . . .'

The youth was frowning. 'Ay, maybe it wasn't such a good ting I come along after all,' he said, which made them both laugh, Nathan refusing to admit the truth of the statement. He pulled the diary from his pocket and looked at the number the Old Man had passed on.

'So wha' we on now?' Garvey asked.

Nathan was punching the digits into his mobile, his levity gone. 'I'm jus' gonna phone Ganemede an' see what's up wi' dat equipment. You got anyting t'do now?'

The Greensider shrugged. 'I gotta cut a sale about twelve in Gol'smit', an' link Sandi later, but dat's about it yuh nuh. I'll ride up to look at dat stuff wid yuh if you can make it after twelve.'

'What time is it now?'

Garvey looked at his Accurist. 'Ten to —'

Nathan held up a hand. 'Hol' on blood . . . Yeah, is dat Ganemede? Yeah G., it's Nathan man, from Greenside, you know the brer dat wanned to set up dat pirate time ago? Yeah man. You still got dat shit? OK . . . OK . . . Where yuh based? Uh huh . . . All right, dat shouldn't take half-hour. Soon come yeah? All right blood, lickle.' Nathan ended the call and raised an eyebrow at Garvey. 'You up fuh comin' Willesden?'

'Yeah man, if you can get hol' of a driver.'

'I dunno . . .'

'Ain' yuh cousin lookin' after dat Swif' Strong an' dem lot got?'

'Yeah man, he is yuh know . . . All right, I'm gonna go an get Ant'ny, phone Mal, den we'll meet at the park in about fifteen yeah?'

'Copa . . .'

They parted company. Nathan headed towards his block with a large smile on his face. Things were looking better than good.

The three of them (Nathan, Garvey and Anthony) trooped into Ganemede's electrical and hardware store half an hour later, each looking determined and ready for action. Ganemede was a huge six-foot plus black man, with shoulders and arms like an American football player – Garvey found himself wondering how much of his size was due to his father's cooking. He was dealing with a customer when they entered, so the youths looked around the various items in the shop until he was done, then Nathan approached the counter and stuck out his considerably smaller fist. It was immediately joined by Ganemede's enormous mitt.

'Yes Nath, come t'look fuh the tings at last,' the older man was saying, nodding and smiling at Anthony and Garvey, who'd been eyeing a powerful Bang and Olufsen stack system on the other side of the shop.

Nathan shrugged. 'Money's a hard ting to come by these days, but if yuh 'ave the determination . . .'

'. . . *Anyting* is possible,' Ganemede finished, looking down on the small youth with a respect that almost made the others envious. Nathan looked back at them and waved a hand their way.

'Dis is my bredrins and business partners – Ant'ny Davison an' Garvey Lammas.'

'Yes . . .' Ganemede rumbled. All three touched fists. Ganemede called out across the shop, and a middle-aged white man came into view; he was bald-headed, red-faced and thin, the shop owner's complete physical opposite. Ganemede introduced the man as Allister, then instructed him to watch over the shop for a while.

He led the trio of young men around to the back of the building, and down some steep steps into the basement. He flicked a light switch. One unshaded bulb lit up the room, which was filled with sheet-covered boxes, large pieces of electrical equipment and tables that bore a carpet of cobwebs. He led them towards the largest pile, uncovered the lot and stood back to let the youths inspect the goods. Garvey stood with him. Anthony and Nathan moved forward eagerly, squatting down and studying names, wattage and age.

'Quad amps . . .' Nathan was saying approvingly.

'Yuh 'ave a mixer fe de twelve tens?' Anthony said in his coarse Jamaican tone.

Ganemede nodded. 'Yeah man, there should be a Gemini in dere somewhere. It's all bin down here so long I can't even remember what went where. But it all came from another pirate dat went bust, so everyting you need should be dere. If it ain' I can get it.'

'None of us are really clear about the broadcast aerial, or how it works,' Garvey was telling the man. 'So would it be possible t'pay fuh everyting except dat, just to see if it works or not?'

Ganemede frowned deeply. 'Lissen man, if you like the stuff, tell me where you're based, I'll drop it round one day when I'm not too busy, an' I'll help set it up. We'll run a tes' broadcast, an' if everyting runs neatly, you can pay me dere an' den . . . Soun' good?'

Nathan returned from his inspection and touched the large man solidly, looking him in the eye gratefully. 'Yeah man, dat soun's wicked, thanks 'Mede, thanks a lot . . .'

'Yeh man, yuh doin' us a real favour boss, jah know . . .' Anthony joined in, also adding his fist. Garvey's was there in a flash.

Ganemede led them upstairs to a little office area. The room was crammed with a broad and battered wooden table and shelves that groaned under the weight of hundreds of box files. The shelves and files filled every wall of the office and huge order books were stacked on the table. Ganemede pushed these to one side until there was enough space to write, then reached for his diary and a pen while the Greensiders got comfortable where they could. Between Ganemede and Nathan, they worked out a day and a place where the equipment would be delivered, then the youths bade the electrician goodbye. They left the shop with hearty expressions on their faces, their bodies full of live energy.

They took a right around the first corner and headed towards the parked Swift in a tight group. Malcolm Walters was behind the wheel, nodding his head to the radio. He saw them coming, and started the vehicle up in his usual unhurried manner. Nathan opened the passenger door and let Garvey and Anthony scramble into the back, before he jumped in the comfy black racing seat, nodding at Mal.

'Respec' cuz,' he said breathlessly. 'Wasn't long was we?'

'Nah mate,' Mal said steadily, his eyes watching the traffic as he slowly pulled out into the main road. 'But I gotta cut a sale up 'Bridge so you man'll affa follow me up dere a while before I can drop you back down Greenside, yeah?'

Nathan reached for the half spliff leaned up in the ashtray, then turned and looked back at the others. 'Yeah man, dat should be safe. Every man can hol' tight a while before we go back innit?'

Garvey and Anthony were nodding casually. 'If you could drop me up Bush, I'd be live,' Garvey said, lounging back in his seat. 'I'll go to Sandi's drum and watch the football on Eurosport.'

'Yeah man, I can do dat,' Mal said easily.

The youths relaxed. Silence fell in the car. Malcolm directed them into a mass of squat grey estates which spread for miles in both directions, up and downhill. This was the Claybridge Estate, North London, every bit as notorious as Greenside, though there was no rivalry between the two places. In fact, commerce flowed regularly between the estates. Malcolm drove to where the looming forest of buildings was thickest, then pulled up in front of two buildings joined by a single walkway, situated high up on one side. He parked in a spot clearly reserved for residents, then told the youths he would be a few minutes, before exiting and disappearing inside the nearest of the houses. Nathan watched his cousin leave, then leaned back in the seat, closing his eyes and breathing a sigh of satisfaction.

'Yeh man, I don' business, tings are goin' exactly as I planned,' he was saying confidently. 'All we affa do is get dat equipment from 'Mede, set the tings up – den we're live, broadcastin' all over London an' the surroundin' counties mate, done know? *Midnight FM!*'

Garvey and Anthony looked at each other and grinned. Nathan was still talking to himself, oblivious to their humour-filled glances.

'Bad bwoy fe dem,' he finished, rubbing his nose roughly before turning around in the seat and facing the others. 'Gimme a light blood . . .'

Garvey passed over his Clipper, then eased himself between the two front seats. 'Hear what now though Nay, we can't be gettin' all excited about equipment an' shit till we get everyting up an' runnin', you know dat innit? Lissen man, you know me star – as soon as I see everyting live an' kosher, I'll be the firs' man to make up bere noise. But until den . . .'

'Ay star, de equipment affa work man,' Anthony said, his face scowling at the thought of things going awry.

Nathan was waving his hand. 'Don' worry yuhself blood, the tings'll work star, trus' me. I dunno, I got a good feelin' about all dis shit man, I can feel it in my bones man, shit's about to go off, an' all we affa do is keep ridin' dat fucker man. We're gonna make it in 'ere blood, believe me . . . God's on our side man, an' I know it's our time man, *I know it's our time*. What, don't tell me you don't feel the same way?'

Garvey and Anthony looked at each other once more, confused expressions on their faces. No one said anything, until Garvey leaned a little further forward.

'Ay Nathan man, whassup wid you, you bin smokin' or suttin', yuh proper hyper star, wha' gwaan? An' yeah – I do reckon big tings ah gwaan, but star, you need to slow down blood, fuh real!'

'Bigga tings ah gwaan though, yes man,' Anthony rasped, adding his two pence worth as usual.

Nathan relaxed in his seat, his eyes tightly closed. His next words were almost to himself again.

'Yeah man, I know why I'm hyper man – I need a *lash* star, trus' me, intermead, if not sooner.'

'Don't worry star, from the way tings look yuh gonna be lashin' the fuck outta the Ol' Man's granddaughter by the en' ah the week, if dat,' Garvey told him confidently, beckoning for the spliff. Nathan passed it over. Beside Garvey, Anthony was reacting in shock to the youth's words.

'Wah, Nat'an, yuh get t'rough wi' dat light-skinned suttin' already?' he was shouting at the top of his voice.

Nathan turned back again.

'Ay keep it down man, you don't affa shout, it's only a Suzuki we're sittin' in blood, yuh goin' on like we're at opposite ends of a limo fuh fuck's sake. Anyway, I ain' got through yet, but I will man, the way the gyal was goin' on. Gyal was all over me star, ah lie Garv's?'

'Nah man, she was properly on it,' Garvey replied casually. 'Let's jus' hope she phones innit?'

'She'll phone man, fuh real . . .'

'So wha', wha' was she sayin'?' Anthony wanted to know, obviously asking for a story. Neither youth intended to let him down.

Nathan told the tale from top to bottom. Garvey filled in and added his own bits and bobs from time to time, with almost as much relish as his friend. Outside the car, as they talked, laughed and made lewd comments, three black youths came walking out of their block, bouncing hard in an attempt to match their peers. One was in front while the other two trailed behind, so they formed a rough-looking triangle. They were dressed in the same style of clothing as the Greensiders – Nike trainers, tightly belted jeans and Umbro sweatshirts that made them look like little men. The two boys trailing the third were shouting what sounded like insults.

Inside the car, Garvey and the others finally noticed.

'Raa, watch dem yout's though, check it – they look like they're gonna rush dat other one, trus' me. *Oooh!* Tol' yuh!'

The two protagonists had caught up with the third boy, argued with him for a while, then punched him to the floor, where they were now beating the life from him.

'Box 'im back nuh, box 'im, box 'im . . . Naah man, dey bruk 'im . . .' Anthony commented without feeling.

As they watched the scene, a few adults started shouting at the boys to stop. The fighters rifled through the third's pockets until they had everything of any value, then they were off, running back into the estate and disappearing among the buildings as only they could. Garvey was shaking his head in sorrow.

'Yuh see dat? Thatcher's kids man. Money, money, money, fuck yuh community, go out fuh yuhself. *Individualism.* The kids even rob off each other nowadays, y'get me . . .'

'Ghetto livin', Jah know . . .' Anthony drawled, unaffected by what he'd seen.

Nathan was looking through the windscreen at the pavement, where the bruised boy was being helped to his feet by a gathering of grown-ups. His nose was bleeding, but other than that he looked fine. Nathan faintly heard the youth talking about getting his older brother for the kids, before he switched off, thinking he'd seen his lot. He'd had enough of watching the fights, the violence, the arrests *and* the desperation.

He looked at his watch and wondered how long it would take for Malcolm to get back.

The next few days went very well for Nathan. Little by little, he managed to goad money from Lionel and Maverick (a promise was one thing – actually getting the money was an entirely different ball game), and Tasha and Ramona had been very successful in securing the support of a number of local businesses. One morning they had arrived at Nathan's house dressed in provocative clothing, each bearing an A4 pad. After telling Nathan what they were up to, they left and came back sometime in the afternoon. Each of them had filled two pages with names, addresses and telephone numbers. Nathan was very impressed.

He managed to get together with Melanie two days after their first meeting. The encounter was even better than he'd hoped. She came over to his house, and after some drinking, smoking and friendly talking, they hit the sack harder than a heavyweight champ beating an outclassed contender. She didn't leave his flat until the next morning, complaining bitterly about the cussing that she was bound to receive from her granddad. Nathan brushed off her dismay, feeling pleased with his performance and unable to keep the pleasure from his face. Melanie gave him her number in Birmingham, making him promise to make the journey north one day.

Ganemede delivered the bulk of the equipment on the following Friday; Nathan had decided to hold a launch party in the flat that was to be Midnight FM's HQ that very night. The station's first actual broadcast was to be the week after. He spread the news by word of mouth, then kept his fingers crossed that the police wouldn't catch wind of what they were up to. On the Friday morning, every single member of the Midnight crew gathered together in the Denver House flat, attempting to tidy it up in time for the party.

'Fuckin' hell, yuh could've chose a better place yuh nuh,' Maverick was complaining, as he pulled on the Marigold gloves Nathan insisted everyone wore. 'Dis's worse than Beechwood man; look, syringes, fuckin' blood all over the walls . . .'

'Yeah man, look a' *dis* . . .' Jarvis intoned.

He was touching a lone sofa cushion with his Reebok, his face filled with disgust. The cushion was splattered with large drops of dry blood. He bent over and picked up a length of curtain lying next to it, showing it to the youths. The curtain was saturated with even more. Sandi gave a little shriek and let go of her mop, clutching at Garvey's arm.

'*Yuk* – wha's dat man?'

Nathan was shrugging. 'We dunno an' we don't wanna know

all right? Shit like dat we jus' stick in dem black bags an' chuck away, yeah? It ain' nuttin' to do wid us.'

Sandi was eyeing the curtain distrustfully.

'I don' like the vibe in 'ere at all,' Tasha joined in from where she was busy attaching soundproofing material to the walls.

Nathan shrugged and came over to inspect her work. 'No gaps yuh nuh Tash. We don't want no one hearin' us up 'ere man.'

'Can yuh see any gaps Nath?'

'Nah, but I'm just makin' sure you know what I want.'

Tasha smiled at that, but remained silent.

'Excuse me though,' Ramona broke in, hands on her hips, cutting her eye at Nathan. 'How come you're jus' stanin' around when everyone else is workin' their fingers to the bone?'

'I'm overseein' tings man – don' bodda watch me . . .'

Ramona kissed her teeth and got back to her soundproofing. Ganemede, Paulo, Omar and Anthony walked into the flat, all carrying heavy-looking boxes.

'Where yuh want these Nath?' 'Mede was asking.

'In dat firs' bedroom, to yuh right . . . Yeah yeah, plonk it down anywhere. I'll soon come an' start hookin' it up.'

By the early evening, the flat had undergone a radical trans-formation. The blood on the walls were faint smudges, the dead animals, drug paraphernalia and used condoms all gone. The youths sat on the floor in the main bedroom, where the turn-tables and speakers were set up, smoking skunk and resting. Ganemede came into the room and handed Nathan a set of keys.

'Dat's yuh locks fuh the front door sorted,' he said, as Maverick passed him a fat spliff. He shook his head, but smiled all the same. 'If anyting, gimme a call when yuh ready fuh the tes' broadcast, an' I'll come right down.'

'Will do,' Nathan replied. 'So yuh not comin' to our lickle do tonight den? It's gonna be live, I'm showin' yuh now blood!'

'Mede was laughing.

'Me nuh know 'bout dat, but me might pass all right?'

'Make sure yuh do man, done know!'

Ganemede laughed some more, then said his goodbyes and left. Garvey sat with his arm wrapped around Sandi, puffing on his zook and looking more than pleased with himself. 'Yeh man,' he was murmuring softly. 'We're almost dere man, almost dere . . .'

Nathan smiled, completely in agreement, but choosing to stay silent. At this point, he didn't want to risk everybody's hard work by jinxing things with silly words.

Greensiders didn't start arriving in force until way after eleven, but by then the music was thumping and the atmosphere more than lively. One of the back bedrooms had been converted into a bar area, where the girls were hard at work selling drinks. A Garage DJ from Shepherd's Bush was spinning ten inchers that had the crowd moving in next to no time. All the local faces were present – Orin and Malcolm, Valerie, Elisha and their crew of friends, Little Stacey, Nazra, Shannon . . . it was very clear that this was a Greenside rave.

Trisha tentatively entered the flat, and was immediately spotted by Valerie and Leonora, who'd been jamming in a darkened corner where their crew was gathered. They intercepted her as she crossed the dance floor and headed for the bar. There were immediate hugs and screams of delight as soon as they saw one another.

'*Oh my God!* Wha' you doin' 'ere Trish?' Leonora shrieked as she squeezed the life out of the former youth worker. Trish was smiling happily and blushing hard at the reception.

'Oh, I got a call from Natasha askin' me to come along, so I thought what the hell . . .' She looked around at the crowd of youths, then smiled and waved, seeing yet another familiar face. 'I'm really glad I came.'

'Do you wanna drink?' Val asked her, steering them towards the bar before she could answer.

'I'd love one thanks. A Red Stripe'll do me.'

'Some tings don't change,' Leonora grinned, as Lilliane, Cassie and Elisha joined them with their own orders.

'Some things *can't* change,' Trisha enthused, grabbing Lilliane's arm, then wrapping her arms around the girl in a tight bear hug. Cassie and even Elisha were next in line.

'I'm proper haps you come back Trish,' Val was telling the woman, as she handed her the sweating can. 'I never got to chat to you dat day, an' when the club got knocked down we thought we'd never see yuh ugly mug again, innit you lot?'

The others nodded and looked at their feet, memories of the club momentarily curbing their joy. Trisha's smile dimmed, but couldn't quite leave her face. It was just so good to see her kids again. At that moment, she knew she could never stay away from Greenside, even if she didn't work on the estate. The Greenside kids would always be *her* kids.

'Yuh hear about Lacey den Trish?'

Cassie, always the most forward of the group, was watching her reaction eagerly. There was another respectful silence. Trisha nodded and popped her Red Stripe; her tears and shock at Lacey's incarceration were not-so-distant memories. Now, almost two weeks later, she could just about deal with the thought of what he'd done, even though she believed it was the most ludicrous idea he'd ever had.

'Yeah . . . Honestly, I dunno what was goin' through the guy's head. Have you bin in to see 'im yet?'

'A group of us went las' week . . .'

Hanging on the edge of the group, not really paying much attention to what was being said, Elisha noticed Orin walking past, at least three heads from where she was standing. She openly stared at him; he caught her gaze and turned at once, recognising her and smiling before coming over.

'Hello you,' she beamed, her eyes on him, her posture relaxed and welcoming. He winked, something she usually couldn't stand, but she admitted to herself that it looked quite good when *he* did it.

'How are yuh den? Enjoyin' yuhself?'

Elisha was nodding. 'Yeah, dis ain' too bad; it's nice to see all the faces from aroun' 'ere standin' in the same place at once. An' they're playin' some *tunes* . . .'

'Yuh *know* dat. Ay, can I get you a drink or suttin'?'

She held up her can of Red Stripe.

'I'm all right thanks. Can I get *you* one?'

Orin shot her a look of shock mixed with sincere pleasure

'Wah! Ah you wid the equality vibe! A true nineties girl are yuh?'

'A true *workin'* nineties girl. It makes all the difference.'

'I won't even be able to drink it wid you still, true I gotta make some movements . . .' He inclined his head towards the DJ set-up, where Malcolm, Nathan and Maverick were gathered, watching him talk. Elisha followed his eyes, then shrugged casually.

'S'all right, do wha' yuh gotta do innit? I'll still buy you a drink – as long as yuh come look fuh me when yuh done.'

'Of course . . .'

They held each other's gaze for a moment.

'What would yuh like?'

'Oh – uhh, they got any E&J?'

'I think so . . .'

'I'll 'ave a brandy an' Coke den please.'

As they went to the bar to get the drinks, Little Stacey and his eight-strong crew bounced past Orin, nodding grimly. They found a stretch of wall long enough for all to lean on, then put their backs against it, passing Rizla, cigarette and ash between them. Benji was shouting loudly in Little Stacey's ear, as usual.

'Ay star I don't business, if Wayne don't come wi' dat edge note we affa bus' my man up, trus' me.'

'He'll come wid the wong man,' Stacey told him confidently.

'Is he comin' 'ere tonight?' Robby asked, his flat, shark-like eyes like deep pools of black tar in his face.

'He fuckin' better, 'cos if he don't, the nex' time I see 'im my man's gettin' bored jus' for the libs he's takin',' Sirus, a Versace-wearing half-caste youth, was saying.

'Lissen, no one ain' borin' my man wivout *me* bein' dere . . .' Benji began urgently, before he looked across the room and saw Sissy, Carolyn and Siân, who'd just made a most welcome entrance. The girls all wore the shortest of skirts, along with tight figure-hugging tops. Benji's jaw dropped. *'Damn* – look at Siân though, lookin' proper buff an' dat. I still don't get a piece ah dat. Girl's goin' on proper stush.'

'Ain' got much up top . . .' Sirus muttered critically.

'Yeah, but look a' dem legs an' dat bumper,' Little Stacey answered, following his own advice. It was a pleasing sight. He licked the Rizla and continued. 'She's cris' differently, done know.'

Benji was peering through the crowd, trying to get Siân's attention. When he caught her eye and received the response he'd been looking for, he touched Stacey's foot with the toe of his Reebok.

'Fancy comin' over – you can chat wid you know who?' he asked, prompting a chorus of 'Who?', 'Who?', from the others. Little Stacey looked over once more, thought about it, then shook his head.

'Nah, dat's long man. Me an' 'er ain' even in nothin' all dese times now y'get me? I'll go over an' gi' yuh moral support if you want, but seriously blood, I'm lookin' suttin' else in 'ere tonight.'

Benji nodded and took no further notice, already moving steadily towards the girls. Sirus took another quick look, then decided he'd join in as well.

'Ay – ay, wha's dat dark-skinned ting sayin' Benzi?'

'She's safe but she's got a man still blood. Yuh know Clive Hanson, goes Avery Park?'

'I ain' watchin' *my man* . . .'

By six am, the Midnight crew knew they'd had a successful night. The flat was mostly empty (there were more crushed beer cans than people) but Garvey was busy playing his second Drum 'n' Bass set. Maverick looked more than happy, as he and Garvey had gone halves on the drinks, of which they'd completely sold out, *and* he'd had a good night with his drugs. Nathan was wandering around clutching the bits of paper he'd been handing out to partygoers, bearing Midnight's proposed frequency – 92.5 VHF. He approached the bar to see how the girls were doing.

'How're you lot den?'

'Safe man,' Tasha blurted quickly. She'd been drinking, but although she was tipsy, she seemed to be under control.

'Wha' we doin' from here?' Sandi was asking as she packed rubbish into black bin bags.

Nathan shrugged. 'Mines I suppose. Leave the clearin' up till tommora, an' we'll go an' have a drink an' a smoke innit.'

'All the drink's done,' Ramona frowned.

'Nah man, Maverick lef' two cases ah Red Stripe at my yard, jus' in case we sol' out.'

'Yuk, I hate Red Stripe,' Sandi complained.

'*So*, come we go man,' Tasha said enthusiastically. 'I'm in the mood to bleach star, blatant.'

The others swapped knowing smiles.

'All right, I jus' gotta get rid ah the stragglers, den we're off!' Nathan grinned, aiming his words at Natasha. The smile he got in return made him tingle from his stomach to his toes. All at once, the moment felt right.

Less than forty-five minutes later, they were all sprawled in Nathan's living room, engulfed in weed smoke and watching *The Box* on cable. Ramona and Sandi were gossiping eagerly. Garvey was half sleeping. Paulo and Omar were watching the bikini-clad girls on the TV screen. Maverick was crowing loudly at anyone who'd listen.

'Yeah man, gi' a fuck, our shit blew up tonight star, trus' me! Dere mussa bin all two hundred man in the dance at one point, ah lie? An' we made a lickle on the door too.'

He prodded Garvey's shoulder. The youth opened his weed-reddened eyes as much as he could, and nodded fluidly. 'Fuh real man, two hundred pounds ain' bad; an' everyone was dere tonight blood. I even see certain man I ain' seen roun' 'ere since school days, y'get me.'

'I see Simon Parrish 'ere wid some flat face gyal,' Omar spoke up, laughing. He turned to Paulo. 'Yuh see 'er P? My girl's boat was squash up boy . . .'

Paulo was nodding and beaming along with his friend. 'I know dat couldn't 'ave bin my man's gyal – I never see Parrish judgin' no bugly lookin' girl like dat!'

'Is the spratt my guy's lookin', dat's all,' Maverick said wisely, while Beth slapped his arm and made wide-eyed faces at him. 'Well it's true innit? All Simon was watchin' was the back off an' the breas' bwoy, he weren't checkin' fuh no boat.'

He was rewarded with another slap for that. He winced, making more of the blow than was necessary, then sat up and called Nathan's way.

'Ay Nath, yuh see Simon in our dance tonight, winin' up wi' dat wedders gyal?'

Nathan was lounging in a quiet corner of the room, talking to Tasha. She looked faintly annoyed at being interrupted, but stayed quiet, a slight smile at the corner of her lips – no doubt due to their conversation. Nathan looked up slowly.

'Yeah man I seen him, but yuh know wha'? Jenny from Goldsmit' was showin' me dat's his girl's cousin or suttin' like dat – so I wanna know what my man's on!'

'On one ah dem bait ones yuh nuh,' Garvey murmured, shaking his head as Sandi smiled.

'My man's creepin' hard,' Jarvis added.

'Dat's wha' yuh call a true family man,' Nathan joked, getting an immediate laugh from everyone. Pleased, he turned back towards Tasha; who was busy watching him while trying hard to pretend she wasn't. He lowered his face closer to hers.

'Suh yuh gonna come in my room so I can chat t'you?'

She pushed at his shoulder. '*Nathan!*'

'What?'

'You *know* what.'

They were both smiling. 'Come man, wha' yuh goin' on frightened for?' He looked at the others to make sure they weren't listening before he continued. 'I got suttin' to tell yuh man, suttin' private, fuh your ears only.'

'Suh tell me here den.'

'I can't, I tol' yuh – it's private innit. It won't take long.'

'*Nathan* – lissen right; we're meant to be friends ain' we?'

'How yuh mean – we *are* friends.' He gave her an intense look.

Tasha lowered her voice. 'Well dat means no matter how much we fancy each other, our friendship's supposed to mean more to us than jus' sex – doesn't it?'

Now their smiles were gone.

'So you admit dere is suttin' between us den?' Nathan asked, knowing deep inside him he'd waited a long time to ask those words. She was blushing slightly, but in spite of her discomfort her green eyes never left his face.

'*Yeaah,*' she drawled reluctantly. 'I thought you knew dat anyway Nathan. I thought we both decided it would be better if we were jus' friends.'

He rubbed his head a little, taking in what she was saying. He looked around the room and saw that everyone was still busy doing their own thing; talking loudly, smoking, or just lying back watching the TV, adding little additions to various conversations whenever they could manage.

Tasha followed his gaze. 'So?'

He shrugged. 'Yuh wanna come nex' door den?'

She wouldn't answer, or even look at him. Her face was held still and stern, as if she hadn't heard. He held out his hand. She glanced at it, looked away, laughed a little – then turned back and suddenly grasped hold with her own. He got up, ignoring the glances of his friends, then led her by the hand and tugged her into his bedroom. Ramona was the only one to protest – but by then, Natasha was already way past the realms of any argument.

They sat on the springy softness of his double bed. He touched her face gently. She blushed once more, then smiled and kissed his hand. They moved closer – their lips touched and their eyes closed. After a long while, Natasha pulled away.

'I'm supposed t'be goin' out wid Alfie at the end ah the week.'

Nathan pulled a face. 'Alfie's safe man, but has he known you as long as me? Y'get me? Are you two as close as we are?'

'*No*; no way, but I like him Nath – yuh know I like him.'

It took him a while to reply to that; it was the truth. She'd told him exactly how she felt about Alfie.

'Are yuh seein' 'im den?'

'No, but—'

There was nothing further to say as far as he was concerned. He kissed her swiftly before she could finish her sentence, then touched her lips with a finger and grabbed her hand.

'Den it don't matter man,' he whispered, knowing there was no going back. They looked into each other's eyes earnestly.

This time, Tasha began the kissing.

He woke up to the sounds of *The Box* playing a loud Heavy Metal tune, the wails, drums and electric guitars invading his sleep.

The bastards never even turned the TV off, he thought grumpily.

The twin aches in his balls and head reminded him of the previous night. He raised himself and looked to his right, knowing what he'd see, even before his eyes settled on the empty pillow. He sighed. There was a deep indentation where she'd rested her head; along with thin ginger strands and the smell of hair grease. He flopped back down on the bed, sighing once more and closing his eyes.

It had been good – more than good – but if he was truthful with himself, things had started to go wrong as soon as the sex was over. They'd clung together for a few moments, talking, kissing and cuddling, before Nathan got out the bed to look for some Rizla. After checking on the sleeping bodies in his living room (Omar and Paulo's – everyone else had given up and gone home), he returned to his bedroom to find Natasha sitting up, holding her head and hurriedly puffing on a cigarette.

He watched her a moment, then climbed back into the bed.
'Yuh all right?'
There was a long pause before her reply.
'Yeah.'
He built the spliff and lit it, aware of the enclosing silence.
Tasha had her eyes shut and was rubbing her head fitfully.
'We was supposed to be friends,' she muttered under her breath.
'Huh?'
Nathan had been gazing into space absently. He looked at
her – not realising what she'd said. Nevertheless, regret was
already seeping through his bones. Tasha shook her head and
slid back under the covers.
'Nothin'.'
'Nah, wha' d'you say?'
'Nothin' man!'
She'd turned on her side and closed her eyes once more.
After that, Nathan had simply smoked the rest of his zook, then
turned over and gone to sleep himself.
He looked at the pillow she'd slept on once more, then
scratched his chin, bad vibes shooting through him. His
headache wasn't the only thing that was hurting him that morning. He hoped he hadn't just lost one of his oldest, closest
friends.

The following Friday they were all back in the Denver House
flat; the whole Midnight crew, including Tasha, Ramona and
Ganemede, who'd been busy climbing, drilling and installing all
night. It was nearly midnight. Tasha and Ramona had been off
with Nathan all day, but he was too busy to notice or even care
very much. His dream was about to come true – his gaze completely diverted by the spinning gleam of the Technics, the
stacked-up power amps and milling Greensiders, who looked as
excited as he felt. Jarvis was in the back bedroom and former bar
with a portable tape deck, waiting to see if their aerial really
worked. Garvey was playing a tape of the adverts they'd
prepared in a friend's studio earlier in the week.

'What's the time, blood?' Nathan asked Garvey.

His friend looked at his watch. 'Five to.'

'Nah it ain',' Maverick countered. 'It's twelve dead.'

'Well I make it two minutes to,' Ramona muttered in her stern manner.

Nathan waved a hand, deciding it was time. He called Jarvis to let him know they were ready, then he nodded at Omar, who grabbed at the mic, looking serious and slightly afraid. Garvey took to the decks. Everyone else was watching and waiting to see what happened.

'All right,' Nathan murmured when the silence was complete. 'Let's do it.'

Garvey leaned over to their Dat machine and pressed play. A deep male voice told listeners that they were in tune to Midnight, broadcasting on a frequency of ninety-two point five FM. When the voice was finished, Omar took to the mic.

'Yes London town, greetin's, greetin's – an' dere you 'ave it – Midnight FM's live an' kickin' fuh the London people dem . . . The firs' ah many broadcasts we hope, an' I can truthfully say, from all of us at the station, we're happy to be here, nuh true?'

A loud roar of agreement from everyone in the room. Nathan gestured at Omar to speed things up.

'Suh all right, our firs' set is due to be a Garage one, fuh all you ravin' man an' sexy gyal out dere, courtesy ah the man like G-Force on the ones an' twos. Fuh shouts an' dedications to yuh people, call in on 0961 668 353, dat's 0961 668 353 all right? G-Force, yuh ready to roll my bredrin?'

Garvey nodded.

'Run tune man . . .' Omar commanded, beginning to warm up. Garvey let go of the record he'd been cueing, while Omar continued to send shouts out to various infamous West Londoners. The youths swayed and nodded their heads to the intro, but as soon as the beats came in they couldn't help themselves – they leapt about the small room, dancing and hugging each other in glee – even Tasha and Ramona joined in. Midnight FM was officially on air.

The mobile Maverick had purchased for the station began ringing. Sandi answered, spoke for a while, then shouted over to Omar.

'Marcia from South Acton Estate wants to sen' a shout out to her man Gerry. She says to tell 'im to get his arse outta bed quicktime, she's roastin'. Also wants to say a yo to Chrissie an' Leoni, an' wish us good luck wi' the station.'

Omar nodded, sending the dedication out over the mic at once. The phone rang again. Nathan suddenly remembered Jarvis.

'Jus' gonna go an' check on our reception,' he told the others, who were still dancing. 'Careful yuh don't bump the decks all right?'

He left the room and went into another, smaller one. This was their chill-out spot – they called it The Restroom. There was a mattress, a radio, a little fridge for drinks, and even a shelf that was stacked with tea, coffee, and sugar. Jarvis was lounging on the mattress, smoking a huge spliff. When Nathan came in, he smiled. Omar's voice was almost bursting from the speakers.

'How's it soundin'?' Nathan asked.

'Cris',' Jarvis replied, giving him the OK sign with his fingers. 'I can hear you man loud an' clear, though the deck volume could go down a bit. Soun's lovely star.'

'Dett,' Nathan said firmly, taking a seat beside the youth. Jarvis passed him the spliff. They listened in silence as he smoked, nodding their heads or laughing whenever Omar sent out a risqué dedication to the female callers. The sound of a small explosion came from the other room. The music from the radio crackled and went dead. Nathan and Jarvis stared at each other quizzically, as an odour of burning and ozone drifted around the vacant flat.

'Fuck!' Nathan shouted, as he got up and ran back into the studio area. One of the amps was spouting a tiny flame and plenty of smoke to go with it. As Nathan burst into the room, Ganemede was throwing a piece of old curtain over the flame. The Greensiders were backing away from the equipment as though in the presence of a man-eating Tiger.

'What's happenin'?' Nathan had to force himself to act calm.

'Amp blew.' Ganemede looked a little stunned by what he'd seen. 'I thought it worked, but I haven't even used it fuh years. From what I can tell, it looks like it must've short circuited or suttin'. Sorry about dat. I would never've sold you the stuff if I thought dis would happen.'

They mumbled amongst themselves, subdued by the loss of something they'd been so happy to own five minutes ago.

'Fire hit the ceiling an' all. Look a' dat.'

Maverick pointed upwards. A dark flower had bloomed on the ceiling, like a black rose. Nathan did a quick check of the other bits of equipment but it all looked fine. The decks were still spinning, and the tinny sound of the record could be heard in the silence that had fallen. Nathan rubbed his head slowly, then set about switching everything off.

As quickly as Midnight FM had begun, it closed down.

Out on the darkened Greenside streets, they all stood underneath Denver House, shoulders hunched, shivering in the cold. The pavement was wet from rain that had just stopped falling. The strong musky smell of it was harsh in the air. Nathan and Garvey came up behind them, pushing through the electric doors to join the group.

'Suh all right,' 'Mede said, repeating his words for the benefit of the rest. 'Lemme check dat shit out an' I'll get back to yuh nex' week OK?'

Nathan touched his leather-gloved fist. 'Yeah blood' jus' gimme a ding as soon as yuh sort it yeah?'

'Yeah yeah – an' sorry about dat you man all right? I'll make sure I get dat shit workin' yeah?' He held each youths eye in turn, making sure they knew how sincere his apology was.

'Yeh man,' they all said, nodding and touching him, letting him know it was all right. Ganemede nodded, then left them, getting in his Mondeo and pulling away. The shuffled about for a moment, no one knowing what came next. In one quick movement Nathan looked up, suddenly realising Natasha wasn't with them.

'Ay where's Tasha den?'

'She went off wid Ramona,' Sandi told him keenly. 'I think she's stayin' at her yard tonight.'

Nathan didn't hesitate a second. 'What Mav, you can gimme a lif' dat way?'

'Yeah man . . .' Maverick's response was a lot like his personality – non-committal, calm and fully composed. 'Yuh ready Beth?'

'Uh huh . . .' She was heading for the Escort already.

'Bell me tommora an' we'll link up!' Nathan instructed the youths. Fists did the rounds, then the young men followed Beth to the car. Maverick let them listen to his fresh Garage mix tape for a second before he started the vehicle. They headed off across the Estate.

'Where's Ramona live?' he said after a minute.

Nathan nodded his head to the music and thought. 'Uhh . . . Flaxman I tink.'

'Yeah, it is yuh know,' Beth joined in.

'OK . . .'

A couple of turns later they were outside the red-brick block. Sure enough, Ramona and Natasha were sitting on her ground floor garden wall, along with a bottle of brandy and a pack of twenty cigarettes. They didn't look too happy to see Maverick's car pull up a short distance from them. Inside the Escort, the young dealer turned to Nathan wearing a serious frown.

'Ay Nath, yuh sure dis's a good idea bro'?'

'I gotta sort dis ting out man; dat's all I can say.' Nathan was busy opening the car door. 'Thanks fuh the lif' blood. Gimme a call tommora yeah?' He got out on to the street. 'See yuh Beth.'

Beth waved while Maverick tooted the horn, then he reversed the car and headed back to Rockwood. Nathan approached Natasha, feeling wary, and conscious of the way she was looking at the concrete floor – as if she was afraid the ground would fall away underneath her feet and leave her dangled in empty space. He moved slower and slower as he got closer to the wall. His hands were held up in the air, in an unconscious gesture of surrender.

'Tash?'

No one would reply to that. He tried again.

'Tash?'

Suddenly Ramona threw her cigarette across the street and got up off the wall. 'I think you lot need to talk. I'll be inside if yuh need me Tasha.'

He nodded gratefully at Ramona, who simply lifted her eyebrows in return, before she pinched another cigarette from the packet and went inside. Tasha took no notice at all. Nathan studied her hard, then hopped up on the wall too, leaving just enough space between them for her to feel comfortable. He touched her arm lightly.

'Ay . . . Ay Tash we affa talk about dis man; yuh know dat innit?'

She turned to him with iron in her eyes. 'I don't wanna talk about it Nathan man. I was drunk, an' summick happened dat shouldn't have, dat's all! Let's leave it at dat shall we?'

'Nah, let's not,' Nathan snapped back. 'I mean, you expect me to leave it at dat when yuh practically tellin' me you slep' wid me 'cos you was *drunk*?'

'*Jesus* Nathan don't shout! An' I never meant dat, you know it. I meant dat I wouldn't have let my urges get the better of me if I was sober, dat's what I meant. Don't start tryin' to twis' the words I *do* say all right?'

Nathan was huffing loudly. The front door opened. It was Ramona. She made a face of apology, grabbed the brandy bottle, then disappeared into the house again. Nathan slowly shook his head.

'I know yuh tryin' t'make me feel better, but you ain' helpin' man.'

'Yeah, well dat's jus' yuh ego luv – it'll pass,' Natasha told him sarcastically, her lip curled in distaste.

'Jesus Tasha man, yuh don't have t'go on like dat! C'mon, am

I trippin' or somethin' or was it a dream dat we actually enjoyed ourselves las' week! I mean, yuh right, we are friends, so I jus' can't see what I did to hurt yuh. An' if I did do suttin', can yuh tell me what it was so I can apologise . . . 'Cos right about now I'm baffed.' He was staring at Natasha now, hurt all over his face. 'I tell yuh suttin' though. I was enjoyin' myself man, so I musta bin missin' suttin' . . . Maybe I got too carried away . . .'

Natasha giggled suddenly, shocking herself, unable to keep it under control. She tried to get serious but her face wouldn't let her; to Nathan's delight, she was beginning to give up.

'I tol' you dat same night Nathan; an' I know I'm as much to blame as you, but I did. It's obvious we like each other, but we gotta be like adults an' keep it under control!'

'Why can't we be like adults an' *fuck*?' Nathan replied, stung.

She gave him a sour glare, then reached over and tugged lightly on his ear. 'Ain' you bin lissenin' cloth ears? 'Cos we're friends, an' if we wanna *stay* friends, we can't fuck each other, OK.' She paused for a second, but for some reason she had to say one last thing. 'Even if it does feel good.'

Nathan didn't even want to reply to that. He sat on the wall, watching her jump off and rub her hands on her jeans roughly.

'Now, as I said, I don't wanna talk about it, so can we done dis conversation please? I need to go in an' get some sleep. I'm bloody tired man.'

'Yeah all right,' Nathan said, reaching for her hand and suddenly feeling his own fatigue take over. 'So what den? We still friends or what? Eh?'

Natasha smiled at him – her full and usual smile – and even though the conversation hadn't gone exactly as he'd wanted, the sight of her bright, dainty grin cheered him. She squeezed his hand and they reached for each other, hugging tightly.

'Course we are,' she said, squeezing him once more and letting him go. 'We'll always be friends, Nathan. I love you yuh know – dat's the bloody trouble. I wanna *keep* lovin' yuh, not hafta hate you one day 'cos our emotions are so screwed up wi' dat relationship shit – you get me?'

Nathan was shaking his head again, a tiny laugh at the edge of his voice. 'You're one pessimistic girl yuh know,' he chuckled. 'How'd yuh know it's even gonna be like dat?'

She shrugged, then looked at her feet, before sighing and backing way. 'I don't – I jus' don't wanna take the chance it will Nath. I'll call yuh tommora OK?'

'Yeah, sure,' he mumbled, suddenly giving up the fight, as though he knew the argument was good and lost. He pushed his hands in his pockets and whistled between his teeth.

'Oh, an' Nath?'

He turned to look at her, surprised that she was still there.

'I jus' wanna tell yuh I'm really sorry the station didn't go on air. It was a shit ting to happen, but you can't give up. Make sure yuh don't give up OK?'

He nodded his head in appreciation.

'Yeah . . . thanks Tash. Goodnight yeah . . .'

'See yuh later Nath.'

The door slammed shut behind her. He rubbed at his head and thought for a while. After five minutes he made up his mind to move. He jumped off the wall, brushed himself down, and checked where he'd been sitting to make sure he had everything. At that moment the phone rang. He looked at it, his face full of confusion, then checked his watch. It was quarter past one. He looked at the caller ID. It was a local number, but not one he recognised. He answered the call.

'Yeah man.'

'Hello you!'

The accent was unmistakable and he smiled as the voice brought back memories. All of a sudden his face was a great deal more animated.

'I 'eard about you an' yuh party,' Melanie was saying. 'Notice yuh didn't invite me den!'

Nathan laughed.

'Everyone was invited man, I thought yuh woulda jus' turned up innit! How come yuh didn't reach anyhow?'

'Ah, me granddad was goin' on funny sayin' I didn't know no

one, so I stayed in to keep him happy. Anyway, I can't talk long 'cos I'm in a call box, but I'm goin' back tommora an' I kinna 'ad a row wid Granddad, so I was wonderin' if I could stay over. Me coach leaves at eleven, so I'll be out yuh hair bright an' early . . .'

He didn't even have to think about it.

'Yeah man, safe,' Nathan replied. 'Are you on the Green?'

'Yeah, the phone boxes by the shops. Where are you?'

'Jus' around the corner . . .' Nathan said casually. He was already walking in the direction of the shops with a brisk and purposeful step. 'Jus' stay put right. I'll be dere in five minutes.'

'OK,' she managed, before she was cut off.

Nathan clipped the phone on to his belt and continued walking. Sometimes things just happened for a reason; some of those things could be seen quite negatively, like the rejection he'd received from Natasha tonight, or Ganemede's equipment breaking down. But ultimately, deep in his heart, Nathan knew things would be all right – he believed life was about turning negatives into positives. He'd get Midnight FM on air next week, even if it took every bone and muscle he possessed. After all, the hardest work was done; all they had to do now was run the thing.

As for Natasha – well, he wasn't giving up on her just yet. She'd told him she loved him, and he believed it was true. He knew where she was coming from about their friendship, but he felt she was wrong. It would take a lot of work to win her over, but Nathan still thought that it was a major possibility.

Despite the morning's drama, he felt he was in with a chance on both counts. Of course, he felt even better when he thought about forthcoming events . . .

Well, let's jus' say dat's fuh my ego innit, he told himself with a grin. He lifted his face to the night-darkened sky and shouted out as loud as he could.

'Midnight FM! Bad bwoy fe dem!'

And no matter how hard the wind blew, it couldn't wipe the smile from his face.

Elisha (IV)

Elisha was in Smallie's kitchen, making some Guinness punch in a huge two-litre jar. As she stirred and added the last touches of cinnamon to the mixture, Jeannie came into the back, a cautious smile on her face.

'Hey 'Lisha – yuh got a man frien' come to see yuh,' she told the younger woman pleasantly. 'I'll give yuh five minutes to talk, seein' as yuh been workin' so hard.'

'Thanks Jeannie,' Elisha replied casually.

She put a cover of cling-film on the jar, then heaved it into the fridge, no sign of anticipation on her face. Boozy was making up beef patties behind her. She was standing on her toes and attempting to peek out into the shop area.

'Who'd yuh reckon it is den?' she beamed.

Elisha was washing her hands.

'Probably jus' Carlos,' she told the girl, shaking off the excess water and walking through into the shop, resigned to the meeting with her ex.

It wasn't Carlos. It was Orin.

'Oh hi!' Surprise made her forget to play it cool and calm. She moved forwards quickly. 'How are you man, I ain' see yuh face in 'ere in a while.'

Orin was on his own, standing with his hands behind his back, looking at her steadily and seriously.

'Safe man, jus' bin busy tryin' to make a change to survive yuh get me? How are you?'

She couldn't help being enthusiastic about how good she was feeling.

'All right yuh nuh, now I got a regular wage.'

'Ay, did yuh enjoy the party the other night den? Dat Midnight ting?'

Elisha brightened. 'Yeah man, dat was a all right little ting yuh know. I tried to lissen to their firs' broadcast, but it sounded like suttin' went wrong. They were only on air fuh about two minutes . . .'

'Yeah, suttin' blew up as far as I know, but they're gonna try fuh nex' week so keep lissenin' out. I know dat station's gonna be live man – it's my bredrin's cousin runnin' it, an' Nathan's sensible,' he answered.

'I saw you all the time at one stage ah the party, den yuh went missin' an' I didn't see yuh fuh the res' ah the night. What happened to you?'

'Ahh, I jus' had to fly out and make some movements yuh nuh. Yuh mussa lef' early, 'cos by the time I come back you was gone.'

'Oh . . . Oh all right den.'

For a moment they just looked at each other, smiling wistfully. Orin took his hands from behind his back. He was holding a single red rose.

'I thought you might like dis . . .'

The other customers 'ahhed' and smiled broadly. Jeannie, who was sitting at the till, made a loud noise of encouragement. Elisha blushed, but took the flower and held it to her nose. The smell was very strong but no matter how much she buried her head in the petals, she couldn't hide her smile.

'Thank you . . .' she managed, embarrassed.

'Cool man. Suh what, wha' time's yuh lunch break an' dat?'

She kissed her teeth. 'My lunch break's done man, I had it

about an hour ago. Yuh come too late, an' I can't even chat fuh long . . .'

'What time you finish den?'

'My shift's done at six. Why, yuh gonna take me out?'

They grinned.

'Yeah man, if dat's wha' yuh on. We could go up Wes' an' fin' a nice wine bar, sip two cocktail y'get me . . .'

He didn't bother saying any more. A million and one possibilities spread out before them. Elisha dipped her head towards the flower once again, breathing deeply. 'Yeah man, dat soun's nice. If yuh come to Bart's aroun' seven, half seven I should 'ave 'ad time to wash an' all dem tings dere . . .'

He snorted and she made a face at him. They laughed.

'. . . Suh I should be more or less ready,' she finished. She noticed the look on his face. He obviously didn't believe a word of it. 'What?'

'Nothin' man. Anyway, I dunno where yuh live innit?'

'Dat's easy . . .' She took a flyer for a ragga rave off the counter, then found a tiny bookie's pen in her pocket, writing her address and phone number down for the youth.

'Dere yuh are,' she said as she gave it to him. 'Gimme a ring about half seven an' I'll be ready by den, trus' me.'

Orin still didn't look too sure. 'Yuh don' mean eight ah clock?' he said dubiously, pocketing the number.

Elisha thought about it. 'Uhh . . . All right, as it goes yuh better make it eight innit.'

They laughed again. Orin's phone rang and he began to back away.

'OK, I'll see yuh at eight den . . . An' yuh better be ready man!' he warned.

'I will be, don' worry! An' thanks fuh the rose!'

He nodded and left the shop. Elisha moved fast, but Jeannie was on her in an instant, despite the fact that she was serving a customer.

'Suh yuh like 'im den? Me know 'im from 'im was a lickle yout' man. 'Im all right still . . . He look nice innit Elisha?'

'Yeah, he's seems OK,' Elisha said vaguely, stepping towards the kitchen.

As soon as Boozy saw the single red rose, she went mad. '*Raa*, ah you Elisha man, Orin gi' yuh dat rose? He *mus'* like yuh star, I never see my man drop dem styles yet!'

Elisha shrugged, still playing it cool, and went to the cupboard to find another jug for more Guinness punch. Boozy put down her half-made patty and frowned.

'Ay – ay wha' yuh doin' girl, yuh better come over here an' tell me what he had to say man, about yuh fixin' up punch! *Come* man, don't look like dat, I waan hear details whassup? Did he ask you out? D'yuh like 'im? When yuh goin' out if yuh do . . . ?'

Elisha made a face and dragged herself over to the girl; deep inside, she knew she was eager to gossip. She brought the large jar with her, then fished in the fridge for three cans of Guinness, knowing she better work while she talked. It had taken a little while, but today, at this minute, for the first time since coming to Greenside, Elisha felt completely relaxed and at home.

She popped the cans, poured the stout, then turned to Boozy and began.